THE
RUINED
HOUSE

THE
RUINED
HOUSE

A Novel

Ruby Namdar

TRANSLATED FROM THE HEBREW BY HILLEL HALKIN

HARPER

An Imprint of HarperCollins*Publishers*

Originally published as *The Ruined House* in Israel in 2013 by Kinneret Zmora-Bitan Dvir Publishing House Ltd.

FIRST EDITION

Designed by Leah Carlson-Stanisic

Library of Congress Cataloging-in-Publication Data has been applied for.

ISBN 978-0-06-246749-2

18 19 20 21   LSC   10 9 8 7 6 5 4 3 2

FOR CAROLYN, LOVE OF MY LIFE,

WITHOUT WHOSE INSPIRATION, LOVE, AND SUPPORT

NONE OF THIS COULD HAVE HAPPENED

BOOK ONE

One clear morning, on the sixth day of the Hebrew month of Elul, the year 5760, counting from the creation of the world, which happened to fall on Wednesday, September 6, 2000, the gates of heaven were opened above the great city of New York, and behold: all seven celestial spheres were revealed, right above the West 4th Street subway station, layered one on top of another like the rungs of a ladder reaching skyward from the earth. Errant souls flitted there like shadows, one alone bright to the point of transparency: the figure of an ancient priest, his head wrapped in a linen turban and a golden fire pan in his hand. No human eye beheld this nor did anyone grasp the enormity of the moment, a time of grace, in which not a prayer would have gone unanswered—no one but an old homeless man who lay on a bench, filthy and bloated with hunger, shrouded in his tatters, wishing himself dead. He passed instantly, without pain. A blissful smile lingered on his face, the smile of a reprobate, his penance completed, granted eternal rest.

At that exact hour, not far away, in a trendy café in the lobby of the Levitt Building, which looked out onto Washington Square Park, Andrew P. Cohen, professor of comparative culture at New York University, sat preparing the opening lecture of his course "The Critique of Culture, or the Culture of Critique?: An Introduction to Comparative Thought." It was required for students majoring in comparative culture, and Cohen taught it every fall.

Cohen specialized in elegantly naming his courses, which attracted students from every department and were always fully enrolled. It was more than just their names, though. His courses were well conceived and well rounded. For all their incisiveness, their main strength lay in the aesthetic harmony of their superbly formulated interpretative models, which were easy to understand and absorb. In general, "elegant" was the adjective most commonly applied to anything bearing the imprint of Professor Andrew P. Cohen. The entirety of him merited it: his dress and appearance, his speech and body language, his ideas and their expression—all had a refined, aristocratic finish that splendidly gilded everything he touched. Although many attributed this special feeling to Cohen's "charisma," they were aware of the cheap inadequacy of the term. Charisma he had, for sure; yet there was something else, too, something elusive. A student of his, Angela Marenotte, a bright young filmmaker who specialized in advanced visual technologies, once articulated it: "He has an aura." This remark was made in the cafeteria following Cohen's weekly research seminar. Cohen hadn't led the discussion that week. He sat alongside his students listening to a guest lecturer from gender studies who spoke about the covert sexual biases in the supposedly gender-neutral world of virtual reality. "You see," Angela explained to the bespectacled doctoral student who had accompanied her through the emergency exit so that she could smoke a forbidden cigarette, "it's not the 'aura'" (her fingers sketched ironic quotation marks in the air) "that the phony New Age mystics talk about. It's more like Hollywood or TV. You see it in celebrities, especially if they're in a private setting away from the spotlight, at a party, or at some restaurant. . . . They have this halo, as if they hadn't removed their makeup and the lights were still on them. They're shiny. Their skin actually glows . . . Come on, let's go back." She threw the burning cigarette butt on the floor and strode inside, the doctoral student on her heels. "They don't look real. That's the thing: they're unreal. They're like wax models of themselves, perfectly executed and lit. I suppose it's an accomplishment of a sort to turn yourself into an icon and become a symbol of who you are or, better yet, of what you are. You know what I mean." The doctoral student, who was slightly in love with Angela just as she was slightly in love with Cohen, nodded eagerly despite not being at all sure that she did in fact know.

In honor of the new semester, Professor Cohen was wearing a white suit that would have looked raffish and pretentious on anyone else. A green tie with scarlet embroidery completed the jaunty, somewhat amused look that he liked to cultivate. His whole person was characterized by a stylish boldness that tested the boundaries of good taste without getting dangerously close to them: the old-fashioned watch on his left wrist, the cartoonishly heavy-framed reading glasses, the Warholian shock of hair with its playful wink of gray. His table stood a bit apart, framed by a bright triangle of sunlight that seemed to elevate it slightly off the floor. Two young, pretty students giggled and whispered while stealing admiring glances at him from afar. Cohen smiled to himself as he leafed through his notes. He was used to the warmth of his female students' adoring stares. But although he probably could have seduced almost any one of them, he was a man of moral fiber and almost never strayed from the ethics of his profession. His eyes flitted across the outline in front of him. He was not one of those professors who prepared obsessively for each lecture. He was a natural teacher, in firm control of his material, and anyway, he was at his best when he improvised.

High above, the celestial spheres went on swirling, one atop the other, each lit by a great, world-illuminating radiance.

Meanwhile, on earth, the cheerful bustle of the first day of the semester continued. Freshmen looked for their classrooms, first friendships forming as they collided in the hallways, guided by the preferences and predilections that would determine their adult lives. Professors strolled back and forth, their self-importance concealed by facades of blithe nonchalance. Department secretaries scowled at anyone who dared enter their offices to ask a question or request assistance. Cohen was the sole person to notice something— something different and momentous that took sudden command of him and moved him inexplicably. He jotted a few words in the margins of his notebook and was about to turn the page when all at once, for no apparent reason, he felt an odd stirring in the pit of his stomach, an aching longing for . . . he didn't know what. His vision clouded. Although he kept staring at his notes, he could no longer read his own handwriting. The outline of his lecture looked like hieroglyphics, a riddle he couldn't make out. His heart felt like bursting; his eyes filled with what appeared to be two large, round tears about to overflow.

The whole strange episode didn't last long—no more than a moment or two. The skies shut and the ascending ladder of light slowly faded. A final glitter of gold flickered in the misty distance, then all reverted to its former state, as though nothing out of the ordinary had occurred. Cohen pulled himself together. His fingers gripped his empty espresso cup, absentmindedly tilting it to his lips. A last, thick, bitter drop rolled onto his tongue and brought him back to his senses. His eyes focused on his notes again. The letters re-formed into words, and the words into sentences. Everything, almost, was as before. The hand he had extended toward the knot in his tie, as though to loosen it, returned awkwardly to the table. What on earth had gotten into him? He hadn't felt so close to tears in years.

2

O Manhattan, isle of the gods, home to great happenings of metal, glass, and energy, island of sharp angles, summit of the world! Have not we all—rich and poor, producers and consumers, providers and provided for—been laboring for generations with all our might, under the direction of an unseen Engineer, to build the most magnificent city ever known to humankind? We lay down more avenues, rule them straight, strive to get the proportions of their buildings right. We pour our lifeblood into the foundations of the skyscrapers, raising them ever higher: the Empire State Building has added two stories in the last decade; the Twin Towers near the Battery will grow by half in the next century. Slowly, imperceptibly, we deepen the rivers encircling our island: the Hudson is twice the depth it was when glimpsed by the first white settlers. The East River would be, too, were it not for the toxic wastes we continuously dump into it, rendering our own efforts Sisyphean. Everything soars, rushes, accelerates: the Dow Jones Industrial Average, the rate of population growth, the bribes needed to flout municipal building codes, the hire of the whores, the price of pedigreed dogs, subway fares, real estate values. The bridges stretch farther and farther; the tunnels linking us to the heart of the continent grow deeper and deeper. The conical water tanks on the rooftops strain toward the heavens, pulling the buildings behind them as if to detach them from their foundations. One day the subway cars will leap off their rails and plunge into the depths of the earth, severing the last cables that anchor the city to the ground. Our island will be torn loose, ripped from its rocky underpinnings; it will ascend into the sky and pierce it like a fast, shining bullet. The rivers will foam and cascade, immense tides pouring into the gaping wound. When calm returns, the quiet will be unearthly. Only large, low-flying seabirds will hover over the face of the depths.

3

September 9, 2000
_____

The 9th of Elul, 5760

Ten a.m. Andrew chooses a CD and slips it into the stereo, which swallows it eagerly. He presses play, waits for the hot milk to finish foaming in the noisy espresso machine, and carries his coffee cup from the kitchen counter to the brown leather couch in the adjoining living room.

An inviting pile of magazines, periodicals, and weekend papers await him on the coffee table. The music fills the large, bright, clean apartment. Sunbeams trickle through the open door of the bedroom. In the living room, four large windows, all facing west, look out onto the familiar view that he loves: the green treetops of Riverside Park and, beyond them, the line of the Hudson, a shimmering strip of metallic blue. The view reigns over the apartment. The river is visible from the front door, the dining room, and even (Andrew attaches special importance to this) the kitchen. When he renovated, he broke down the walls with a daring that was determined, undaunted by the tyranny of what was, to uncover the promise of what lay behind it. The former owner, a retired elderly Jew who had moved to Florida and sold him the place for a price that now seems ridiculous, had never thought of turning his cramped New York dwelling into the unified, free-flowing space that Andrew crafted. He can stand in the kitchen cutting vegetables, making coffee, or have his breakfast on the bar stool at the slate countertop, with the light-filled view spread out before him,

appearing and reappearing in the living-room windows like a
landscape painted on four panels. The light changes by the hour: a
modernist experiment in texture and color. Winter strips the trees
of their foliage, leaving them nakedly somber and gray against
the steely backdrop of the river. On long summer evenings, the
sunsets are theatrically stunning, throwing their golden-orange
shadow on the dark water and turning the ugly industrial buildings and residential towers across it into yet more elements in a
breathtaking work of art. Although Andrew has been living with
this view for eight years, it keeps revealing new secrets. He has
never gotten entirely used to it, not really.

Saturday mornings are his favorite time of the week. He likes
to spend them alone and refers to them as "my quality time with
myself." The slowly sipped coffee, the tastefully chosen music,
the enjoyable leafing through of the weekend papers—all are a
kind of meditation by which he experiences, undisturbed and un-
distracted, a heightened sense of self that recharges him with the
creative energy needed for the rest of the week. A fierce, silent bliss
runs through him on such mornings. He does all he can to prolong
them, congratulating himself, sometimes almost explicitly, on his
wisdom and courage in having left home, with its ceaseless, cloying clamor of family life, for the personal and aesthetic indepen-
dence of the marvelous space inhabited by him now. His apartment
stands in sharp contrast to the feminine clutter that symbolized,
more than anything, his life with Linda: the furniture, the rugs,
the bric-a-brac; the framed snapshots of the children, the photographs in color and black and white; the bright cushions with
their wool and linen tassels, the patchwork quilts, the swatches of
embroidery; the bookends shaped like rabbits, frogs, and bears;
the flowerpots, the vases, the hammered copper trays, the carved
wood, ivory, and mother-of-pearl jewelry boxes; the elongated,
black metal dachshund shoe scraper by the front door; the little

bird's nest with its three indigo eggs; the old ceramic pots from Morocco, the painted tiles from Mexico, the nude African women carved in ebony. Each piece was elegant and authentic—Linda's taste was consistently excellent—but as her New York Jewish penchant for exaggeration increased with the passage of time, so did the objects that filled the house to bursting until it resembled one of those self-defeating, overcrowded antique shops that drive their customers away to their competitors.

The more Andrew felt asphyxiated by his marriage, the more insufferable the house had become. Linda, as he once put it to his therapist, was trying to be her own mother by clinging to the aesthetics of the suburban respectability she had grown up with. The content, to be sure, was different: ethnic rugs instead of synthetic carpets, original paintings rather than reproductions, rustic wood furniture, not plastic and Formica. Yet the structural essence remained the same. Even had he wanted to, Andrew could never have spent his life chained to the tedious mediocrity of such bourgeois domesticity. Eight years after his divorce, it still exhilarates him to step out of the shower each morning, a large towel wrapped around his waist, and stride to the espresso machine on the kitchen counter through the uninterrupted, almost empty expanse of a living room elegantly punctuated by a few handsome, carefully selected items: the large screen of Chinese calligraphy whose vertical characters spelled the Mandarin word for "serenity"; the art deco chest of drawers; the carved oak china cabinet; and of course, the costly collection of antique African sculptures and masks hanging on the eastern wall. The startling, almost sterile spotlessness of the place is a statement, too. Not that Linda's house wasn't clean, but its cleanliness was of a kind that had to be worked at and maintained by Carmen, the Colombian housekeeper who scrubbed, dusted, and vacuumed three times a week. Andrew's apartment seems to clean itself, as though repelling every last speck of dust and dirt, politely but imperiously driving it, properly shamed, back to the raucous street it had come from. His own housekeeper, Angie, once said, "I just come here to do the laundry and look at the view. There's nothing to clean here, this place is always spotless."

Ten thirty. Although he is having ten guests for dinner the next evening, Andrew is unfazed. He will shop for food later in the day and have everything, as always, ready in time. Settling onto the couch, he puts down his coffee and pleasurably surveys the pile of publications and periodicals with their sensuous wealth of paper and fresh, deliciously crisp words in all sizes, shapes, and colors. Each typeface has its aroma and hidden semantic field. The thin, ascetic newsprint of the *Times* contends with the glossy sheets of slick magazines that made him think of the leather seats of luxury cars; the creamy leaves of professional journals lay beside the recycled, wrapper-like paper of avant-garde reviews whose fuzzy print, an iconic replication of the typewriter's, suggests the quintessence of the American writer, popularly imagined (closed blinds, a bottle of whiskey, cigarette smoke); and in the midst of all this, curled embryonically among the other magazines, is the latest issue of the *New Yorker*, concealing an article written by Andrew himself. Although he went over the proofs only two weeks ago and had his research assistant fax his last corrections two days before the issue went to print, Andrew pretends to be surprised by it, both to heighten his anticipation and to hide the slight embarrassment he feels each time he is overcome by a childish joy at the sight of his name in print above words recognizable as his own. Prolonging the sweet suspense, he sifts through the pile, sampling a headline, a masthead, or half an editorial before putting each down.

His coffee is slowly getting cold. Andrew takes short sips of it, conscious of the small red triangle that forms the tip of the *New Yorker*'s cover. Continuing to ignore it, he pursues his regular Saturday morning routine of going through the heap, selecting what interests him, marking passages with improvised bookmarks, and returning some items to the pile while discarding others. Only now, no longer able to tolerate the pleasurable suspense, he puts down his empty coffee cup and reaches for the prestigious weekly as though it were a fresh, red, perfectly chilled fruit. With a slight shiver of pleasure, he opens it, inhaling the intoxicating scent of its print, and begins to leaf casually through it, proceeding at a leisurely pace through the front of the book until he comes to the table of contents.

By now his embarrassment is long gone. The tingle of uncertainty with which he searches for his name reminds him of his childhood birthdays, the excitement of getting out of bed in the morning intensified by the titillating fear that *this year* he had been forgotten. Slowly, he would descend to the ground floor with its pile of presents and smell of blueberry pancakes made especially in his honor. Every time, encountering the printed name of Andrew P. Cohen seems a distant echo of his heart's wild leap when he saw his first published article, which appeared only after an editorial board had put him through all the hellish rituals of the academic tribe. The manuscript had been returned to him for "improvements" no less than eight times, and each time he had been forced, in those pre–word processing days, to type its twenty pages all over again. The changes demanded were so great that every draft became a new article, every iteration increasingly devoted to the scholarly work of one of the editors. He still remembers his fascinated reaction when he first began to publish and saw his words transformed into a definitive presence, as if given an objective validity by the printed page not had by them before. He puts this experience to use in the classroom in order to illustrate the concept of "reification." He asks a research assistant to collect samples of a class's writing and then returns these printed and bound with the request that the students spontaneously record their feelings at having their work "made official." They would remember it long after graduation.

Andrew sits up and turns to his latest piece with satisfaction, reading it as carefully as if going over the proofs one more time. The clarity and originality of his phrasing—his own yet no longer his own—pleases him greatly. From time to time, on Saturdays between the hours of ten and twelve, he indulges in a small, harmless dose of vanity.

4

September 10, 2000

The 10th of Elul, 5760

The wind gusting from the river carves imperceptible signs on the soft limestone cornices of the buildings' facades. It howls between the glass and metal cliffs of midtown Manhattan, shrieks in the hollows of the Gothic pilasters of the cathedrals, and charges around the capitals of the soaring towers that glisten against the melancholy blue of the evening sky, ringing the unheard bells of the great city and waking the gargoyles from their slumber on the old rain gutters, causing them to suddenly seem menacing and malevolent. The deep, dark wind of Time itself rises and demands its due.

Yet in the empty apartment, an absolute, majestic silence reigns. The windows keep outside and inside, cosmos and chaos, apart. The walls glow in the orange sunset; the polished parquet floors gleam; the rectangular screen of the computer glows in the twilight as if a small sliver of the river were brought in and carefully placed indoors. The day battles against its own shadows, but in vain. The outcome is foretold. The light will be vanquished; darkness shall cover the earth and a dim, damp mist will blanket the river. The last glimmers will retire from the face of the water. The strongly pronounced faces of the wooden masks will be flattened and swallowed by the shadows. The masterful brushstrokes spelling "serenity" will be gathered one by one on the darkening wall. It is time to rise, illuminate the room, fill it with music, uncork a bottle of wine. No sun ever truly sets. Light is eternal. Far away, a golden dawn is breaking, shedding its light on nameless islands. White ships sail into it, awash in the fresh radiance of a day reborn.

5

September 10, 2000

The 10th of Elul, 5760

Six p.m. Although his guests will soon be arriving, Andrew lingers in the kitchen. He is as attentive to the presentation of the food as he is to its flavor and texture. He loves to cook. His dinners have an almost regal reputation and not just because of the outstanding food and expertly chosen wines: like everything on the menu, the guests are carefully selected, in a way that creates a perfect balance between stimulation and relaxed intimacy. His cooking is creative without being provocative, so much so that someone once remarked that its proportions resembled a Mondrian, almost perfectly geometric. Furthermore, his impressive collection of cookbooks does not deter him from improvising and enjoying himself in the kitchen. Although his Italian, especially Tuscan, dishes are superb, he sometimes flirts with French cuisine and even conducts controlled experiments with Asian fusion. But surprisingly, his true specialty is meat. It is indeed strange that a man like him, so ethereal and aloof, would so masterfully work with such rough and bloody material like beef, bison, lamb, and venison; there is an almost visual contradiction between his thin, delicate form and the large cuts of dry-aged Black Angus that he seared to perfection.

Andrew's renowned dinner parties are served with a semi-comical, theatrical relish that is part of the experience. The guests are long seated, a third bottle of wine opened, and the appetizers quickly consumed as the conversation becomes more and more lively—but the host is shut in the kitchen with the meat, a large cut of which lies on a gray granite slab. Sipping the wine around which he has planned the meal, Andrew stares at the cut as though to penetrate its inner being; then, suddenly, he puts down his glass and attacks the meat with sharp, sweeping movements, cutting it, spearing it, sprinkling it with pepper and coarse salt, beating the spices into it, and lovingly massaging it with olive oil and seasoning. Anyone observing his single-minded intensity at such times might think him an avatar of an ancient hunter or tribal shaman charged with sacrificing to the gods. The oven is now at the right temperature and the large wrought-iron skillet, purchased from a restaurant equipment wholesaler in Chinatown, is red-hot. Taking a deep breath, Andrew seizes the meat with both hands and flings it at the skillet's center. The effect is cinematic. A loud sizzle explodes in the kitchen and a tidal wave of mouthwatering scent quickly spreads through the apartment.

The fire sputters with glee. The seared flesh cries out in pain, writhing in the skillet as though struggling to escape while Andrew stands over it with merciless concentration, pinning it to its fiery bed of torture with a double-pronged fork. The searing sound begins to fade, the meat surrenders to the flame. Turned on its other side, it rages and resists again, but its defiance is short-lived, and its soul, fleeing the infernal flames, withdraws to its interior, turning into a hot, heavy, bloodred essence that oozes onto the serving tray and mingles with lemon juice, ground pepper, and olive oil as Andrew carves the roast expertly, the knife in his hands fluttering lightly over it as if it has a life of its own.

The guests, transfixed by this ceremony with its smells and heathenish display of succulent slices of meat wallowing in their juices, singed black at the edges and reddish-pink at the center, hesitate a bit before cutting and biting into it. The warm blood fills the mouth and feels as though it is trickling down the neck and throat. It ignites them with its raw saltiness, its soul trans-muted into theirs. Andrew stands by, expressionlessly, small beads of sweat glistening on his forehead. Long seconds pass in silence, until someone (usually, a woman) gasps in astonishment: "Oh my god, this meat is divine." Now all join in, breathlessly. "Fantastic!" "Amazing!" "Unbelievable!" Only then does Andrew snap out of his trance, his face relaxing and reverting to its usual amiable ex-pression. He refills the wineglasses with wine, takes his seat, and cheerfully welcomes his guests.

6
September 18, 2000

The 18th of Elul, 5760

Ten a.m. Though the morning music has finished playing, its last notes still float in the apartment before fading into the walls, ceiling, and furniture. Andrew sits at his desk, wrapped in his silk robe, his reading glasses playfully perched on the tip of his nose. Two or three books, a laptop, and a coffee cup lie on the desk. The keyboard, its keys like little mice dancing mischievously, click away almost inaudibly. Before beginning to work, he decided to record a dream in a special notebook kept for that purpose, an old habit retained from the psychoanalysis he completed several years ago. *A huge, splendidly uniformed warrior, blood-drenched and enraged, strides with giant steps toward a sunrise. Everything is in black and white, as in a Kurosawa movie. The uniform is like a samurai's magnificent armor.* Oddly, he awoke with a wonderful feeling. There was something powerfully liberating, almost comforting, about the warrior. Whom did he represent? A transposed father figure, most likely.

Ten twenty. The apartment is still. Andrew is hard at work, whistling merrily with a slight smile on his lips. He has never been a pedantic library rat. Scholarship is an art form for him. His light, airy manner suggests a painter or sculptor working in a spacious, well-lit studio, whistling to himself as he works. Most academics of his generation, products of the ecstasies of the sixties, translated their once-youthful rebellion into political radicalism, but that did not necessarily lead to methodological creativity. Andrew had never succumbed to the cheap temptation of being a professional rebel or playing the exhibitionistic role of the university enfant terrible. Although well versed in the standard critiques of capitalist society and proficient in teaching them to his students, he had never fallen prey to the anger and bitterness that characterized many of his colleagues. The buoyancy of his ideas keeps them afloat. From above, they can easily shift perspective, sometimes tumbling into creative free fall like Alice down the rabbit hole.

At ten thirty his answering machine comes alive with Linda's voice. "Hi, Andy. About Thanksgiving. We're making it at four as usual. Everyone will be there. There's no need to bring anything. Alison says hello. Bye." As always, Linda plans things months in advance and doesn't trust him to remember them. Her mention of Alison makes Andrew smile: she is such a sweet child, he wished he saw more of her. The damned thing about life in New York is that it never leaves time for what really matters. He will bring flowers and a bottle of good wine. No, not wine: chocolates. A big box of Belgian chocolate truffles. There is a new Godiva store on Broadway and 84th Street. It's settled, then: Belgian chocolates and flowers. Linda never filters her incoming calls the way he does. Like an anxious, obedient clerk, she answers the phone whenever it rings. Blinking and bleary-eyed, she lets salesmen wake her early on weekend mornings and friends bare their souls to her far into the night. It never occurs to her that she need only pick up the receiver when it suits her.

Ten forty. Andrew's fingers are still poised over the keyboard. He opens a book, turns its pages, finds what he is looking for, and replaces it facedown on the table. Ten fifty. Now the commanding voice of the legendary Ms. Harty—the department secretary— sounds in the apartment. Would he please get in touch with her today? No, it isn't urgent, but she will be waiting to hear from him. Andrew grunts something, picks up the book again, compares a quote with the original text while noting its page number and publication date, shuts the book again, and returns it to its pile. Although he is considered a fashionable thinker, this isn't because, as is commonly thought, he strives to be one. His detractors who accuse him of being a popularity hound are wrong. Projecting their own dogmatic selves onto his, they fail to grasp his true motives, exactly as they fail to guess a step ahead as to where the academic fashion is heading. The au courant character of his thought, with its playful language and quick, unmediated transitions between seemingly unrelated assumptions and discourses, is a sign not of glibness but of a mercurial, Peter Pan–ish nature that makes other, often much younger scholars, though still at the beginning of their careers, feel stodgy and conservative by comparison. Coupled with their annoyance at the poetic liberties he allows himself is their objection to what they call his "Popular Science" approach. (One cultural critic, a neo-Marxist who failed to get tenure in New York and was forced to wander to a state university an hour and

a half from the city, called this "the school of the soft academy.")
In this, too, they are mistaken. There is nothing opportunistic or
designed to inflate his list of publications in the wide range of subject matter and media that engross him. He simply has an open and
curious mind that refuses to be restricted to any one field. In his
fashion, he is a true Renaissance man.

Eleven twenty. The hesitant voice of Bert, his teaching assistant, requests clarification of Items 1 and 7 on the reading list. Bert
speaks quickly and nervously; well aware that Andrew screens his
calls, he has trained himself not to be insulted, but he is nevertheless at a loss each time he is ignored. Next come the chiming tones
of a young woman, obviously a junior secretary: "Hello, Professor
Cohen?" She is inviting him on behalf of the administration to the
opening of an exhibit the following month. Andrew goes on writing. Almost any message beginning "Hello, Professor Cohen" is
immediately ignored. Every few days he takes all these calls and
answers them from the phone in his office. Sometimes he entrusts
the job to his young research assistants, who, Andrew observed,
feel the same excitement at such moments that is felt by a small
child bursting with pride at having been asked by his parents to
perform a grown-up task. At other times he asks Bert to confirm
his participation in some event or apologize for his inability to attend, while in special cases he even avails himself of Ms. Harty—
behavior deemed by his colleagues to violate the laws of nature, all
the more so inasmuch as she complied with it even before rumors
of his imminent appointment, expected to be announced in September, had begun making the rounds of offices and corridors. Yet
neither openly nor in private does anyone protest his presumption
in asking to be freed of the annoying everyday chores whose very
existence, so it seems, are at odds with Andrew's aristocratic image. No one feels exploited, not only because, unfailingly polite and
respectful, he never crosses the lines of fairness as others in the

department occasionally do, but because of the precious, heady, even addictive nature of the time spent alone with him while receiving instructions or reporting back.

Eleven forty. It takes Andrew a moment to recognize the voice of the rental agent. "It's all arranged. The house in Montauk is yours for the third weekend of December. You and your lady friend" (does he detect a smirk?) "can have it starting Thursday. Enjoy yourselves!" Andrew grunts his approval: he likes the romantic charm of off-season vacation spots that are otherwise insufferable. It will be nice to be alone, just the two of them, with some privacy and quiet before the bustle of the winter holidays and the spring semester.

Twelve ten. The cautiously friendly voice of Shirin Zamindar, one of his recently graduated research students, catches Andrew off guard. She is so sorry to disturb him, she knows how busy he is, but she hopes it's okay to ask him whether he read her last article, recently published in *Theory Revisited*. She is very eager to know what he thinks. She is waiting to hear back from him, okay? Andrew frowns in discomfort. No, he hadn't had the chance to read it yet, and was sort of dreading it, not knowing what to say if he didn't like it as much as she wanted him to like it. He must do it soon, though. He must read the damn thing and find something nice to say about it—he can't keep her hanging in the air like this forever.

Twelve fifteen. A loud, clear feminine voice rings through the apartment: "Hi, Dad, I know you're there!" Andrew rouses himself. Rachel. He hurriedly presses "save," runs to the telephone, and grabs the receiver. The sudden exertion makes his "Hello" sound rushed, hoarse, and out of breath. "Hi, Dad, is that you? For a second I thought you really weren't there."

7

Rachel resembled neither of her parents. Linda liked to joke that she must have been switched at birth. She was long-legged and thin with a stark, angular beauty that made one think of Byron's or Heine's Hebrew maidens and rabbi's daughters, a beauty that was so diametrically opposed to the image of the China-doll, blue-eyed, and blond-haired all-American cheerleader that it seemed to deliberately challenge it. She inherited her father's aristocratic aura, but hers was not cool and collected; rather it was dark, fiery, and nervous. When she was angry her nostrils flared dangerously and her lips curled in an alluring, cruel smile that had a chilling effect. Her precise, articulate staccato made short shrift of anyone daring to contradict her, snappily dismissing all arguments as blundering and childish. Yet the other side of her, the opposite pole of the same intense equation, was an unrestrained and tender sweetness that stayed with those lucky enough to have kissed her long after she had lost all interest in them and discarded them by the wayside of her trail of romances. In Andrew's presence, she almost grudgingly softened even more. Her smiles became bigger and lost their all-knowing sarcastic quality, and sometimes, bursting into loud laughter, she would rub her cheek against her right shoulder in a manner that brought them both back to the bright, adorable five-year-old daddy's girl she once was, when they had spent hours playing word games and competing at intricately invented nonsense rhymes, amazed by their ability to stretch the boundaries of language and even of reality itself, creating and destroying fabulous worlds with wild giggles. Their favorite book was *Alice in Wonderland*. They delighted in its endless, mercurial imaginativeness, conversed in quotations from it, and felt as at home in its pages as if they themselves had written them. How Linda loved looking at them then, taking so much joy in the father-daughter bond that had seemed a protective wall around the blessed togetherness, the impregnable wholeness, of family life.

8

The divorce was devastating for Rachel. She was fourteen at the time, an unusually sensitive, intelligent child able to read her parents' distress signals before even they dared to do so. She had seen the disaster approaching and had realized, with the maturity precociously imposed on her, that having Alison was their last desperate, irrational effort to keep their disintegrating family together. Still, her feelings of shock and betrayal were as great as her mother's when Andrew finally left home and moved into a studio apartment in the faculty housing between Bleecker and Houston. For hours on end she shut herself up in her room, stretched out on her bed with her headphones on, listening to music so loud that it could be heard all over the room. Linda, who—for a while—feared she was having a nervous breakdown, was a wreck, too shattered to pay Rachel any attention. Her maternal instincts barely sufficed to care for Alison.

Rachel went through adolescence like a species in the wild, learning the ways of the adult world by trial and error, at once totally irresponsible and shouldering responsibilities far beyond her years. Her schoolwork suffered; she cut classes and spent her time smoking pot, listening to music, and making out, sweaty and glassy-eyed with random boys, her age and slightly older. At night she was often left alone to feed and bathe Alison, read her a bedtime story, and put her to sleep, after which she sat up waiting in the kitchen, sometimes until the small hours of the morning, for a sometimes drunk and disheveled and other times inappropriately ecstatic mother who would tell her, down to the most intimate details, about her date with a colleague from work, a new divorcé, or a sworn bachelor, a friend of a friend. Once, at the height of her abandon, it was even a stranger she met at a party. Rachel lost her virginity too early, slept with too many boys, and developed too sophisticated an exterior. Femininity seemed to her a crossroads that pointed in one of only two directions: humiliation or anger, and she chose anger. She despised weakness. It took years for her feelings for her mother to mellow and warm.

In the end, Linda got over it. Her career as a social worker resumed its central place in her life and Rachel learned to respect her again, though more as a peer than a daughter. When, four years after her divorce, Linda met George, a charming psychotherapist, amateur gardener, and lover of literature and music, and married him a year later in a modest civil ceremony in the Brooklyn Botanic Garden, Rachel was thrilled for her and delighted to be her unofficial bridesmaid. Not even Andrew's having been invited to the celebratory dinner party held in the private room of a nice Italian restaurant could cause her to lose her composure, at least not outwardly.

9

October 1, 2000

The 2nd of Tishrei, 5761

There was something special about those lazy Sunday mornings, which didn't start until the afternoon. True, it felt a bit absurd to be bringing home bagels, cream cheese, and orange juice at an hour when the sun was already listing heavily westward, dappling the river with the first intimations of sunset. Nodding hello to the doorman, Andrew stepped outside and paused as usual by the

two male figures flanking the entrance of the building, carved into
the soft limestone. Its facade was studded with gargoyles, which
once, in medieval Europe, may have symbolized something but
were symbols only of themselves in America. Half-naked, muscular, and neoclassically handsome, they held up the building with an
infinite, Atlas-like fatigue in their tormented faces. Andrew's nod
to the doorman was a salute to these figures as well.

It was a warm, humid autumn day, a consequence no doubt
of global warming. The street echoed with sound, which was
strange, because Sundays were generally quiet. Something was in
the air, something unusual that invoked in him an odd yearning, a
pang of unclear desire. His heart swelled; his eyes misted and felt
about to overflow. As though borne by an unperceived wind, jagged trumpet blasts could be heard in the distance, the bleat of rams'
horns tipped with pure silver. A walled city, round-bellied like a
pregnant woman, stood by a river crossing. Its walls would fall on
the seventh day, crumbling to dust. Where were those notes coming from? Was there a parade today? An open-air performance
by a wind orchestra? A familiar song reached his ears, a song he
knew well: Neil Diamond's "Shilo." Was it drifting through an
open window on a lower floor? *Young child with dreams, dream every dream on your own.* It had been their theme song for an entire
summer, the unforgettable summer of 1970. Smooth black fins, one
after another, emerging from the sea's metallic blue, overlapping
each other in a dreamlike silence, forming a series of perfect arcs
in the milky mist of the dawn. But could it really be their song? It
no longer sounded like "Shilo." And those trumpets! So many of
them, a hundred or more, all blaring together.

Papa says he'd love to be with you if he had the time. Young child
with dreams, young child of joy: it wrenched his heart each time
he heard his name. Wake up! What in the world was happening to
him? Why all these bizarre thoughts? Gradually, the mysterious

excitement was wearing off, leaving a vague sense of emptiness. He ran his fingers through his hair and scratched his head vigorously, the hard contact restoring him to his senses. What was going on? He had never felt so emotional for no reason. It was over now, though . . . almost. The distant sounds had faded, blending into the ordinary din of the city. Quiet at last. But why was the sun so burning hot when it was already October? Bagels. Right: bagels. The Absolute Bakery and then orange juice. He mustn't forget the orange juice!

Andrew turned left and started up 110th Street toward Broadway. A Jewish family passed by in the other direction, the father's suit jacket open and his tie loosened. Behind him slowly strode a few young people with yarmulkes and prayer books, heading for Riverside Drive. *Tashlikh*, Andrew told himself, smiling fondly with sudden understanding. It was Rosh Hashanah (the word came to him in its old East European pronunciation, a relic of his distant Sunday school days) and *tashlikh* at the Hudson, with its colorfully symbolic casting of sins into the water, was an entertaining annual ritual that the Upper West Side was known for. Andrew had once gone to see it with a friend, a somewhat practicing Jew who lived in the neighborhood. He had enjoyed the colorful assortment of different clothes and lifestyles with its variety of skullcaps worn by men and women, interspersed with an occasional Orthodox black hat and even a *shtreimel*, a traditional Hasidic fur hat, that looked—against the background of the green trees and the white sails of the boats on the river—like an exotic, wild animal.

Rosh Hashanah reminded him of Yom Kippur. That had to be soon, didn't it? Andrew paused to write a reminder in the PalmPilot he drew from his jacket pocket: "Confirm Yom Kippur attendance. Check tickets and payment." He read on, scrolling with a pencil point to check the coming two weeks. While all New York universities were closed on Yom Kippur, he wanted to make sure he had no other appointments. There it was. *Monday, October 9*: "10 a.m., Yom Kippur services." That was seen to, then. Below it, though, appeared: *Monday, October 9*: "6 p.m. Friends of New York Opera Society. Maria Callas. Lecture and rare recordings." Of course. Callas. He would have to leave the synagogue early. The lecture, with its never-before-heard tapes of the legendary soprano, promised to be fascinating. Open only to members of the society, it had probably sold out long ago, but Andrew had connections with more than a few cultural institutions in the city. He had written about their activities, had sat or was sitting on their boards, organized joint research projects—getting hold of two invitations would not be a problem. Ann Lee would be so happy! The thought of Ann Lee curled up on his brown leather couch in his spectacular silk robe, which clung to her thin, naked body, watching a TV program recorded the night before on some amazing high-tech innovation that her generation took for granted, sent a wave of warm desire through his body.

10

The way Andrew and Ann Lee met seemed stolen from a movie. In the second week of April 1999, the spring issue of the *New Yorker* had had an unusually stunning cover illustration of a good-looking young couple—an embodiment of the anorexic chic of the late nineties—kissing in the street while locked in an embrace that brimmed with youthful sexuality. The nipples of the girl's breasts were taut against her thin T-shirt; her hair was gathered with fashionable little pins. The boy's shirt was hiked up past his flat stomach, his sharply outlined pelvis showing above his low-slung pants. Their long, passionate kiss, which deserved a place in the hall of fame of iconic invocations of Eros, had a surprisingly powerful effect on Andrew, who first saw it on one of those Saturday mornings when he sat relaxing on the couch with his papers and magazines, his hair still rumpled from sleep and his cappuccino smelling of hot milk and cinnamon. There was something extraordinary about it, able to penetrate the defenses of a man exposed to large and frequent amounts of art—something enticing, rousing, even moving. Yes, moving. Andrew was moved. For the first time in years, something had touched him to a core that lay buried beneath many layers of knowledge and experience. His eyes glued to the cover, he studied its perfect depiction of the woman's petite breasts, the round curve of her cheek, and the tilt of her swanlike neck. Even the body of the young man stirred him in an odd, unfamiliar way. It wasn't strictly sexual; it had to do with something deeper, more elementary, of which sex was only a part. His entire person felt triggered into action: his muscles tensed, the small hairs of his body bristled, his skin tingled. Everything was suddenly alive. Andrew shut his eyes. Disjointed thoughts ran through his mind. He stretched, feeling the seductive kiss work its way into him and course through his veins. He pressed the sole of his bare foot against the couch, pleasurably probing its cool, rich leather. Something throbbed pleasantly between his thighs. Looking down, he smiled in wonder at the warm, boyish, almost full erection prodding his cloth pajama bottoms.

That whole day and the day after that, Andrew continued to feel the same arousal. It carried over to Monday, too, with its promise of rejuvenation that, had he tried to find a word for it, he might have called in his playful manner "Renaissensual." And then on Tuesday, which happened to be a warm, balmy spring day, at exactly ten thirty a.m., he was surprised, almost startled, to see Ann Lee sitting by herself at a front table of the Hungarian Pastry Shop.

The women Andrew had gone out with since his divorce had been strikingly similar. All resembled feminine versions of himself.

He had met them through the tightly woven network of professional New York intellectuals who commanded the city's institutional intersections of knowledge and power: female professors, magazine editors, literary critics—well-groomed, attractive, elegant women in their early forties with imposing presences and sharp minds, most of them trim, tall, and athletic. The dynamic of his short-lived relationships with them was repetitive to the point that it might have been deemed an intrinsic part of courtship. A first, Saturday-night date. Dinners at upscale restaurants so alike that one couldn't tell them apart: the same Chardonnay, Sauvignon Blanc, or Pinot Grigio with the appetizers; the same Cabernet Sauvignon, Merlot, or Pinot Noir with the main course; the same cognac, grappa, or amaro to round off the meal. Such evenings almost always ended in the woman's apartment, which, once he made out the unifying idea behind its multiplicity of detail, was like all the others. So was the enjoyable but never exciting sex that inevitably began—too soon and almost out of necessity—on the first date. It was followed, on the woman's initiative, by a romantic weekend at a vacation home (a beachfront property or mountain lodge, depending on the season) belonging to her or a friend, or else jointly owned, in the Hamptons, Fire Island, the Berkshires, or the Poconos. Indeed, these occasions found Andrew surrounded by the woman's friends, cooking for them, entertaining them, and impressing them with her choice of the ideal partner—soon after which their relationship invariably came to its painless, tearless, unprotested, and perfectly routine end. Had anyone invented a fictional version of Andrew's love life, carefully constructing it to have as many complications and contradictions as possible, he could not possibly have imagined anyone so unlike these companions for a week or two, so much their polar opposite, as was Ann Lee.

He had gotten to know her the previous autumn in his weekly research seminar. Her regular seat was opposite him at the end of an oval table, and although she was far from his most active student, Andrew felt that her presence and the partially verbalized communication between them were the class's hidden axis, not only for him but also for all its participants.

Nearly every teacher has a student who becomes the class's center of gravity. Something in his or her look—a vital, almost telepathic spark—forges an unspoken bond that is a bit like falling in love, except that it is the love of pure knowledge. It is an ad hoc infatuation that should exist only for the duration of the lesson and under no circumstance be given other expression. There can be no greater mistake than the attempt to preserve it beyond the boundaries of the classroom.

Yet sometimes, less frequently, it happens as well that a student, by virtue of physical beauty or sheer sexual magnetism, has a magical, hypnotic, almost obsessive effect on a teacher. The heady power of youth links up with that of professorial authority, reinforced by a strict, inviolable taboo, a powerful stimulant in its own right, hovering over the classroom like a threatening bird of prey.

Ann Lee's case was a good example. Each time that Andrew—who, like an actor, picked up every vibration from his audience and adjusted his performances accordingly—surveyed his students, his involuntary glance came to rest on her, forcing him to tear his eyes away before they both were equally embarrassed. She was gorgeous. Her face and proportions gave her beauty a rare, unmistakable quality that Andrew might best have described, had it not been so politically incorrect, as exotic. Young and unspoiled, she had lustrous skin and a willowy frame. Her head was a bit too large for her body, which sometimes lent her the look of a child. And she indeed looked a bit like a child, when Andrew saw her on that warm, balmy Tuesday as she sat, encircled by a softly glowing halo, at a front table of the Hungarian Pastry Shop.

11

The Hungarian Pastry Shop, a pleasant, dimly lit café opposite the Cathedral of Saint John the Divine on Amsterdam Avenue, was the perfect place to sit and write. It hadn't been renovated in years, which only heightened its homey charm in the eyes of its regular customers. Its old-fashioned decor had a sweet-and-sour, European flavor. The walls, last replastered in the 1980s, were covered with dozens of naive, semi-primitive paintings of the kind once popularly referred to by the vague label of "modern art." A single artist had painted them all, and all, without exception, had a single subject: angels—or, more precisely, the angelical. Well-built, flaxen-haired, and broad-shouldered, the rustic, Slavic-looking women bore hefty wings protruding from their muscular backs through flimsy garments. The café's motley clientele of Columbia University students and professors, would-be actresses working as waitresses, and not-yet-though-no-doubt-soon-to-be-famous writers was interspersed with a handful of slovenly, unshaven eccentrics, relics of the neighborhood's previous incarnation, who sat nursing a single cup of coffee all day while devouring cheap tabloids that, like them, seemed to have emerged from a time capsule.

Andrew liked the Hungarian Pastry Shop. He came there to work, to meet colleagues, or just to read. Paradoxically, he found the continual hubbub of public places conducive to his inner quiet and creativity. Yet this quiet was disrupted that spring Tuesday upon seeing, to his surprise, Ann Lee sitting with a large notebook at a front table by the window, radiantly pretty. A cup of red herbal tea stood carefully aligned with the notebook, its vapors that rose to mingle with the sunbeams completing a perfect composition. It was their first encounter outside the seminar's protective, neutralizing walls, which symbolized the endless prohibitions, justifications, and rationalizations that circumscribed his infatuation with her and ruled out the slightest possibility of doing anything about it. She was dressed with the same stylish nonchalance as she had been in his classes; her brightly colored, flared pants, which came almost to the ankles and were a throwback to the fashions of the seventies, made her even more attractive, invoking youthful memories as visceral as the strip of belly revealed by the midriff's cunningly provocative cut and as innocent as her green kerchief and the two long braids descending from it. Resurrecting long-lost sensations: the foam on the waves, the sun's warmth on bare skin, the salty-sweet kisses tasting of the ocean. Andrew was bewildered by the pounding of his heart and the quickened pulse at his temples, adolescent sensations that his body, seemingly long immunized against them, had allowed itself to forget. The previous Saturday's spring fever, triggered by the kiss on the cover of the *New Yorker*, overcame him again with full force, augmented by a new urgency, a sense of alarm verging on panic. Adrenaline flooded his body. His footsteps slowed as he passed her table. Yet not daring to stop, he swallowed hard and made his way inside, pretending not to have seen her, though he had no idea whom he was trying to fool. Was it sensible to ignore her? Should he have said hello? Sat down next to her? He felt an itchy, nervous annoyance with himself that he hadn't experienced in years.

Andrew continued unsteadily to the back, managed to find an empty table, and sank heavily into a chair, careful to position himself behind a large column. Although suffused by a sour, physical sensation of missed opportunity, he couldn't muster the courage to return to her table and make up for his lapse, couldn't even conceive of it. He simply went on sitting there, huddled in his hiding place until he saw her get up and leave. A worn, brown suede jacket, a leather handbag slung across her back. Not until she was gone did he dare rise and go to the counter to order his coffee. At last, his rational defenses swung into action just as his brain finished processing the visual data transmitted to it in the split second he had paused by her table. The notebook was a musical score. She had been reading music.

12

Andrew was sure he was dreaming when he heard her voice over the telephone that same evening. He recognized it at once, despite her failure to identify herself. With a casual, even amused assurance, like someone talking to a confidant, she invited him to a concert to be given by her choir. "It's tomorrow night at seven, at Saint John the Divine. Can you make it?" Andrew was at a loss for words. His mouth dry, he groped for something to say before finally blurting the requisite "Yes, of course" in the choked, raspy voice of a frightened teenager.

He groomed himself for the concert as he hadn't done in years. For nearly an hour he stood before the mirror, putting on and taking off shirts, staining their stiff collars with perspiration mingled with blood from an overly close shave. In the end, he decided on black with a black jacket and gray tie, a worldly look that suited his crisp shock of hair. Confused by his excitement, he tried standing apart from it and putting it in perspective with a wry, paternal smile, only to be forced to acknowledge (his sweaty palms were the final giveaway) that he couldn't remember when, if ever, he had last been so nervous before meeting a woman—none of which prepared him for the thrill of her intoxicatingly clear, siren-like voice that was threaded with the finest gossamers of silver. Like a precious metal, it had a perfection born of itself and comprehensible only on its own terms. Andrew stared at her with mounting emotion, his eyes on her mouth. He was in a state of lucid euphoria, last experienced by him in a younger, less jaded, more pristine time of his life. Nor did he expect the spontaneous, behind-stage hug he was given when the performance was over, or the salty, touchingly large tears that trickled from her tightly shut eyes.

He still felt warm all over late that night, long after she had fallen asleep, nestled in the crook of his neck, her heavy childlike breathing tickling him. He could feel her kisses everywhere, on his neck, on the folds of his stomach, on places whose existence had long been forgotten: the kisses of a young woman for whom sex was not yet a routine, who put all her desire, infatuation, and curiosity into each embrace. He lay awake, his arm around her thin body, full of wonder at the speed and intensity with which it had all happened. Only months later, again late at night, in the gentle fog of presleep, did he mention having seen her alone at a table that morning, studying a score.

"Yeah," she said. "You were so cute."

Andrew turned to her in sudden, wakeful surprise. "I used to go there all the time."

Ann Lee laid a tender hand on his cheek, stroking his earlobe and neck. "I know you did. I was there to run into you."

Propped on his elbows, he looked at her. "Is that true?"

"Of course it is," she said with a loving smile. "What did you think? It's not like they have such amazing coffee."

13

October 9, 2000

The 10th of Tishrei, 5761

Nine a.m. The Yom Kippur service was on the Lower East Side, and Andrew wanted to be on time, especially since he would have to leave early. Rachel's announcement that she would join him had touched and gladdened him even more than he was willing to admit. He wasn't sure he understood her reasons, especially since it meant coming into the city from Princeton, but questioning her would only have put her on the defensive and forced her to rationalize.

Broadway was less crowded than usual. Yom Kippur made itself felt all over the city, most of all on the Upper West Side. On his way to the subway he glanced, as he did every morning, at his homeless man on the corner, as though to make sure he was still there. He was one of the neighborhood's iconic lunatics. His obese, grotesque figure complemented that of the skinny, half-mad black preacher who liked to stand on the same corner, always wearing the same hat and suit, holding an unidentified book—the New Testament, no doubt, or else some ancient apocalyptic text—while rocking back and forth and shouting rhythmic 'allelujahs in his Creole accent. His homeless man never shouted or lost his composure. On the contrary, he seemed perfectly pleased with his station in life. He sat expansively on his bench in a broad-brimmed hat, wrapped in woolen blankets that formed a filthy gray poncho while carefully balancing in one hand a chessboard set for a game that never took place. Like a cruel parody of the proverbial swallow, he appeared annually on the first day of spring and vanished on the first day of autumn, borne away by his grime-encrusted blankets as though on the gray wings of a huge, slow-moving migratory bird.

The skinny preacher was in his regular place, bobbing up and down as always while straining with his hornlike voice to be heard. Andrew's homeless man, on the other hand, did not display his usual calm. Eyes wide with apprehension behind smeared glasses that were held together by Scotch tape, he was mumbling something unclear, his immense frame shifting restlessly on his bench, throwing off the heap of blankets covering him like a mass of molten magma. His agitation could be felt. Its frantic contortions got under Andrew's skin, forcing him to slow down and stare, mesmerized, at the heavy, pitiable figure. The flaps of the blankets lifted, revealing a pair of unexpectedly spread massive thighs, between which Andrew saw a huge, bloated member suggestive of a strange, beached sea creature. Quickly, he looked away from the repulsive sight, his heart beating faster; what should have been compassion had turned into an inexplicable anxiety. The penises of drowned men, he imagined, must look that way, sickly hunks of pale, swollen meat. *Who by fire, who by water*: wasn't that a Leonard Cohen song?

Andrew hurried down the subway stairs. Only when he had descended a few steps and put himself at a safe distance did the standard New York fantasy occur to him: Why not bring the man home, wash the filth from him, cover his nakedness, give him a roof over his head, and restore him to the human race? Yet no less a part of this ritual, these thoughts were followed by the cold voice of reason: No, that was out of the question, not even remotely possible. As if smelling something bad or spoiled, Andrew involuntarily bit his lips and quickened his pace, trying not to think of the obscene sight he had witnessed, letting it dissipate in the sea of impressions in which his mind swam. How does one get to the Lower East Side? It was at the other end of the world. He would have to take the 1 or 9 train to 14th Street, follow the underground passage that led to the orange lines of the F, B, or D train, and continue to Lower Manhattan, making sure to get off at the right stop. A year ago, immersed in a book, he had missed it and found himself in Brooklyn.

14

What was left of the old Lower East Side Jewish ghetto? Not much. The neighborhood had been abandoned to low-income housing projects and depressingly ugly high-rises standing in seemingly random lots. Miraculously, the clock of the old Forward Building still showed the right time. On its edifice, the paper's Yiddish name survived, carved in block gilt letters like those of an ancient prayer book. The large synagogue on the corner of Forsyth and Delancey, a grand structure that once had been the pride of the Jewish community, was now an Adventist church. A huge white cross adorned the facade, centered on the rose window with its former Star of David. And there were still a few Jewish eateries: Yonah Schimmel's knishes, Kossar's Bialys, Nathan's kosher hot dogs, which had never really been kosher. Old-time New Yorkers still recalled Bernstein's kosher Chinese restaurant on Essex Street with its Chinese waiters and their greasy black yarmulkes, its customers offered gift packages of salami for their sons in the armed forces with the motto "The gift you'll love to give." Mysteriously burned down a few years ago, it had been replaced by a nameless, nondescript office building. As for the renowned Essex Street pickle sellers, they became a tourist trap and branded themselves a "New York institution," as advertised by a sign above the entrance. Now delivered all over the United States, the pickles were sold from hermetically sealed red plastic containers, which are far more economical than the old wooden barrels.

And yet the restless ghosts of the poverty-stricken immigrants who worked themselves to the bone in sweatshops or at miserable outdoor stands still haunt the streets where they had led their slavish lives, seeking their redemption in the old buildings, the basements that once had housed workshops and the lofts of the shut-down synagogues, amid rotting piles of old parchment, torn scraps of sacred books, and Yiddish ads for the Second Avenue Theatre.

15

Andrew did not go to synagogue on Yom Kippur for nostalgic reasons, or at least so he had told himself. Nor did he do so out of guilt. Ethel Cohen was the complete opposite of any stereotype—comic or tragic—of the Jewish mother. Guilt was not her thing. She deeply disliked sentimental Judaism, of the hora-dancing "Hava Nagila" variety, along with the Jewish mothers who behaved as though the medical degrees of their sons and the nice Jewish girls they were married to were their own achievement. When Andy chose to go to the progressive, even radical University of California in far-off Berkeley, Ethel's protests were strictly for the record; deep down she was pleased to see her youngest son continue the westward trek of his ancestors, break the last chains of the East Coast ghetto, and leave behind the world of doctors, lawyers, Harvard graduates, and Mama's boys for a new, more "American" path in life. Perhaps, too, the fact that her older son Matthew had gone to law school and joined a prestigious firm made it easier for her to cast off her generation's prejudices and take pleasure in the non-Harvard education of her nondoctor son pursuing a non-lucrative field. So tolerantly accepting was her outlook that Andrew was ready to swear—it was his and Linda's private joke—that she was even a bit shocked ("Disappointed," Linda corrected him once the humor of it had begun to wear off) that her Andy had brought home a Jewish girl. It was from his mother that Andrew had gotten his aversion to the narrow-mindedness of the Jewish middle class and to what he called in an interview with the *American Review* "the empty matrimonial obsession of contemporary Judaism . . . a materialistic, visceral reaction that is fully focused on the nuptial bed, the fetishization of which has stranded it in a symbolic vacuum like a hot air balloon floating in space after the basket holding its passengers has detached itself and crashed."[*]

Why, nevertheless, did he go to synagogue one Yom Kippur after another? Not knowing the answer to this question, Andrew declined to ask it too often. It was neither a rational decision nor the outcome of lengthy debate, but an unthinking, almost absentminded choice. Congregation Anshei Shalom, the synagogue he attended, was particularly progressive, even avant-garde. Except for a few Hebrew verses retained for their poetic value by the editors of *The New Holiday Prayer Book*, nearly the entire service was in English. ("We see no spiritual advantage," proclaimed the congregation's founding declaration of principles, "in the rote repetition of an ancient liturgy that fails to resonate with the speech of our daily lives.") Constantly adapting, it was at the cutting edge of the egalitarian, multicultural, humanistic, left-liberal politics of the day.

Anshei Shalom occupied the premises of an old synagogue, dating to the early twentieth century, which shut down in the 1970s when the last congregants died or left the neighborhood. Due to budgetary difficulties, the church to which it was converted shut its doors after a while. Thereafter, the building sat empty for several years and served as a hangout for drug dealers and the homeless; eventually, it was taken over by a group of young Jewish artists and intellectuals who had moved into the neighborhood, the gentrification of which had begun to attract bohemian types.

---

[*] J. L. Goldstein, "Identity as a Case of Group Dynamics"—Interview with Andrew P. Cohen, author of *I Spy Me: The Changing Rules of the Game of Identity*, *American Review* 14, Spring 1989, pp. 82–84.

The group's religious leader, Abby Rosenthal, was an energetic
and charismatic young rabbi, a fellow at the Koenig Institute for
Advanced Cultural Studies. One of the founders of the small but
dynamic Fringe Theater Troupe, she had also recently published a
book of poetry to critical acclaim. In addition to being intellectually gifted and creative, she had a talent for administration and politics that had enabled her to obtain not only permission to use the
old building but a municipal grant for its renovation. For reasons
aesthetic (and financial), this restructuring had only been partial.
Some of the decaying stained-glass windows and gilded molding
had survived, lending the space a brooding theatrical charm that
suited its sophisticated congregants.

The decision to retain Anshei Shalom's old name was more a
matter of whimsy than of any heavy, humorless argument on behalf of cultural continuity. While far from traditional, the congregation's services had none of the group singing, guitar playing,
colorful prayer shawls, and embroidered yarmulkes that had replaced the organ and priestly rabbinical garb in most Reform temples. Abby's wit, passion, and powerful presence were enough to
keep attendees in a permanent state of spiritual alertness. She liked
to refer to her style of leading a service as "eclectic," a blend of
mysticism, meditation, and the latest scientific theories that left
open the question of God's existence. (Many of the congregation's
members were atheists or agnostics.)

"Dad, Dad, over here!" Rachel was waving with a smile while
pointing to an empty seat beside her. A warm feeling welled in Andrew's chest, as it did whenever he caught sight of her, his baby
daughter who had grown to be such an attractive and impressive
young woman. It was strange, though, to see her here. As a rule,
she shrank from anything Jewish, and he himself was hardly a regular. He was puzzled even more by the open interest she took in the
proceedings. Yet curious though he was, this was not the time to ask

her about it. He let the hypnotic rhythm of the singing and chanting carry him along, half-concentrating on the motes of dust swirling in the colored shafts of light that pierced the stained-glass windows.

One thirty. The service was taking longer than usual—longer than he remembered, at any rate—and Abby Rosenthal hadn't yet begun her sermon, the high point of the day for most congregants. Restlessly, Andrew glanced at his watch; he didn't know how much longer he could stay. He had to meet Ann Lee at five if they were going to make it to the opera on time, which was a shame, because he liked to hear Abby speak. Should he stay a while longer and catch the sermon's beginning? No, it would be rude to walk out in the middle. "I have to go," he whispered to Rachel, leaning slightly toward her. "Do you want to come with me?" Surprising him again, she chose to stay. "I've heard all kinds of interesting things about this rabbi of yours," she whispered back. Yes, Abby was interesting. Maybe he would read her sermon later, on her website. He rose, kissed Rachel on the cheek, and headed for the exit. Strange, how her eyes had lit up when talking about Abby Rosenthal. He stepped into the corridor, returned his yarmulke to its basket, picked up his coat from the coat check girl, tipped her a dollar, and left. He could grab a quick espresso and get home in time to rest and change before meeting Ann Lee.

16

Abby Rosenthal mounted the podium holding an intriguing, old prayer book with gilded pages. "I want to share something with you this year," she began after a long moment of silence. "It's an unusual reading experience: a description, in great technical detail, of a remarkable theatrical performance staged every year on this very day, the day of Yom Kippur, the day of atonement. An audience of thousands watched it with baited breath, itself a participant, everyone's energy converging on a single figure—a single actor, if you will, the star of our pageant. It's set in the Temple in Jerusalem. The time is the Roman period. The chief protagonist bears the title of High Priest. It's a suspenseful, passionate, exacting drama. The climax comes at a highly charged moment, a symbolically explosive one, when the High Priest enters an inner room, the most mysterious and secluded of all the rooms in the Temple, which no one would dare enter on any other day of the year. Its enchanting name: The Holy of Holies."

Abby let her last words echo, then continued in a less dramatic, more personal tone: "I know that some of you cringed when you heard me say 'the Temple in Jerusalem.' I know that for most of you, myself, too, those words are instinctively off-putting. I can remember one year, when I was eleven; my father was a visiting professor at a university in Boston and the nearest synagogue was Conservative, not Reform. Everything was different there—it was a whole other world. Every week they prayed for the Temple, the Temple . . . *Build the Temple again, God!* It went in one ear and out the other. It was all a lot of white noise, meaningless words, an incomprehensible mantra that had lost its suggestive power—or perhaps nothing but its suggestive or auto-suggestive power remained. Maybe I had to journey a long way and feel sufficiently grounded in the here and now before I could take the time to listen to this ancient voice that tells me about a house destroyed two thousand years ago. Our text for today was deleted from the prayer books that you and I grew up with by the nineteenth century. This year I rediscovered it. Its aesthetics, structure, texture are as fascinating as are its contents. It's old, strange, fascinating, inspiring. It moves me greatly to share it with you. It's called"— she pronounced the words in Hebrew, in a deep, musical, guttural voice—"*Seder ha-Avodah*, Order of the Ritual."

[Leviticus, Chapter 16, Verses 1—2] And the LORD spoke unto Moses, after the death of the two sons of Aaron, when they drew near before the LORD, and died; and the LORD said unto Moses: "Speak unto Aaron thy brother, that he come not at all times into the holy place within the veil, before the ark cover which is upon the ark; that he die not; for I appear in the cloud upon the ark cover."

ORDER OF THE RITUAL

[Mishna, Treatise Yoma, Chapter 1, Mishna 1] Seven days before the day of atonement the High Priest was removed from his house to the cell of the counselors and another priest was prepared to take his place in case anything happened to him [the High Priest] that would unfit him [for the service]. Rabbi Judah said: Also another wife was prepared for him in case his wife should die. For it is written, and he shall make atonement for himself and for his house. "His house" that means "his wife." They said to him: If so, there would be no end to the matter.

[Babylonian Talmud, Treatise Sanhedrin, Folio 22a] Rabbi Eliezer said: For him who divorces the

Now in Jerusalem, there was a certain priest whose name was Obadiah. He served in the Temple and was devoted to its sacred rites, being a pious, God-fearing man and jealous for the Lord. Where there is love, there is jealousy, and where there is jealousy, there is love.

There came the week between the festivity of the New Year and the Day of Atonement in which the sages of Israel and the priestly elders seclude the High Priest in the Temple to rehearse with him the order of the ritual, the offerings and sacrifices made on the awesome day. Among those chosen to attend him and be his acolytes was Obadiah. Long before the High Priest arrived in his chambers, these hummed like a beehive. Priests ran to and fro, sparing no effort to make them fit for a king. Floors were scrubbed, lamps polished, drapes hung, and linens taken out to be aired, for while not all High Priests were greatly versed in Tradition, great power was vested in all High Priests.

[Babylonian Talmud, Treatise Yoma, Folio 6a] THE HIGH PRIEST WAS REMOVED. Why was he removed? [You ask] why was he removed! [Is it not] as you have said, either according to the derivation of Rabbi Johanan, or to that of Resh Lakish?——No, this is the question: Why was he separated from his house?——It was taught: Rabbi Judah Ben Bathyra said: Lest his wife be found under doubt of being a menstruant and he have congress with her. Do we speak of wicked people?—— Rather, perhaps he will have congress with his wife and she will then be found to be doubtfully a menstruant.

first wife, the very altar sheds tears, as it is written [Malachi, Chapter 2, 13]: *And this further ye do, ye cover the altar of the Lord with tears, with weeping and with sighing, in so much that he regardeth not the offering any more, neither receiveth it with goodwill at your hand.* And further it is written [Malachi, Chapter 2, 14]: *Yet ye say, Wherefore? Because the Lord hath been witness between thee and the wife of thy youth, against whom thou hast dealt treacherously, though she is thy companion and the wife of thy covenant.*

The Gate of Rebirth:
Know that the physical body is but the soul's outer garment!
Let us begin with our Sages of blessed memory having said that the soul has five names. From the lowest to the highest, these are: *Nefesh,* or Vital Soul; *Ruach,* or Intellectual Soul; *Neshamah,* or Spiritual Soul; *Chayah,* or the living soul; *Yechidah,* or the unique core of the soul.

[Mishna, Treatise Yoma, Chapter 1, Mishna 2] Throughout the seven days he sprinkles the blood and burns the incense and trims the lamps and offers the head and the hind leg; on all other days he offers only if he so desires; for the High Priest is first in offering a portion and has first place in taking a portion.

On the day he was brought to the Temple, the High Priest was met at his front door by the elders of the Sanhedrin, who escorted him through the streets of Jerusalem like a bridegroom. The city's youth ran ahead of him to clear his path; musicians marched behind him with their music; young priests sang as they led the bull of the sin-offering that would be sacrificed by him on the Day of Atonement. As they neared the Temple's western gate, the Levites, hurrying to conclude their preparations, spread a damask carpet for him to tread on and stood in rows on either side of it as though for the arrival of a potentate. Obadiah took his place among them, beads of sweat on his brow. He looked at the noisy crowd of old and young priests elbowing and jostling one another by the gate until the voice of the Superior announced, "Make way for the High Priest!"

[Babylonian Talmud, Treatise Yoma, Folio 8b] TO THE CELL OF THE COUNSELORS etc. Rabbi Judah said, Was it the "Chambers of the *Parhedrin* [counselors]," was it not rather the "Chambers of the *Buleute* [senators]"? Originally, indeed, it was called the "Chambers of the Senators" but because money was being paid for the purpose of obtaining the position of High Priest and the [High Priests] were changed every twelve months, like those [Roman] counselors, who are changed every twelve months, therefore it came to be called "the Chambers of the Counselors."

[Isaiah, Chapter 57, Verses 16—21] For I will not contend forever, neither will I be always wroth; for the spirit that enwrappeth itself is from Me, and the souls which I have made. For the iniquity of his covetousness was I wroth and smote him, I hid Me and was wroth; and he went on frowardly in the way of his heart. I have seen his ways, and will heal him; I will lead him also, and requite with comforts him and his mourners. Peace, peace, to him that is far off and to him that is near, saith the LORD that createth the fruit of the lips; and I will heal him. But the wicked are like the troubled sea; for it cannot rest, and its waters cast up mire and dirt. There is no peace, saith my God concerning the wicked.

[Babylonian Talmud, Treatise Abodah Zarah, Folio 5a] Rabbi Jose said: "The [Messiah] Son of David will only come when all the souls destined to [inhabit earthly] bodies will be exhausted, as it is said, *For I will not contend forever, neither will I be always wroth, for the spirit should fall before me and the spirits which I have made.*"

[Babylonian Talmud, Treatise Yoma, Folio 53a] Our Rabbis taught: And he shall put the incense upon the fire before the Lord: i.e., he must not put it in order outside and thus bring it in. [This is] to remove the error from the minds of the Sadducees who said: He must prepare it without, and bring it in. What is their interpretation?——For I appear in the cloud upon the ark cover "that teaches us that he prepares it outside and brings it in." The Sages said to them: But it is said already "And he shall put the incense upon the fire before the Lord." If so for what purpose then is it stated "For I appear in the cloud upon the ark cover"? It comes to teach us that he puts into it a smoke-raiser. Whence do we know that he must put a smoke-raiser into it?——Because it is said: So that the cloud of the incense may cover the ark cover. But if he did not put a smoke-raiser into it, or that he omitted one of its spices, he is liable to death.

[Babylonian Talmud, Treatise Yoma, Folio 18a] Surely it has been taught: And the priest that is highest among his brethren, that means he should be highest among his brethren in strength, in beauty, in wisdom, and in riches. Rabbi Assi said: A Tarkab full of golden Denars did Martha, the daughter of Boethus, give to King Jannai to nominate Joshua ben Gamala as one of the High Priests.

———————

[Babylonian Talmud, Treatise Yoma, Folios 4 a—b] We have a teaching in accord with Resh Lakish: Moses went up in a cloud, was covered by the cloud, and was sanctified by the cloud in order that he might receive the Torah for Israel in sanctity, as it is written: "And the glory of the Lord abode upon Mount Sinai." [. . .]

There was a hush. No one dared utter a sound. Two elders of the Sanhedrin appeared in the gateway of the Temple, leading a man of handsome mien and proportions. He had a fine carriage. His hair was coiffed, his beard neatly trimmed, his cloak of the very best cloth. Glowing, he cut a courtly figure as he entered the Temple precinct, stepping like a man without a care, a person of substance and sway who knew not the meaning of want. Obadiah cast a jaundiced eye on him. He thought of his own poverty, of his many labors under the sun, of all the barbs and insults he had had to suffer in his lifetime, and he said to himself: "Here comes one to lord it over us! Why, just look at the curl of his lip: no zealot he! He might even be a subverter of the sacred rites, a secret heretic, a Sadducee who will light the incense before entering the Sanctuary rather than inside it. Then none will be atoned for."

Rabbi Nathan says: The purpose of Scripture was that he [Moses] might be purged of all food and drink in his bowels so as to make him equal to the ministering angels. Rabbi Mattiah ben Heresh says: The purpose of Scripture here was to inspire him with awe, so that the Torah be given with awe, with dread, with trembling, as it is said: "Serve the Lord with fear and rejoice with trembling." What is the meaning of "And rejoice with trembling." Rabbi Adda bar Mattena says in the name of Rab: Where there will be joy, there shall be trembling.

The Gate of Rebirth:

Know that the *Nefesh*, or Vital Soul, is from the World of *Asiyah*, or the World of Actions, and that the *Ruach*, or Intellectual Soul, is from the World of *Tetsirah*, or of Creativity, and that the *Neshamah*, or Spiritual Soul, is from the World of *Beriah*, or of Creation. Most of us have a Vital Soul alone, which exists on different planes, for the World of Actions has five aspects, all of which must be perfected if the Vital Soul is to be conjoined with an Intellectual Soul from the World of Creativity. Therefore, one must first labor to perfect oneself in the World of Actions, for the World of Creativity is higher.

The sermon lasted over half an hour. Rachel was surprised to find that she didn't lose interest once. There was something about Abby Rosenthal that she liked, something that made her decide to stay until the end of the service, or at least until the afternoon break. Should she approach her afterward and introduce herself? She couldn't remember whether she had her cards in her bag. She searched for one, taking advantage of the opportunity to peek at a mirror and refresh her lipstick. It was odd to think of getting to know this unusual rabbi. But it was also, for some reason, exciting.

17

October 9, 2000

The 11th of Tishrei, 5761

A conductor once told me I was a reincarnation of Maria Callas," Ann Lee said, continuing out loud a conversation she had been having with herself all evening. Her bare, cool, smooth thigh lay on Andrew's. "I didn't believe him. He just wanted to get me into bed." She giggled. "And he almost did. But not because of Maria." Her small hand hovered over Andrew's body. The wind instruments played a new phrase, their bronzed, golden notes giving her goose pimples. "I don't think I'm her reincarnation. I think I'm a reincarnation of a Chinese opera singer, a docile little virtuoso whose voice and soul were bound just like her tiny feet, forced into a closed circuit that recycled her energy inward rather than outward." She paused. "I know, I know." Ann Lee gave a little squeeze. "There's nothing Chinese about me. I'm the exact opposite and always was. No one could be less Chinese than I am. But that's why I feel that that's who I was in a previous life. I'm the other side of her, all she had to suppress. I was born to make up for her life, to go to the other extreme, so that together we're one harmonious, redeemed soul. It's as if my story isn't complete without hers, or hers without mine."

Andrew smiled and nodded, half-listening. "What were you in your former life? You don't believe in any of that, do you? Neither do I." Miles Davis's golden trumpet reached new heights, scaling the walls and raising the ceiling. "I don't believe in astrology, either, absolutely not. And not in feng shui or crystals or numerology. It's just a pose. I can get away with it because I'm young and beautiful, mostly beautiful." She gave him a mischievous, teasing smile and kissed him full on the lips. The wind instruments joined the trumpet like a polyphonic echo. Andrew shut his eyes and allowed himself to be immersed in her kiss.

18
October 14, 2000

The 15th of Tishrei, 5761

Crimson, boiling blood coursed through the streets: the besieged city had fallen. The screams of raped women mingled with the shrieks of their pregnant sisters, whose bellies were slit open by the soldiers competing to see who could most skillfully slice a baby in half with a single stroke. The possessions were plundered and divided up within the very walls. Looters ambushed each plundered house like a pack of wolves bringing down a gazelle and tearing it to pieces. The giant warrior loomed on the horizon in full battle dress, his enormous legs astride the high mountain to the city's east, uprooted olive trees were strewn over its slopes like stacks of cheap Christmas decorations. A tremendous, ear-

splitting explosion rent the air, splitting the mountain in two. A
great valley appeared between its halves, thrusting them north
and south. The fleeing populace headed for it, seeking the pro-
tection of the warrior. The day was black, its light frozen, but the
night would be lit by a precious radiance. Living water, erupting
cold and pure from the depths of the earth, would wash the blood
from the streets and the rocks' jagged edges and flow on, half to
the outmost sea and half to the Ancient Ocean. A flow without
end, by day and by night, in winter and in summer, pure, clean,
and forever.

19
October 22, 2000

The 23rd of Tishrei, 5761

Four p.m. The early, end-of-October twilight gilded the green
latticework framing the main entrance to Wave Hill Estate,
limning the dark red ivy and causing its leaves to glint mysteriously, like precious stones. Andrew and Ann Lee, both dressed
in black, walked up the crunchy gravel path that led to the gate,
holding hands. Pausing for a moment to admire the fiery beauty of
the ivy that was at the height of its autumn color, they exchanged
conspiratorial glances before unlacing their fingers, composing
their faces in an appropriately blasé expression, and entering the
grounds.

WELCOME TO THE BRONX BIG RIVER CHURCH HAPPENING, said
a sign. "Our local community," the mailed invitation had read, "in
collaboration with the Juilliard School of Music, invites the public
to a musical and culinary event to be held on the grounds of Wave

Hill. The artistic program will include a joint musical performance
by Juilliard students and the Big River Church choir. All proceeds
will go to the development of music education programs for the
children of the Bronx and scholarships for young musicians."

The guests strolled on a large lawn with a dramatic view of the
Hudson and the Palisades beyond it. The Juilliard Wind Orchestra filled the air with loud strains, accompanying a church choir
that was singing a spiritual whose words seemed tarnished by
time. *Jordan River, I'm bound to go, bound to go, bound to go.* The
white-clothed tables, adorned with orange and yellow gourds,
were heaped with a stylized assortment of traditional African and
African American dishes. All kinds of tea were available, as was
African coffee spiced with cinnamon, cloves, and something that
tasted like allspice. There was even wine—organic, to be sure and
not of the highest quality, but wine nonetheless, which wasn't bad
for a church affair.

"Meet my dad! I'm just joking. This is my friend Andrew," Ann
Lee laughed, wrinkling her nose, in that charming and provocative
way of hers. She had a taste for parody, pastiche, and the grotesque.
She seemed to draw some twisted pleasure from these jokes; it tickled something within her. Her friends, all also in their twenties,
echoed her laughter. Looking around him, Andrew thought that
Wave Hill on this particular day looked like the animated campus
of a school for the arts, brimming with young people dressed in a
hand-me-down chic, which declared that they were—if not artists
themselves—their future patrons. He felt a current of—no, not
exactly of nervousness—but of a definite unease. He wasn't accustomed to appearing with Ann Lee in public. On the rare occasions
when they had allowed themselves to be seen together, a vague but
caustic fantasy had lurked at the back of his mind like an incom-
plete hologram or the remembered fragments of a bad dream. An
aging professor at a New England college, a dust-coated old owl in

a faded tweed jacket, spins his sticky web around a helpless, tender young student thirty years his junior. Although the semester is over and everyone is on vacation, he forces her to remain with him on the empty campus and to invent lies to tell to her friends and parents, robbing her of the summer's adventures: the wilderness treks, the beach parties, the healthy romances with boys her age. Compulsively, desperately, he sleeps with her again and again, clinging to her young body, plying her with his desiccated old man lust, holding her prisoner in his love, chaining her to him, sucking the youth from her while injecting her with his fustiness, his decrepitude, the death already forming within him. Such moments never lasted long. One glance from Ann Lee, a single syllable uttered in her voice, was enough to return him to the easy, light-hearted flow of their relationship. The unmistakable happiness this gave her, the love and passion she showered on him, were reassuring in the cold light of reason. The guilt was driven underground, to lie buried until the next time.

Four twenty-five. When was the concert supposed to begin? The sun, a big, ripe, orange pumpkin itself, was already sinking in the west, dangerously close to the toothed crags of the Palisades. Andrew broke away from the crowd and strolled past the estate's buildings, greenhouses, and gardens, instinctively drawn to the hedge overlooking the river. A fresh breeze blew in his face, ruffling his thick shock of hair. He drained the last drops of wine from his glass, placed it on a stone parapet, and leaned forward to examine the splendid view.

Although a lifetime seemed to have passed since then, he had been, by chance, in this exact place just two months ago, at the wedding of Linda's nephew Jason. Linda had arranged to pick Andrew up on her way from Brooklyn. Expertly maneuvering her station wagon through the Manhattan traffic, past yellow cabs madly cutting in and out of lanes, trucks parked in the middle of streets, and pedestrians dashing from sidewalks without warning, she arrived in her endearing, it's-just-family-anyway manner, a mere half an hour late. Sweating lightly in his summer suit, Andrew spotted her car two blocks away; he knew her by her driving, its particular combination of determination and hesitancy that reminded him of his own mother's driving. Linda recognized him at a distance, too. His dignified shock of gray hair, perfect posture, and, of course, white summer suit all stood out from the drab street like the Rock of Gibraltar rising from the sea—who else but Andrew would stand like this in the middle of Broadway, at three in the afternoon? His daughters, dressed in evening gowns, waved to him as the car approached, and even George could hardly suppress an affectionate smile.

"Hi, Dad! You look great."

"Look who's talking, you bevy of beauties!"

Andrew squeezed into the backseat between his two daughters, giving Alison a big hug, Rachel a kiss, and George a warm handshake.

"Sorry we're late. You wouldn't believe the traffic in midtown." Linda glanced at him in the rearview minor, her unapologetic apology another ritual. "Are you okay back there? George volunteered to sit up front—isn't he the perfect gentleman! After all, someone had to do the dirty work of guiding us through the infinite gridlock known as Manhattan."

Andrew smiled back at the mirror. "I'm fine. There's enough room back here for a whole family. It's good to be crowded together, going nowhere fast in this high yellow afternoon light. That's our neighborhood Jeremiah, over there. He's outdoing himself today. On his knees in the street, arms out and eyes lifted to heaven—it's pure Hollywood. You're best off taking Broadway to 125th and making a left to the northbound entrance of the parkway. Can you believe Jason is getting married? And in Wave Hill, just like his parents! If anyone had told us when he was in rehab two years ago that he would end up working for a big-time ad agency and marrying a girl who looks like a magazine cover, we would have thought it was a bad joke. What's she like, by the way? Has anyone met her?"

"Yes, Dorothy. She said she and Jason seemed very well suited to each other. Coming from her, that doesn't sound like a compliment. How exactly do we get there? We were told to come early for photographs before sunset. It's lucky it didn't rain today, it's so nice outside on the lawn. George, do you have the map?"

"No, Alison has it. How do you think we made it so far?"

That had been two months ago, only two months, but everything had changed since then. Andrew let his gaze take in the grand view of the river. It flowed lazily, sprawled like an old hippopotamus between dark green cliffs speckled with the orange, yellow, and scarlet of autumn leaves. Glossy angel's trumpets stood regally in heavy terra-cotta pots, their large, sensuous flowers hanging mouth-downward. The evening light painted the pine trees a deep green, filling him with a mixture of melancholy, elation, and something else . . . might it be longing? For a moment, the unseen matrix holding the disparate elements of the universe together seemed to have become visible, its unspoken promise suddenly within reach. Consider the ripe fruit of autumn, in which is conserved icy Februaries, fickle Mays, and lethargic, heat-stricken, desire-laden Augusts; recall the unclouded intoxication of your twenties, the intense activity of your thirties, the joys and anxieties of fatherhood, sex, ambition, honor, success—all now of one piece with the white wedding cake you stretched an eager finger toward when you were four, the pale neck of the girl who sat in front of you in sixth grade, and the soft, almost transparent, old woman's skin of your mother's sun-weathered hands; reflect on the searing, tormenting beauty of your older daughter and the still incipient graces of your younger one; see the blaze in the heavy boughs of the pine trees and the sparkles dancing on the river like fish in a net. An elderly, almost doddering man was pointing with an ungainly walker at a magnificent tree whose lower leaves had turned an incandescent yellow, while its upper ones, still a fresh green at their center, held gamely on. How beautiful are the hundred and one yellow-to-scarlet hues burning on the hills across the river? It's not just the wine. It was that, too, but not just.

"Aha, there you are, my brooding philosopher! Come on, the concert's starting."

The smile in Ann Lee's voice was infectious. Andrew roused himself from his musings, gave her his hand, and let himself be led back, not forgetting to take his empty wineglass from the parapet while wondering whether there would be time to refill it before the concert began. The wind instruments had fallen silent. The seated members of the church choir were carefully sampling teas, coffees, and assorted pastries never before seen on the near side of the Atlantic. A flock of gray and white pigeons performed an aerial somersault in midflight, circling the ancient slate roof of the estate manor like a small, elusive rain cloud. The air grew thick and electric. A storm was brewing. There was a stir around him. The audience regarded with anticipation the five stately black women who mounted the small stage in majestic silence. The lead vocalist, her large figure looking as though it were carved from granite, stepped to the front of the stage, took a deep breath, and began to sing in a deep, spine-tingling voice that might have been chiseled from ancient rock, too. *Nobody knows when the sun goes down what's going to be in the morning.* The other women answered with a moan that seemed to come from deep in the ground. *No, no, nobody knows.* The bass rumbled like an avalanche, the alto quivered: *nobody knows. Nobody knows, nobody knows,* crooned the tenor. It was a song from the depths, the music of existence. The women drove their voices to the limit, wailing like a wind blowing down a canyon. *Nobody knows! Nobody knows!* Where were those voices coming from? From the bowels of the earth, from the world's heart. *Nobody knows when the sun comes up what's going to be when it sets.* They were almost visible, those voices. Granite and basalt, copper and iron, silver and gold. *Nobody knows when the dawn breaks what's going to be in the evening.* The day suddenly grew dark. The sun foundered all at once on a crag across the river. Would it drown in the great waters, never to be seen again? The reds, yellows, and oranges on the other side of the Hudson vanished, melting rapidly into the muddy brown that descended on the Palisades. A damp, restless wind began to blow, lifting the flaps of Andrew's light jacket. His thin shirt clung to his body and he shivered. Where had the fiery glory of the golden afternoon gone? *Nobody knows when evening comes what the dawn's going to bring.* How, as though from an ambush, has autumn waylaid us?

END OF BOOK ONE

[Mishna, Treatise Yoma, Chapter 1, Mishna 3] They delivered to him elders from the elders of the court and they read before him [throughout the seven days] out of the order of the ritual. They said to him, sir High Priest, read you yourself with your own mouth, perchance you have forgotten or perchance you have never learnt.

[Babylonian Talmud, Treatise Yoma, Folio 2a] We learned elsewhere: Seven days before the burning of the [red] heifer the priest who was to burn the heifer was removed from his house to the chambers in the northeastern corner before the Birah. It was called the Stone Chamber. And why was it called the Stone Chamber? Because all its functions [in connection with the red heifer] had to be performed only in vessels made of either cobblestones, stone, or earthenware. What was the reason?[...] The Rabbis ordained that only vessels made of cobblestones, stone, or earthenware——which are immune to impurity——should be used in connection with the heifer, lest the ceremony thereof be treated slightly.

All week long, the High Priest resided in the Stone Chamber and performed each day's rites. He offered the incense, tended the oil lamps, sprinkled the blood of the sacrificed animals on the corners of the altar, and laid their heads and legs on the fire. The elders reviewed the traditions with the High Priest and read to him from the sacred books to make certain he understood his duties. All week long he was kept apart from the world in sanctity and holiness, excepting one moment when he was given an unclean creature to touch and sprinkled with cleansing waters to keep the Sadducees from claiming he had never been purified. His fellow priests did not leave him alone for a minute, lest his mind stray to sinful thoughts. They came and went all day in his chambers, bearing slaughtering knives and coal scoops, chalices and stoups. The commotion they made was joined to the whisperings of the elders, the bleating from the stockyard, and the singing of the Levites at their posts.

[Mishna, Treatise Kelim, Chapter 1, Mishnayot 1—4] These are the origins of impurity: creeping creatures, semen, any person who came in contact with a dead body, lepers [...], purification water that is not sufficient for sprinkling. All these defile humans and vessels upon being touched. Earthenware vessels defile once lifted in the air, but not while being carried. [...] Above them [in the hierarchy of impurity] are: the carcass of a dead animal and purification water that is sufficient for sprinkling. [...] Above them: him that hath marital intercourse with a menstruant. [...] Above him: the discharge of him that hath an issue, his spittle, his semen, his urine, and the menstrual blood. [...] Above him that hath an issue is she that hath an issue, for she defiles anyone with whom she has marital intercourse. [...] Above she that hath an issue is the leper, for he defiles anyone with whom he has marital intercourse. Above the leper is a [human] bone that is as small as a grain of barley, for it defiles for seven days and seven nights. And above them all, a dead man, for it defiles all that is in the tent with it, unlike the rest of these things, that do not defile [all that is in the tent].

[Mishna, Treatise Kelim, Chapter 1, Mishnayot 6—9] There are ten rungs [levels] of holiness: The land of Israel is holier than the rest of the lands. [...] Towns that are surrounded by walls are holier than the rest of the land [of Israel] since the lepers are sent out of them, and the dead, once taken outside of their walls, are not permitted to be brought in again. The area inside the walls [of Jerusalem] is holier [than other towns that are surrounded by walls] since one may partake in sacrificial feasts within it. The Temple Mount is holier, since it is forbidden for he or she who have had a discharge, for menstruants, and for those who have recently given birth to enter it. The Exterior Court is holier, since foreigners and those whose hair is uncovered are forbidden to enter it. The Women's Court is holier, since not even a person who has immersed in a ritual bath may enter it before sunset. The Israelite Court is holier, since no man who was not atoned for may enter it, and if one enters he must bring a sin offering. The Priests' Court is holier, for it is forbidden for mere Israelites to enter it. [...] The area between the Great Hall and the altar is holier, since bearers of blemishes and those whose hair is uncovered are forbidden to enter it. The Sanctuary is holier, since one may not enter it without washing the hands and feet. The Holy of Holies is holier, since only the High Priest may enter it on the Day of Atonement, at the designated time of the offering.

[Mishna, Treatise Yoma, Chapter 3, Mishna 2] Those of the House of Garmu did not want to teach anything about the preparation of the showbread. Those of the House of Abtinas did not want to teach anything about the preparation of the incense. Hugros ben Levi knew a chapter [concerning] the song but did not want to teach it. Ben Kamtzar did not want teach anyone his art of writing [the holy name of God].

———————◆———————

[Babylonian Talmud, Treatise Yoma, Folio 39b] Rabbah bar Bar Hana said: From Jerusalem to Jericho it is a distance of ten parasangs. [. . .] The goats in Jericho used to sneeze because of the odor of the incense. The women in Jericho did not have to perfume themselves, because of the odor of the incense. The bride in Jerusalem did not have to perfume herself because of the odor of the incense. Rabbi Jose ben Diglai said: My father had goats on the mountains of Mikwar, and they used to sneeze because of the odor of the incense. Rav Hiyya bar Abin said in the name of Rabbi Joshua ben Karhah: An old man told me: "Once I walked toward Shiloh and I could smell the odor of the incense [coming] from its walls."

Most of all, they instructed the High Priest in the preparation of the incense, a demanding task that few were adept at. Each priestly clan had its secrets and all vied to see whose incense was more fragrant and whose sent up greater billows of smoke. There were elderly priests who had spent their entire lives grinding the spices for the incense and had gone mad from breathing the dust. [This story was told by Bar-Kozbai: "My uncle, my mother's brother, was an elderly priest. One day when he was grinding saffron, he began to laugh. At first all thought he was laughing because of an amusing thought. Some said he was in his dotage. But when the minutes passed and his laughter continued, they approached and saw that he was clutching his stomach in agony and laughing too hard to stand up. They tried to make him stop and could not. No physician or healer was able to help. He laughed for three days and three nights until he took leave of his senses. God was beseeched for mercy and he died."]

[Babylonian Talmud, Treatise Yoma, Folio 38a] Our Rabbis taught: The house of Abtinas were expert in preparing the incense but would not teach [their art]. The Sages sent for specialists from Alexandria of Egypt, who knew how to compound incense as well as they, but did not know how to make the smoke ascend as well as they. The smoke of the former ascended [as straight] as a stick, whereas the smoke of the latter was scattered in every direction. When the Sages heard thereof, they quoted: "Everyone that is called by My name, I have created for My glory," as it is said: The Lord hath made everything for His own purpose, and [said]: The [priests of the] house of Abtinas may return to their [wonted] place. The Sages sent for them, but they would not come. Then they doubled their hire and they came. Every day [thitherto] they would receive twelve minas, [from] that day twenty-four. The Sages said to them: What reason did you have for not teaching [your art]? They said: They knew in our father's house that this House is going to be destroyed and they said: Perhaps an unworthy man will learn [this art] and will serve an idol therewith.——And for the following reason was their memory kept in honor: Never did a bride of their house go forth perfumed and when they married a woman from elsewhere they expressly forbade her to do so lest people say: From [the preparation of] the incense they are perfuming themselves. [They did so] to fulfill the command: "Ye shall be clear before the Lord and before Israel."

[Babylonian Talmud, Treatise Berakhoth, Folio 3a] Rabbi Eliezer says: The night has three watches, and at each watch the Holy One, Blessed Be He, sits and roars like a lion. For it is written: The Lord does roar from on high, and raise His voice from His holy habitation; "roaring He doth roar" because of his fold. And the sign of the thing is: In the first watch, the ass brays; in the second, the dogs bark; in the third, the child sucks from the breast of his mother, and the woman talks with her husband. What does Rabbi Eliezer understand [by the word "watch"]? Does he mean the beginning of the watches? The beginning of the first watch needs no sign, it is the twilight! Does he mean the end of the watches? The end of the last watch needs no sign, it is the dawn of the day! He, therefore, must think of the end of the first watch, of the beginning of the last watch, and of the midst of the middle watch. [. . .] And for a man who sleeps in a dark room, and does not know when the time of the recital [of the morning prayers] arrives. When the woman talks with her husband and the child sucks from the breast of the mother, let him rise and recite. Rabbi Isaac bar Samuel says in the name of Rab: The night has three watches,

In the middle watch of the week's final night, a cry from the Gallery echoed through the Temple precinct. The High Priest, unaccustomed to such sounds, woke and exclaimed, "Who screamed?" The priests laughed. "It's a Levite," they said. "All night long the Officer of the Watch goes from post to post with his lantern. If a watchman does not greet him with 'Peace be upon you, Officer of the Watch,' he is assumed to be sleeping. The officer strikes him with a stick and has leave to set his bedclothes on fire." And the Superior added with a frown: "The Levites are gluttonous; they eat and drink too much. Food and drink lead to sluggishness and sluggishness leads to drowsiness. Go back to sleep, my liege. The night is still long."

But the High Priest, having been startled from his sleep, was unable to resume it. All that week his slumbers had been troubled by images of jetting blood, the sound of bellowing bulls, and the jangle of musical instruments. [*Aristobulus once said: "One year when I was High Priest, I did not sleep a wink from the Day of Atonement to the Feast of Tabernacles because of all the blood I kept seeing."*] When he saw that all were fast asleep, he thought: "Perhaps a breath of fresh air will do me some good and allow me to fall asleep, too." And so he rose and left his chambers.

and at each watch the Holy One, Blessed Be He, sits and roars like a lion and says: Woe to the children, on account of whose sins I destroyed My house and burnt My temple and exiled them among the nations of the world.

[Mishna, Treatise Berakhoth, Chapter 1, Mishna 1] From what time may one recite the Shema in the morning? From the time that one can distinguish between blue and white. R. Eliezer says: between blue and green. And he has time to finish until sunrise. R. Joshua says: until the third hour of the day, for such is the custom of kings, to rise at the third hour.

At that very moment, Obadiah was standing by the western gate, having gone to relieve himself outside of the Holy compound. He stood in the bracing night air and gazed at the sky that stretched overhead like a silken screen embroidered with stars and constellations. Then he glanced back at the silent city. On any other night, sounds of Torah would have been heard from the study houses and snatches of song from the taverns, but tonight all were asleep, conserving themselves for the great and terrible day of the Lord. As it is written: "They that wait upon the Lord shall renew their strength." Obadiah stood thinking until he began to feel chilled. He gazed upward again. The moon and stars had fled. He looked to the east and saw that the morning star had risen. Yet there was still not a ray of light, not even enough to tell blue from green at an arm's length. Somewhere a cock crowed. In the stillness, it sounded very near.

Just then Obadiah heard footsteps and trembled like one caught trespassing. He peered into the darkness and saw a dim figure emerge from it. It might have been a dog, a wolf, a man, or even a demon, and he would have fainted dead away had he not known that demons lose their power once the cock crows. Still, he stood rooted to the spot, shivering with fear as the figure approached. It was, he saw, none other than the High Priest. Where, Obadiah wondered, could he be going by himself in the night? Why had he left his chambers and his companions? Was he on his way to a rendezvous with a fellow Sadducee? As he stood wondering, the High Priest recognized him and greeted him cordially. Obadiah returned the greeting meekly with a pounding heart as if something fateful had taken place.

[Babylonian Talmud, Treatise Berakhoth, Folio 9a] What is the meaning of BETWEEN BLUE AND WHITE? Shall I say: between a lump of white wool and a lump of blue wool? This one may also distinguish in the night! It means rather: between the blue in it and the white in it. It has been taught: Rabbi Meir says: [The morning Shema is read] from the time that one can distinguish between a wolf and a dog; Rabbi Akiba says: Between an ass and a wild ass. Others say: From the time that one can distinguish his friend at a distance of four cubits. Rabbi Huna says: The ruling is as stated by the "Others."

The Gate of Rebirth:

And in the same manner, one must perfect oneself in all aspects of the World of Creativity before being conjoined with a Spiritual Soul from the World of Creation. Know, too, that the souls of the righteous who have departed this world can cleave to the souls that are in it, assisting them in the worship of the Almighty, may He be blessed.

BOOK
TWO

1

October 23, 2000

The 24th of Tishrei, 5761

Out for an early-morning bike ride, Andrew surrenders to the breeze, the light, the air, the sheer motion. He speeds past an avenue of ancient gray trees standing stiffly at attention like an honor guard of old soldiers, swerves to the right onto the curving underpass beneath the West Side Highway, and strikes out, in his own private dawn Eden, on the bicycle path leading north by the edge of the river. Mist rises from the ground into the sweet-smelling air, bathing him in its cool, moist freshness.

He breathes in the morning deeply and pedals swiftly, effortlessly. In the phosphorescent light of late October, all seemed pure and primeval, a marvel to behold. The gray rocks are half-sunk in water. Fresh patches of grass sprout from the turf. The sky blue of the river meets the watery blue of the sky, divided only by the thin filament of the George Washington Bridge, stretching from bank to bank like the hint of a knowing smile: The day would come when all would return to what it had been and the world would revert to chaos. Water would cover the earth, the earth would be a vast sea. Sun, moon, and stars would flicker out. Day would turn into night.

The sky above him is a yawning abyss. The bicycle whirs; celestial beings clamor; the heavens stare down with all their hosts. The ground beneath him growls, like a hungry monster. The dead seethe in its swollen belly like undigested food. Adam, a gorgeous giant the size of the universe, lies like a babe on the earth that bore him; Divinity lovingly licks the dirt from his tender skin as a doe licks the afterbirth from her fawn. Cain rises against Abel to strike him dead in a field and flees in ignominy, a curse hanging over him like a storm cloud. The voice of Eve is heard on high, the lamentation and bitter weeping of the Great Mother for her children, the living and the dead. But Andrew hears and sees none of this. He flies along weightlessly as though on the wings of the wind. Soon, soon, he would shed his last material traces, leaving only pure motion, a perfect, bow-like arc like the line of the bridge in the pure blue haze above the river.

2

October 25, 2000

The 26th of Tishrei, 5761

Morning, Private Andrew!" A perfect row of white teeth flashed from the rugged face that seemed lit from within by a childish smile. "Up, up, up . . . How's your energy today? You all warmed up?" Andrew Wilson, Andrew's personal trainer, had the jovial innocence of those who are at one with their body. There was something refreshing about it, especially for Andrew, whose relations with his trainer had an unmediated quality missing from his contact with others. "Let's go, Private Andrew! Up, up, up . . . Follow me, Private!" Wilson began to run in place, his big, muscular frame pounding in what might have been a spoof of a military sitcom. It never ceased to amuse him that he and Andrew had the same name. Hence, his insistence on "Private Andrew" and on himself as "Sergeant Andrew," though Andrew never called him that and hardly spoke to him at all in the course of their weekly sessions.

The woman trainer standing nearby gave Andrew an embarrassed smile and shrugged like a young mother apologizing for her wayward toddler—in this case, a powerfully muscled one standing over six feet tall. Andrew smiled back with friendly forbearance. There was always a woman around, usually young and good-looking. Sergeant Andrew liked to flirt, carrying on in his Caribbean lilt, never missing an opportunity to lay a large hand on the arm or shoulder of someone a head or more shorter, a habit that struck no one as intrusive because he seemed to have a child's natural delicacy.

A whole hour of total, meditative yielding to his physical well-being: Andrew liked Equinox with its slate floors, burnished wood benches, and piles of white towels in the showers; its dozen different televisions tuned to as many different channels; its long, symmetrical rows of machines and apparatus, and its exactly right amount of enough, but not too many, beautiful people. He liked his training sessions with Andrew Wilson, too. They went from machine to machine and from one set of exercises to another, his trainer's soft, unceasing patter like harmless white noise as he was put through his paces. He enjoyed feeling his body, which was still reasonably strong, supple, and healthy at the age of fifty-two. "Okay, Private Andrew, that's it for today. Roll call next week at ten sharp. Dismissed! And don't forget your cardio." Andrew smiled good-bye and headed with a rolling gait for the gleaming line of machines whose long levers protruded like the antennae of giant insects.

Sweat trickled down his neck onto his T-shirt; his arm and leg muscles tensed and relaxed rhythmically; he breathed harder. The television screens danced in bright array, their monotonous stream of Technicolor information absorbed by his steady, trancelike breathing. These twenty minutes were an opportunity for Andrew, who had no patience for TV, to catch up on contemporary pop culture. Three or four times a week were all his incisive mind

needed to process and distill their dominant metaphors, which he
would transform, in the calm of his work space or while facing a
classroom, into theoretical and scholarly insights.

Now, he found himself watching a reality show on one of those
bubbly, music-driven, youth-oriented channels that homogenized
the global scene while raking in billions for their shareholders.
Its contestants were unfortunate-looking people from all over the
country who sent in videos meant to persuade the viewers and a
panel of judges that they, of all contestants, deserved the coveted
prize: free plastic surgery. Wanting to be beautiful, however, was
not enough; they were also required to name the celebrity they
most wished to resemble. One overweight woman aspired to be
Jennifer Lopez, while a heavyset, moonfaced man with huge ear-
lobes that hung down like bell clappers, dreamed of passing for
none other than George Clooney. There was also a pair of adolescent, identical twins, obviously Jewish. Large-nosed, scrawny-
necked, and anemic-looking, they had something touching about
them, an unforgettable, infinite sadness that hid behind the gawk-
ing optimism with which they faced the camera. Though it was not
a nice thing to say, they truly were hideous; they made one think
of birds of prey—no, of vultures, with their long, hooked noses,
pointy chins, and exaggeratedly prominent cheekbones, generously strewn with bloody acne. Aaron and Jason. Like wretched
caricatures from *Der Stürmer*, the fact that they were identical
twins made them twice as monstrous and revolting. And in whose
image did they desire to be re-created? Brad Pitt's, of course!

Who would win the coveted operation? Tune in next week. And
now a break for commercials. Andrew turned disgustedly away
from the flickering screen. It was unbelievable what junk the popular channels fed their audiences. He glanced at the clock hanging above the mirrors on the wall. Eleven fifteen—his session was
over. There was just enough time for a few minutes in the sauna,

a shower, and a shave. The post-rush-hour subway ride would not pass unpleasantly with time for a quick look at a new book sent to him for review, followed by a short, invigorating walk from the Christopher Street station to the Tisch Building. His class started at twelve thirty. The weather was gorgeous, more springlike than autumnal.

3

October 26, 2000

The 27th of Tishrei, 5761

Four p.m. Andrew exited the subway and headed down 110th Street, sifting through his mail as he walked and deciding which envelopes to keep and which to throw out before getting home. Amid the brown paper wrappings, a white manila envelope from Israel with English, Hebrew, and Arabic print caught his eye, and he stopped near his building to open it. It was the annual report of the Israeli human rights organization B'Tselem (the awkwardly transliterated word gave him a prickly, uncomfortable sensation), accompanied by an invitation to a three-day conference of Israeli, Palestinian, American, and European scholars on human rights violations and restrictions on academic freedom in the West Bank and Gaza. Although there was nothing unusual about it—he received dozens of such notices every year—something, perhaps it was the sight of the square Hebrew letters printed on the envelope, caused his pulse to quicken as though it were an unexpected letter from the tax authorities or an old lover.

A loud, merry noise made him turn its way. Looking up from the invitation, he saw an unshaven man in his thirties, his ultrathin designer glasses a comical contrast with his rough-hewn face, leave the building across the street and head for the park with two dogs. One white and one brown, they chased each other as though playing tag, winding their leashes around him while he laughed encouragement in a foreign, half-familiar-sounding language. Greek? Arabic? Persian? Andrew racked his brain, studying the broad, swarthy face. The dogs went on romping while their owner continued to laugh, addressing them fondly. Now, Andrew identified the language. It was Hebrew. What an odd coincidence! He was from Israel, he's an Israeli.

Andrew had first visited Israel in 1969 with a student group organized by the Jewish Agency. The trip now seemed to him a dream or hallucination. The savage outpouring of light that reflected violently off Jerusalem's stone walls had blinded him and coated his memory with a pinkish haze like the discoloration in an old photograph that gradually reduces it to a single, blurry hue. Whenever he thought of the Dome of the Rock, or of the blazing stone ruins by the Western Wall, he envisioned them as just a snapshot.

Throughout their tour, young Andy and his fellow students had been unable to shake off a nagging, almost intimidating sensation of having been hijacked. Their Zionist guides wouldn't leave them alone for a minute. Loud and hyperactive, they had all looked alike, too: suntanned, energetic, and arrogant, their voices laced with disdainful laughter. They all sported the same awkward style, as if it were a uniform: an open shirt whose collar was folded, for some reason, over that of a cheap sports jacket that never matched their pants. Their self-confidence bordered on the pathological; they listened to no sentence to its end. Sweepingly dismissive, they appeared to doubt the masculinity of anyone who wasn't an Israeli and expected the women in the group, having met real men at last, to fall into their arms like ripe fruit. Their speech sounded prepackaged, its scolding superiority based on an absurdly simplistic conception of something called "the Jewish soul"—a formula composed in equal parts of guilt, sentimental nostalgia, and a no less mawkish nationalism. While this approach might have worked with the generation of their parents, it left Andy and his friends cold. They did not feel guilty about anything, disdained patriotic rhetoric, and had no ready-made Jewish sentiments to play on. The transparent emotional blackmail practiced by their hosts aroused their scorn, which they expressed in their wry North American manner by referring to them all by a single Israeli name, Avi: "The Avi is waiting by the bus." "The Avi wants us here at five."

It was a form of passive, unspoken resistance to the crudeness of it all. For three weeks they followed their guides like sleepwalkers, stooped beneath a fiery sun, their weary eyes fixed on the ground as if refusing to partake in the visions imposed on them by their tireless hosts, straggling beneath an incandescent sky, stopping abruptly from time to time, like the jostled sheep of a capricious shepherd, beside some ancient column that supported nothing, or the soot-blackened floor of what had once been something and would surely be it again, since history demanded no less of us! For a while, a few of them made the effort to listen to the loud, heavily accented explanations of that day's Avi, but eventually they, too, gave up trying to follow or find meaning in any of it and let themselves be herded, stupefied and indifferent, from one scalding archaeological ruin to the next.

The Arabs they met were small, dark, and defeated-looking. They spoke a broken English and never looked their conquerors' American guests in the eye. Yet while the body language of the older ones suggested an absolute, almost inhuman submission, the younger ones exhibited the first stirrings of rebellion. Once, by a roadside souvenir stand, an Arab boy, unable to resist, had reached out to pinch the bare thigh of a blond female student wearing shorts. Their Israeli guide fell upon him, slapped him roundly, and berated him in a Hebrew hoarse with rage. The boy cringed like a frightened animal, and his father, the stand's owner, began slapping him, too. It wasn't clear whether he did so simply to appease the enraged tour guide or in order to shield his trembling son from the arrogant stranger's aggression with his own, familiar one.

And there was another memory, too, a wondrous one, of a round red moon rising from the desert and hovering very close to the Dome of the Rock, which looked like a mysterious, blood-orange, lunar apparition itself. The sacred mount, with its large mosques couched like magnificent, dusty old lions, exerted a strange pull. Yet this enchanted moment, too, was dissipated by the stench of the Old City. The food was greasy, the showers were cold, the hotel corridors crawled with cockroaches. Even the hash was different from the mellow pot Andrew was used to smoking back home. Heavy, wet, and sticky, it tasted like the thick tongue of the girl from Brooklyn, who had all but forced him to half undress her one night, a charm necklace strung with Stars of David, crosses, and crescent moons suspended between her heavy breasts.

Since then, he had been to Jerusalem many times as a guest of the Hebrew University, the Mishkenot Sha'ananim Conference Center, and the Van Leer Jerusalem Institute. Yet though most of these visits had gone well, the alienation of those three awful weeks remained in the back of his mind, and after the outbreak of the First Intifada he had taken fewer trips to Israel. As the Jewish state began losing its legitimacy in the family of nations, his attitude toward it, particularly in regard to its treatment of the Palestinians, became increasingly ambivalent. Even after the signing of the Oslo Agreement, he repeatedly found himself shying away from invitations to various lectures and conferences there. And this time there was no need for excuses. His new appointment would take effect in early September, leaving his schedule too crowded for a trip to Israel.

He slipped the invitation back into its envelope. On Monday, he would ask Ms. Harty to decline, with regrets, on his behalf.

4

October 27, 2000

The 28th of Tishrei, 5761

Nearly noon. Ann Lee, in a good-natured, perfect parody of Andrew's gentlemanly manners, insisted on going to get the car. In return, Andrew, still luxuriating in the laziness of the weekend morning, handed her the keys with mock fatherly hesitation, drily spoofing the latent oedipality of their relationship. For a few more minutes, he remained seated on the brown leather couch, paging through the Arts and Leisure section of the Sunday *Times*. Then, finishing his second cup of coffee, he went downstairs with the bags and gifts. The lobby was deserted. Andrew peered out at the street. Ann Lee must have forgotten where she had parked the car, or else stopped to buy something. Still drowsy and loath to part with the cozy quiet of the lingering morning, he smiled at the doorman's greeting without making his usual attempt at small talk and absentmindedly studied the decorative bosses on the walls and ceilings.

They would be driving upstate, to the small house two hours from the city in which Ann Lee's mother, Donna, and her new husband lived. Ann Lee's father, a Chinese American artist, had been living in California for the past eight years with a woman twenty years his junior, with whom he had a daughter younger than Alison. The stated purpose of the trip was to bask in the glory of the autumn foliage, which was particularly spectacular in the

Catskills, and though it was already two weeks past its prime, Ann Lee refused to attribute any other motive, obvious or hidden, to their excursion. Who would believe that they had been together for seven, almost eight months?

The quick, cheerful honk of a horn roused Andrew from his reverie. Smiling vivaciously, Ann Lee was waving through the car window.

A deep gray sky hung low over the Hudson, caught on the crags of the Palisades. Ann Lee drove easily, humming an unidentifiable tune, one hand on the steering wheel and the other playing lightly on Andrew's thigh as if it were a piano. Andrew smiled down at the strumming hand before trapping it in his own larger and older one. They were both in a strangely quiet, dreamy mood. As they neared the bridge, Ann Lee removed her hand from Andrew's knee, leaving behind a residue of warmth, gripped the wheel firmly, and nimbly maneuvered their little car in and out of the exits and overpasses that led to the northbound thruway. Quickly, they passed the monotonous projects of the South Bronx with their windowless buildings that looked more like factories than residences. Ann Lee tuned into some jazz on the radio, its ragtime contrasting with the depressing grayness around them. Lulled by the rhythm of the music and the monotonous hum of the motor, Andrew leaned back against the headrest. The last urban construction yielded to the more vivid rural scenery of the towns along the Hudson. Together with the jazz and the hum of the motor, the Westchester landscape invoked dim, dreamlike memories. He felt a thick, dark, maple-syrupy nostalgia for something indefinable. *You know how proud your father is of you, don't you?* The soft, gray wool sweater snugly fit Walter's broad chest and straight back, his always straight back, as if he had taken a deep, proud breath and would not let go of it.

"Hi, Andrew, rise and shine! We're almost there." Ann Lee's voice made him sit up with a start. He turned to her, blinking. She smiled back. "Were you sleeping?" He ran a hand over his face and through his hair, checking to see if it needed combing. "Not really. Well, yes. Maybe a bit."

They had been driving for an hour. Though the road the car was climbing was unromantically wide, their surroundings grew wilder as it got steeper. Once they were over the top of the mountain, the American continent, vast and endless, came into view. Strangely menacing, the somber tower of Mohonk Mountain House rose from jagged peaks, a fit home for a prince of darkness. The atmosphere in the car had changed, too. There was now a tension in the air. The lively jazz that had accompanied them most of the way was gone, its place taken by nameless, small-town stations whose grim religious preachers and twangy country music came and went. Although she could have played a tape, Ann Lee, suddenly brooding, kept both hands tightly on the wheel and let the radio blare away inanely, its chaotic farrago of noise reflecting her state of mind, which worsened as the familiar comfort of the city receded. She had deliberately, it suddenly struck Andrew, worn the least attractive of her everyday clothes, as if to deprive their visit of any special significance. Her doubts about its wisdom, increasingly evident as they neared their destination, reinforced his own. What was the point of it? Why, all of a sudden, had she wanted him to meet her mother? Without bothering to explain, she had set a date and informed him. Now, though she strove to appear nonchalant, he could tell from her coldness how stressed she was.

Andrew did his best to be sympathetic and relieve Ann Lee's anxiety, but she was unresponsive, as if punishing him for the situation that she herself put them in. Her face was contorted, almost pained. She was driving too fast, pulling out to pass every car in front of her. Belted into his seat, he felt helpless, a caricature of the normal, healthy father who drives his daughter's friend to the train or brings the babysitter home at night. Here, on this highway, removed from the protective bubble of their daily lives, the social categories that distanced them had reasserted themselves. Ann Lee's youth now struck him as exaggerated, indecent, almost pornographic. His mood darkened. Something nagged at him, a dim sorrow tinged with an edgy sensation he couldn't explain. Not even the flame of the autumn leaves, which showed them with their full splendor as the car left the highway for a narrow, winding country road, could penetrate the car's closed windows. That their surroundings looked like a stage set only made their venture more absurd. His nervousness, which might have been likened to that of a boy meeting the parents of a girl he was dating, was in fact the opposite: what had been right and proper at that age now gave him the hollow feeling of something gone unaccountably wrong. The phantom college professor and his student flickered in his consciousness and vanished, leaving a bitter, medicinal aftertaste.

His main concern, he was forced to admit, was the approaching encounter with Ann Lee's stepfather. As irrational as it was disconcerting, it had to be faced. The jealous, judgmental shadow of the father hovered vulture-like over their little car. Although being introduced to Donna's new husband wasn't as bad as meeting Ann Lee's biological father, Andrew didn't look forward to it. All he knew about the man was that his name was David and that he was an ex-musician now working as a not particularly successful sound technician. As far as Ann Lee was concerned, the marriage, which she rarely talked about, was just another one of her mother's childish whims. Yet Andrew, who hated the look that he saw in the eyes of whoever, no matter how liberal or progressive, was aware that he, a fifty-two-year-old man, was sleeping with a woman barely half his age. Projected onto him, he felt, were not only sexual fantasies but all the hidden patriarchal defenses of the tribe. It was natural, of course, he thought with a glance at his watch. As if he didn't have such instincts himself! Two fifteen. How could anyone live so far from the city? The area wasn't even a pastoral one of white churches, red barns, and farmhouses. It was depressingly poor, dotted with old industrial buildings and decrepit trailers that looked as if they were left over from the Depression era. The opaque, misplaced names on the road signs—Goshen, Rehoboth, Bethel—made the place feel even more oppressive.

Ann Lee swung the wheel sharply to the right, having nearly missed the turnoff. The car swerved like a tacking boat. On the left, an inscription on a redbrick wall in English and Hebrew said "Eretz HaChayim Cemetery." Beyond the wall, heavy gray tombstones ran up a hill, their square letters too small to make out from a distance. A Jewish cemetery, here? How come? But of course: they were at the heart of what had once been the Borscht Belt. Still, it was hard to imagine Jewish life (or any life, for that matter) in such a godforsaken place. How awful to die and be buried by the side of a road in the middle of nowhere! What time was it? How much longer, damn it, would it take to get there?

5

Donna must have been a beauty when she was young. Even now, in her late forties, she had the good looks of a younger woman. Andrew knew her type: she had the eternally pubescent appearance of a former Flower Child forever arrested in her teens. And there was something else that he was familiar with: a lack of confidence that was tangible in her movements and expressions, the physical apology of a woman, left by a husband after long years of marriage, who never stopped excusing herself even though she was lucky enough to have started a new life with someone else. For a brief, painful moment, the thought of Linda flashed through Andrew's mind. Donna's smile was too wide, too inviting. No sooner had Donna begun begging them to forgive her husband's not joining them for lunch than, conscious of the distress emanating from Ann Lee like a cold draft blowing through a broken window, Andrew interrupted her with a disarming smile, took her by the arm, and led her inside as if he, not she, were the host while promising, "Don't worry, I'm sure we'll have plenty of time to spend with him." Ann Lee walked behind them, stunned and lethargic, limply carrying the bags and the wrapped presents.

Lunch was more suited to summer than to fall: a cold soup, a salad, and a vegetable quiche accompanied by an over-chilled white Burgundy. While Ann Lee fiddled silently with her food and hardly ate anything, Andrew, as though eating for the two of them, kept asking for seconds. The wine, surprisingly, was first-rate. Were Donna and her husband real connoisseurs or had she simply bought something expensive in order to impress him? Andrew and Donna had to talk nonstop to fill the vacuum created by Ann Lee's silence. Enveloped by the light fumes of the wine, Donna's behavior at the table, while not exactly flirtatious, excluded Ann Lee and made it seem that she and Andrew were the parents, and Ann Lee their prickly, capricious adolescent daughter. Nodding enthusiastically as he spoke, as if hanging on every word. Compared to an engaging man-of-the-world like himself, he was sure, her husband must seem to her a compromise. Rather than flatter him, however, this thought weighed on him. He tried putting it aside by asking about David's work, making appreciative sounds as he was told about it. It wasn't easy. Ann Lee was in a world of her own and left it all up to him. Keeping the conversation going was exhausting. Again and again he found himself glancing at his watch, wondering when he could politely excuse himself and take a nap.

The opportunity came unexpectedly. When Donna inquired at the meal's end if they would like a hot drink and Andrew asked for coffee, nothing turned out to be available but decaf and herbal tea.

Donna was flustered and Ann Lee, though blushing at her mother's embarrassment, said, "But, Mom, we do need *real* coffee." The cruel *real* bordered on rudeness. "But what about the cake?" Donna protested weakly. Ann Lee's eyes flashed angrily. "No, thank you. We're fine. Andrew doesn't like desserts, especially if they're made without flour or sugar."

AT THE FIRST TRAFFIC LIGHT, after several minutes of driving in silence, Ann Lee killed the motor, unbuckled her seat belt in a single motion, and flung herself at Andrew, holding him tightly and showering his face and neck with fierce, quick kisses. Andrew hugged her back, surprised. Her wild gratitude startled him. He had misjudged her. All along he had thought that she dreaded Donna and David's opinion of him—or rather of her, the young lover of an uncommitted middle-aged divorcé with nothing to offer her. Now, he realized it was the other way around. It was *his* opinion that she feared—of them, and ultimately of herself. Ann Lee felt like an orphan. Her parents' infantile narcissism had robbed her of her childhood. It was she who had had to raise them, to be the responsible adult while they went on being children. She despised their hippie mannerisms, their refusal to grow up and accept the role of being parents. All her sandals, tank tops, and kerchiefs were a costume, a disguise concealing her parentless soul.

"It all started with my name. My dad meant it as a tribute to Edgar Allan Poe." Ann Lee was sitting on a bench outside the local Starbucks draped in a shapeless gray coat, holding her second cup of coffee in one hand and a lit cigarette in the other. "Or so he said. I always thought my mom wanted to call me Honnah Lee because of that stupid Peter, Paul and Mary song . . . you know the one I mean? You must, it's from your generation." (She forced a provocative giggle.) "Do you know what turned out, though? The idea wasn't my mom's, it was my dad's. He thought he was calling me

Annabel Lee—you've heard of *her*, right? Or was she after your
time?" ("Ha-ha, very funny!") "It's just that he was stoned out of
his mind at the naming ceremony they made for me. There was
an African drumming circle and dancing in the moonlight and all
that shit. He got that from TV, from that *Roots* series. It made a
big impression on him—I'll bet he was stoned when he watched it,
too. He could hardly stand on his feet, but he was shouting 'Anna
Lee! Anna Lee!' as if he were Kunta Kinte. They were all drumming and so wasted that no one knew what was happening and no
one cared. Every time they've told me about it, they've laughed
as though it were a good joke. When I was old enough to go to
school, I insisted on being called Ann instead of Anna. Everything
around me was weird enough as it was, and at least Ann Lee was
a normal-sounding name. It wasn't exactly like living in the East
Village here, as you can see. Are you done with your coffee? We'd
better go back. I'll bet my mom's made a flourless leek quiche for
supper, or something equally disgusting. . . . I can't believe that I
still have two more days here. It's like *Little House on the Prairie*,
but minus the good-looking dad. . . . Look how dark it already is.
It'll be night before we know it."

6

*Midnight. A last measure of light sifts through the thin crack of
a crescent, late-month moon. Tomorrow or the day after, it will be
gone from the sky. The gates of the Eretz HaChayim Cemetery are
wide open. Who comes and goes there? Ghostly shades of those who
are cast away from the city, people of the field, those who were buried in foreign shrouds, in coffins of pine and oak. The souls of our
dead lie scattered upon the earth, drifting over fields and forests like
gray patches of fog, snagged on bushes, carried onward by the cold*

wind that blows from the mountains, sucked into the vacuous wake
of cars and trucks that travel in the dark from north to south, from
east to west. Strewn like night soil upon the earth, our souls await
their redemption. How many more cycles must we pass through,
how long shall we look for the secret tunnel leading back to our orig-
inal source? Who knows? Perhaps a thousand years. Perhaps a sin-
gle day. The gates of the cemetery are wide open, but no one comes
or goes. A cold wind blows from the mountains. Trucks travel in the
darkness from north to south, from east to west.

7

Nine a.m. Andrew blinked in the bright light. The frilled, flowery curtains on the windows were more for show than utility, and the autumn sun flooded the room, fading the patchwork quilts and embroidered cushions. Half-awake, he looked around. It took an uncertain minute or two to recall where he was. From the moment of his and Ann Lee's arrival, it was clear that she would sleep in her old room and he in the guest room. The idea of them spending the night together in her childhood room, with her teddy bears, posters, and cheerleader's paraphernalia, seemed bizarre if not perverse. It was as if the house had decided on its own to class him as a grown-up and Ann Lee as an alternately genial and thorny teen. Leaning toward him at the dinner table, she had whispered in his ear: "Don't forget to leave your door open tonight. I might want to check you haven't thrown off your covers." The titillating thought of her stealthily tiptoeing to him past her parents' bedroom made both of them feel they were back in high school. Yet dinner had ended late and Andrew, fatigued and slightly drunk, fell asleep at once and didn't wake up until late.

He stretched in bed and surveyed the room. The walls were

paneled in light pine. Knickknacks crowded the shelves. A robe and slippers had been set aside for him by the bathroom door. He smiled, pleased by their declaration of intimacy. His shower lasted longer than usual; unaccustomed to the faucets, it took a while to figure out how to regulate the hot and cold water. Nor did he know whether Ann Lee was already awake and in need of some time with her mother, in which case it would be better to linger in his room. Deciding to do so, he availed himself of a comfortable arm- chair and a shelf of old New Age books that clearly hadn't been looked at in years.

When he finally came down to breakfast a little after ten, An- drew was surprised to find no one but Ann Lee's mother. David— who, it seemed, worked on weekends, too—was already gone. "He wishes you a nice day and hopes he'll see you again soon," said Donna. Andrew gave her a cordial smile. Although last night's dinner had been perfectly pleasant, his real reason for not coming down sooner, he had to acknowledge, was his only half- unconscious reluctance to spend more time in David's presence. "Where's Ann Lee?" he asked. "Isn't she up yet? It's a quarter af- ter ten!" Donna, wearing a silk print dress more suited to an after- noon tea party than a family breakfast, poured him coffee. It was excellent, though a bit weaker than he liked. Stung by yesterday's fiasco, she must have run off to the coffee-bean counter and bought the most expensive blend there was. Did she do it late yesterday evening or early this morning?

Ann Lee, her hair mussed and wearing a faded T-shirt she had slept in as a teenager, came down a bit before noon, still brush- ing the sleep from her eyes. The sight of her small breasts pushing through the thin, worn material of the old T-shirt made Andrew involuntarily avert his gaze. As if their fantasized midnight tryst had actually taken place, she gave Andrew a secretive smile that caused him to blush like a boy while hoping Donna didn't notice.

Their breakfast, Andrew's second, was washed down with more coffee, after which, despite the warm atmosphere, he found himself peeking at his watch as if to ascertain when etiquette would permit him to say what a marvelous time he had and how sorry he was to have to leave, pack his things, and head back to the city by himself. Although he hadn't really suffered in Donna's company, he still felt a great need to get away. There was no point in staying for dinner. They had all eaten together yesterday and he didn't like to drive at night, especially on poorly lit country roads. Besides, she and Ann Lee must want some time for themselves, mustn't they?

8

After ten or twelve minutes, I never remember exactly how long it takes, start keeping an eye out for the high-tension wires crossing the road. That's where you get off the highway on a shortcut to Route 112. I don't know why there isn't a sign, because everyone gets confused there. . . ."

Andrew had had trouble paying attention. Donna's directions were long and far from consistent, the hour was late, and he was anxious to be off. He would manage to find his way. In the end, all roads led to the city.

"Okay, Mom, he got it. He's very smart, remember?" Ann Lee was impatient, too. Eager to get over an awkward situation, she couldn't wait to be free of the exhausting, ambiguous role that his presence had imposed on all of them. Donna, who had to be in the city Monday afternoon for a workshop she was giving on the uses of meditation in childbirth, or some such thing, would bring her back then.

Andrew waved good-bye while backing the car out of the driveway, trying not to trample the flower beds alongside it. The strange

family ménage had gone on long enough and he was glad to get
back to reality. With a last look at Ann Lee and her mother as they
stood watching him with their arms around each other, he swung
the car onto the road. In the distance, they looked more like two
friends the same age than mother and daughter. They suddenly
seemed relaxed and happy to be together, as if the tension between
them had been dispelled by a magic wand.

Andrew drove with concentration, unsuccessfully trying to recall
Donna's complicated instructions. He was shocked by how clumsy
he felt behind the wheel. Anyone not knowing he had grown up in
New Rochelle and gone to school in California might have thought
that he had never left Manhattan in his life and that his entire experience of private motor transportation consisted of sitting in the
back of a New York City taxicab. As part of his self-reinvention
as an urban being, so it seemed, his body had rejected an aptitude
he was practically born with. Linda, on the other hand, still drove
like a suburban housewife even though she now lived in Brooklyn,
skillfully navigating her oversize station wagons full of children and
dogs from one school, shopping center, and playground to the next.

Andrew reached out instinctively to switch on the radio, but
now, too, it couldn't stay tuned to the same station for more than a
minute or two. Either something was the matter with it or the reception in the area was bad. How could anyone live so far out? For
some reason it didn't occur to him to play one of the tapes that lay
around the car, and he kept getting the same distant, sentimental
Muzak with its cloying piano adaptations of old pop songs, letting
the radio spew out its musical pap. He drove slowly, the missed
shortcut to 112 already behind him, regretting not having listened
more carefully to Donna's vague explanations. As though in a
maze, the road signs kept repeating themselves: Goshen, Bethel,
Canaan. None bore the shield-like symbol of Route 87, which
would take him straight to the city.

It was getting dark. Andrew pulled off the road, took a map from the glove compartment, and spread it out on the wheel. The old air conditioner, while producing little in the way of cold air, droned like an old airplane, especially after the radio, which hadn't stopped its insipid emissions, was turned off. Looking at the map, he tried seeing where he was in relation to the boldly colored, diagonal line of 87. When did he become so helpless on the road? He was surprised to feel, despite the cold evening air, sweat running down his neck. Route 87 crossed the Tappan Zee Bridge and merged with 287, which ran nearly to the Hutchison River Parkway. He knew "the Hutch," as it was called in his youth, well. The main route running through Westchester County, it connected New Rochelle with Pelham, Yonkers, and ultimately, Manhattan. And yet how far-off his New Rochelle childhood and adolescence now seemed to him, so unconnected to the person he had become that his memories of them could have been someone else's or from a previous incarnation. Linda had never felt the need to choose between the two worlds, but Andrew's survival as an urban creature had depended on cutting himself off from suburbia. Transplanted to the metropolis, he had put his old self behind him as surely as some species lose their flippers or the ability to fly.

Andrew folded the map, stuck it back in the glove compartment, signaled, and returned to the road. Linda! More than once over the weekend he had thought of her. The frilly curtains, the rustic furniture in the kitchen, the walls paneled with cheap pine—her provincial sense of elegance, which he couldn't abide, would have approved of it all. The tastes of some of the primitive tribes he had encountered in his research were more congenial to him than that of the attractively arranged home he had just been in. And yet that, too, was *human, all too human.*

Andrew had to smile at the phrase's aptness, even while chiding himself for plagiarizing Nietzsche. There was a time when he had constantly repeated it—to himself, to his therapist, in his conversations with Linda, and, most of all (as she once complained to him), in talking to her friends in the weeks after leaving her. "The curved line is human," he had written in his journal in a moment of euphoric insight. "It is finite, limiting, and limited. The straight line is infinite, not just as a negation of the finite but in and of itself." Flowers on the wallpaper, on the sheets, and on the pillowcases. Flowers on the tablecloths and on the napkins. Flowers in flowerpots and on the rims of dishes. Flowers with round, toothed, and lobed petals, with small and large leaves, with twining stems in treacherous swamps of bright color, snakes biting their tails. Like Alexander the Great, he had had no choice but to cut the Gordian knot all at once, to cast off the chains of everything curved, respectable, domestic, and feminine for the open, masculine, geometric spaces of freedom.

He had been driving for a long while, and the more he drove, the less he knew where he was. The total, pitiless darkness of the countryside would soon descend, swooping down on his car to throttle him. A dim, paralyzing fear seized Andrew by the throat, constricting his breath. It was impossible to match the map's information with the road's reality. None of the exits he passed were marked on it, the junctions appeared without warning, the forks led nowhere. Looming before him on the wrong side of the road like a toothless mouth, the open gate of the Eretz HaChayim Cemetery turned his anxiety into near panic. The oncoming night would be black, moonless. Ghostly shades flitted in and out of the gate. *The souls of the dead lay scattered upon the earth, drifting over fields and forests like gray patches of fog, sucked into the vacuous wake of cars and trucks that traveled in the dark from north to south and east to west. How many more cycles must we pass through, how long shall we look for the tunnel leading back to our first source? Who knows? Perhaps a thousand years, perhaps a single day!*

It seemed slightly less than miraculous when the road ran the little car all at once into the southbound side of Route 87 and thence to the Tappan Zee Bridge and the familiar embrace of the Hutch. From that point on, the car seemed to drive itself, taking care to reach the city just as darkness was falling. The Palisades on his right, lit by the last rays of twilight, angled sharply upward from the gray mist that had swallowed the river. He smiled as he crossed the narrow bridge leading from the Bronx to Manhattan. Had he unconsciously planned his dramatic arrival all along? Was there some conspiracy to return him to the city at exactly this hour? The artificially lit profile of the George Washington Bridge shone majestically in the gathering dusk, making his chest expand and his heart beat steadily again. Opening the window, he let the cathartic evening breeze flow past him as if it were a river and he a gray rock in its midst. The regal glass towers of the city, with all their lights, rose to welcome him back to the city he loved.

9

November 3, 2000

The 5th of Heshvan, 5761

An alternate universe is reflected in the dark glass of the buildings. The yellow cabs flow from top to bottom, crawling on their surface like heavy drops of rain. Pedestrians stride diagonally across a tenth-floor window, obeying the unwritten laws, the pure style, of New York's skittish yet precise choreography: waves of jaywalkers crossing on red lights, slanting columns of steam rising from the street corners, giant graffiti ascending the walls, darting messenger boys zigzagging in and out of traffic, taxis jumping lanes without signaling—all exist in a state of perfect harmony.

And yet how stable is the rock foundation on which everything

rests—as heavy, strong, and gray as the river on an overcast day.
And in the midst of all this, somewhere along the line between rest
and motion, gravitational pull and release, a perfectly ordinary-
looking yellow cab cruises slowly down Broadway, all four windows wide open in spite of the late autumn chill, its radio blasting
with the precise, pedantic diction of a digital-age preacher, "And
they said, Let us build us a city and a tower whose top may reach
unto heaven." Thundering with impatience at the blindness of the
unrepentant, the insistent voice that drowns out all else like the
sound track of a movie. It rams the buildings, shaking their glass
panes and reverberating in space. "And the Lord came down to see
the city and the tower which the children of men built." The light
turns red. The driver, a middle-aged man of unclear national origins who converted his empty taxi into a giant loudspeaker for the
enlightenment of the sinful masses, sits motionlessly inside it, staring straight ahead with the blank look of the born again, a look that
is single-minded to the point of mindlessness. "And the Lord said,
Behold the people is one, and they have all one language, and this
they begin to do, and now, nothing will be restrained from them
which they have imagined to do." How can he sit there amid all
that noise? Is he deaf? His lips are clenched in tight fury. Clearly,
he believes every word of the uncouth text with which he is bom-
barding the city. "Go to, let us go down and confound their language, that they may not understand one another's speech." The
flint-hard verses strike like pickaxes, like mighty hammers splin-
tering the rock foundation. Unseen fissures ran through the walls
of the buildings, streams of doom that would flow to the great Sea
of Obliteration. The copper water pipes sluiced up the bloodred,
corrosive rust that was coating their insides like plaque. A trillion
tons of metal, glass, and stone are slowly, invisibly, crumbling.
The city's fatigued heart is giving out. "So the Lord scattered them
from there upon the face of all the earth, and they left off building

the city." The light turns green. The driver, perhaps loath to exit the marvelous stage at whose center his commandeered taxi had placed him, lingers for a moment before heading for the next intersection, there, too, to spread the tidings to the great city.

10
November 6, 2000

The 9th of Heshvan, 5761

Eleven p.m. The interior of the apartment was pleasantly dim. A light, bluish halo enveloped the screen of the computer. Andrew's fingers skim lightly over the keyboard and grip the elongated mouse. He is checking his e-mails for the third time that day. What an enchanting new medium, so captivatingly noncommittal! Words appear from nowhere and vanish into thin air, lacking the least physical dimension. Throwing a letter into a wastepaper basket, let alone tearing it up or shredding it, was a positive, almost declarative act compared to deleting an e-mail, whose text disappeared without a trace at the slightest, all but immaterial touch of a fingertip. Important and trivial messages, personal correspondence and junk mail—Andrew clicked away at the keyboard, effortlessly sifting and sorting his communications.

A yellow icon blinked: important mail. Rachel. It was Rachel. She was sitting right now just like him, in her charming little apartment in Princeton, answering her mail. *Hi, Dad. The department is sending me to New York for a three-day conference. Don't worry, I have a place to stay on the East Side, it belongs to friends who are out of town. Let's get together if you can find the time for me. Love you, Rachel. P.S. Take a look at this link when you get a chance.*

Andrew smiled. The department was sending her? Not bad. Her

offhanded way of letting him know amused him. From time to time, partly to celebrate their joint interest in contemporary culture and partly to challenge him by testing the boundaries between them, she sent him links to unconventional and even provocative sites, and before beginning one of the virtual tête-à-têtes they engaged in, he double-clicked on the blue outline of her latest selection. The computer whirred faintly; the screen went momentarily blank, then logged on to a strange, disturbing site entitled *Back to the Foreskin*. Andrew paged down it, his discomfort growing as he scanned its text and images, the photo journal, kept for the past half year, of a thirty-eight-year-old Jewish man from Brooklyn who had recorded his persistent efforts to retrieve his lost foreskin and become again what he called "a whole man." In the spirit of the times, his pursuit of the holy grail of epidermal restoration had become a psychological and spiritual quest exhibiting every up and down, revelation and blank moment, euphoria and depression. Andrew had to squirm. The ritualization of selfhood in modern society, with its compulsive public exposure of what once had been private, was totally bizarre. This particular pilgrim was touchingly pathetic: an emasculated male, an overgrown infant with the tenderized flesh of a castrated bull whose sole interest was his puny little circumcised penis. The site was illustrated with odious close-ups of the longed-for, never-again-to-be-had flap of skin, whose strange membranous inflorescence made Andrew think more of a female sexual organ than a male one.

Andrew shut down the site. He felt soiled, intruded on. What on earth compelled her to send him this vile link? To his dismay, he found himself wondering—no, not really wondering, it was just an idle thought—whether Rachel's boyfriend, Tom, was circumcised. True, he came from a Catholic family, but weren't nearly all Americans circumcised nowadays?

Ridiculous. What possessed him to think about such things?

Chasing away the annoying gnat of introspection, he decided to say nothing about the link and wrote:

Hi, sweetie.

It's great that you're coming. I'm sure you'll be very busy, but we must find time to have lunch or a quick coffee together, just the two of us. I need some quality time with my little girl.

Love you,
Dad

11

You know, all that fake warmth, that 'we must find time to have lunch together,' is just his way of saying that that's all the time he intends to give me." Rachel and Tom were in bed, nestled under the sheets. "And the way he puts it, as if the one who's so busy is me! It's always been like that. He'll never say it's him who has no time or finds it inconvenient. That's not his style. His method is to make you feel embarrassed for wanting to bother him. It's passive-aggressive, which I don't think anyone has ever told him or even thought of. But that's what he is: passive-aggressive! And you know what's the most amazing part of it? No one is ever angry at him! No one can be, because no one sees what he's doing. I mean, we all feel it, but we can't put it into words—not when he's so nice and sexy and sensitive and such a good listener. And that includes me. I play along with him like everyone else. We all belong to the prestigious little club of his protégées who know the rules. We do the work for him, we protect him from our own demands, we make an ice circle around him and guard it as though we were its priests. Did I ever tell you about his doctorate? He finished writing it when I was a baby, right after I was born. Would you believe it? The last act of the dissertation, the one that's famous for its nervous breakdowns, suicide attempts, and divorces, when suddenly, a week before your deadline, you're handed a ten-page list of required corrections, and then at the last second, after you've made them all, a request to change the typeface of the chapter headings and renumber them, and, oh, yes, the margins need to be one-point-two and not one-point-three inches . . . and there he is, sitting up all night in their little apartment, two days after I was born, surrounded by baby bottles, pacifiers, and dirty diapers, rewriting his fucking footnotes. What powers of concentration, right? Well, let me tell you something. It's not concentration, it's sheer egotism. He doesn't see anyone, no one exists for him but himself. And do you think my mom ever complained about it? That she ever felt neglected or marginalized? Forget it! If you ask her about those days, she'll tell you they were the best of their marriage, an absolute golden age."

Tom nodded silently. He didn't exactly get it. He had grown up in a lower middle-class Irish home whose tough, devoted mother chain-smoked menthol cigarettes, made supper seven times a week, and knew at any given moment just where all her six children were and what they were up to. Passive-aggressive parents lay outside his experience.

12

November 16, 2000

―――――――

The 19th of Heshvan, 5761

Ten p.m. Outside it was raining, but the apartment was warm and cozy. Set against the easy patter of the rain, the soft light of the floor lamps suggested a crackling fireplace, which the apartment never had. Andrew was at work at his desk, debating whether to use a quotation from a *New Yorker* interview with Robert Altman as the epigraph for an article that he hoped to finish by the following afternoon. "Culture and politics have become incestuous," Altman had said about Fellini's *Dolce Vita*, which was interesting, definitely interesting, but how much did it communicate? Never mind, he could put it off until tomorrow. A good epigraph could springboard an entire piece, even if you erased it afterward. Recently, Andrew had been even more prolific than usual. He had to publish a lot this year, especially in light of his increasingly likely appointment as director of the Asch Interdisciplinary Program in Contemporary Cultural Studies—a prestigious, handsomely funded enterprise considered by many to be the department's flagship.

He glanced at his watch. Ann Lee should be back by ten thirty, and he wanted to finish at least one more paragraph before then. Taking a quick look at Mark Eisenstein's *On the Nature of the Fantastic*, he returned the book facedown to his desk and went on writing:

Fantasy is not necessarily that which we yearn for but never dare realize—this is the vulgar and trivial meaning of the word. Fantasy is the testing of the boundaries of possibility in both its positive and negative sense, the sometimes painful stretching of the frontiers of the imagination. The oedipal fantasy, for example, is not the actual desire to sleep with your mother or daughter but rather the fear that such a frightful thing might happen, and the obsessive, perfectly human urge to imagine what it would be like if it did. By the same token, the nightmares and terrible daydreams that devoted parents have of their children dying are not repressed wishes. They are toxic, compulsive experiments in examining the extent of their emotional dependence on the offspring they love.

Suppose we take, for instance, the expression "Sodom and

Gomorrah," which has powerfully engaged religious fanatics through the ages. These are not places that most of them would like to be in, especially since they mainly associate by them with mass homosexual orgies. They simply mark the upper limit of what their limited imaginations can conceive of. The existence of these mythological sin-cities, far-fetched and fantastical as it may be, remains for them a seminal metaphor enabling them to live what they consider to be respectable and sinless lives. A more classic, perfectly formed fantasy than that of these ancient twin cities of sin would be hard to come by.

The doorbell rang gaily, cutting short his train of thought. Ten forty: here she was. Andrew, going to open the door, was overcome all over again by Ann Lee's unspoiled beauty. Wet from the rain, eyes sparkling, she smiled radiantly and threw her arms around him, dampening his clothes. Her cheek was smooth and cold, sprinkled with sugary drops of water. Her small feet must be frozen. "Some cocoa?" he asked. "Cocoa with a touch of rum? Maybe some wine?"

She wriggled out of her raincoat by the door, leaving its stylish black puddle of rayon on the floor beneath her long, wet, black wool scarf. "Wine, thanks. Is there any red?" She was full of life: the concert must have gone well. As lithe as a ballerina, she sat on the rug, kicked off her shoes, and tossed them into a corner. Andrew, uncorking a bottle of wine, heard the sound from the kitchen. Next, she stripped off her black stockings, tossed them after the shoes, rose gracefully, and began to circle the room, drying her wet, cold feet on the thick rugs. Noticing the lit screen of the computer, she went over to it, scanned a few lines in silence, and read aloud in a pompous, professorial voice: "*Rare is the man who has not dreamed at least once of having sex with his daughters. Sometimes this is transposed into an encounter with a strange, desirable woman that suddenly turns into a tabooed, incestuous act.* Very interesting. Ve-ry interesting. You know you could be arrested for this, don't you?"

Andrew, returning from the kitchen with a large glass of wine in each hand, strode—not exactly hurrying, but with a slightly faster gait than usual—to his desk, handed Ann Lee her wine, and shut the lid of the computer, burying its lit screen in the keyboard. "Bad girl," he said. "Weren't you taught in school that it isn't nice to read someone's writing without permission?"

Ann Lee threw him a sharp, amused look. "And being a dirty old man is nicer?" She embraced him, gave him a long kiss, and whispered in his ear: "Had any other interesting dreams you've forgotten to tell me about, Daddy?"

13
November 17, 2000

The 19th of Heshvan, 5761

The lamps on the living-room tables cast a warm, orange-tinted light on the floor, leaving the space beneath the ceiling in dusk. From the dining room came sounds of conversation and laughter. The guests were assembled there, waiting for Cora, Linda's mother, to bring her renowned Thanksgiving turkey to the table. Someone rapped a fork on a wineglass to signal the start of the toasts. Putting her glass down, Linda snuggled up to Andrew on the couch in a way that took him twenty years back to the first days of their relationship. The sudden intimacy of it confused him, his emotion mixed with an unease that made his heart pound and his fingertips and facial muscles tingle. When had they last been together like this, so close to each other? And where was everybody? Suppose someone came and saw them?

Linda gave him a long, significant look. Her hair, dyed red, fell in straight lines on both sides of her face, reframing it in a mysterious way. Andrew had to overcome the frightened instinct to back away and keep the correct distance they had maintained since the divorce.

"I loved you, do you know that?" Linda paused, letting the full weight of her words resound in the charged quiet of the room. "I loved you very much. Sometimes I think I still do, even now." She fixed her green eyes on him, their burning intensity not at all like her usual, self-incriminating smile. "Don't get me wrong, Andy. It's not that I have any regrets. But you're still the best-looking man I've ever met." She laid a gently provocative, cruelly sensual hand on his. Andrew recoiled as if bitten by a snake. Sharp and searing, her unexpected touch ran through him like an electric shock. He raised himself on his elbows, head jerked from the pillow. What the hell! The gray window sash stood out against the black wall. Where was he? The square numbers on the alarm clock glowed green in the dark: 4:24. He stared at them in disbelief, his mind unable to bridge the gap between sleep and wakefulness. Where was Linda? Where had everyone gone? The clock let out a small digital hiccup. The green numbers faded. Then their cold fire returned: 4:25 a.m.

14

November 23, 2000

The 25th of Heshvan, 5761

Autumn. The trees are bare and seem like they'll never come to life again. How they take us by surprise each year anew. Thanksgiving is upon us. The Macy's Thanksgiving Day Parade is set to march on Thursday, but its huge floats are already lurking, like grotesque, brightly brindled prehistoric beasts, between Columbus

Avenue and Central Park West. Once more we will stand in rows to
see them go by; once more the sudden cold will find us unprepared,
as if we had hoped this year would be different. The blue is gone
from above; gray reigns over the palette. A pewter sky glowers in
the leaden river, its sole ornament the brittle, slate-colored trees. The
asphalt, a fresh black in spring, has aged and grayed, too; gray are
the puffs of smoke rising from the town houses in which the first
fireplaces have been lit. Their brownstone facades alone grow richer
from day to day, as though the cold were distilling an utterly, unbearably beautiful essence from their bloodred veins.

Kenny and Robin were the first to arrive. Sean, their eldest, was
already—can you believe it?—twelve. Incredible how time flies!
With Kenny's brown eyes and wavy hair, he looked like a slimmer
version of his father. Blond little Tessa, lissome and delicate, her
blue eyes the color of distant oceans veiled by a dreamy mist, had
Robin's Nordic beauty. And let us not forget Barnabas, their old
Labrador, limping in after them: he's part of the family, too. Cora,
as every year, remembered to tell about the Thanksgiving when
Robin asked, "Kenny, have you seen the puppy?" A minute later,
suspicious sounds came from the kitchen. What did we see? Little
Barnabas, dragging behind him a turkey drumstick twice his size!
"And what does Mom do?" asked Kenny, supplying the time-worn
punch line. "Without losing a beat, she says to Barnabas, 'Hey, just
a second, you forgot the cranberry sauce!'"

"Hi, Linda." Robin kissed Linda. "Hi, George. I didn't mean to
overlook you. Is Andrew coming? It's your big bourbon day, you
must be impatient to see him. Hi, Mom, good to see you. Where
should I put the cake? Sean, say hello to your grandma."

Eric arrived at four fifteen, accompanied by the same girlfriend
he had come with the year before, who was as pretty and thin—
perhaps a bit too thin—as a model. Linda, who couldn't remember her name, kissed her warmly and avoided talking to her until

Amy arrived and could be asked. Sean and Tessa joined Alison in the family room, sprawling out on the couches to watch TV while quietly devouring the appetizers on the coffee table. Barnabas plopped down beside them on the rug and fell asleep until the water bowl Robin had put there for him was mistakenly kicked over, its contents spilling on the parquet floor.

Kim and Larry rang the doorbell at a quarter to five. Kim had to lean over a large bowl of fruit salad to kiss Linda. "We left really early, but there was terrible traffic. You wouldn't believe it." Larry brandished the bottle of expensive single malt scotch he had brought; he liked to impress people with exotic blends and rare vintages. "It's time we put some style into this affair! What do you say to a twenty-one-year-old Glenlivet? They age it in sherry casks. We bought it in the duty-free in St. Thomas—you can't find it in local liquor stores. Our local dealer has never even heard of it."

"Hi, Kimmy," said Robin. "Hi, Larry. I wish you luck with the single malt, but I'll probably be your only customer. Kenny's waiting for Andrew to start their annual bourbon binge."

George thanked Larry, took the bottle, and placed it on the bar beside the snacks, ice bucket, and bottles of wine, whiskey, soda, and juices. At five, Rachel walked in with Tom. "Hi, sweetheart," Linda murmured to her, giving her a big hug. She hugged Tom, too, standing on tiptoe to give him a kiss. At home in her house, he shook the hands of the men standing by the bar and accepted a generous glass of scotch from Larry. Rachel went to the kitchen with Linda to say hello to Grandma Cora and get the lowdown from Aunt Amy, who had just walked in, on Eric and his girlfriend. "They met at Amherst. She's lovely. She's majoring in music. No, I don't like her weight, either. I wouldn't call it an eating disorder, but she's super-skinny. It's nothing I can talk about to Eric, though. You know what he's like . . ."

"Hi, George." Rachel hugged George, who had come to fill

the basket of blue corn chips and the bowl of salsa. Yes, there was some tension between them during the first years of his marriage to Linda but what would you have expected? It was long gone now and she was genuinely fond of him.

As usual, the last to arrive was Andrew. Dressed in an elegant black suit, he carried a big bouquet of white lilies and a large golden box of fancy chocolates. Robin, who was standing with the men by the bar and drinking neat ("it's too good for ice") scotch with Larry, was the first to spot him. "Hi, Andrew. Making your usual dramatic entrance, hey? Kenny was about to start in on the bourbon without you."

Rachel was startled to feel her heart leap at her father's appearance. Everyone seemed to have the same reaction. The dynamics of the room changed completely, as if its center of gravity had shifted all at once; yet no less striking than the electric effect on her was the inner resistance it aroused. Andrew made straight for the kitchen, hugged her, and asked how she was before turning to kiss Linda. Her heart skipped another beat as she saw her parents' eyes meet. He kissed Amy and Cora, his ex-sister- and mother-in-law, and gave George a warm handshake; if the presence of his wife's ex-husband made him feel the least bit uncomfortable, George was careful not to show it. Kenny, who was standing at the bar, shook Andrew's hand happily, hesitated, and then gave him a big, clumsy bear hug. Larry shook his hand, too. Pots and pans clattered in the kitchen. The white lilies were put in a vase and placed at the center of the table. Where do the chocolates go? Just put them over there, with the desserts, the cookies, and the pumpkin pie.

Andrew excused himself for a minute and went to look for Alison. Though he had a good idea where she was, he wandered absentmindedly through the house, peering into bedrooms, opening the door of the game room, and leaving the family room for last.

Alison was absorbed in a movie. Wrapped in a blanket with her shoes kicked off and her chin propped on a fist, she was such a darling that only his fear of embarrassing her kept him from sweeping her up in his arms with fierce longing. He stood there watching her quietly, this child he felt so close to and knew so well. What an amazing combination of Ethel, Cora, and Linda she was, but with her own wisdom and goodness! He reached out to stroke her hair. "Dad!" Startled by his touch, she jumped up bright-eyed and pressed her cheek to his. "We're watching a movie. Want to see it with us?" Andrew kissed her on the forehead and playfully rumpled her hair. "I'd love to, but the grown-ups are waiting for me. Another time, okay?"

15

It's odd, Rachel thought, setting forks and knives on the table beside the folded napkins by each plate, how on Thanksgiving the men in our family sit and eat and the women serve. It's odd because it isn't usually that way. Dad cooks, and George cooks, and Kenny cooks, and Robin hasn't cooked a thing in her life, but the deep patriarchal structure surfaces on Thanksgiving even in our liberal, intellectual family. For a single afternoon we live the old fantasy: the men at the table, red-faced and tipsy, and the women bustling in the kitchen, giddy with the excitement of being the housewives they never were. Old-fashioned queens of hearth and home, they parade proudly out with their turkey and stuffing and sweet potatoes while the men cheer them on like overgrown children. If Dad would follow Mom in, standing tall behind her and the turkey, it would make a perfect Norman Rockwell painting.

Rachel finished setting the table and, instead of returning to the kitchen to see what else she could do, went to the bar to pour herself a second bourbon. Though she drank scotch on occasion, savoring the subtle gender-bending statement of ordering it in public, bourbon was a drink she never had learned to like. Its crude, corn-mash odor didn't appeal to her. Even Andrew drank it only on Thanksgiving, and no one else she knew touched it at all; as far as she was concerned, it was strictly for Republicans and Confederate flag flyers. Downed in one gulp, the rough, faintly honeyed liquor stoked the resentment that had been building up in her all afternoon, an anger, dark and deep, laced with bitter nostalgia and longing that had kept her on the verge of tears. Feeling dizzy and flushed, she banged her empty glass on the table as if she were in a Western and casually poured herself another drink.

"Mom, Mom! Sean switched channels to a football game in the middle of the movie!" Alison tugged at Linda's skirt while Linda stood by the open oven with Cora, probing the browned, mouthwatering bird with a thermometer to see if it was done.

"Not now, Alison sweetie, okay?"

"But Mom, he grabbed the remote and started switching channels, and now we can't see the end of the movie."

"Why don't you go play the piano?" Linda suggested with sudden inspiration. "Show Tessa how you play. You play, too, Tessa, don't you?"

The thermometer registered 180 degrees. "All right, darling," said Cora to her daughter, "you can tell everyone to come to the table."

"I can't believe you made this!" Robin called across the table to Cora. "We've been eating the same Thanksgiving turkey for fifteen years, year after year, and I still can't get over how tender and juicy it always is."

"That's right, Mom," said Kenny, his mouth full of food. "The turkey's fabulous."

"And the stuffing!" Larry had to shout to make himself heard above the animated conversation, the scrape of silverware on china, the unmelodious chimes of the piano, and the roars of the crowd from the television in the family room. "It's great!"

Cora smiled broadly. "Butter. The secret is butter. I squirt tons of it under the skin. Just don't tell my doctor, he'll kill me. Or the rabbi at my synagogue."

Everyone laughed. Linda came from the kitchen with a large tray of steaming sweet potatoes baked in their skins. "Girls!" she called to the living room. "Girls, can we have a little quiet? Alison, sweetie, why don't you play the piano later?"

"I'd like to propose a toast," Larry shouted, ringing his fork on his wineglass to the chorus of assent that sounded like a musical accompaniment. "Here's to our host Linda! And to George, of course! And to the four-star chef Aunt Cora! And to this whole wonderful family!"

The toast was greeted with a cheerful clink of glasses. "So what's new, Andy?" asked Kenny, filling Andrew's extended glass with more bourbon. They were standing at the bar, slightly apart from the other guests, who had retired to the couches at the other end of the living room to drink coffee and listen to Alison and Tessa's "holiday concert," a stumbling, four-handed duet that convulsed the two girls in giggles while earning them a merry ovation. The bourbon ritual, by now a family joke, had started years ago when Kenny, Linda's younger brother—a would-be poet who had settled for an assistant professorship at Bard College teaching English and writing a bit of verse on the side—had declared that nothing but bourbon should be drunk on Thanksgiving because it was "the very soul of America." Andrew tipsily took him up on it, and ever since then, in the mysterious way that passing incidents have of becoming time-honored traditions, their bourbon brotherhood was part of the day. Each year Linda made sure to buy a squat bottle of Maker's Mark with its red plastic top that resembled a wax seal and indeed sealed a pact of quiet affection between the two men, who never saw each other from one Thanksgiving to the next.

"The situation in our department is intolerable," Kenny said without waiting for an answer. "There's been a rash of promotions and everyone is now entrenched in a tenured position. We've had to turn down a ton of job applications, some from men and women with lists of publications almost as impressive as yours . . ."

They exchanged smiles. Kenny's gibe was aimed more at himself than at Andrew. He had never made his peace with his academic career, which he had continued to rebel against passively even after getting tenure himself. Andrew nodded in agreement. He liked Kenny's company. Despite the differences between them, they shared an unspoken bond, as unspoken as the strange illusion, re-created each Thanksgiving, that Andrew and Linda were together again with George as an older, harmless, likable uncle.

Without waiting for Andrew to empty his glass, Kenny reached for the half-finished bottle and refilled it. *He's nervous*, Andrew thought. *There's something he wants to tell me and doesn't know how.* Andrew supposed he knew, or at least could guess, what it was. "You know," Kenny said, refilling his own glass almost to the rim, "Robin and I have been having problems lately." Andrew nodded sympathetically, every bit the discreet friend. He was used to it. Since his divorce, quite a few men had tried making him their confessional priest, assuming that having "been through it" himself, he would understand them and have some advice for them, a magic formula to rid them of their guilt and let them have it both ways. "I don't know if Linda told you, but I moved out for a couple of weeks and went to live in the apartment of some friends who were abroad." Andrew kept nodding, waiting for the confession to come. "I had this really brilliant doctoral student, a young woman who was writing a dissertation on intertextuality as a reflection of . . ." *Here we go*, thought Andrew, feeling suddenly bored and drunk. "They called her Lolita . . ." But although Kenny went on confiding in a tone no less proud than distressed, Andrew was no longer listening. Something he couldn't put a finger on was nagging him. "Now Robin and I are back together again, and it's wonderful. Wonderful! She's a fantastic woman. She took me back and hasn't nursed a grudge. You know something? Paradoxically, it's even better than before. It's like there's an electricity between us that we haven't had in years. As if it had all been part of a plan . . ."

"Well, look who's here!" The loud, hoarse voice came from nearby them. Kenny fell silent at once. Neither of them had seen Rachel approach. "If it isn't Dad, Uncle Kenny, and Tennessee Williams!" Rachel pointed a sardonic chin at the almost empty bottle of bourbon. Andrew looked at her in shock. She was drunk. There was a coarseness about her, a defiant vulgarity, that he had never seen in her before. A vulnerability, too, which only made it worse, as if he were seeing his grown daughter without her clothes on. He felt almost compelled to avert his eyes from her. "Wouldn't you know it!" Rachel took the bottle from the bar and held its diminishing contents up to the light. "Pretending to have a man-to-man talk so as to polish off the bourbon!" She poured herself a brimming glass and self-assuredly, almost coquettishly, two more for the men, enjoying their discomfort at her provocative reversal of the gender roles. "It's my turn to make a toast." Her loud voice drew stares from the far end of the living room, stilling its conversation. She raised her glass, the bottle in her other hand. "To the great Native American genocide that we're here to celebrate! To the hypocrisy of liberal America and to the self-absorbed radical intellectuals who sold their souls to . . ."

You could hear a pin drop. No one said a word. The last notes of the piano hung in the air. So did the end of Rachel's sentence, which froze on her tongue and refused to be spoken. Her fingers gripped the glass as if to break it. Although the tense silence lasted only a few seconds, time seemed to have stopped, leaving her suspended and looking down from above, from an angle of forty-five degrees. All at once, like a river whose dam has broken, she made a retching sound, put down her drink, murmured "Excuse me" as if to herself, and hurried from the room while struggling to keep her balance. Tom, who had been sitting on the couch with Kim and Larry, excused himself and quickly followed her into the hallway.

"Isn't Rachel sweet!" laughed Cora, defusing the tension and restarting the flow of conversation as if nothing had happened. "I remember the first time Linda came home drunk. She was fourteen. She tried sneaking off to her room without being seen, but she smelled like a distillery. The whole neighborhood could smell it."

"God, that was awful! I barely made it to the stairs," Linda said.

"I have to tell you a story," chuckled Larry. "Would you like to know what my father said to me the first time I came home drunk in tenth grade? He . . ."

Linda didn't stay to listen. Leaving the living room, she headed for the bathroom in the hall. Tom, his lanky frame crouched by the shut door, was listening to the gagging, sobbing sounds coming from its other side. Linda knocked. "It's me, sweetheart. Can I come in?"

There was no answer. Linda waited. After a minute, the door opened a crack and Rachel's pale, tearstained face appeared. With an apologetic look at Tom, who remained standing in the hall, Linda slipped inside and shut the door behind her. "Come, darling," she whispered, hugging Rachel, in a voice reminiscent of other, distant times. "Come, I'll make you some coffee. Everything's all right. Everything's all right now."

"Do you get what I'm saying?" Kenny was saying at that moment to Andrew in the living room, speaking too quickly, almost defensively, as if called upon to justify his bourgeois existence. "Intellectual maturity, if you ask me, is the ability to live simultaneously on different levels of consciousness. When you're young, you think that only a hypocrite who's sold out gives up critiquing the social construct and accepts it as reality." He lectured as if to soothe the inner wound caused by Rachel's words, which he was sure were meant for him. She must have known that at her age he had published an underground edition of poems, written in the narrative voice of the Native American, calling upon America to face up to its genocide of the Indians and make Thanksgiving a national day of reckoning.

Eight p.m. Eric, tired and already slightly hungover, had left with his girlfriend, a long ride ahead of them. Larry, far from sober himself, was having a second coffee while saying, "It's better to get home late than get into an accident, isn't it?" Tessa was sleeping in Robin's lap, and Alison, too, had fallen asleep on the couch, her head propped on Andrew's thigh. Linda sat dreamily at the piano, her wineglass beside some sheet music, amateurishly picking out an old, familiar duet. What was it? Of course, Gershwin, *Porgy and Bess*. Did you know he, too, lived on West 110th Street? That's where he composed his *Rhapsody in Blue*, on a small upright piano, in a little apartment looking out on the backyard. Cora, peering over her glasses to read the music, was singing the female voice in a husky contralto while Kenny crooned the male part in an off-tune tenor. Where was George—in the kitchen? He could never sit still when there were dirty dishes in the sink, he always had to sneak into the kitchen and do them. What a lovely evening. Too bad it would soon be time to say good night. Outside, in their parked car, Rachel is weeping, her head burrowed deep in Tom's lap, staining his brown leather jacket with hot tears of shame and self-pity.

16

Eleven p.m. The kitchen is squeaky clean, the dishes are washed, and the house is back in perfect order. The turkey leftovers, wrapped neatly in tinfoil, are already in the refrigerator, ready for the next day's sandwiches. George and Linda lie reading in bed, in their pleasantly lit bedroom, surrounded by colorful pillows, magazines, and stray parts of the weekend paper. "God, George," says Linda suddenly, as if picking up the thread of a dropped conversation, "could you believe Andrew, with his black suit and white flowers?"

George looked up from his magazine with a smile. "Yes. He's been prolonging his twenties longer than anyone I know."

Linda giggled and poked him in the side. "Don't be mean!" She sighed. "Rachel worries me, though. I don't think she's happy with Tom. There's something missing there, don't you think?"

George put down the magazine. "I don't think it's about Tom. It's much deeper than that. She's harboring a lot of rage toward her father; she is very conflicted and has all kinds of mixed feelings about their relationship. She doesn't dare attack him directly because she's afraid to endanger his love, so she took it out on Kenny. The poor guy is an easy target with all his frustrations and guilt."

Linda put down her book, too. "Do you really think it's all about Andrew?"

"Of course," George said. "Transference, a classic case."

17

Nighttime. A night of unleashed fury, of dark dread, of the shadow of death. Demons are conjured, ghosts come to you in your dreams. The Harpies raise their bloodcurdling cries and the horrible howls of Cerberus reverberate to the dark horizon. There is a river, called the Sambation, which could smash an iron mountain; six days a week it roars with sand and stones, and on the eve of the seventh, as darkness descends, cloud covers it and it is hidden from men until the Sabbath departs. Angels' wings beat to the hoarse cry of the phoenix, revived again and again from its ashes. Stray souls migrate endlessly, flying in all directions like the slivers of a shattered pot, ricocheting, changing course, colliding again. The migrations quicken; hence, the ancients lived longer than we do. Adam. The generation of the Flood. The generation of Babel. The soul of Abel, of Cain, of our Father Abraham, of Moses, may he rest in peace, of Aaron the priest, of Nadab and Abihu, of Phineas, son of Eleazar, pure and zealous for the Unutterable Name, of the prophet Elijah of blessed memory. Souls big and small, black and white, unclean and holy; rebirth without end; flashes of light in the darkness of oblivion; entire lives, transmigrations, go by; lives many years long flicker for a moment and go out, their burning, speeding brilliance tracing a thin arc of fire that curves through space and is gone like a meteor shower; infinite motion. A man, a priest, walks between the drops, his head wrapped in a linen turban, a gold fire pan in one hand.

18

November 24, 2000

———————

The 26th of Heshvan, 5761

Three a.m. Andrew was awakened from a troubled sleep by a splitting headache and a sour feeling of nausea. Jerkily, as

if beamed by an old movie projector, the image of someone in a
wheelchair danced before his half-opened eyes, a figure from a
dream whose fragments squirmed like maggots: Walter Cohen,
Andrew's father. A venerable old man, he shivered feebly from
cold beneath the layers of clothing piled on him by Maria, the devoted housekeeper at his assisted living unit in Miami.

Walter's low blood pressure made him feel cold all the time, and
Maria, touchingly maternal, kept straightening out his brown wool
sweater that had expanded shapelessly with Walter's body until,
tattered and threadbare, it hung on him like a second, elderly skin.
Walter hated Florida and refused to get used to its manicured, artificial, ever-air-conditioned world. Absurdly, he found it colder
than the Westchester he had lived in and would have liked to die
in, and where, so his will laid down with unchallengeable precision, he wished to be buried.

Andrew was on a sabbatical in Paris with Linda and Rachel
when he received the news of his father's death and hurried to buy a
ticket to Miami. Only at the last minute was he told that the funeral
would be in New York, Walter having insisted on being buried
in the Westchester grave that he and Ethel had paid good money
for, in the place where he had lived and raised his children, the
place that he loved always. Westchester was his Promised Land,
his America, the place that enabled him to re-create himself as the
man he always wanted to be. New Rochelle was the polar opposite
of the Lower East Side ghetto that he wished to escape in his death
just as he escaped it in life. Was it really a misunderstanding, an
administrative error, that landed the grave site he bought outside
the fence of the designated Jewish plot?

Sunk in grass, his no-frills headstone, looking more like a memorial plaque than the top of a grave, was tucked away among the
megalomaniac tombs of granite and marble that surrounded it.

It wasn't planned that way. Ethel so took it for granted that he would be buried among Jews that she hadn't bothered to confirm it before boarding the flight from Miami that bore his coffin. But the funeral was rushed; sleet cast a foggy pall over everything; and not until later was it discovered that Walter's grave had mistakenly been dug in the nondenominational part of the cemetery. The family hadn't wanted to make a fuss. The thought of exhuming and reburying Walter was unimaginable, nor was anyone up to threatening the management with a damage suit. The fact was that he not only wouldn't have minded what happened, he probably would have preferred it. He felt completely American and had no use for the Jewish tribalism that struck him as an Old World relic. He would have come back from the Beyond, Linda not unaffectionately joked, just to make sure that, as she put it, "Ethel didn't stick him in a ghetto of the dead."

Should Andrew have felt guilty he wasn't with his father in his last moments? That was difficult to say. Walter had faded and become a shadow of his old self, and even in better times, the communication between them was strained. Andrew was a guest lecturer at the Sorbonne that year; the news reached him at the last minute; he could hardly have been expected to fly back to America three days before the end of the semester. And even had he arrived in time, Walter had lost consciousness and could not have been counted on to recognize him. His brother, Matthew, was there, and in a way (not that Andrew held it against him, at least not in so many words), Matthew was closer to his father, just as Andrew was more his mother's boy.

Linda and Rachel did not attend the funeral. There was no point in dragging a small child back and forth across the Atlantic. He stood at the fresh grave by himself, his jet lag and emotional exhaustion compounded by the wet and cold that penetrated the thin soles of his shoes. No one cried. Even in death, Walter was not

someone in whose presence one cried easily. Andrew flew back
right after the funeral. All he remembered was the strange, dreamlike silhouette of the airplane in flight, the long, lingering sunrise,
and the French accents of the Air France stewardesses. The plane
was almost empty and he had an entire row to himself, wrapped
like a mummy under layers of blankets and still shivering in his
only black suit; meant for all seasons, it didn't suit a single one
of them. Although he desperately wanted to sleep, he wasn't able
to. Not even a double Johnnie Walker Black Label, the standard
airborne scotch, had an effect. The trivial things one remembered
twenty years later! The thought of the whiskey sent a surge of bile
up Andrew's throat, making him gag. Stumbling to the bathroom,
he groped in the dark for something against heartburn. There was
nothing. What did he expect to find? He almost never suffered
from reflux. Another wave of acid scorched his esophagus. For a
moment he half-seriously thought of dressing and going down to
the corner drugstore, but the damp, the dark, and the cold outside rid him of the unreasonable impulse. Perhaps a glass of milk?
They said it helps.

19

November 24, 2000

The 26th of Heshvan, 5761

Eleven a.m. Andrew, shocked by the late hour, gathered himself wearily and forced himself to get out of bed, stumble to the
kitchen, and turn on the espresso machine. He wasn't accustomed to
being hungover. Moderate by nature, he didn't take well physically
to extremes. The headache and fatigue caused by the bourbon were

joined to the sour taste of last night's events. He mulled it over, as if trying to solve a puzzling riddle. Rachel's strange outburst. Poor Kenny! What had gotten into her? What was bugging her? He had never seen her lose her self-control like that before.

Andrew turned to go to the bathroom. Another memory, of something similar, was coming back to him . . . right: that time she came back from Israel. He took off his boxers and stepped into the shower, trying to remember the exact year in which this trip had taken place. Her group, composed of Jewish students from several large universities in the New York area, had also gone to Jordan, to Petra. The refreshing downpour of hot water on Andrew's head and shoulders helped dispel the vile feeling he had woken with. They had visited some mountain where local tradition claimed that Aaron, the biblical priest, was buried, and their Israeli guide had jokingly told Rachel, "Young Miss Cohen, it's your great-great-grandfather we're talking about." Andrew shut off the faucets, stepped out of the shower stall, and reentered the bedroom. Rachel was not amused. *That poor guide*, Andrew thought with a smile, *he didn't know what he was getting himself into.* Her anger still resounded when she returned home in late August and told him about it, expecting him to share her indignation at the guide's pretentious naïveté. "How could he believe in such crap? Doesn't he know the Ellis Island immigration officials called Jews Cohen and Levi because they couldn't cope with all those long, strange East European names? None of that biblical stuff can be proved, and anyway, it's a scientific fact that there's no such thing as a genetically pure people. All that talk about bloodlines . . ." Andrew's mind wandered. He felt vaguely uneasy. All the arguments and counterarguments were known to him, as was Rachel's way of thinking. It wasn't what she was saying. It was how she was saying it. It was crude and nasty, full of unconcealed anger. "Anger at what?" Andrew wondered. "At whom?"

20

December 22, 2000

The 25th of Kislev, 5761

How easy it sometimes was to love New York! A sunny, clear, balmy winter day. You might almost have thought the weather this year had decided to skip winter entirely and begin spring in December. Riverside Drive's curvaceous elegance next to the solemn, ruler-straight line of the Hudson was like the other, sensuous, feminine side of a single whole. Broadway hummed with life like a country fair. The used-book sellers were out in force on the gray sidewalks, streaking them with loud, bright color. Andrew and Ann Lee, slightly intoxicated by a night of wild love and the irresponsibly late hour at which they had risen, walked hand in hand down the street on their way to a late, a *very* late, breakfast at Tom's Diner. How nice it all was, a small campus town in the middle of the city! An old, deluxe edition of Thomas Mann's *Joseph and His Brothers* caught Andrew's eye. The tall, gilt, cathedral-like Gothic letters stamped on its heavy binding bespoke respect, morality, ambition, dignity, and severity, all qualities Mann would have approved of. Andrew toyed with the thought of buying the book from its savvy vendor but decided in favor of a bottle of German wine. Its label, in Gothic print, too, was like a drunken parody of Mann's novel, with a comical, pseudo-medieval-style illustration, as though taken from Boccaccio's *Decameron*, of a fat, debauched friar seated by a barrel while two young urchins poured a tankard of wine down his gullet. The wine was cheap and probably not very good, but Ann Lee liked the label. She also liked a dramatically striped dress hanging in the window of the Liberty House clothing and gift shop.

"Would you like to try it on?"

"Yes! No. Maybe later. I'm starving. Let's go eat."

Tom's Diner, New York's most world-famous diner thanks to *Seinfeld*, was a real place. Standing on the northeast corner of Broadway and 112th Street, it was also a congenial one, at least for anyone with a taste for Americana. The winning banality of its decor, with its soda fountains, large tin coffee urn, and gleaming round metal stools at the counter, their cheap varnished wooden legs and fake pink leather seats reminding one of a Queens wedding hall or an emigrant aid society in Little Italy, was an accurate re-creation of the neon diner aesthetics of the 1950s. The only challenges to its mirage of authenticity, greatly prized in Manhattan, were a signed poster of the TV series' four stars above the cash register and a large portrait of Kramer, the most popular and beloved of them. Although these gave cause to suspect an ambition to be a New York institution, itself reason to be denied such a status, it was enough to glance at the broad-faced old matriarch dozing by the cashier in her black widow's clothes and cheap, ugly plastic glasses when not chatting with or scolding in Greek—over the heads of the diners—her son standing by the entrance, to be reassured: greater authenticity was nowhere to be found.

21

December 26, 2000

The 29th of Kislev, 5761

Early morning. A gray light glinted through the windows. Thin snowflakes swirled against them, cradled by a heavy fog. Andrew took pleasure in the lull before the day's storm, savoring it to the full: the burble of frothing milk, the throaty tone of the cello, the smell of fresh coffee, and the streaks of frost on the window-panes, which made one want to press one's nose against them in a momentary reversion to childhood. A dull thump made him stir. The morning delivery of the *Times* had landed on the doormat. He rubbed his hands in a tingle of anticipation: the timing couldn't have been better. Just when the coffee was ready!

He went to the door, lazily shuffling over the wooden floor in his woolen slippers. *Come round me, little childer; / There, don't fling stones at me.* Where was that from? It was so familiar. *My man was a poor fisher, / With salt lines in the say.* It was on the tip of his tongue. *And sometimes from the saltin' shed / I scarce could drag my feet, / Under the blessed moonlight, / Along the pebbly street.* Damn it! Where? *I'd always been but weakly, / And my baby was just born; / A neighbor minded her by day, / I minded her till morn.* Of course. "The Ballad of Moll Magee"! Yeats. How could he have forgotten? *I lay upon my baby; / Ye little childer dear, / I looked on my cold baby, / When the morn grew frosty and clear.* Terrible! What had made him think of it? *A weary woman sleeps so hard! / My man grew red and pale.* When had he read it? Thirty years ago or more, in college. Maybe even in high school. *Pilin' the wood or pilin' the turf, / Or goin' to the well, / I'm thinkin' of my baby, / And keenin' to mysel'.* So many years and he still was moved by it. *So now, ye little childer, / Ye won't fling stones at me; / But gather with your shinin' looks / And pity Moll Magee.* What was it all about? Why now? It astounded Andrew that the poem still had such power over him. He took a deep breath, steadied himself, opened the door, and bent to pick up the newspaper.

22
December 27, 2000

The 1st of Tevet, 5761

The fall semester is over. The term papers have been submitted. The bureaucratic procedures are out of the way and the students have gone home for the holidays. They will sleep in their old beds, on familiar, time-softened mattresses; eat Mom's food, which tastes as good as ever even though Mom rarely makes it anymore and prefers to buy it at the take-out counter; have uncomfortable, awkwardly intimate talks with Dad; explain to a high school boyfriend or girlfriend why they yielded to temptation despite pledges of loyalty; quarrel with their parents, sulk, make up, embrace, cry, and smoke a joint in the guest bathroom.

Those bittersweet winter vacations! How much longing they arouse! We, too, will go away. We will take time out for a trip to the wintry sea. There, to the strains of a melancholy string quartet, a dim maritime light will fall like dew on the gray day's yearning. Swift storm clouds will race across the sky. Distant thunder will rumble, lightning will flash. An electric crackle will rend the air. Coffee, cigarettes, sweetly astringent liqueurs. The feel of a naked body, the feel of a cold fresh sheet. Light filtering through the shutters, sketching pale webs on the wall. The rain will beat against the shut windows and we will lie, cuddled like puppies, beneath a sea of blankets, among a mountain of pillows.

The tip of Long Island, the tip of the continent, a long finger thrust into the ocean, pointing back toward the Old World. The ostentatious mansions of East Hampton and its vacationing celebrities gradually give way to older homes that were once, twenty or thirty years ago, loudly pretentious, too, but that have been weathered by time, painted over with the peeling pastels of nostalgia that bathe them, like distant hills glimpsed in twilight, in a violet, soulful haze. Here and there, remnants of the island's former, agricultural life are still visible: rusting tractors, red barns, cornfields, fruit and vegetable stands brightened by vividly, almost shockingly orange, jack-o'-lantern-colored gourds. But then the fields vanish, the highway narrows, and the ocean's light-drenched, sandy, austere presence begins to be felt.

The island's end is rimmed by a dramatic ellipse, a curved road that bounds it like sacred ground. The moment your vehicle turns onto it, the trip becomes ceremonial, symbolic, almost ritualistic. In the distance, a large lighthouse sits on a grassy lawn like a diamond cushioned in velvet. Beyond it, in the far background, swells the Atlantic. Great whales prowl its depths, past old naval mines, skeletons of shipwrecked vessels, and lost continents. Andrew, wearing a felt hat, and Ann Lee, in a bell-shaped flapper's bonnet, stand, two long, thin silhouettes, looking down from a cliff at the foaming water. A white seagull is perched on a wooden pole. The rusty frames of the lighthouse's windows stand out against its white walls. Between the stormy sky and the stormy sea runs a clear, metallic strip of immense silence. If only you could frame the moment and hang it on the wall.

END OF BOOK TWO

On the eve of the Day of Atonement in the morning they place him at the Eastern Gate and pass before him oxen, rams, and sheep, that he may learn to know and become familiar with the service.

[Babylonian Talmud, Treatise Yoma, Folio 61a] Rabbi Simeon said: Just as the blood of the he-goat [the rites of which are] performed within obtains atonement for Israel in all matters of impurity touching the Sanctuary and its holy things, thus also does the blood of the bullock obtain atonement for the priests in all matters of impurity touching the Sanctuary and its holy things; and just as the confession over the he-goat-to-be-sent-away obtains atonement for Israel with regard to all other transgressions, so does the confession over the bullock obtain atonement for the priest for all other transgressions.

[Babylonian Talmud, Treatise Yoma, Folio 18a] ON THE EVE OF THE DAY OF ATONEMENT IN THE MORNING: A Tanna taught: [They would pass before him for inspection] also the he-goats. Why has our Mishna not mentioned the he-goats?——Since they are meant for sin [offerings], he might feel discouraged. If it be so: does not a bullock, too, come for a sin [offering]?——Since that comes for himself and his brethren the priests, [there is this advantage] that if there be one among his brethren the priests with whom there is something the matter, he would know it and bring him back to repentance, but would he know that with all Israel? Rabina said: This is what the popular proverb means: If your sister's son has been appointed a constable, look out that you pass not before him in the street.

On the eve of the Day of Atonement, the High Priest was brought early in the morning to the Temple's Eastern Gate, where bulls, rams, and sheep were passed before him. A linen canopy was spread above him to shield him from the sun, as he would need all his strength on the morrow; the success of whose rites depended on him. Young priests surrounded him, this one bringing him a drink of cool water and that one fanning him to refresh him. Obadiah watched him bear himself like a king, dressed royally with a retinue at his beck and call, and he thought: "O ye high and mighty! The Lord makes rich and makes poor, He raises up and casts down."

The Gate of Rebirth:

Now, without a doubt the Intellectual and Spiritual Souls of the righteous who have departed this world are bound in the Bond of Life in God's presence in the Worlds of *Atzilut*, or the World of the Sublime, and *Beriah*, or the World of Creation, each according to its station. From there they do not descend. Yet in the Worlds of *Yetsirah*, or the World of Creativity, and *Asiyah*, or the World of Action, they remain below without ascending and can assist other souls by cleaving to them in an act of impregnation.

[Leviticus, Chapter 21, Verses 16—23]
And the LORD spake unto Moses, saying, Speak unto Aaron, saying, Whosoever he be of thy seed in their generations that hath any blemish, let him not approach to offer the bread of his God. For whatsoever man he be that hath a blemish, he shall not approach: a blind man, or a lame, or he that hath a flat nose, or anything superfluous, or a man that is broken-footed, or broken-handed, or crookbacked, or a dwarf, or that hath a blemish in his eye, or be scurvy, or scabbed, or hath his stones broken; no man that hath a blemish of the seed of Aaron the priest shall come nigh to offer the offerings of the LORD made by fire: he hath a blemish; he shall not come nigh to offer the bread of his God. He shall eat the bread of his God, both of the most holy, and of the holy. Only he shall not go in unto the veil, nor come nigh unto the altar, because he hath a blemish; that he profane not my sanctuaries: for I the LORD do sanctify them.

(Babylonian Talmud, Treatise Yoma, Folio 54a)

Rabbi Nahman said: It was taught that the Ark was hidden away in the Chamber of the wood-shed. Rabbi Nahman ben Isaac said: Thus were we also taught: It happened to a certain priest who was whiling away his time that he saw a block of pavement that was different from the others. He came and informed his fellow, but before he could complete his account, his soul departed. Thus they knew definitely that the Ark was hidden there. What had he been doing? Rabbi Helbo said: He was playing with his ax. The school of Rabbi Ishmael taught: Two priests, afflicted with a blemish, were sorting the woods when the ax of one of them slipped from his hand and fell on that place, whereupon a flame burst forth and consumed him.

It so happened that Obadiah had a distant cousin who was of the priestly caste, too. The man was an invalid with a leg as withered as a dried palm frond that he dragged behind him like the tail of a fox. He went about on a crutch, half-walking and half-hopping like a crow. "Old Crow" was indeed what all called him, at first behind his back and in time to his face, for his beard was black and his brows were black and his face beetled blackly with the anger that he vented on all who crossed his path. In the end, no one remembered his true name. Since he was barred from the sacred rites, it being written "The man with a blemish shall not come nigh to offer an offering to the Lord," he was given work in the Temple woodshed deworming logs, since no wormy log was allowed to be burned on the altar. He also performed such odd jobs as chopping wood and carrying water, even though he hardly had the strength for them. He worked like a dog and ate like a crow of the crumbs that fell from God and man's table. All day long his mouth was filled with curses and imprecations, for his soul was bitter and his heart raged within him.

[Babylonian Talmud, Treatise Ta'anit, Folios 20a—b] It once happened that Rabbi Eleazar ben Rabbi Simeon went from the tower of Gador, where resided his master, riding on an ass. He rode leisurely on the banks of the river, being greatly rejoiced and feeling very proud on account of the wealth of knowledge he had accumulated from his master. On the way he met a man who was terribly ugly [of face]. That man greeted Rabbi Eleazar respectfully, and said to him: "Peace be with thee, Rabbi!" The rabbi did not, however, return the greeting, and, moreover, said: "Vain man, how terribly ugly art thou! Are all thy townsmen as ugly as thou art?" And the man replied: "That I know not; but it would be seemly if thou wert to go to the Creator who formed me and say to Him: 'How ungainly is the creature Thou hast made!'" Realizing that he had offended against the man, Rabbi Eleazar dismounted and, making an obeisance, said: "I have sinned against thee—— forgive me, I pray!" But the man refused, saying: "Nay, I shall not forgive thee until thou shalt go to the Creator and say to Him: 'How ungainly is the creature Thou hast made!'" Rabbi Eleazar, however, would not leave the man, and followed him on foot until they reached the city where Rabbi Eleazar dwelt. As soon as the townsmen perceived him they thronged toward him with greetings. "Peace be with thee, Rabbi, Rabbi! Master, Master!" The ugly man who preceded Rabbi Eleazar asked them whom they were addressing as "Rabbi" and "Master," and they answered: "The man who is following thee." Said he: "If he be a rabbi, may there not be many like him in Israel." And they asked: "Why not?" So he replied that thus and so had he been served by him. They then pleaded with him: "Still forgive him, for he is a great man in the study of the Law." And he said: "For your sakes I will forgive him, but upon the condition that he shall not do likewise again."

Now, the flesh of the offerings was cut up and boiled in a cauldron. As was the manner of the priesthood, the pieces of meat were speared with a fork and one given to each sacrificing priest. So great was the stir on the eve of the Day of Atonement, however, that Obadiah was given an extra portion by mistake. He recalled his unfortunate cousin, who could not afford meat at all, and he thought: "The Day of Atonement is here and the poor fellow has nothing to eat and will be too weak to get through the fast. Let me bring him some meat to fortify him. He's a living soul, too, and an Israelite like the rest of us, and we're all children of the LORD."

When Obadiah's cousin saw the meat, he fell on it like on a rare treasure and gnawed it to the bone as though he had been fasting since the last Day of Atonement. Even as he chewed, he railed at his woes and his foes, denouncing the evil times and their degenerate ways. He worked himself into such a fit that he stood on his good foot, waved his crutch in the air, and nearly toppled over while denouncing the wealth and the pelf of the filthy rich, who bought high office in the Temple with gold Denars, sold their poor brothers for copper pennies, and trafficked in the High Priesthood itself. They were the wicked of whom Simon the Just had said that they did not merit living out the year, and their heirs were as haughty as they were. Of them it was written in Scripture, "Thou shalt not bring the hire of a whore nor the price of a dog into the house of the Lord thy God."

[Babylonian Talmud, Treatise Yoma, Folio 9a] Rabbah bar Bar Hana said: What is the meaning of the passage, "The fear of the Lord prolongeth days," but the years of the wicked shall be shortened? "The fear of the Lord prolongeth days" refers to the first Sanctuary, which remained standing for four hundred and ten years and in which there served only eighteen High Priests. "But the years of the wicked shall be shortened" refers to the second Sanctuary, which abided for four hundred and twenty years and at which more than three hundred [High] Priests served. Take off therefrom the forty years which Simeon the Righteous served, eighty years which Johanan the High Priest served, ten, which Ishmael Ben Fabi served, or, as some say, the eleven years of Rabbi Eleazar Ben Harsum. Count [the number of High Priests] from then on and you will find that none of them completed his year [in office].

The Gate of Rebirth:

Know that if a person has acquired all three souls, *Nefesh, Ruach,* and *Neshamah,* and subsequently damaged them by sinning, they must be reborn to repair what he has damaged. Yet once his Vital Soul has been repaired and is again perfect, his damaged Intellectual Soul cannot be conjoined with it. Rather, it must be reborn in a second person and conjoined with the latter's Vital Soul, just as the first person's Spiritual Soul must be conjoined with a third person's Intellectual Soul. Meanwhile, the first person's Vital Soul is conjoined with the Intellectual Soul of a fourth person who has departed this world with many merits, and this becomes his own in every respect. In the same manner, once he has perfected this Intellectual Soul, it is conjoined with yet another meritorious person's Spiritual Soul. This is the hidden meaning of the saying of the Sages that "the righteous are greater in death than in life."

[Babylonian Talmud, Treatise Yoma, Folio 19b] Our Rabbis taught: There was a Sadducee who had arranged the incense without, and then brought it inside. As he left he was exceedingly glad. On his coming out his father met him and said to him: My son, although we are Sadducees, we are afraid of the Pharisees. He replied: All my life was I aggrieved because of this scriptural verse: *For I appear in the cloud upon the ark cover.* I would say: When shall the opportunity come to my hand so that I might fulfill it. Now that such opportunity has come to my hand, should I not have fulfilled it? It is reported that it took only a few days until he died and was thrown on the dung heap and worms came forth from his nose. Some say: He was smitten as he came out [of the Holy of Holies]. For Rabbi Hiyya taught: A noise was heard in the Temple Court, for an angel had come and struck him down on his face [to the ground] and his brethren the priests came in and they found the trace as of a calf's foot on his shoulder, as it is written of the Angels: *And their feet were straight feet, and the sole of their feet was like the sole of a calf's foot.*

As he spoke of the opulent classes who bought and sold honors in the Temple like cows in the marketplace, Old Crow spat on the ground. A strand of his spittle landed on Obadiah's cloak and sizzled there. Had he not been loath to shame his cousin, he would have run off to scrub and launder his cloak at once. Old Crow observed his silence and thought: "So he, too, is in their clutches! He's fallen for their lucre and their lies." And out loud he croaked: "You're no better than they are, you lummox! You have eyes and see not. Of you and the likes of you it is said, 'A stick is not enough to thrash a fool with.' You're all led by the nose like mooncalves. Who knows how many Sadducees are among you, waiting to tear down everything holy? The High Priest is one of them, but you and your ilk cozy up to him and say amen to his every word. If I had two good legs, I'd give you a taste of a heretic's wages! If only I had my strength, you'd see what a Sadducee deserves!"

Old Crow stood waving his crutch like a sword and shouting at the top of his lungs: "The Lord of vengeance appeareth! He hath requited the proud! How long will the wicked rejoice?" He was still shouting when he lost his balance, fell flat on his face, and lay writhing on the ground like a fish. Tears of humiliation ran down his cheeks. He was like a boy struck down by his father with no mother to comfort him or help him to his feet. Obadiah marked his words well. Their venom bubbled in his veins. From then on, he knew no peace. Each time he saw the High Priest, he scrutinized him and thought, "Can it be that the elders can't see beyond their own noses?"

[Mishna, Treatise Yoma, Chapter 8, Mishna 1] On the Day of Atonement it is forbidden to eat, to drink, to wash, to anoint oneself, to put on sandals, or to have marital intercourse. A king or a bride may wash the face, and a woman after childbirth may put on sandals. This is the view of Rabbi Eliezer. The sages, however, forbid it.

[Mishna, Treatise Yoma, Chapter 8, Mishna 2] If one eats the bulk of a large date, the like thereof, with its stone included, or if he drank a mouthful, he is culpable. Any foods complement one another in making up the bulk of a date, and all the liquids complement one another in making up a mouthful, but what a man eats and drinks does not go together.

That afternoon, as the Day of Atonement drew nigh, the elders brought the High Priest to the incense maker's quarters and tested him to make sure he would not depart from what he was taught or offer the incense in the manner of the Sadducees. The ordinary priests, who took no part in this, went off to catch some sleep, grab something to eat or drink, and obey the call of nature, for the day was short and there was still much to do. Whoever did not attend to his earthly needs now would end up adding them to the deprivation of the fast.

[Babylonian Talmud, Treatise Yoma, Folio 81b] *And ye shall afflict your souls, in the ninth day of the month.* One might have assumed that such affliction commences on the ninth of the month already. Therefore the text reads: "At even." If from "at even," one might have inferred that one must afflict oneself only after it gets dark, therefore the text reads: "In the ninth." How is [this to be explained]? He should commence to afflict himself whilst it is yet day. From here we learn that we add from the profane time to the sacred one. [. . .] Hiyya, the son of Rab, of Difti taught: "And you shall afflict your souls in the ninth [day of the month]." But is one fasting on the ninth? Do we not fast on the tenth? Rather, it comes to indicate that, if one eats and drinks on the ninth, Scripture accounts it to him as if he had fasted on the ninth and the tenth.

[Isaiah, Chapter 58, Verses 1—11] Cry aloud, spare not, lift up thy voice like a horn, and declare unto My people their transgression, and to the house of Jacob their sins. Yet they seek Me daily, and delight to know My ways; as a nation that did righteousness, and forsook not the ordinance of their God, they ask of Me righteous ordinances, they delight to draw near unto God. "Wherefore have we fasted, and Thou seest not? Wherefore have we afflicted our soul, and Thou takest no knowledge?" Behold, in the day of your fast ye pursue your business, and exact all your labors. Behold, ye fast for strife and contention, and to smite with the fist of wickedness; ye fast not this day so as to make your voice to be heard on high. Is such the fast that I have chosen? The day for a man to afflict his soul? Is it to bow down his head as a bulrush, and to spread sackcloth and ashes under him? Wilt thou call this a fast, and an acceptable day to the LORD? Is not this the fast that I have chosen? To loosen the fetters of wickedness, to undo the bands of the yoke, and to let the oppressed go free, and that ye break every yoke? Is it not to deal thy bread to the hungry, and that thou bring the poor that are cast out to thy house? When thou seest the naked, that thou cover him, and that thou hide not thyself from thine own flesh? Then shall thy light break forth as the morning, and thy healing shall spring forth speedily; and thy righteousness shall go before thee, the glory of the LORD shall be thy rear guard. Then shalt thou call, and the LORD will answer; thou shalt cry, and He will say: "Here I am." If thou take away from the midst of thee the yoke, the putting forth of the finger, and speaking wickedness; and if thou draw out thy soul to the hungry, and satisfy the afflicted soul; then shall thy light rise in darkness, and thy gloom be as the noonday. And the LORD will guide thee continually, and satisfy thy soul in drought, and make strong thy bones; and thou shalt be like a watered garden, and like a spring of water, whose waters fail not.

The Gate of Rebirth:
Moreover, when the first person passes from the world, his Vital Soul remains with its new Intellectual and Spiritual Souls and reaps its reward with them. Yet when his original Intellectual Soul is entirely repaired, too, his Vital Soul says in the words of the Prophet Hosea, *I will go and return to my first husband*, and it leaves its second Intellectual Soul to rejoin its first. And so it is with the Spiritual Soul.

[Mishna, Treatise Yoma, Chapter 1, Mishna 3]
The elders of the court handed him over to the elders of the priesthood and they took him up to the upper chamber to the house of Abtinas. They adjured him, took their leave, as they said to him: Sir High Priest, we are messengers of the high court and you are our messenger and the messenger of the high court. We adjure you by him that made his name to dwell in this house that you do not change anything of what we said to you. He turned aside and wept and they turned aside and wept.

[Psalms, Chapter 56, Verses 2—9]
Be gracious unto me, O God, for man would swallow me up; all the day the warriors oppress me. They that lie in wait for me would swallow me up all the day; for they are many that fight against me, O Most High, in the day that I am afraid, I will put my trust in Thee. In God——I will praise His word——in God do I trust, I will not be afraid; what can flesh do unto me? All the day they trouble mine affairs; all their thoughts are against me for evil. They gather themselves together, they hide themselves, they mark my steps; according as they have waited for my soul. Because of iniquity cast them out; in anger bring down the peoples, O God. Thou hast counted my wanderings; put Thou my tears into Thy bottle; are they not in Thy book?

But Obadiah did not join them, as his mind was not set on food or sleep. He hid at the bottom of the staircase to the incense makers' quarters like a watchdog, straining to hear. He failed to make out a thing, for the elders, who swarmed around the High Priest like bees around a bear come to steal their honey, spoke in low voices. Was this not proof of an intrigue? The longer Obadiah stood there, the more convinced he became that the sages of Israel were ensnared by the High Priest's lies and could not tell truth from falsehood. Although he dared not speak out, he thought: "Just wait and I'll show them what a true priest is like! Woe to the generation that has such wise men! Woe to the generation that has such leaders!" Yet when the elders took their leave of the High Priest, Obadiah saw that they were tearstained with sorrow for having doubted him, and that he himself remained behind, facing the wall with heaving shoulders like a child bullied by his companions. Seeing him sobbing, Obadiah pitied him and thought: "Can I have suspected him unfairly? He may be as guiltless as he seems to be."

[Babylonian Talmud, Treatise Yoma, Folio 19b] HE TURNED ASIDE AND WEPT AND THEY TURNED ASIDE AND WEPT. He turned aside and wept because they suspected him of being a Sadducee, and they turned aside and wept, for Rabbi Joshua ben Levi said: Whosoever suspects the righteous will suffer [for it] on his own body. Why was all this [solemn adjuration] necessary? Lest he arrange the incense outside and thus bring it in, in the manner of the Sadducees.

[Babylonian Talmud, Treatise Shabbat, Folio 105b] Rabbi Simeon ben Pazzi said in the name of Rabbi Joshua ben Levi in Bar Kappara's name: If one sheds tears for a worthy man, the Holy One, blessed be He, counts them and lays them up in His treasure house, for it is said [Psalms, Chapter 56, Verse 12]: Thou countest my grievings: Put thou my tear into thy bottle.

The Gate of Rebirth:

If a Vital Soul has not been perfected in its first stay on earth, it must return as often as is necessary to perfect itself. Even when it has done so, however, it must be reborn one more time to be conjoined with an Intellectual Soul. In the same manner, the Vital and Intellectual Souls must return together as often as is necessary for the Intellectual Soul to be perfected, after which they must be reborn one more time to be conjoined with a Spiritual Soul. The Spiritual Soul must then be reborn until all three have been perfected together, after which they will return to earth no more.

BOOK
THREE

Late December. While the days are cold and short, the fast-falling evenings are festive and gay. A week before Christmas, the taciturn Canadian lumberjacks, who appear every year, unloaded their different sizes of Christmas trees at the corner of Broadway and 110th Street, perfuming the air with the pungent, familiar fragrance of a young forest. The doormen, excited by the prospect of generous Christmas tips, placed little decorated trees in the lobbies alongside electric Hanukkah menorahs, an additional flame-shaped bulb of which lit up on each of the holiday's eight days. The shop windows were covered with paper cutouts of snowflakes, menorahs, dreidls, merry Santa Clauses, and red-nosed reindeer. The same mawkish Christmas songs were played and replayed so often in the crowded stores that the whole city seemed to be running on a single sound track. Would there be a white Christmas? An innocent question, asked by children and grown-ups alike.

A year ago, the apocalyptic shadow of the Y2K bug clouded the celebrations of the new millennium. As always at such times, the notorious figure of Nostradamus, the false prophet of Rotterdam, was invoked, his name sending chills down the spines of chronic worriers. The anxiety was like the bitterness in a fine whiskey, or the pale scent of danger at a medieval carnival. At midnight, thousands assembled in Times Square to watch the fall of the traditional crystal ball. At the stroke of twelve, a great shout burst from tens of thousands of mouths. The ball fell slowly, gliding down the column of light on Times Tower. A year had gone by. Another had begun. A century had passed. A thousand years went by—and now there would be a thousand more. The lights shone on. The neon signs continued to blink on their giant billboards. Mouths reeking of alcohol, steak, and mentholated breath freshener met in the midnight kiss. The world had not come to an end. Nostradamus was proven wrong once again. The universal relief was tinged with a touch of disappointment. Nothing had happened. Everything was the same as before.

This year was more ordinary, less histrionic. Andrew gave Ann Lee a New Year's gift of a lovely, burgundy-colored organza scarf from Bergdorf Goodman. Ann Lee gave Andrew a gorgeous, coal-black cashmere scarf from Barney's. Andrew reserved a table at Harry's New York Bar. They had a wonderful dinner, washed down by a bottle of 1985 Château Latour that justified every one of the superlatives lavished on it over the years, and then strolled hand in hand down a Fifth Avenue lit by the magic twinkle of thousands of gaily colored glass baubles. Carefully sidestepping the human swarms heading for Times Square, they managed to position themselves, exactly at midnight, in front of the main display window of Saks Fifth Avenue for a long, elegantly executed, cinematic kiss. What a way to start the new year!

2

Day follows day, season follows season. The quality of the light, the peculiar quality of the air, the cycles of growth and decay: all keep changing. Cold and warmth, summer and winter, day and night have no end. Was not this the promise? Innumerable clocks tick the flow of time: the white steam eddying up from the manholes to the frosty azure above, its shadows dancing on the red and white brick of the old apartment buildings; the parade of flowers filling the front shelves of the Korean delis; the different blues of the sky that merge with the blues of the river only to part from them again. This year, too, there will be buds on the naked branches that had seemed beyond resurrection. The trees will groan again in late summer under the weight of their dense, heat-stricken foliage. The world will once more catch fire with autumn flames that blaze for weeks until quenched by the cold, gray rains of November. Everything will be as it was the year before.

Everything will proceed as usual, as it always does. Colorful catalogs of winter clothing will arrive in the mail, followed by even more colorful catalogs of summer clothing. Old shoes will wear out and the children will need larger sizes. Just let time's peaceful flow go on, let nothing interrupt its routine! Yellow daffodils will reappear in the buckets of the florists and make way for red tulips and purple, white, and pink hyacinths. Saturdays in Central Park. Social events. The premieres of much-touted movies. Now and then a good meal, an especially fine bottle of wine. On Valentine's Day long lines will form in the flower and confectionary shops. Sturdy red roses will open in glass vases; the light, shining through their petals, will make them glow like gemstones; in a few days they will wilt and be thrown down incinerator chutes. In spring we will go to the Hamptons, the Berkshires, and the Catskills, spending long hours in the mythological traffic jams of Friday afternoon and Sunday evening. In August the city will empty. In September the bedlam will begin again. In October, right after Halloween, the holiday season will be back with its hectic preparations and Christmas jingles that return to the stores and malls. Day follows day, year follows year. Slowly, imperceptibly, our lives' spans are running out.

3
January 2, 2001

The 7th of Tevet, 5761

Early afternoon. A fine day. Andrew, his right hand resting casually on the steering wheel of Ethel's old Roadmaster and the fingers of his left hand drumming to the beat of the music on the radio, followed the green, night-glow exit signs. Exit 12, Mount Vernon. Exit 16, New Rochelle. It was so familiar, it could have been yesterday. His memories were sharp and clear. Tiny, seemingly trivial details stood out in them like the sugar crystals on a gingersnap: the place where the road made a wide curve as if sketching an imaginary circle, the loud tick of the directional signal drilling at his brain like a merciless plastic mosquito. How could he not have been here for so many years? Had there been no opportunities, no need, to return? He steered the big car, which made him think of a large barge, toward Exit 16. The old Roadmaster knew the streets so well that it practically drove itself. Here was the house: the lawn, as trim as ever; the picket fence, still a spotless white; the garage door, rolled all the way down, just the way his father liked it.

Andrew turned into the gravel driveway, careful not to trample the flower beds. He stopped a yard short of the garage door to keep from blocking it, switched off the ignition, and leaned back against the leather headrest while observing, to his growing astonishment, that nothing had changed. Nothing at all, as if time had stood still. It took him a moment to realize why his heart was beating as fast as the blinker signal that wouldn't turn off. What an idiot I am. What an idiot. He's alive! Dad is alive! He's been here all along, living his quiet, honorable life, without complaints, without demands, without anger at the son who never visited, who never returned home. A torrent of emotion swept over him like a flood wave threatening to burst a dam. He wouldn't be able to hold it in much longer. Dad's been alive all this time and I haven't known it! How could I not have known it? What kind of son have I been? I have to hold it in. I have to. Breathe regularly. Breathe deeply. Don't cry. Whatever you do, don't cry. If there is one thing Dad can't stand, it's crying!

Andrew let out a groan. As if released by a hidden spring, his eyelids snapped open. Confused and disheveled, he sat up in bed. The large green, night-glow digits on the alarm clock showed the hour: 6:13 a.m. How could it be? So many years without a sign of life. With no contact. What kind of a son would do that? Enough, he must wake up! His chest heaved frightfully, spasmodically, his arrhythmic heart out of control. He must wake up now! Get out of bed, splash cold water on his face, and wake up.

The darkness was thinning. His eyes, growing used to it, made out the shadowy, half-recognizable details of his bedroom. What had happened to the garage and the gravel driveway that crunched under the big tires of the car? Hadn't they sold the old Roadmaster years ago and bought a new, smaller, more gas-efficient Dodge? His father had adamantly refused to buy a Japanese car. American industry, the country's backbone, had to be supported.

His chest calmed. His heart beat more slowly. Andrew got out of bed and went to the living room. Although it was getting light out, the day had yet to begin. The opaque curtain of a gray dawn covered the windows. It was 6:35, too early for his morning coffee. Should he try going back to sleep? Aimlessly, he wandered around the apartment, not knowing what he was looking for, preferring to remain in the pale, ghostly dawn light rather than switch on a lamp. The last fragments of his strange dream, though still hovering at the porous edge of consciousness, were now distinct from waking reality.

It grew lighter. Andrew kept up his search. Opening the old, exquisitely carved eighteenth-century cabinet with its family mementos and expensive china, he found what had eluded him: an antique silver goblet, inherited from his father, standing on a shelf. It was an old Kiddush cup, early nineteenth century by the looks of it, with signs of Russian workmanship. He couldn't recall whether Walter had ever used it. Perhaps for their Seders? They did have a Seder each year, that much he remembered. How little was left, just a few items: the Kiddush cup, an old wristwatch, several photographs, a certificate of honor from an old, now defunct labor union. A handful of keepsakes, the nostalgic shards of a man who never expressed the least nostalgia for anything. Andrew reached for the glass door, desiring to hold the Kiddush cup, to feel its weight and examine its silver filigree, but his hand froze on the way to it. No, not now! It was too melodramatic, too pregnant with meaning. What time was it? Seven. Too late to go back to sleep. Coffee, a shower, to work!

4

January 3, 2001

———————

The 8th of Tevet, 5761

Ten a.m. Even the weather had put on its best face for the first day of the spring semester. The air was crisp and clear, invigorating, not cuttingly cold. The colorful jackets, scarves, and woolen caps of the students brightened up the brown lawns and gravel paths, creating the illusion of springtime in bloom. Andrew, smartly dressed, his new cashmere scarf wrapped around his throat, left the Christopher Street station and headed for campus. Although his first class was not until two, the university president's

secretary had phoned him the week before to ask him to come earlier for an important meeting. She had divulged no details; contacts
with the administration had been enveloped in recent years in a
strange mantle of diplomatic secrecy more appropriate to the corridors of big business and politics than to the noisy hallways of a
New York university. Andrew supposed the call had to do with his
new appointment, which was already regarded as a fait accompli.

Bernie Bernstein, the president of New York University, elegant in a black cashmere coat worn over an expensive black suit,
stood at the main entrance of the Administration Building, his
hands youthfully stuck in his trouser pockets, taking note of the
lively scene with the expression of a shrewd, worldly man of means
pleasurably surveying his many assets. Behind him, a large bronze
plaque engraved with the names of the university's prominent donors majestically framed his burly figure, as if in tribute to his winning ways that had seduced many a woman and philanthropist.
Spotting Andrew in the crowd, Bernie flashed him a hearty smile
that Andrew returned with genuine affection. They knew each
other well. Both belonged to the same generation and were products of the same intellectual and cultural milieu. Bernie, the boyish
enfant terrible of the frightfully straitlaced Sociology Department,
had an unpredictable, razor-sharp mind, vocal left-wing opinions,
and a long list of romantic conquests that included, in the best egalitarian tradition, students, professors, women administrators, and
bored faculty wives. Although his colleagues were surprised by his
meteoric rise in the university's administrative hierarchy, it would
have been just as difficult to imagine him spending the rest of his
career under the cold fluorescent light of the library, bent over a
stack of stuffy academic articles.

Andrew climbed the steps and shook the big, rough hand extended
to him from afar. For a moment or two, they stood looking out at the
vibrant flow beneath them while permitting themselves an intimate

silence. Bernie stirred first. His smile broadened and he touched Andrew lightly on the elbow. "Let's get out of here and go have some
coffee. I have something to talk to you about that will interest you
greatly." His tone of sly, unstated complicity piqued Andrew's curiosity, as did his choice of an off-campus location. Something was
going on. What, though? Just more of the absurdly self-important
wheeling and dealing that had infected the institution's top echelons
since Bernie took over, their hush-hush, semi-conspiratorial tones
more suited to a Byzantine court than an American university?

Bernie had begun to talk about the reasons for their meeting in his deep, radio announcer voice. Andrew, however, soon
abandoned his initial effort to follow him. There was something
unclear, devious, in his remarks, something convoluted that concealed more than it revealed, as if purposely hiding its true motives. Half listening, Andrew concentrated more on its tone than
its contents. Long practiced in the art of politely dull conversation
and trusting himself to identify the moment when, his formal pro-
logue concluded, Bernie got to the point, he let his mind wander
while transmitting automatic signals of interest and attention. A
slight but irritating tiredness, the result of waking prematurely
from an interrupted sleep, weighed on his eyelids. From the depths
of forgetfulness, a fragment of a week-old dream came back to
him. In it, seven Rubenesque women, well favored and fat fleshed,
had emerged from the lazy waters of the river to loll unsuspect-
ingly on its grassy bank while he, a bare-assed, hairy satyr, having
deftly infiltrated their ranks, swam like a playful guppy in and out
of their sweet white voluptuousness.

Andrew smiled at the pleasurable if not unembarrassing memory
and blinked in the cold winter light, thinking of a large latte with an
extra shot of espresso. Should he have it with a biscotti? Perhaps an
almond croissant? Bernie, a man of infinite appetites, would surely
eat something, too. He was quite capable of ordering and devouring

a pastry without knowing what it was called or what was in it, let alone to what tradition of baking it belonged. All Bernie had eyes and taste buds for was power, influence, and more power. Nothing else mattered. But didn't this make him like all the great sovereigns who were makers rather than spectators of history? Andrew himself knew all there was to know about biscotti. He was versed in its different varieties, could tell you where to buy the best of each, and had even successfully baked them himself. His command of life's details was a reason for satisfaction—a kind of power, too. He was proud of his ability to scan the cultural scene in all its aspects, major and minor, and quickly to identify its hidden structures and covert pathways of meaning. His entire career, he reflected, was based on this gift—and as careers went, it wasn't a bad one . . .

He was surprised to find himself thinking so apologetically. Something in the meeting with Bernie, which had started out well, was turning sour. Bernie's vitality made him feel, weak, childish, and circumscribed, more concerned with minutiae than with the larger picture. Andrew studied him. He hadn't stopped spinning his dense web of thoughts, unaware that Andrew had long ago lost track of them. His suit was of a high-quality fabric; well cut, too; from time to time, it shone in the sunlight like silk; it was obviously tailor-made. Did Bernie choose his own clothes? It was hard to imagine someone like him keeping abreast of fashion or expending the energy needed to dress well. And how did his expensive tastes go with his radical views, which had earned him the reputation of a social maverick?

Andrew took a deep breath and tried refocusing on the words of the president, who was droning away like the public speaker he was. "We have to face up to there being other forces at work behind the scenes. It's not entirely up to us, if at all . . ." Andrew perked up. At last Bernie was getting down to business. Yet just then, at the very moment his intuition told him it was time for the mental alertness he was noted for, a strange, disquieting sound distracted him again. Distant yet near, unrecognizable but unaccountably familiar, it came from all sides, its deep, bestial roar bringing to mind the bellow of a huge, primeval beast. Andrew's eyes grew wide. A surge of adrenaline signaled the presence of something momentous, solemn and formidable. He glanced around, trying to curb his unrest. They had left the campus and were walking down one of the quietly charming side streets of the Village. Everything looked normal. There was nothing unusual—nothing but a strange light shining on the street's northeast corner and becoming brighter as the sound grew louder. Andrew couldn't take his eyes off it. Whatever it was, it was weird. Bernie was still talking, but Andrew no longer heard a word. A shiver ran through him. His entire being was in a hyper state, one that he hadn't experienced in a long time. The shaft of light grew more intense, more concentrated, configuring a precise circle on the gray sidewalk that glowed with a heavenly radiance. What could it be? A super-powerful spotlight? Was someone filming? Filmmakers, especially cinema students, used these streets as a site all the time.

A huge, snow-white bull appeared from around the corner and strode slowly to the center of the circle with a regal, dreamlike gait. Between its horns stretched a red streak of wool, a wonderfully luminescent carmine ribbon. Its sudden manifestation was followed—from where Andrew couldn't tell—by a second figure, no less startling and impressive: a bearded man, cloaked from head to toe in white linen garments, his head wrapped in a white linen turban. Advancing at the same slow, ceremonial pace as the bull's, he brandished a long, hypnotically gleaming knife. Andrew held his breath in fascination. Never had anything aroused in him such a mixture of joy and alarm, longing and awe. More figures appeared, dressed in colorful garb, prancing and whirling around the white bull and the priest who led it. A powerful, penetrating, irresistible music filled the air, drowning out the everyday sounds of the city. What was it? Andrew racked his brain, feeling his heartbeat quicken. An ethnic parade? A Hare Krishna–like cult? Half walking, half dancing, the brightly dressed crowd kept streaming around the corner, blowing large, conched horns, plucking primitive-looking stringed instruments, and beating drums. Its guttural, mesmerizing song, dreamlike, too, swept all before it. The shaft of light moved slowly down the street, toward its far end. Andrew searched for the vehicle carrying the projectors, cameras, and sound equipment needed for such an extravaganza, but none appeared. He glanced overhead. Could there be a helicopter? An absurd thought. Any helicopter flying so low would be deafening. Where, then, for goodness' sake, was the light coming from? A window? He turned back to the street. The bright circle was gone, leaving only a fading circumference. The exotic figures had vanished, too. For a brief moment, the shadow of the last of them flitted in the distance: an ancient priest, his head wrapped in a linen turban and a golden fire pan in his hand.

Andrew pulled himself together. He was tingling with a strange excitement the likes of which he had never felt. Although the whole thing couldn't have taken long, it seemed to have lasted an eternity, as if another dimension of time had sucked him into its whirlpool and cast him back out like a fish washed up on the shore. He had to tear his gaze away from the empty corner at the street's end to fix it on Bernie, who was saying with a puckish smile, a smugly amused, Machiavellian twinkle in his eyes, "In short, my friend, you had better keep an eye on what's happening under your nose, right under your own nose! I can't tell you more than that. You're a big boy and a pretty shrewd player yourself, we've known each other for a long time. . . . Here, let's try this café, I'm famished! In half an hour, I have an international conference call. It's something big, but I can't go into the details."

Andrew nodded mechanically. The bright light had hurt his

eyes, causing them to blink and smart as though filling with tears. The hypnotic jangle of the instruments still echoed in his ears. He studied Bernie's face, trying to see what impression the strange event had made on him, but it registered no emotion, as if nothing out of the ordinary had happened. How could that be? Was he the only one who had seen the bizarre pageant? He struggled to come to his senses and resume his part in the conversation, the crux of which, he realized as he regained his grip on reality, he had missed. Yet as crucial as it was to reconstruct the gist of Bernie's·curious insinuations and extract something concrete from him, the substantive part of their conversation was clearly over.

Well, no need to be upset. He had other contacts in high places and would find a way to clarify the matter. But where, damn it, had the spotlights and sound equipment been? Wait a minute. Yes, that was it: on the roof! They must have placed the projectors on the roof of the building on the southwest corner. There was no other way for it to have followed the procession around the corner and down the street.

He felt exhausted. His head ached and he could hardly keep his eyes open. But how could he possibly cancel the first class of the semester and go home to sleep? He needed some coffee, a double espresso. No, not an espresso. He couldn't handle anything that bitter. A cappuccino, with lots of milk. Perhaps even a biscotti.

5

January 16, 2001

———————

The 21st of Tevet, 5761

I am lying on a bed in a dirty, dimly lit room, in an old, half-ruined hotel, like a scene in Stephen King's The Shining.

Something terrible is happening: a dark force that keeps shifting its shape is pressing on me, about to crush me. It wants to kill me. I can feel the terror squeezing my heart like a giant pincers. A murderous angel is staring insanely at me. Its unshaven chin is as sharp and strong as a razor. It's a young Jack Nicholson. Linda is wearing a wedding dress. She's in an advanced stage of pregnancy. Her swollen belly protrudes through the thin material of her white bridal gown. Her bride's veil is spattered with blood like in a cheap horror movie. She holds a huge kitchen knife and screams: "I'll save you! I'll save you!" She picks up the baby, holds it in the air, cuts off its foreskin, and throws it at my feet. The little foreskin wriggles on the sheet like a worm cut in two. The blood stings my toes. The angel cringes. Its frightening face shrinks, bursts like a soap bubble, and disappears. The pressure on my chest is released. I can breathe again. Linda hugs my legs. Her face, smeared with blood, presses against my bare thighs. "I've saved you!" she says, sobbing. "I've saved you! You're my bloody bridegroom! You're mine again!"

6

January 19, 2001

The 24th of Tevet, 5761

Winter. The grand facades of Riverside Drive stand, austere and angular, against the frosty light. Their cornices, jagged turrets of a fortified ancient city, rise skyward with a sharp cry. The sun's rays are hard and cold. The ice creaks underfoot. The air is as brittle as crystal. A young hawk screeches above the treetops, suspended in midflight like a snagged pendulum. Small, transparent beads of ice dot the naked boughs of the trees like buds. A thin, dry layer of snow accumulates on the shattered slabs of limestone lying like discarded altar tops in the rear of the Cathedral of Saint John the Divine. Dumped there and forgotten, their inanimate memory preserves the stages of sedimentation and recalls the quarry they were hewn from long ago. So, too, the blind eyes of marble statues hoard what they have seen. Line upon line, dot upon dot, here a little, there a little. Nothing vanishes. All is stored in inanimate memory. Large, bluish-white ice floes, cleaved by winter's mighty ax, drift on the current of the river. Swiftly they pursue their southward course to the great ocean, there to be swallowed, it would seem, forever. Mark this wonder, though: hours later they are shockingly moving northward, pushed back up the river by the tide toward their hidden source, in the dreamily mist-covered core of the continent. The sea has spat them out. Yet a recollection of its depths remains, for more hours pass and they drift by again, on their way to the ocean once more. How do the trees avoid dying in this cold? How do they manage every spring to come to life?

7

January 20, 2001

—————————

The 25th of Tevet, 5761

Ten forty a.m. If not for the quiet of these Saturday mornings, how would one ever stay sane? Ann Lee left early to go to the gym, after which she planned to meet friends. Her rhythms were a perfect match for his. Their need for solitude and space was so alike that it almost seemed like their own private pleasantry. The friction that should have been caused by the age gap between them never made itself felt, nor did this surprise either of them. They

made an effort not to take each other for granted or to let their lives
be routinized. Sometimes they left it up to the mysterious hand of
fate to decide their next meeting, preserving something of the addictive, intoxicating danger of a love affair's first days by keeping
a whimsical distance from each other. It was a game that he, they,
liked to play. It made him feel young and adventurous.

What was in the *New York Review of Books* today? A new book
on Freud's *Moses and Monotheism*. Another book on Freud? The
old man refused to die. He was the incarnated God of the psycho-
analysts, if not of Abraham, Isaac, and Jacob. What better subject
is there for a Freudian reading than Freud's own obsession with
Moses? All that hysterical rhapsodizing in front of Michelange-
lo's sculpture that betrayed more than anything the drama of self-
hatred raging in his assimilated Viennese Jewish soul and the need
to kill his inner father, the greater Moses, so that he, the lesser Moses, might take his place. Angst-ridden, he can't take his eyes off
the disproportionately long beard twisting itself over the muscular
stomach of the marble lawgiver like a giant sea monster caught in
the depths of the oceanic feeling of Freudian theory—that magnificent beard whose tip disappears in the lower abdomen to merge
with his pubic hair in an allusion to the inflated threat (a double
entendre, that!) lurking beneath the toga so nonchalantly draped
over the loins of the titan of monotheism. He should write about it
sometime. No, better not. As if the world needed another scholarly
article on Freud . . .

Andrew put down the *New York Review of Books* and glanced
at the wall clock in the kitchen. It was 11:10, time for a shave and
shower. At noon he was meeting friends for lunch at Le Monde,
the new French café on Broadway and 113th Street. From there
he would go straight to the Guggenheim. Its new exhibit, *The
Man in the Mirror: Installations and Performance Art*, was opening
next week. He had been asked to review it for *Harper's* and wanted

to have a look at it before deciding whether to accept. Ann Lee wouldn't be back before late afternoon or evening. They might eat out, or order in, open a good bottle of wine and watch a late-night film at his place. Although they sometimes went out together, they generally preferred staying in. Not that their relationship was a secret, not really. They just didn't flaunt it. They both guarded their privacy. For obvious reasons, Andrew could hardly introduce Ann Lee to his circle of friends as his partner, and she, too, must have felt no need to present him to her acquaintances or to appear with him in public. Far from harming their relationship, its semi-clandestine nature only enhanced it by making it more exciting and less matter-of-course. Was there time for another cup of coffee? No, he had to run. He would have it at Le Monde. Hopefully, their coffee would be up to the French bistro ambience they were trying so hard to create.

8

February 12, 2001

_____

The 19th of Shevat, 5761

Eleven a.m. There was a knock on the door of Andrew's office. Its diffidence told him who it was even before Bert's awkward figure appeared in the doorway holding a large stack of Xeroxed documents. Andrew's teaching assistant (or "valet," as he was unkindly referred to behind his back by both staff and students) was a pale, pudgy young man with granny glasses and the weak, wounded look of someone constantly about to burst into tears. Hesitant and stammering, he stored a thick layer of hurt under his skin, enflamed by the slightest friction; his restrained body language, which made him seem like he never dared flex a muscle or limb to the full, struck Andrew as typical of a "nice Jewish boy." It made him think of the domesticated elephants of India that he had read about while working on an essay challenging the myth of human-animal bonding.* The elephants' trainers, or so legend had it, would wait for the monsoons to come and then tie their little charges to a tree, fully exposed to the elements for days. Hungry and terrified by the fierce storms, they would repeatedly try to break loose until, helpless and exhausted, they collapsed on the soggy ground. No matter how large or powerful such an animal grew to be, it would never know its own strength or go beyond what its chains had permitted during those few terrible days.

"Hi, Bert. How are you?" Andrew smiled cordially.

"Hi, Andrew. I'm good, thank you." Bert's tongue tripped over itself each time he had to utter Andrew's first name. He found the fashionable democratization of names and titles unnatural and would have much preferred the old "Hello, Professor Cohen," had it only been acceptable. "I Xeroxed the reading list and left copies of the books on the reserves shelves in the library. I left two with Ms. Harty, too."

He spoke with the touching pride of a child eager to please and thirsting for approval. He liked running errands for Andrew and invested more time and energy in them than was justified by any rational calculation of their benefit to a research assistant like him-

---

* Andrew P. Cohen, "'Best Friends': The Myth of Inter-Species Symbolic Symbiosis," *Contemporary Culture* 5, Fall 1990, pp. 48–56. "Symbolically, the human being creates the animal in its image. Anthropomorphism is an integral part of humanity's relations with the animal kingdom, as with all other non-human aspects of the universe. When we observe and interpret animal behavior, we are actually observing nothing but our own selves. The observed animal is simply one more object onto which we project our own subjectivity. We look at it as though looking in a mirror, inventing what we see to suit our needs while simultaneously reinventing ourselves in the process" (ibid., p. 52).

self. Never did he broach the possibility of publishing a joint article with Andrew or angle for invitations to the conferences or
meetings of academic organizations. Even Andrew's proposal that
he lead a class in "The Critique of Culture" course was accepted
only after much soul-searching. Though a boost to Bert's ego, his
adulated teacher's faith in him was also the cause of paralyzing
self-doubt. Well-organized and not unlikable, he had no reason
to fear facing a classroom. Yet the contrast with Andrew's magical presence made him think twice about it, and there were even
some jaundiced souls in the department who dared hint that he was
picked for the job not in spite of his painful lack of charisma but
rather on account of it, having absolutely no chance of ever out-
shining his master.

"Professor Cohen." The voice on the intercom was Ms. Harty's.
"Rachel called. She said she's on her way but will be delayed by
a few minutes." Andrew glanced at his watch and leaned toward
the speaker. "Thank you, Ms. Harty." At the mention of Rachel,
Bert, who was filing documents at a side desk, gaped behind his
glasses, his hands moving more quickly but to less purpose. He
was hopelessly in love with her. He had stubbornly been so for
years, ever since they had shared notes and studied for exams together as college sophomores. His feelings for her, though he had
never dared express them, were an open secret. Loyal and obedient, he followed the twisting tracks of her stormy and anguished
love life, meeting her latest boyfriends and the more casual acquaintances allowed by her for some reason to be her short-term
lovers. Introduced, he shook their hands with a limp, sweaty palm
and timidly declared he was glad to meet them while regarding
with languishing looks their possessive arms around her shoulders
and the self-assured sexual gleam in their eyes. Each time he felt
that something had died in him anew and been buried deeper and
more futilely than the last time.

"Hi, Dad. Hi, Bert." Rachel entered the office as light and bright as a butterfly, passing by Bert's desk to reach her father and give him a long hug.

"Hi, Rachel," Bert muttered. He had to fight back an involuntary urge to look the other way when he saw them embracing. His hands still gripping their stack of documents, he hunched his shoulders and slumped in his chair, his head thrust forward until his neck was barely visible, once again the submissive freshman he had been when he first met her. Rachel glided across the room to him and grazed his cheek with a kiss. He blushed, eyes darting behind their glasses. "How's your dissertation going?" she asked.

"Oh, okay." Bert seemed to flinch even more. His dissertation, a thorough and thoroughly trite work, was going slowly. He sometimes thought his only reason for sticking it out was not his studies or an academic career but the allure of Andrew and the craving to remain in his orbit. It was as if some part of Rachel had rubbed off on her father, making the crumbs of attention he scattered on Bert, however remotely, a substitute for her affection. "How are things at the Hillel House? How are all your lovely admirers?"

Bert chuckled self-consciously. He was active in the Jewish students' union, helped organize its lectures, conferences, and weekends, traveled to Israel nearly every year, and was a cautiously reliable supporter of the American Jewish mainstream causes. The female students who frequented Hillel—nice, friendly, unfortunate-looking girls—considered him a good catch, a future companionable husband and devoted father. Some were aware of Rachel's shadow lurking in the background, her unruly coal-black curls so unlike their dull brown hair that was as tamed and stiff as their behavior, her tempestuous, almond-shaped eyes the reverse of their own lusterless, bovine ones.

Bert felt a pressing need to change the subject. Although he hated what Rachel's presence did to his voice, this was not something he acknowledged even to himself. "Hasn't the semester at Princeton begun yet?" he asked.

"It did, yesterday, but I decided to play hooky in the city and take Daddy dear out for lunch. You know Tom and I have split, don't you?"

It wasn't clear at whom the surprising last sentence, which shot through the room like a meteor, was directed. Rachel felt no compulsion to expand on it. She offered a gentlemanly arm to Andrew, who smilingly accepted it with a ladylike grace. "Bye, Bert. Nice seeing you again. Good luck with the dissertation."

Bert, heart racing, went on clutching his stack of documents. Murmuring something indistinct, he watched Rachel and Andrew leave the office arm in arm. From the rear, they looked more like a pair of young lovers than a twenty-something-year-old woman and her fifty-something-year-old father. They were almost gone from sight when Andrew turned to look back with a quick, encouraging, almost paternal smile. Bert's tense muscles relaxed, his nearsighted eyes blinked quickly. He responded with a big, childish smile of gratitude.

9

The apartment Rachel would be staying in belonged to a successful musician from a Long Island Jewish family who had gone to study in India, fallen for a guru like so many educated young Westerners, become an observant Hindu, and changed his name to Krishna Ram. Now, encouraged by his teacher to revert to an American lifestyle so as better to spread enlightenment, he performed in its name all over the United States. His place was on the third floor of a brick walk-up on 84th Street between Second and First, sandwiched between two East Side brownstones.

Rachel, to whom it had been described as "a cute little place" with an exotic aura, traipsed up the stairs gaily, key in hand, curious to see it. Andrew followed her up the narrow staircase, dragging her heavy suitcase. By the time he reached the third floor and found her standing in front of the door with a sarcastic smile on her face, his white shirt, fresh that morning, was damp with sweat. "That must be the guru," she said, pointing to a photograph taped to the peeling door of a fat, bald, mustached Indian man who was sprawled on a low wooden bench, completely naked except for a small loincloth. Far from radiating a refined spirituality, he had a self-satisfied, hedonistic expression that was accentuated by his corpulent belly, which hung over the bench and practically reached the ground. Andrew turned away from the repellent sight, half-aware of the urge to protect his daughter by covering it.

The door opened after a brief struggle and Rachel, in that youthful, almost euphoric spirit of adventure that excuses all faults and even turns them into virtues, entered the apartment. Perspiring and out of breath, Andrew came after her. He hadn't worked up a sweat in his ordinary clothes, as opposed to his gym and bike suits, in years and the incongruity of it caused him to feel a faint, semi-conscious, physical distress. He stood in the middle of the main room, which was hardly bigger than his own bathroom, squinting uncomfortably at his surroundings while gripping the suitcase as though afraid to soil it by putting it down. The room was long, dark, and narrow. A thick layer of dust and neglect, palpable despite the shut blinds, lay over everything. It evoked in him none of the nostalgia that comfortably off adults sometimes feel when encountering the squalor often chosen by the young as a backdrop for the drama of youth. Andrew wasn't one of those middle-aged men who mourn their lost youth. At the age of fifty-two he had the same youthful vigor he had had thirty years before, which caused others, even if younger than him, to feel an envy comparable to what they might have felt at the sight of the dark, dingy, devil-may-care space he was standing in. Something was bothering him, something indefinable. It wasn't just the dust or the darkness or the smell of mildew exhaled by the walls. It was the vague sense of a hostile presence, as if somebody or something were lurking in the dim apartment and observing them malevolently.

Rachel groped for the light switch. A dusty, low-wattage bulb clicked on. As soon as it did, something strange happened to the walls, which began to twitch as if thousands of roaches, lizards, or spiders were crawling over them. For a moment, Andrew felt he was in a Grade B horror movie. Heart pounding, he fought off his consternation and strained to see. The twitching grew less frantic. He took a deep breath and looked around. The walls, every one of them, were plastered with posters, photographs, and postcards of dozens, if not hundreds, of Hindu gods and holy men, so madly crowded together that hardly an inch of bare surface showed through. Exaggeratedly drawn in the lurid colors of Indian print art, demons and misshapen semi-human monsters regarded him from every direction, a glut of alien symbolism in their too sloe-eyed, too ferocious stares. Most unnerving of all was a face that appeared repeatedly in a bizarre variety of sizes and poses, a weird half-breed, whether an illustration or a photograph he couldn't tell, with the flattened nose and broad mouth of a chimpanzee, rouged cheeks, and large, feminine human eyes painted with a whorish black mascara. Bedecked with gold jewelry, the repugnant creature wore an array of kerchiefs from which greasy black curls hung down to its shoulders. The bile surged in Andrew's throat. The creature's dark eyes seemed to come moistly to life and rest on him. He broke into another sweat, a clammy one that seeped into his shirt. He now found himself, the situation aggravated by its absurdity, in a schoolboy's staring game with the uncouth, malignantly powerful creature on the wall, who was coming close to breaking

his will and forcing him to lower his eyes. This demented clash
lasted for only a few seconds before Andrew managed, with no
small effort, to tear himself away. He felt that he was trapped in a
nightmare, but that also, not quite rationally, he had been rescued
at the last moment from a horrible, demonic fate.

He struggled to get hold of himself, breathing deeply while
waiting for his highly developed rational defense mechanisms to
return him to reality. Meanwhile, he scrutinized the wall facing
him, involuntarily averting his glance from his repellent nemesis
until he recognized a familiar figure: the heavyset, semi-humorous
elephant god Ganesha, whose picture was displayed on the packs
of beedies, the smelly Indian cigarettes sold on Berkeley street
corners to students flaunting their opposition to all things Western. Andrew smiled as if meeting an old friend. The elephant god
Ganesha! He and the monkey god Hanuman, like an old comedy
team, had recently starred in a fascinating novel by a promising Indian author named Vikram Chandra, which Andrew had praised
in *Harper's* for its sophisticated juxtaposition of Western and native
Indian narrative techniques. Reading the book and writing the
review had made him feel drolly intimate with these two Hindu
gods, who were now inextricably linked in his mind with the author's brilliant portrayal of them.

Andrew threw back his shoulders with a sigh of relief, his sense of
unreality dispelled. His reassurance, however, did not last long, for
now the illustration of Ganesha, too, came alive and began to move.
Its brutish eyes, set on either side of its thick trunk, flashed wick-
edly. The trunk began to gyrate, wrapping itself around the beast's
swollen abdomen like the tentacle of an octopus. Before his eyes, the
friendly trickster god Ganesha was turning into a horrid, contorted
ogre. A new wave of nausea swept over him. Afraid that the slightest
contact with the pictures on the wall would release a flood of vomit,
he shut his eyes, groped blindly for the door, and leaned against its

cool, bare wood to let his tension drain. He realized now who the terrifying creature in the first illustration was. It was the monkey god Hanuman! Of course: Ganesha and Hanuman!

Andrew felt a searing, childish resentment. But it couldn't be Hanuman! Hanuman had always been so funny and likable. He now felt more menaced than before. The grotesque faces of the Indian gods aroused an ancient, primordial animus. Something buried deep in his unconscious had surfaced with no way for him to cope with it or even know what it was. His head was swimming with it all: the guru's naked belly, Ganesha's prominent belly button, the penetrating feminine eyes of the monkey man and the dumb brutish ones of the elephant man, the mouse hiding underneath Ganesha's swollen belly like a tiny male organ, and the guru's huge sex, barely concealed by the thin loincloth beneath the stomach that hung casually over the bench and almost reached the ground. How vile, how intolerably vile! A strange, startlingly inappropriate thought suddenly invaded Andrew's tormented mind: Were Hindus circumcised, or not?

"Dad, are you okay?" Rachel's voice seemed to come from afar. "You're pale. And sweating! What's the matter?"

Andrew looked at her wide-eyed, as if waking from a bad dream. The walls stopped twitching and came to rest, ordinary-looking in the weak light of the electric bulb. "Could you please open the window?" he asked. "I'm suddenly dizzy. I don't feel well."

Rachel hurried to the window, alarmed but also a bit excited by her father's appeal for help. The window was jammed. She wrestled with it briefly, gave up, and switched on the air conditioner, which began to rattle like an old tractor, then returned to her father, guided him to a desk, and tried getting him to sit. Andrew resisted wordlessly and remained standing, leaning on the dusty Formica desktop. The irrational, indefinable feelings stirred up in him were not ones he recognized. "Other!" he thought. "Other!"

The word, lacking all context, repeated itself stubbornly in his mind. "You don't have to stay here if you don't want to," he said. He straightened up, brushing the dust from his hands. "I don't think you'll like it here."

Rachel was startled by the almost panicky urgency in his voice. "Why not stay with me? My apartment has all you need. There's a pull-out couch in the living room and plenty of space for us both. I'm hardly ever home. And it's only for three days. Come on, let's take a taxi, now!"

She looked at him in shock. Such a combination of nervous energy and overprotectiveness was something she was used to in Linda, but she had never expected to see it in her father. "But Dad! What's the matter with you? I'd hate to impose on you. It's perfectly nice here. It just needs to be cleaned and aired a bit. You yourself said it's only for three days. And look at the wild pictures on the walls!"

She felt pulled in two directions, the need to assert herself balanced by an exuberantly warm rush of childish glee, as if she had been waiting for such an invitation all day—no, since telling her father she was coming to the city—no, longer than that, for long, long years, for as long as she could remember.

"Absolutely not!" Andrew was surprised by his own firmness. "I want you to come to my place. Come on, let's go. How do you turn off this air conditioner? What a racket! Have you ever seen filth like this?" Busily, he circulated through the apartment, lowering the blinds, turning off the air conditioner, and lifting the suitcase while grabbing the keys from the desk. Rachel stood staring at him in astonishment. He was behaving like a different, unrecognizable person. Like Linda.

10
February 13, 2001

The 20th of Shevat, 5761

An endless hospital corridor. All sorts of oddly, indecipherably named wards. Wing after wing, an exitless maze of forking hallways that all look alike. A pervasive smell of urine, disinfectant, tears, and clotted blood. The green curtains only partially hide beds on which lie old, half-undressed women, their liver-spotted skin hanging like worn sacks. Why aren't the curtains closed all the way? Anyone passing can see their pitiable nakedness. The metal parts of wheelchairs glitter in the cold, clinical light. More corridors. Where's obstetrics? There must be someone to ask. But the corridors are empty. There's no one. Elevators go up and down at a snail's pace. There are no signs, no directories. Excuse me, miss. How do I get to the obstetrics ward? The name is Cohen, Linda Cohen. I'm looking for Linda Cohen. Yes, she's my wife. We have a new baby. Yes, today, now, a few minutes ago. Where is she?

The door opens with difficulty and swings silently shut on its hinges as if in a strange dream. Be quiet or you'll wake the sleepers. Rachel is lying in a bed. She's totally exhausted, she's lost a lot of blood. Her pale face is the color of the sheets but her eyes burn with a dark, flickering fire. Gently she presses the red, wrinkled face of the new baby to her white cheek, shuts her eyes, and inhales its fresh scent. The baby is wrapped in a red-and-green-striped flannel blanket. From the little cotton bonnet on its head protrude a few dark, damp curls. It's a beautiful baby. What a perfectly formed face. Rachel's black curls are damp, too, as if she, too, has just been born. It's a boy! We have a boy! A wondrous little boy, glad tidings of redemption, reconciliation, eternal peace. How good everything is suddenly. What bliss.

11
February 13, 2001

The 20th of Shevat, 5761

Eight a.m. Rachel opened her eyes lazily. She felt more cozy and relaxed than most mornings, far more than she had expected to feel. To wake in Dad's apartment, on his famous leather couch! Who would have guessed that it opened into a bed, let alone such a comfortable one?

Rachel stretched, luxuriating in the unanticipated pleasure of her slow awakening while sleepily surveying the large space of the living room, which was already bright, despite the early hour, with a festive gray light. The stylish expanse of the room was impressive, especially given the city's housing shortage and the wild jump in real estate prices. None of the New York apartments she had recently been in were anything like Andrew's. Although in its former existence it had had a second bedroom and a maid's room, Andrew had done away with these inner divisions, leaving a minimum of structural elements and a large, loftlike space more reminiscent of Tribeca or SoHo than of the Upper West Side. Perhaps its lack of a guest bedroom was his way of protecting himself against unwanted visitors—not that anyone would dream of barging in on Andrew without an invitation . . .

Rachel smiled wryly. She was just pretending to be critical. She loved being in this place, so close to her father. He had made her feel wanted, totally at home. She rose, pulled the crocheted blanket from the bed, and wrapped it around her like a cape or a prayer shawl. Was he still here? The door to his bedroom was shut and no sounds came from its other side. Noiselessly, she tiptoed across the waxed parquet floor, once again a nine- or ten-year-old sneaking into her parents' room, and put a slightly embarrassed ear to the door. Not a peep. He was out. Since when was he in the habit of leaving so early? How had he slipped away without waking her? She didn't know if she was disappointed or not. But there was no point in indulging in pointless introspection, and she chose to enjoy the peace and clarity, so unusual for her, by which she was surrounded. Barefoot, she glided across the room, the blanket half trailing on the floor behind her like a lacy train. The view from the windows was sensational. A low winter sky grazed the bare branches of the leafless oaks and plane trees. Bluish-white ice floes, like polar bear cubs playing tag, chased each other on the river. Everything was so clear, and clean, and orderly, so therapeutically spotless.

She turned to the counter separating the open kitchen from the living room, slowly emerging from the dreamlike, enchanted fog she had been in since opening her eyes. A key! The sudden, discordant thought broke the blissful gray flow of the morning. I don't have a key. If I go anywhere, I'll be locked out. A moment later, discord yielded to childish joy as she spied a key on the counter, resting on a note whose handwriting she could have recognized a mile away.

Hi, sweetie,

I have a bar mitzvah party tonight for a second cousin—would you like to come with me? It'll be fun. We'll stop at Barney's this afternoon and buy you a nice dress. There's a great restaurant there on the eighth floor, the perfect place to celebrate.

Love,
Dad

Her joy mounted to an almost infantile exhilaration when, next to the small pot of hot coffee left for her in the espresso machine, she noticed a square of a yellow sticky note with the words from their favorite book, the one she had never tired of asking to be read from as a child: "Drink me!"

A long, hot shower and a leisurely lull in front of the mirror. A real morning off. Curious, Rachel investigated the bathroom shelves and sink. There was not a sign of Ann Lee, her father's girlfriend. Although she had heard a lot about her, she had never met her, which could not have been an accident. There was no forgotten cosmetic case, no woman's shampoo, not even a box of goddamn tampons hidden somewhere. Didn't she ever sleep here? She must have hid it all—maybe in the cabinet beneath the sink, or in the handsome, French country-style pannier beneath a shelf whose white towels were stacked as neatly as in a hotel. While it didn't demand a superhuman effort on Rachel's part to avoid peeking— she was not by nature an eavesdropper or voyeur—it did call for some restraint.

She dressed, carefully put on her makeup, poured herself the rest of the coffee, and sat facing the view in the living-room armchair. Not until she felt totally ready did she take a slip of paper from her purse and dial a number on the cordless phone, her nervous fingers reluctant to acknowledge that she already knew it by heart. She unconsciously counted the number of rings, feeling like an adolescent. There were butterflies in her stomach. Her mouth was dry. She had rehearsed her opening line. "Hi, Abby. It's me, Rachel. Yes, I'm in town."

12

February 13, 2001

The 21st of Shevat, 5761

A large color photograph of the bar mitzvah boy stood on an easel at the entrance of the synagogue, welcoming the guests in their tuxedos and evening gowns. The lobby had an old-time splendor with its marble floor, gilt armchairs, and oversize fireplace, framed in ornamental marble, too, that quite evidently had never seen a fire. The guests strolled among the tables of hors d'oeuvres, one hand holding a cocktail and the other free for handshakes. The quantities of food were overwhelming. Servers in white chef's hats stood by steaming-hot cuts of meat set on wooden trenchers, carving portions and carefully placing them on the outstretched plates. Entire salmons lay on their sides, garnished with thin slices of cucumber. Oily Chinese stir-fry glittered in large woks. A sushi chef, who, too, was Chinese, swiftly rolled and cut his fare, trying hard to keep up with the demand for the new and exotic delicacy, only recently discovered by American gourmand wannabes. There was even a kosher hot-dog stand for the children, the bar mitzvah boy's cousins and schoolmates.

"This is some bar mitzvah," Rachel whispered to Andrew. "You don't see this much food at a wedding. Wow, look at that! There's even a sushi bar, over there. And what a line!" She narrowed her eyes in disgust, leaning on his arm.

"Look who's here! It's Andrew!" Michael, the bar mitzvah boy's father, appeared in their path, hearty and heavyset in his black tuxedo, his sweaty face aflame. Giving Andrew a long, back-thumping, familial hug, he left one hand resting on his back while extending the other to Rachel. "Isn't it ridiculous to say 'My, how

you've grown!' each time we meet?" Rachel smiled neutrally and
shook his surprisingly firm hand, stunned to see someone, an almost stranger, touching her normally remote and untouchable father with such intimate nonchalance. "And this is David, our bar
mitzvah boy, star of the evening." Michael's voice boomed in the
jovially stentorian tone of a seasoned host. David held out a polite
hand, clearly flustered. In his black formal attire, he seemed disguised, like a little boy trying on his father's oversize tuxedo. *He's
such a cutie*, Rachel thought, *a real cutie. The poor kid, does he have
to wear that silly-looking yarmulke all the time?*

Andrew gave David a warm smile. Someone handed him a
white paper skullcap, unlike the ones brought from home by most
of the guests, and he adjusted it carefully on his head, smiling at
his awkwardness. "Get a load of Rabbi Cohen!" Michael joked.
"We'll make an Orthodox Jew of you yet." He thanked Andrew
and Rachel for having come, promised to bring Grandma Henya
to them when he saw her, and encouraged them to eat and drink.
"Don't worry, everything's kosher," he quipped, disappearing,
shiny tuxedo and all, in the crowd. Andrew and Rachel exchanged
knowing looks, linked arms, and strode mock-ceremoniously into
the noisy ballroom.

At nine o'clock the reception ended and the guests were invited
to the dining area. "I thought that *was* dinner," Rachel protested in
a low voice. "There was enough meat at the reception to feed every
child in Africa." The dining area was hot, crowded, and animated.
A wedding band played synthesized klezmer music full blast, the
electric guitars twanging, the clarinet slithering like a black snake,
and the jazz trumpets sounding their golden notes. A vocalist in a
modish suit and black velvet yarmulke accompanied himself on a
synthesizer. The old Hebrew words, amplified to electro-metallic
heights by the sound system, made a surrealistic impression. Waiters in red uniforms ushered the guests to round tables festooned

with flowers and balloons, took their orders for the main course, and poured kosher champagne into their glasses.

Andrew sat in his assigned seat and took a sip of the wine. To his surprise, it wasn't so bad—for a kosher wine, that is. He reached for the bottle and inspected the label. Baron Herzog. Andrew smiled in pleasant surprise, as if he had bumped into an old friend. Saul Bellow's cocky smile and dandyishly tilted fedora flickered before his eyes for a second. What would good old Herzog think of this bar mitzvah? He leaned back, took another sip of the wine, and regarded his surroundings, contemplating their angular, abstract modern architecture that was characteristic of American houses of worship—churches, synagogues, even mosques. There was something paradoxical about it, something that contradicted the idea behind it. It took him a while to connect what he saw to what he remembered: the space he was in was the prayer hall of a synagogue. Surely, he had realized that all along, hadn't he? His eyes sought and found the Ark, a tall, rectangular structure— ultramodern, too, of course—of wood and glass. Although such contrasts of old and new, sacred and profane, were always jarring, he liked them for their challenge to time-worn assumptions. His critical mind, always on the lookout for subversive points of view, took note of its own conventional recoil from what it instinctively classified as "desecration," and of the tacit power of the socializing process of religion over even a secular person like himself.

He studied with interest the Hebrew writing on the wall opposite him. Its square, stern-looking letters, both familiar and strange, were the same ones his Westchester Sunday school had striven to inculcate in him, only to be rebelliously rejected and forgotten after his own bar mitzvah. His memory was jogged by a word spelled with the characters *Yod Heh Vav Heh*. These were, he knew, the four letters of the tetragrammaton, God's holy, unutterable, numinous name that was spoken aloud once a year, on the Day of

Atonement, by the High Priest in the Holy of Holies. Andrew had
to smile. How obsessively the biblical scholars and archaeologists
insisted, whether it was relevant or not, on pronouncing this name
unnaturally loudly in their conferences and lectures like children
pleasantly shocking themselves by saying a forbidden word.

The guests circulated among the tables, taking each other's
seats, talking in loud voices, and engaging in the collective disorder so deeply woven into the fabric of Eastern European Jewish culture. How different it was from the exemplary decorum of
Protestant weddings that had become—for most Jews, too—the
American ideal. A generation or two of small, undramatic decisions, Andrew thought, sipping some overly fruity kosher white
wine, was all it took: the move to the suburbs with their big house
and garden, the enrollment in the Reform synagogue that was
closer to home, the minimal Jewish education because the mortgage payments were high and ate up the family budget. Small,
semiconscious, semi-voluntary deviations whose cumulative effect
was that of an off-course missile, multiplied exponentially from
generation to generation until huge, unbridgeable chasms were
created. It wasn't a matter of conscious religious or ideological
choice. The truly significant differences had to do with things like
body language, aesthetic taste, and sense of space. And they'll go
on growing until the last thin strands connecting us to each other
fray and snap like old violin strings. For a moment, Michael and
I, two aging, sentimental Jewish men, can make one last attempt
to join hands across the divide. But although our fingers may still
touch, it's an optical illusion. A genuine embrace, even a genuine
handshake, is no longer possible. Rachel acts as though she were
here at gunpoint, critical and estranged, as if it had nothing to do
with her. Once Michael and I are gone, there's not a chance that
she and David will stay in touch, or have a common ground of any
sort.

A blinding halo of artificial illumination, like a little island of
sunlight, surrounded the photography crew as it went from table
to table. The men and the women danced separately. Rachel had
never seen anything like it. The women circled with precise, measured steps. The men, on the other hand, spun wildly in a compact,
ecstatic mass, pressing and leaning their full body weight against
each other. Some, swept away, shut their eyes and sang along with
the loud vocalist at the tops of their voices. Andrew was fascinated,
equally attracted and repelled by their openly celebrated, unapol-
ogetically flaunted male bond. He was reflecting on the oddity of
adult men in expensive suits and ties dancing this way in twenty-
first-century America when, out of nowhere, two powerful hands
gripped him and playfully propelled him into the circle. Startled yet
excited by what was a sign of acceptance no less than an invasion of
his privacy, he let himself be carried along by the dithyramb of human bodies pulsing with humid body heat. Heavy hands gripped
his shoulders while his own rested on an unfamiliar, perspiring
back; its sweatiness could be felt even through the heavy fabric.
The dancing wave tossed him this way and that, lifted him off the
marble floor, and finally set him down in the circle's center, face-
to-face with his cousin Michael—who, sweat pouring out of him
like water, was in a kind of trance, dancing with an abandon that
bore no relation to his shrewdly practical, pragmatic everyday self.
Eyes half-shut, he held his hands out in front of him. Andrew, not
knowing what to expect, did the same, and soon his fine, delicate
fingers were in the grip of his cousin's large, fleshy ones. With a
bearlike gentleness, Michael led him in a clumsy but not charmless
jig. Their shoulders swayed back and forth; their bodies rocked
from side to side, now on one foot, now on the other; their sweaty
hands were stuck together.

An intense light shone on them from above. The video crew
had reached the circle and was aiming powerful spotlights at its

center. Eyeglasses, cuff links, and bald spots glittered with every step. The song reached a crescendo. Michael and the other dancers joined in, whooping the Hasidic tune in a triumphant chorus. Andrew danced and danced. Although his senses felt battered by the close physical contact, its intrusiveness aroused not the antagonism he might have anticipated but a pleasurable, hypnotically intimate sense of warmth. Most striking was his reaction to so much masculine sweat not his own. The sensation was one he couldn't place. His body could remember the salty, vaginal-tasting sweat of wild lovemaking, the perspiration of long hikes, the damp curls of a baby lifted from her crib after an afternoon nap. This, though, took him further, deeper . . . A kiss? Yes, it was a little like a first kiss with its repulsive thrill of someone else's sweet saliva. No, it went even deeper than that. It was liberating, cathartic. It was like surrendering to a summer downpour that ran down one's face and soaked one through and through. The sopping wet clothes. Time ceased to exist. All inhibitions were gone. All was one and One was All.

His pas de deux with Michael ended as abruptly as it began. Swept back up by the flow of bodies, he spun briefly in its orbit before being flung out of it and deposited, sweat-drenched, in the very spot he had entered it from. The insistent beat of the music was like a second pulse driven by his pounding heart. How much time had elapsed? A minute or two, it couldn't have been more. His body still shook with the wild rhythm of the dance. Relief was tinged with disappointment. Part of him would have liked to plunge back into the circle, to reimmerse itself in the storm that had swept his senses and surrender to it unconditionally. But another part, more stable and familiar, was already leading him, short of breath, out of the storm to safety. He stood between the circle of dancers and his table, not knowing which way to turn. His heartbeat slowed, and, with it, the everyday Andrew took command. For another minute, he remained standing. Then, his legs weak, he walked to the table at which the waiters were serving the second course.

"Hi, Dad. Having a good time?" Rachel's sarcasm was annoying. Irritably, she threw herself into a seat by his side and reached out for her no-longer-bubbly flute of champagne. Andrew murmured a vague answer. His emotional, semi-ecstatic state surprised him. Its strange, dreamlike, yet not unpleasant stimulation was like being drunk. The perspiration now drying on his skin, the loud music, the obscene quantities of food, the heat, the wine: all merged in a sensation as utterly new as it was terribly old. The rhythm of the dance was still beating in his veins, low and primitive like an ancient drum. It had a thrilling, primeval, almost pagan feel. Rachel muttered something that failed to register on him. He glanced again at the Hebrew on the wall. Something about it tugged at him, like a secret code that suddenly seemed painfully familiar. He couldn't take his eyes off it. A strange, wistful longing overcame him, for what he didn't know. His heart brimmed. His eyes felt like they would soon fill with tears, and his breathing kept growing deeper.

There was a flurry of excitement. An orchestrated clash of cymbals announced the return of the red-uniformed waiters with large, steaming trays of grilled prime rib on their shoulders. The vapors swirled toward the Holy Name, whose letters seemed to shimmy with life on the wall. The pungent smells of perfume, sweat, breathy exhalations, and the repugnantly appetizing grilled meat assaulted Andrew's nasal cavities, making him dizzy and unsure where he was. *Lo, the foundations of the thresholds shook and the house was filled with smoke. The walls were moving apart, farther and farther from each other, lifting like stage curtains to reveal the gleaming white marble facades of a huge, ravishingly beautiful shrine crowned with gold. The song of Levites surged and spiraled upward in a deep, ancient chant in which, as though from the first days of Creation, the world's soul was enfolded. The Temple's golden gates shone in the*

pinkish-violet light of the desert twilight. A thick, upright column of
smoke rose from the burning logs on the altar, oblivious of the evening
breeze that blew as though to dislodge and disperse it to the four winds.
Men of piety and men of deeds danced with hymns of praise and the
Levites on the fifteen steps leading to the Women's Gallery from the
Gallery of Israel played their zithers, dulcimers, cymbals, and divers
instruments. A barefoot, nimble old man dressed in a gold-embroidered
cloak juggled eight torches in the air, catching one and throwing another
back in the air. Never did one touch another.

13

Eleven thirty p.m. The highway is empty and the car gulps the
miles like a horse eager to return to its stable. It had just begun
to snow. The radio warns of a rapidly approaching blizzard that
threatens to cut off the city. They do not want to get stuck in it on
the highway. Rachel, the alcohol wearing off and giving way to a
predictable headache, is getting the toxic remains of the evening
off her chest. "All that celebrating doesn't convince me. It's artificial, forced happiness. They've been brainwashed. Those women
with their ten-thousand-dollar nose jobs and anorexic daughters!
And their Gucci and Prada bags, and three- and four-carat en-
gagement rings, and Madison Avenue hats and dresses! It's disgusting, perfectly disgusting! All they talk about is clothes, home
appliances, and shopping. It's unbelievable, like a pious parody of
our consumer society."

Her voice, though, is growing softer, almost accepting. The last
thing she would have admitted to herself was that she had actually enjoyed their little adventure. Enough with the news channel. A golden-black saxophone is playing on the jazz station. The
New York skyline rises regally to their left. The green lights of the

Triborough Bridge are already winking ahead of them. Andrew drives silently, his face and neck still coated with warm, dry, sticky perspiration. His mind hadn't stopped reeling from the awesomely powerful vision. Its last traces, though their bright threads were already unraveling, continued to reverberate. He reached for the radio, as though intending to turn up the volume, then retracted his hand. What was this about? What was happening to him? This wasn't the first time. He was having more and more of these strange visions. They came from nowhere and had no explanation, not even a hypothetical one. This wasn't the time to think about it, though. He was too tired, confused, and overstimulated. It could wait till tomorrow. He had to concentrate on his driving. He bent over the wheel, as though to grip it better. Bright flares keep arcing before his eyes, eight fiery torches, dancing nimbly in the dark night's air.

14

February 14, 2001

The 21st of Shevat, 5761

A heavy white snow covers the city like a gleaming satin blanket. Seen from above, Riverside Drive has been stripped of its innumerable, confusing details. Nothing is left but a fresh coat of pure form. For a moment, the perfection we spend our lives in pursuit of has become a reality. Soon, the sacred stillness will be broken. There will be sounds of traffic. Snowplows will clear the main arteries. Doormen will bustle up and down the sidewalks with little carts of salt, scattering its corrosive grains in front of their buildings to melt the snow and sting the soft paws of dogs. Later, closer to eleven, a wonderfully lively commotion will resound from Riverside Park, the merry voices of children sledding down the hill at 108th Street. A tantalizing smell of fresh rolls, hot chocolate, and simmering soup will emanate from the cafés and next-door apartments—the smell of winter with its almost unbearable longing.

Meanwhile, the silence is unbroken. The air from the river is cold and crisp and little snowflakes ripple wavelike through the air. The trunks and branches of bare trees look even darker against the all-white backdrop. The world is an abstract painting whose missing element is provided by the small figure of an old Asian man, wrapped in a tattered black overcoat, walking slowly down the Drive. A Zen monk? A poet? A crazy person? From time to time, he pauses to meditate on a virginal bank of white snow. Then he inscribes on it, with a cheap metal hanger that has been straightened into a stylus, large, mysterious Chinese characters that appear to conceal a great, transcendent secret.

15

February 18, 2001

The 25th of Shevat, 5761

Five p.m. Last week's snow had half melted, leaving behind dirty piles of slush. Andrew returned home slightly earlier than usual. He stood at the kitchen counter, sorting the mail while absentmindedly listening to the messages on the answering machine. The one from Linda took him aback, both in its content and in the urgency, bordering on impatience, in her voice. "Hi, Andy. I'm calling again about the Cape. Can you get back to me with your exact dates? I need to plan the summer. Thanks."

What's the rush? Andrew wondered. We're still in the middle of

February. He erased the message and scrawled on the back of an envelope: *Linda, dates for Cape Cod*. He was proud (as in the end Linda had come to be, too) of the amicable divorce that had allowed them each to retain half of their summer home on the Cape. Linda had the use of it in July, while in August it was his. Sometimes her duties as a clinical social worker forced her to remain in the city, and then Andrew could spend the whole summer there. Their joint ownership subjected the house to an odd kind of suspended animation in which their unraveled relationship was perpetuated. Each of them was careful to preserve the aesthetic status quo: not one of the cracked dishes, yellowing sheets, frayed beach towels, rugs stained with children's pee, or place mats with twenty years' worth of chocolate milk, lemonade, and wine stains on them was ever replaced. Everything had been frozen since the day of their divorce: the Danish-modern living-room furniture, the batiked fabrics fashionable in the seventies and early eighties; the big brass bed in the master bedroom whose comical creaking had enlivened their midsummer nights' lovemaking; the rafters and wooden shingles on the roof, now gray with age; the bushes stubbornly sprouting along the sandy descent to the beach. And yet none of this seemed the least bit shabby. On the contrary, all was enveloped in an aura of longing, cushioned by the tenderness of children's laughter, hot corn on the cob, and blueberry pie with vanilla ice cream. Sometimes it seemed that sharing the house was just an alibi, for which they were grateful, for keeping their memories alive.

Andrew smiled. It was odd to think of the Cape now, in a New York February. A grainy scene, as if shot with an old Super 8 Kodak, passed before him: white sails glinting in a blue haze, the ferry for Martha's Vineyard, broad amidships, heading into the deep bay. Whiskey! Andrew suddenly craved a drink. He looked at his watch: a quarter after five. Was it too early for alcohol? What was it about the Cape? You couldn't be there without leaving part of yourself behind to haunt the empty beaches and gray stone fences, the stubby lighthouses and old saltbox homes. It had an ascetic splendor, a power born of the sun and the whiplashing wind, the salt air and the violent thunderstorms. Andrew poured himself a scotch and settled down on the couch. The mere mention of Cape Cod sent a shiver of belonging through him, as though it were the name of a native city or an old country his ancestors came from. His connection to America was natural, direct. He felt completely at home in the WASP world of New England with its white colonial houses fronted by well-tended lawns and flags, its spring Easter egg hunts and summer lemonade stands. He saw its false consciousness, of course, the deception wrought by its pretense of frugality and mannered Puritan simplicity, behind which the influential rich hid their power and greed, privileging the rocking chair on the porch over the fancy yacht and marble-columned mansion because it better expressed the spirit of the place. And why shouldn't they love the spirit of the place? They had appropriated it for their advantage, tamed and domesticated it as their forefathers had tamed the wild horses, the unnavigated rivers, and the virgin forests. Yes, he saw all that. Still, something in him swallowed its romantic lie hook, line, and sinker and hankered for every last local pose and posture. Take, for example, those weathered decoys that filled the souvenir shops: little ducks blackened by age, long-necked Canada geese, and green-headed mallards, once used by hunters to lure in and slaughter whole flocks of birds and now, like old swords and ancient pistols, household bric-a-brac. He liked them even though they were the worst kitsch, liked the nondescript mementos that embodied all the yearning of the vast country. The old buoys. The bleached, sand-and-wind-blasted oars. The cuff links, letter openers, and snuffboxes carved from yellowing scrimshaw. He went to the counter, poured himself some more whiskey, corked the bottle, returned it to the liquor cabinet, reconsidered, and took it with him back to the couch, setting it on the coffee table while the blues, greens, and grays of the seashore went on drifting evocatively through his mind.

The Atlantic's colors were so different from the Pacific's. The Pacific was almost theatrically dramatic with its gigantic blue waves, its breathtaking cliffs, its sandy black beaches, its clear, celestially pure sapphire light. The Atlantic was more gently, more humanly shaded, ranging from blue to green and gray to dune yellow. The Pacific faced west, continuing the outward sweep of the continent toward the unknown. The Atlantic looked longingly back toward the Old World, striving to bridge a widening cultural abyss. In his young, innocent, stormy California years, he had had a passionate romance with the Pacific. The youthful, joyous potency of life—the freely available sex, the drugs, the contact with nature, the delight of self-discovery and self-love—had all been colored with the Pacific's bright hues. Once, from a cliff at Big Sur, very early on a far-off summer morning, young Andy had seen a sight that branded his tender soul: wondrous and without warning, a southbound school of black-finned whales, their sleek backs gleaming like dark pebbles, overleaped each other in dreamlike silence, forming a series of perfect arcs in the milky mist of the dawn. Now, though, in maturity, the grayer, less spectacular, duller Atlantic was more to his liking. Viewed in retrospect, the exaltation produced by the Pacific struck him as an overly intense, even slightly vulgar adolescent infatuation. The capable, successful, handsome, middle-aged Andrew of today loved the Atlantic with its warmth-breathing Gulf Stream and its fat, amiable whales lounging out of sight the way one loves—undemonstratively, peacefully, gently—a long-wed wife.

The ring of the telephone roused him from his lyrical mood. "Wow! That was some happy hello!" Ann Lee sounded happy, too.

"Yes." Andrew smiled uncertainly, as if waking from a nice dream. "I may be a bit drunk."

16

Sunday, ten thirty a.m. The city was still half-asleep. The clean, quiet streets gleamed in the bluish light. In front of the building, a no-longer-young father in a baseball cap was teaching his son to catch a fly ball. Even such an absurdly urban scene, the narrow strip of sidewalk a makeshift outfield, bespoke the freedom of an America that refused to be fenced in. So, for thousands of generations, hunters and warriors had handed down their skills in mime and movement, just like this father enacting the major league center fielder for his son who lapped it up eagerly, leaning forward with his tongue sticking slightly out.

Ann Lee's car was parked near the corner of 108th Street. Andrew, thinking with a smile of her girlishly sweet body still cuddled beneath the blanket, had to move the driver's seat back to squeeze into it before readjusting the rearview mirror. Walter had taught him and his brother, Matthew, to play ball, too, displaying the same expertise he had mowed the lawn with every Saturday in a white polo shirt, his tanned biceps visible beneath its short sleeves. Tall and proud, he had mowed one precise square of grass after another without having to look down. The car glided along Broadway. A few early customers sat in the sidewalk cafés and restaurants, first swallows of the flocks that would wait their turn for Sunday brunch in long lines. How many years had it been since he first read *Portnoy's Complaint*? The grotesque description of the Jewish father whose attempts to play ball with his son only revealed his un-American ineptness. A wonderful, masterly bit of prose! Andrew had taught it several times in classes dealing with the body as a vehicle of social identity. It was hard to imagine a greater antithesis to Roth's caricatured father than Walter Cohen. You couldn't have been ashamed of Walter even had you tried to be. He had the body language of America, the entire American lifestyle, down pat. Left at 96th. Amsterdam Avenue. Columbus. Right on Central Park West. The flower stands of the delis were celebrating the early spring. Is 96th Street open through Central Park on Sundays? Better to cross at 86th and turn right past the Met. Their lawn was always trim. New Rochelle wasn't the Lower East Side, not by a long shot. It was no place to look for what his mother called "your typical Jewish shambles." Until when were her visiting hours? Alison gets out of Sunday school at twelve. If we leave Linda's at two, we'll be at my mother's by three or three fifteen.

Alison's attachment to Andrew's mother was amazing. By the time she was old enough to know the difference, Ethel was already a shadow of her old self. Lately, she had even started calling her "Bubby." Where did that come from? We never called her that. Can she have picked it up in Sunday school and decided every Jewish grandmother is a Bubby? When did she begin reinventing her Jewish roots? Right on Fifth. How nice this part of town is. The Met's first visitors were drinking coffee on its steps, soaking up the sunshine before entering. There's an exhibit of the latest Thorntons and the new installation center was opened yesterday. Eileen wrote something about it for the *Times*, I have to talk to her. All of New Rochelle's houses had identical lawns, as if planned by a single landscape architect. E Pluribus Unum. What better proof could there be of the vitality of the American dream than its big suburban lawn? Since the sixties, we've been aggressively socialized to believe that individualism is good and conformity is bad, but there's another side to it—the freedom to assimilate that was every immigrant's thanks to the uniformity of the now derided American melting pot, the target of every armchair social critic's barbs. Who dares speak today of conformity's liberating power, of the blessed sameness of American life that freed one and all from

Europe's constricting categories of class, religion, and ethnicity? It's precisely the alleged prison of middle-class homogeneity with its mass-produced neighborhoods and jobs that made possible America's unrestricted, unprecedented, almost anarchic freedom of choice. Whoever wanted to join the New Society could do so. The only price of admission was mowing the lawn every Saturday in a white polo shirt. Left at 65th and east all the way to York, then south on the FDR to the Brooklyn Bridge. It was eleven o'clock. The streets were still almost empty. There would be time to stop at the bakery in Park Slope and buy the bagels Linda had asked him to bring.

17

The standard gift of IBM shares that Walter and Ethel Cohen gave their newborn sons was less a calculated economic investment than a symbol of the normative, responsible, middle-class ethos of work and saving. For the young Cohens as for most of their generation, the idea of freedom, so central to the American experience, meant above all freedom from want—or, to put it differently, from anxiety about tomorrow. Along with the archaic dress, the docile body language, and the ceaselessly muttered prayers of the ghetto, the new American Jew had put aside the grinding, never-ending worry of his forebearers, who scurried frantically through the narrow streets of the shtetl—no more than a rural slum, really—without knowing from where, if anywhere, their children's next meal would come. The farthest ahead they could think under such unimaginably difficult circumstances was the coming Sabbath, for which they hoped to scrape together enough for a piece of carp, the cheapest of fish, so pathetic it would be sent back to the kitchen of any American restaurant if served as a main course. The savings plan and the life insurance policy, however pitifully small, became the icons of American Jewish culture. Their symbolic value was huge, almost religious; into them was funneled all the spiritual energy once concentrated on ritual objects. Their almost fetishistic power expressed the determination of men and women who had experienced hunger, deprivation, and an uncertain future to make sure these never recurred and to shield their children, if need be with the headlong aggressiveness of animals protecting their young, from the demon of scarcity that had plagued their parents and robbed them of their own childhoods.

The slow but steady rise in the value of IBM shares spelled the fulfillment of Walter's middle-class dream. The stock's success, which lifted many a Jewish family through the glass ceiling separating the lower-middle from the middle class, strengthened Walter's bourgeois values by endowing them with an objective, pseudoscientific validity. It was ironic, therefore, that the one impulsive, spur-of-the-moment investment he ever made, a purchase of Conair stock against his better judgment, was to determine more than anything the economic fortunes of his family.

What happened next was also taken from a Philip Roth novel. Walter was irritated when Ethel's younger brother Jake, who had landed a job as an assistant broker on Wall Street (the vague nature of which caused Walter to relabel it as "assistant *goniff*"), talked him into buying, on the basis of what he presented as inside information, one hundred shares of Conair for each of his two sons. The stock's subsequently fabled, meteoric rise seriously undermined Walter's view of the world. Although in hindsight it might have seemed predictable, a sensible investment that worked out exceptionally well, it was a poisoned apple for Walter Cohen. Conair's dizzying success raised a specter from the grave that his entire respectable, middle-class life had been a bulwark against: the speculator's dream of easy profits, the eternal mirage of the shtetl's

luftmensch. Chaplinesque, a pauper's wild throw of the dice, such
gambles were the behavior of those ready to bet everything on the
first harebrained scheme to come along because they had nothing
to lose anyway.

But there was no arguing with success. When Jake, by now
an independent broker living with his wife Mira in a nice colonial house on an acre and a half in Scarsdale, recommended one
day that Walter sell Conair and immediately buy, without delay,
all the RTC shares that he could, resistance would have been futile. Since then the years had gone by, the children were grown,
and the mortgage on the New Rochelle house was paid off. Jake,
having traded his black Lincoln for a silver, latest-model Cadillac
and bought a summer place in Cape May, called every few weeks
to chat with Ethel before asking for Walter and recommending the
purchase, without delay, of this or that stock for his sons. Matthew's
and Andrew's portfolios prospered, especially once—for now, too,
success could not be gainsaid—they were put entirely in the hands
of Uncle Jake, who had meanwhile divorced Aunt Mira, married Ms.
Robertson, his twenty-seven-year-old secretary, bought her a Mustang convertible, and moved to a mansion in Greenwich. Inasmuch
as Walter had invested in Jake's tips none of his own hard-earned
money, which he put not in stocks but in the solidest of savings plans
and insurance policies so that his family would have the maximum
protection against illness, accidents, and death that any responsible
husband and father could give it, the paradoxical situation ensued
that his two sons, even before going to college and without having
worked a day in their lives, were richer than forty years of wise, responsible, day-in-and-day-out work had made him.

Walter stayed in the same house, in the same neighborhood he
had raised his children in, even after it lost its charm and began
to deteriorate. An independent man proud of his achievements, he
refused to accept the help that his sons would gladly have given

him, at no great inconvenience to themselves, for the purchase of
a nicer, more modern home. He had even insisted on buying the
assisted living unit in Florida, to whose large, attractive two bedrooms he and Ethel moved after his retirement, entirely with his
own savings, using them to make up for the depreciated value of
the New Rochelle house. Only after his death, when Ethel's Alzheimer's worsened and it was decided to bring her back to New
York, did Andrew and Matthew participate in the cost of a nursing
home—and even then their contribution was largely symbolic,
since together with the medical insurance, the remainder of Walter's savings, the nest egg put away dollar by dollar by a strong,
unyielding man, covered the expense. Their nominal payments,
it sometimes seemed to them, had been carefully planned, like everything else, so that they could chip in at no real cost to themselves. Walter had no more wanted money to be an issue after his
death than before it.

A subject never discussed, Andrew's portfolio remained active
in the investment house. Like a fireplace in winter, it crackled quietly away with a warm flame. Without radically changing his life,
it enhanced it. He lived modestly, or at least modestly enough not
to be a conspicuous spender, getting along for the most part on
his professor's salary, that of a tenured position at a major American university. Yet something about the easy, aristocratic way he
carried himself had a whiff of wealth nonetheless. The confidence
provided by the safety net of his substantial assets helped give him
the aloof, ethereal air of a man so utterly disinterested in financial matters and material possessions that he never even thought of
them. The idea of Andrew P. Cohen dwelling on or even uttering
the word "money" was inconceivable—and it was as odd to picture him depositing a check or coming out of a bank with a wallet
full of bills as it was to think of a monk ordering a meal in a restaurant or buying a ticket for the theater. Imagining him conferring at

length with his investment adviser about increasing the returns on his capital seemed little short of obscene.

This adviser, Mitchell, was an old friend from Berkeley, an ex-California beach boy who had gone through college as a spaced-out rebel with flowers in his curly hair, his hands pawing his latest girlfriend at this or that love-in having more to do with politics than love, only to be reincarnated as a financial genius, a Wall Street wonder child. So vertiginous was Mitchell's ascent in the world of finance that he had no time to lose his winning hippie ways, which included, while schmoozing about underground politics, alternative culture, and ecology, smoking the obligatory joint (the best, homegrown sinsemilla, nothing less) whenever he and Andrew met to discuss investment strategy. It made them feel like they weren't taking the making of money too seriously, turning it into a kind of game.

Rachel, whose own investment portfolio, opened for her by her parents when she was young, made her a financially secure graduate student, toyed for a while with moving her stocks and bonds to a socially and ecologically aware firm that promised to invest none of its clients' money in companies exploiting third-world workers, damaging the environment, ignoring international treaties and regulations, or operating in corrupt and dictatorial countries. The firm's directors, so its promotional literature declared, were prepared to forgo a modest, not unreasonable amount of profit to avoid compromising their own and their clients' beliefs. Rachel's desire to transfer her account, and with it, she implied, her family's, created an awkward situation, since the progressive views she had been raised to hold by her parents clashed with other values, such as loyalty to the family adviser and the need for a responsible managing of funds that were an unearned heirloom. Thinking of them as her own private property to be disposed of as she wished was rather embarrassing, and although Andrew did not openly disapprove of her initiative, she concluded it was best to put it off. This decision came as a relief to her, though not one she was willing to acknowledge.

18

P ark Slope, a neighborhood of well-maintained two-story town houses dating back to the start of the twentieth century, looked lovely as usual. The trees lining its streets were kept neatly pruned, their leaves bright against the brownstone buildings. There were small backyards, front steps flanked by flowerpots, mosaic door-mats, cafés and restaurants, and old jewelry and fashion boutiques. Vibrant and safe, it was an island of upper-middle-class contentment in the gray wilderness of Brooklyn's vast slums. Andrew found a parking spot right across the street from Congregation Beth Elohim—a large, impressive building with Gothic windows and a broad entrance—which was nothing short of an urban miracle.

What a wonderful morning! The balmy air was seasoned with sunshine and the scent of flowers. He felt limber and full of joyful energy, the way one can be made to feel by a glass of chilled white wine in the summer. The unexpected gift of fifteen long minutes was like a sudden, leisurely vacation. He felt an eager sense of an-ticipation that was concentrated for some reason in his mouth, as if he had sniffed a freshly baked pastry or was about to sit down to a holiday meal. The bakery, he thought. I have time to go to the bakery. The word "bakery" aroused in him the ravenous, carefree appetite of a child. Andrew loved his younger daughter, Alison, greatly. The time the two of them spent together was a joy for him. The friendly, liberal-minded arrangement he had with Linda made life easier. It would have been pointless to make the child divide her time between two homes. It wasn't necessary and she wouldn't have liked it, anyway.

Ten to twelve. Andrew clutched the brown paper bag full of baked goods to his chest. The stairway to the synagogue's second floor exhaled its usual cavernous coolness. Muffled sounds of laughter. Children singing. Sounds of prayer. Her classroom was empty. Could they be below, in the sanctuary? Drawings hung on the walls, the names of the children scrawled on them in touchingly uneven letters. Long rows of chest-high coat hangers. Windows with grilles. Hebrew letters on the blackboard. An old wistfulness came over him. A child's hands traveling down a smooth banister. Knees pressed against a hard desk. The square, backward, right-to-left letters. The strange, guttural sound of the *Heth* and the *Kaph*. Blessed art Thou, O Lord. Bagels with cream cheese and jelly. Syrupy orange juice in paper cups. Little League baseball. Dressing rooms. The nice, itchy feeling of the inside of a fielder's glove. Mom's big old wood-paneled Roadmaster that cruised the roads like an old ship. She piloted it like a captain, its big wheel held tightly in her delicate, energetic hands.

"Good morning, Professor Cohen. You're a bit early today." Betty, the secretary, never skipped an honorific in addressing a parent. "The children went to prayer early because we had an emergency evacuation drill, and you know what it's like to get them back upstairs when they love running around so much. It's our third drill this year. That sounds like a lot, I know, but you can't be too careful. You can wait here if you'd like, or else in the small hall on the ground floor. Alison must have taken her things with her. She knows that today is your day to come for her." Betty liked to demonstrate her command of the schedules of the children's families, especially when the parents were divorced or separated.

The sound of singing grew louder as Andrew approached the doors of the sanctuary, chimes of bright laughter punctuating the lilting voices. For a minute, he stood outside the shut door. Then, unable to resist temptation, he peered through its glass panel. A brisk young woman rabbi with a knit yarmulke led the prayer, accompanying herself on a guitar. The children sat in rows on either side of the aisle, in old wooden pews with prayer book racks. The front rows, closer to the podium, were reserved for the younger ones, while those approaching bar and bat mitzvah age sat farther back, pinching and tickling each other or otherwise evincing the disinterest that came with their age. The same smell, the same stained-glass windows with their Judaized neoclassical illustrations of sturdy men with long beards and robes standing in heroic positions, the same Hebraic-looking English letters spelling *Tsedek*, *Emet*, and *Chesed*. Justice, Truth, and Charity. Rabbi Schindler in his three-piece suit and broad, brightly striped tie. Always the same suit and tie. Oreos. The religious families said they had lard and wouldn't let them into their homes. We ate them secretly during prayer. Held them in our mouths without chewing, letting them slowly dissolve on our tongues without moving the jaws so that Rabbi Schindler wouldn't see. I hope Alison doesn't turn around and see me. I'd have killed my mother if she'd done this, peeking through the window to see her. How many years since my bar mitzvah? Thirty-nine, no less.

The tremulous feeling he had had all morning was growing stronger, closer to something like tears or a fever. He had goose pimples. Longing churned in the pit of his stomach. Other eyes and ears were seeing and hearing for him. The singing was becoming more distant, but also very near, clear and uniform. The jangly, unpracticed chords of the guitar grew more harmonious, were joined by the strains of deep, poignantly yearning voices. He felt he was no longer in his body—not entirely, anyway, not enough to keep him from noticing how the real and the unreal had merged. *Golden flecks of light glittered on the walls of the temple. Bright shafts of sunshine streamed in, fiery spears piercing the clouds of incense midway between the gold altar and the ceiling of the sanctuary. The blood stormed in his veins. An aromatic scent swept his nostrils and went to his head. The song rode the incense as a ship at sea rides the waves.* Row after row, the children stood praying, bowing deeply, comically poking each other mischievously with stifled laughs. Andrew stared at them, stirred by the sight of another, primal reality that shone through their fragmentary movements—the Whole that lay behind the broken bits of a vessel that now seemed never to have been smashed. *The temple was bathed in majesty. Multitudes. They filled the gallery. They stood shoulder to shoulder, hardly able to move, yet there was room for them all when they prostrated themselves on the ground, as if space had stretched itself for them. A voice was heard on high. A great voice rumbled like thunder down the desert's declivities to the distant green treetops of Jericho. The voice of the High Priest declaiming the Holy Name on the Day of Atonement. Where was it coming from? It sounded so close. It was coming from within him, from himself! Whence these sounds, these scorched, seething syllables? He was making them! He was uttering the great Name aloud, stressing its consonants and lengthening its vowels as taught to do by the whispering elders, closeted with them in an inner chamber. And when the priests and the multitudes in the gallery heard the awesome and venerable Name emerge whole from the High Priest's mouth in holiness and in purity, then fell they to their knees and upon their faces and did cry: Blessed be the glory of His kingdom forever and ever. Shaken, in a tumult, he thought his heartstrings would snap. Happy is the eye that has seen all this, happy the people that such is its lot.*

The heavy wood doors of the sanctuary swung forcefully open, almost knocking Andrew over as he stood with his eye to the glass panel. He jumped back, abruptly returned to a humdrum reality, his eyes searching wildly for the other, glowing world he had glimpsed through the panel. A strange yet familiar face appeared in front of him. It belonged to a Mediterranean-looking man in his thirties whose designer glasses contrasted risibly with his rough-hewn features. Leaving the sanctuary, he removed the skullcap from his head and tossed it nonchalantly into a basket by the door. For a moment, his and Andrew's glances met, lingered on each other, and passed on. Who could he be? Andrew was sure he knew him from somewhere. The man paused for another fraction of a second, as though debating whether to say something, then thought better of it and turned to the corridor leading to the street. Andrew watched him go, trying to remember where he had seen him. Although he couldn't explain or make sense of it, he felt their encounter had something unusual, perhaps even crucial about it. He thought of the overwhelming pageant he had seen, ejected from it by a swinging door. Who opened doors like that, wham, without thinking who might be on their other side? The man. It was he who had opened it. He was a foreigner, not American. That explained it. An Israeli, he spoke Hebrew! The man from 110th Street with the two playful dogs, one white and one brown. What could he be doing here in Brooklyn? Did he teach Hebrew or something?

"Dad, what are you doing here? Don't you know you're supposed to wait outside?"

Alison. His darling Alison! Dizzy and out of breath, he knelt to give her a hug, blocking the children who now burst through the door, flinging their prayer books onto a growing pile on the table by the door and expertly aiming their colored skullcaps at the basket as if warming up for a game. Although sensing Alison's dismay, Andrew couldn't let go of her and prolonged his embrace. "Come on, let's go, sweetie," he said at last, getting a grip on himself. "Mom is waiting for us."

19

"Hi, Ethel, look who's here!" Jamila, Ethel's private nurse, had a southern accent that seemed perpetually on the verge of laughter. The old woman went on staring unblinkingly ahead of her. If something in her still was able to recognize her visitors, she gave no sign of it. "Hey, baby," Jamila persisted. "Don't be like that. Say hello to your guests. It's Alison! Don't you remember Alison?" She put a thick arm around Ethel, its plump ebony protruding from the sleeve of her starched white uniform, and sat her up in her wheelchair, patting her thinning gray curls with an instinctive, maternal motion. *She treats her like an infant*, thought Andrew not unresentfully. The morning's memory of his mother's delicate hands on the big wheel of the Roadmaster, swinging it left and right with a confidence that seemed boundless to a child, came back to him. Automatically, he glanced at his watch. Three minutes. It happened every month. No sooner had he arrived than he felt a great need to be gone, as though he had been here for hours.

"Good, Bubby, very good." Alison wiped the dribbled applesauce from Ethel's chin. "Want some more? One more spoon, okay?" Ethel's lips remained tightly shut, ignoring the spoon, then opened just enough for Alison to slip it between them. *Eleven years old and she's already feeding her grandmother, all that spittle doesn't bother her*, Andrew thought, ashamed to find himself sitting on the edge of his chair, as if afraid to stain his clothes or catch something. Jamila ate Alison up with proud, endlessly loving eyes. They called each other "baby," too. When did it begin, all that "baby" business? She had already made Jamila promise to come to her bat mitzvah. "Come with Bubby. I want you there, baby, you've got to come." He watched them silently, struck by their feminine devotion that left him outside its circle of compassion. He missed Ethel, missed the keen, peppery person she had been before her Alzheimer's walked off with her—leaving behind the unresponsive old woman sitting motionlessly in her wheelchair and staring past him as if he weren't there. Again he felt the urge to get up and leave. He fought it back uncomfortably, wedging his rear more firmly against the back of his seat.

"O-*kay*, Mr. Cohen, you'll have to excuse us now." Jamila took a towel and clean pair of pajamas from a drawer of the dresser and handed them to Alison, who had lately begun to assist in Ethel's daily bath and now sponged her gently with a washcloth and helped Jamila shampoo her hair. Andrew didn't care for the idea. He had been sure, had even hoped, that the administration would forbid it, only to be told to his surprise by the divisional head that she not only did not object to Alison's participation but was all for encouraging it. Without noticing, she had begun in their meetings to address her remarks more to Alison than to him, turning to her as respectfully as if she were the adult responsible for the patient. While Alison's maturity gave Andrew a kind of confidence in her, it also worried him. She was only eleven. How had she grown up so fast?

Jamila bent to lift Ethel from the wheelchair. In the nurse's arms, his mother resembled a pale, pink-eyelidded baby bird peering out from a black nest. Alison ran to open the bathroom door and the strapping nurse carried Ethel's frail little body through it like an infant's. Now, too, Andrew had to control himself, this time to keep from whisking Alison urgently away, as if there were some imminent danger or ill omen in the old woman's withered, moribund body. Never seen by him in the bathtub, he imagined it floating on a layer of soap bubbles, its white, shriveled skin hanging loose. Feeling a helpless anguish, a bitter longing for his lost mother, he tore himself from his seat, slipped into the hallway, and walked eagerly to the cafeteria like a man who hadn't eaten or drunk all day. He had been in it many times, invariably fleeing to it even though its coffee was mediocre and its pastries weren't fresh. It happened on every visit. The admonishing pangs of his hunger for life would make him suddenly crave choice coffee, expensive wine, red meat. Sometimes, sipping the cafeteria's acrid, lukewarm brew, he dreamed of dapper suits, oceanic cruises, even a sporty new convertible, or else experienced sudden and bizarrely intense sexual desires. Uncharacteristically ogling the young nurses, he had feverish, pornographic thoughts that left him with a bad feeling and a sour taste in his mouth. He glanced at his watch: fifteen minutes. Only fifteen minutes since arriving! He couldn't go on sitting here any longer. He had to go outside, to the lawn, for a breath of fresh air.

Andrew sat on a wooden bench at one end of the lawn, his untouched coffee getting cold in its Styrofoam cup, his eyes roaming over the sea of naked branches below the nursing home. It was a private, expensive, well-run institution, one of the best in Westchester. His mother had loved Westchester no less than did his father. She hated Florida, too. What had ever made them move? It was totally absurd.

Feeling vulnerable and on edge, he took deep, regular breaths, trying to calm himself. His head spun with the jetsam of memory, the flotsam of thought, the driftwood of emotion. They coursed through it as though on a river on which floated words from a half-remembered song. Stubborn and elusive, they bobbed up and down, surfacing and sinking on the restless water: an old song, taken from some musical that hadn't played in years or a radio program that had stopped being listened to long ago. What was it? What was its name? It suddenly seemed the key to everything. If only he could remember its words. *Why haven't I told you?* Where was that from? What time was it? Half an hour already. He had better get back.

Ethel sat on the bed with her back to the door. Her green pajamas, which buttoned in the back, were half-open, revealing a broad triangle of naked skin. Jamila had just finished massaging her back with baby oil. "It keeps her from getting bed sores," she explained to Alison, who nodded seriously. Andrew approached slowly, his eyes on his mother's bare back that was slowly disappearing behind the green pajama top with every button that Jamila deftly did up. "Come, baby, help me comb her hair. Easy does it, baby, easy does it. She doesn't like knots in her hair." The thick fingers ran nimbly through Ethel's thin gray hair, plaiting pickaninny curls. "I sometimes do this for her. She likes it. You see? Like this! Next time, baby, I'll make them for you, too. Look how pretty Ethel is today. Isn't she, Alison?" Andrew circled the bed, staring at the old woman lying there. He stiffened as though from an electric shock. Eyes shut and head thrown back like a petted baby, she was loving it. A slight, live, almost impish smile played over her thin lips. For a moment, just for a moment, she looked like his mother again, like Ethel.

20

Five p.m. Time to head home. Alison fell asleep in the front seat, curled on her side, one arm hiding her face. Although he couldn't be sure, she seemed to be sucking her thumb like she did as a toddler. Appearing from nowhere, heavy, leaden, low-lying clouds hung over the car. Andrew drove silently. He didn't want to turn on the radio. It might wake Alison, and besides, he didn't want any outside noises. The loaded silence was good for him. He needed peace and quiet. The stubborn fragment of the melody that had haunted him all afternoon wouldn't leave him alone. Something unremembered, unsolved, was at work. *Why haven't I told you?* The hungry craving felt in the nursing home had abated, leaving the emptiness of the drive back, which made his body ache as if coming down with the flu or getting out of bed after a sleepless night. *I've told every little star.* A round, heavy raindrop fell on the windshield directly in front of him. Another and another followed. The rain beat down, knocking on the windows desperately, humanly, as if begging to be let into the car. Although his field of vision was blurred, he didn't bother to turn on the wipers and let the unimpeded sheets of rain run down the windshield. *Why haven't you told me?* Ethel was dancing with Rachel in her arms, singing to her. *I've told every little star just how sweet I think you are.* A sentimental, artfully naive song, possibly a lullaby or children's rhyme.

I've told every little star
Just how sweet I think you are.
Why haven't I told you?

He was aching, aching all over. The memory jabbed like a needle. Twenty-five years. The melody wavered, not in sync, like the sound track of an old movie.

I've told ripples in a brook,
Made my heart an open book,
Why haven't I told you?

The beautiful voice she had had. Had she ever thought of being a singer when she was young? Or an actress? She never talked about it. She never talked about such things at all. Never. But wasn't that everyone's dream back then? Broadway, Hollywood, the klieg lights. She was a redhead, smoked, liked boys, loved to dance. Her delicate, fragile-looking hands on the wheel, gripping it tightly, steering the old Roadmaster determinedly down the wet, winding road.

> *Friends ask me am I in love,*
> *I always answer yes,*
> *Might as well confess,*
> *If the answer's yes.*

Cheek to soft baby's cheek, cradling her in a slow dance, singing with her eyes shut. Rachel's open eyes blind, unseeing, as if trying to hear with them, to take in all she could of Grandma's pretty song.

> *Maybe you may love me too.*
> *Oh, my darling, if you do,*
> *Why haven't you told me?*

His eyes smarted, their ducts filling with tears. Everything wanted out: the regret, the compassion, the guilt. Why guilt? Guilt for what? Time had been allowed to go its way as if it meant nothing. No attempt was made to stop it. None! Now it was too late. It was over. Mom was dead. Her skin was thin enough to see through. Little pickaninny curls in her gray, matted hair. Another minute and his heart would break. Too late to do anything. What a rain. He mustn't wake the child. If only I could cry now.

END OF BOOK THREE

[Leviticus Chaper 15, Verses 6—7] And if the flow of seed go out from a man, then he shall bathe all his flesh in water, and be unclean until the even. And every garment, and every skin, whereon is the flow of seed, shall be washed with water, and be unclean until the even.

[Deuteronomy; Chapter 23, Verses 11—12] If there be among you any man that is not clean by reason of that which chanceth him by night, then shall he go abroad out of the camp, he shall not come within the camp. But it shall be, when evening cometh on, he shall bathe himself in water; and when the sun is down, he may come within the camp.

[Mishna, Treatise Yoma, Chapter 1, Mishna 4] Throughout the seven days they did not withhold food or drink from him. But on the eve of the Day of Atonement near nightfall they would not let him eat much because food brings about sleep.

[Babylonian Talmud, Treatise Yoma, Folio 18a] THROUGHOUT THE SEVEN DAYS THEY DID NOT WITHHOLD etc. It has been taught: Rabbi Judah Ben Nakussa said: One fed him [cakes] of fine flour and eggs in order to produce [speedy] elimination. They answered him: Thus you will induce the more excitement. Symmachus said in the name of Rabbi Meir: One does not feed him [. . .] citron, nor eggs, nor aged wine. And, according to others, [. . .] neither citron, nor eggs, nor fatty meat, nor aged wine; some say neither white wine because white wine induces impurity in man [i.e., may cause him to have a nocturnal emission].
Eleazar Ben Phinehas said in the name of Rabbi Judah Ben Bathyra: One does not feed him milk, nor cheese, nor eggs, nor wine: [. . .] neither soup of pounded beans, nor fatty meat, nor muries [a brine or pickle containing fish hash and sometimes wine]. "Nor any other foods that induce impurity"——What is that meant to include?——It is meant to include what our Rabbis taught: Five things induce impurity in man, they are as follows: garlic, pepperwort, purslane, eggs, and garden-rocket.

The priestly elders went off to their homes, for the day was waning and they had yet to eat the last meal before the fast that would give them strength on the morrow. On a word from the Superior, a table of gold and seat of fine linen were brought to the High Priest's chambers. Bread and water were set before him with condiments of herbs and olives to cool his body's humors, lest he fall into a deep sleep and pollute himself with a nocturnal emission. He ate and blessed God for the food, his eyelids drooping, for he had been awake much of the previous night and had stood long hours in the hot sun. Although he was permitted to drowse a bit to restore himself, no sooner did his head drop to his chest and his breathing grow heavy than a young priest snapped two fingers in his ears, waking him as though bitten by a snake.

[Babylonian Talmud, Treatise Yoma, Folio 88a] A scholar recited before Rav Nahman: "To one who experienced a [nocturnal] pollution on the Day of Atonement, all sins will be forgiven." But it was taught: All his sins will be arranged before him?——What does 'arranged' mean? His sins are arranged to be forgiven. In the School of Rabbi Ishmael it was taught: One who experienced a [nocturnal] pollution on the Day of Atonement, let him be anxious throughout the year, and if he survives the year, he is assured of being worthy of the world to come. Rabbi Nahman ben Isaac said: You may know it [from the fact that] while the rest of the world is hungry, he is satisfied. When Rav Dimi came, he said: He will live long, thrive, and beget many children.

[Mishna, Treatise Yoma, Chapter 1, Mishna 7] If he sought to slumber, young priests would snap their middle finger before him and say: Sir High Priest, arise and drive the sleep away this once on the pavement. They would keep him amused until the time for the slaughtering [of the daily morning offering] would approach. If he was a sage he would expound, and if not, the disciples of the sages would expound before him. If he was familiar with reading [the Scriptures] he would read. If not, they would read before him. From what would they read before him? From Job, Ezra, and Chronicles. Zechariah ben Kubetal said: Often have I read before him from Daniel.

[Babylonian Talmud, Treatise Berakhot, Folio 3b] Rabbi Oshaia, in the name of Rav Aha, said: King David said: Midnight never passed me by in my sleep. Rav Zera says: Till midnight he used to slumber [lightly] as does a horse, from

[Babylonian Talmud, Treatise Yoma, Folio 19b] IF HE SOUGHT TO SLUMBER, YOUNG PRIESTS WOULD SNAP THEIR MIDDLE FINGER BEFORE HIM [...] Rabbi Huna demonstrated it [the snapping of the middle finger] and its sound could be heard in the whole academy. AND THEY WOULD SAY: SIR HIGH PRIEST, ARISE AND DRIVE THE SLEEP AWAY THIS ONCE. Rabbi Isaac said: [Show us] something new. What was that?——They said to him: Show us how one performs the *kiddah*. [Commentators: And what was the *kiddah*? Pressing both big toes against the floor, bowing and kissing the pavement, and rising without moving the feet——this difficult performance was called the *kiddah*——the bowing to the ground.]

AND THEY WOULD KEEP HIM AMUSED UNTIL THE TIME FOR THE SLAUGHTERING WOULD APPROACH. A Tanna taught: They kept him amused neither with the harp nor with the lyre, but with the mouth. What were they singing? Except the Lord build a house, they labor in vain that build it. Some of the worthiest of Jerusalem did not go to sleep all the night in order that the High Priest might hear the reverberating noise, so that sleep should not overcome him suddenly.

From now on, he was allowed to sleep no more. Each time he was about to nod off he was told, "My liege the High Priest, stand for a minute on the floor," and the chill of the cold marble awakened him. He shivered and sneezed, and the Superior whispered to Obadiah: "The man is delicate. He mustn't catch cold. When you draw his ritual bath in the morning, mix it with hot water so that he comes to no harm." The High Priest's shoulders were covered with a woolen shawl and a scribe read to him stirring passages from the books of Ezra and Job. Not that he couldn't have read them himself, but the Superior said, "Let others read to him. He'll need his voice tomorrow and mustn't strain it." All night long the High Priest was kept occupied. The young priests sang him psalms about the Temple, such as the one that begins *Except the Lord build the house, they labor in vain that build it.* As the darkness deepened, the night's air was filled with the sound of study and prayer. The nobles of Jerusalem rose from their beds at midnight and recited their lesson loudly, in order that the High Priest might hear their voices and not be overcome by sleep.

thence on he rose with the force of a lion. Rav Ashi says: Till midnight he studied the Torah, from thence on he recited songs and praises. [...] But how did David know the exact time of midnight? [...] David had a sign. For so said Rav Aha bar Bizana in the name of Rabbi Simeon the Pious: A harp was hanging above David's bed. As soon as midnight arrived, a north wind came and blew upon it and it played of itself. He then arose immediately and studied the Torah till the break of dawn.

The Gate of Rebirth:

Know, however, that a perfected Vital Soul that is reborn so that it may be conjoined with an Intellectual Soul can no longer be damaged by its possessor's sins and need not itself return to earth because of them. Rather, the damage is to the Intellectual Soul alone and henceforth the two souls must continue to be reborn together until the Intellectual Soul is perfected, whereupon they are joined by the Spiritual Soul. Similarly, if their possessor now sins again, it is the Spiritual Soul alone that is damaged, as was previously so with the Intellectual Soul.

[Mishna, Treatise Yoma, Chapter 3, Mishna 1] The officer said to them: go forth and see whether the time for slaughtering [of the morning sacrifice] has arrived. If it had arrived, then he who saw it said: It is daylight! Mathia ben Samuel said: [Thus would the officer ask:] The whole east is alight. Even unto Hebron? And he answered yes. [Ibid. 3:2] And why was that [considered] necessary? Because once, when the light of the moon rose, they thought that the east was alight and slaughtered the continual offering, which afterward they had to take away into the place of burning.

[Mishna, Treatise Yoma, Chapter 1, Mishna 8] Every day one would remove [the ashes from] the altar at the cockcrow or about that time, either before or after. But on the Day of Atonement at midnight, and on the feasts at the first watch, and before the cockcrow approached, the Temple Court was full of Israelites.

[Babylonian Talmud, Treatise Yoma, Folio 21a] Rab Judah said in the name of Rab: When the Israelites come up [to Jerusalem] for the festivals, they stand pressed together, but they prostrate themselves, with wide spaces [between them], and they extend eleven cubits behind the back wall of the Holy of Holies. What does that mean? It means that although they extended eleven cubits behind the back wall of the Holy of Holies, standing pressed together, yet when they prostrated themselves, they prostrated themselves with wide spaces [between them]. This is one of the ten miracles that were wrought in the Temple, for we have learned: Ten miracles were wrought in the Temple: No woman miscarried from the scent of the holy flesh; the holy [i.e., sacrificial] flesh never became putrid; no fly was ever seen in the slaughterhouse; no pollution ever befell the High Priest on the Day of Atonement; no rain ever quenched the fire of the wood-pile on the altar; neither did the wind ever overcome the column of smoke that arose therefrom; nor was there ever found any disqualifying

The first watch of the night made way for the middle watch and the middle watch for the last watch. The cooled ashes of the previous day's sacrifices were cleared from the altar. Dawn had not yet broken. Every minute seemed to last an hour. The elderly priests, fearful of the Day of Judgment, thought: "Would it were morning and we could begin to do the deeds that will save us from the fires of Judgment!" The young priests, anxious to get started, thought: "Would it were morning and we could perform what we have studied and see the High Priest at his work!" Obadiah, too, was impatient. "Would it were morning," he thought, "and we could know, for better or worse, what manner of man this is!" Only the High Priest remained tranquil. If he was concerned with what the dawning day would bring, he showed no sign of it.

At last the cock crowed and the Superior said to Obadiah, "Go see if it is time for the dawn sacrifice." Obadiah stepped outside to look at the sky and reported, "The morning star has risen!" "Wait a moment and look again," the Superior told him. Obadiah waited, looked again, and saw that the dawn was breaking. "There's light in the east!" he called out. "Does it reach as far as Hebron?" asked the Superior. "Yes, as far as Hebron," he replied. The Superior rose and said, "My liege the High Priest, it is daylight! The time has come for the day's first offering."

defect in the *omer* or in the two loaves, or in the shewbread; though the people stood closely pressed together, they still found wide spaces between them to prostrate themselves; never did serpent or scorpion injure anyone in Jerusalem, nor did any man ever say to his fellow: The place is too narrow for me to stay overnight in Jerusalem [. . .] There are two more [miracles wrought] in the Temple. For it has been taught: Never did rains quench the fire of the pile of wood on the altar; and as for the smoke arising from the pile of wood, even if all the winds of the world came blowing, they could not divert it from its wonted place.

[Leviticus, Chapter 16, Verses 3—4] Herewith shall Aaron come into the holy place: with a young bullock for a sin-offering, and a ram for a burnt-offering. He shall put on the holy linen tunic, and he shall have the linen breeches upon his flesh, and shall be girded with the linen girdle, and with the linen miter shall he be attired; they are the holy garments; and he shall bathe his flesh in water, and put them on.

[Mishna, Treatise Yoma, Chapter 3, Mishna 4.] The High Priest was led down to the place of immersion. [...] He stripped off [his garments], went down and immersed himself, came up and dried himself. They brought him the golden garments. He put them on and sanctified his hands and feet. They brought him the continual offering, he made the required cut, and someone else finished it for him. He received the blood and sprinkled it.

[Mishna, Treatise Yoma, Chapter 3, Mishna 5] If the High Priest was either old or of delicate health, warm water would be prepared for him and poured into the cold, to mitigate its coldness.

[Babylonian Talmud, Treatise Yoma, Folio 31a] FIVE IMMERSIONS AND TEN SANCTIFICATIONS: Our Rabbis taught: The High Priest underwent five immersions and ten sanctifications on that day, all of them on holy ground, in the Parwah Cell, with the exception of the first, which took place on profane ground, on top of the Water Gate, lying at the side of his [private] chamber. [...] And he shall bathe all his flesh in water, i.e., in the waters of a ritual bath, in water which covers his whole body.

Even before the cock's crow, the Levites and priests had been called to their positions and the Gallery of Israel was full. The crowd stood pressed together, all eyes on the High Priest as he was led to the ablution pool at the Hide Skinner's Quarters. The young priests brought large vessels of warm water and emptied them into the ritual bath. They spread a linen sheet between him and the onlookers, who stared at the ground for an extra measure of modesty, and the High Priest undressed, bathed, and dried himself. He donned gold vestments and washed his hands and feet in a golden basin. The morning's sacrifice was brought to him. For a second, he stood with his knife as if debating. Then he roused himself, gripped the animal firmly, and slit its throat in the prescribed manner. Leaving the cut to an attending priest to finish, he hurried to catch the blood in a gold stoup.

[Babylonian Talmud, Treatise Yoma, Folio 32a] Rabbi said: Whence do we know that the High Priest had to undergo five immersions and ten sanctifications on that day? Because it is said: He shall put on the holy linen tunic, and he shall have the linen breeches upon his flesh, and shall be girded with the linen girdle, and with the linen miter shall he be attired; they are the holy garments; and he shall bathe his flesh in water, and put them on. Hence you learn that whosoever changes from service to service requires an immersion. Moreover, it says, "They are the holy garments," thus putting all the garments on the same level. Now there are five services; the continual offering of dawn, [performed] in the golden garments: the service of the day [the Day of Atonement], in linen garments; of his [the High Priest's] and the people's ram, in the golden garments; [the taking out] of the censer and coal pan, in white garments; the continual evening offering in the golden garments.

[Mishna, Treatise Yoma, Chapter 3, Mishna 4.] He went inside to smoke the incense of the morning and to trim the lamps; [afterward] to offer up the head and the limbs and the pan-cakes and the wine-offering.

[Mishna, Treatise Yoma, Chapter 3, Mishna 5] The morning incense was offered up between the blood and the limbs, the afternoon [incense] between the limbs and the drink-offerings.

[Jeremiah, Chapter 3, Verses 14—17] Return, O backsliding children, saith the LORD; for I am a lord unto you, and I will take you one of a city, and two of a family, and I will bring you to Zion; and I will give you shepherds according to My heart, who shall feed you with knowledge and understanding. And it shall come to pass, when ye are multiplied and increased in the land, in those days, saith the LORD, they shall say no more: The ark of the covenant of the LORD; neither shall it come to mind; neither shall they make mention of it; neither shall they miss it; neither shall it be made anymore. At that time they shall call Jerusalem the throne of the LORD; and all the nations shall be gathered unto it, to the name of the LORD, to Jerusalem; neither shall they walk anymore after the stubbornness of their evil heart.

From that moment, the High Priest had no time to think. He hurried from task to task, sprinkling blood on the altar, burning incense, trimming the wicks of the candelabrum, placing the head and legs of the slaughtered animals on the fire, and offering the flour cakes and wine. Thousands of eyes bore into him. No one spoke even in a whisper. Every tongue cleaved to its mouth in fear of God's judgment. Suppose the High Priest's hand trembled on the knife and spoiled the sacrifice? Suppose he stumbled or forgot what he had been taught by the elders? Suppose he were a heretic who deliberately made changes, leaving the people unatoned for and abandoned to a year of tribulations? The very air in the Temple was like the finest glass vessel that can shatter to pieces at a mere sound.

[Mishna, Treatise Yoma, Chapter 5, Mishna 7] Concerning every ministration of the Day of Atonement mentioned in the prescribed order: if one service was done out of order before another one, it is as if it had not been done at all. If he sprinkled the blood of the he-goat before the blood of the bullock, he must start over again, sprinkling the blood of the he-goat after the blood of the bullock. If before he had finished the sprinklings within [the Holy of Holies] the blood was poured away, he must bring other blood, starting over again and sprinkling again within [the Holy of Holies]. Likewise, in matters of the Sanctuary and the Golden Altar, since they are each a separate act of atonement. Rabbi Eleazar and Rabbi Simeon say: wherever he stopped, there he must begin again.

[Babylonian Talmud, Treatise Hagigah, Folio 15a] After his apostasy, Aher asked Rabbi Meir: "What is the meaning of the verse: 'Gold and glass cannot equal it; neither shall the exchange thereof be vessels of fine gold?'" He answered: "These are the words of the Torah, which are hard to acquire, like vessels of fine gold, but are easily destroyed like vessels of glass." Said [Aher] to him: "Rabbi Akiba, thy master, did not explain thus, but [as follows]: 'Just as vessels of gold and vessels of glass, though they be broken, have a remedy, even so a scholar, though he has sinned, has a remedy.'" [Thereupon, Rabbi Meir] said to him: "Then, thou, too, repent!" He replied: "I have already heard from behind the Veil: 'Return ye backsliding children——except Aher.'"

The Gate of Rebirth:

Now it may happen that the Vital Soul, in the course of being perfected, is refined to such a high degree that it is not required to be reborn with the Intellectual Soul. In such a case, it remains bound in the Bond of Life and the unperfected Intellectual Soul is reborn without it. Yet since the Intellectual Soul cannot exist on earth by itself, it must be conjoined with another Vital Soul until it is perfect. Only then may it be reborn with its original Vital Soul, after which the two can be rejoined to their Spiritual Soul, which must run the same course. It may also happen, however, that the Intellectual and Spiritual Souls are perfected apart from their original Vital Soul and reunited with it only once they are perfected, whereupon all three dwell together in the Bond of Life.

BOOK
FOUR

1
March 6, 2001

The 11th of Adar, 5761

One p.m. Andrew entered the apartment, carrying two large, brown paper bags while pushing ahead of him, with one foot, a case of wine that the delivery guy from Martin Brothers had left with the doorman. The spotless apartment smelled pleasantly of detergents and air fresheners: Angie had finished cleaning early, leaving him to enjoy in solitude his favorite pastime of making dinner for guests. It was too bad Ann Lee wouldn't be there. She had left the day before with her ensemble for the West Coast—for a long time, almost two weeks. Not that she would have come anyway. Lately, she had avoided what she called his "adult evenings," sparing them both the discomfort of appearing together in public.

A wave of longing swept over him. Desire, like God, was in the details. A few days ago he happened to glance inside her pocketbook, stirred by the sight of her touchingly small, almost girlish bra, folded next to a dog-eared copy of *The House upon the Top of the Mountain* and an alluringly forbidden red pack of cigarettes. Now, though, the deliciously long amount of time spent at the meat counter, vegetable racks, and wine shelves had aroused the inner chef in him. It would be a fabulous feast: a deboned, largely cubed leg of lamb, lavishly seasoned with cinnamon, cardamom, white pepper, and powdered ginger, braised with carrots, white raisins, and halved walnuts; served on a bed of homemade couscous; a small salad with a simple olive oil vinaigrette; a crisp, fruity Alsatian Riesling with the main course; and a nice, deeply golden Sauterne with the dessert—an upside-down apple tart, a tarte tatin with subtle hints of cinnamon and cardamom as to continue the arc of flavor, served with a scoop of ice cream.

Andrew kicked off his shoes, put the bags on the counter, went to the bedroom to change into shorts and a T-shirt, and returned barefoot to the kitchen, eager to get started. First came the wine. He opened the case and took out the bottles, putting some in the wine cooler and the rest in the pantry. It was a common mistake, especially in America, to chill white wine to death. An hour or two in the cooler was all that was needed, especially with such a fine Riesling. Uncorking a bottle, he poured himself a bit and left the glass on the counter; he liked pre-tasting the wines he planned to serve with the food. Next came the music. Choosing a CD, he slipped it into the slot of the player. Marvelous, simply marvelous! And now to work.

Although the recipe called for marinating the lamb overnight, Andrew, reluctant to overpower it, had put half up the previous evening and half that morning. Taking the cubes of now slightly grayish meat, he laid them on a paper towel to dry while pouring the equally gray-colored marinade into a pot. He would bring it to boil and let it simmer until it had partially steamed off, leaving a rich stock to bring out the best in the meat and vegetables that would stew in it.

The violins played a sweeping passage. Andrew caught himself humming along and smiled: humming or whistling while he worked was a sign of concentration. Yet it was not the same once he grew conscious of doing it, and he stopped after a few more bars, a bit embarrassed. He sipped some warm wine (it was truly

a first-rate Riesling, with a hint of melon and a faint herbal aroma
that was just right for this time of year), took a handful of couscous, and scattered it carefully in a big, handsome skillet whose
heat-retaining copper surface hardly needed any cooking fat. He
wanted to toast the couscous a bit before steaming it, to lend it a
nutty, almost smoky, touch. Couscous was a delicate grain. If allowed to sponge up even a bit of oil, it lost its lightness and turned
greasy.

The toasting couscous filled the kitchen with its subtle aroma.
It was done: half a minute more and it would be brown and overcooked. Emptying its contents into a large glass bowl, he carried
the skillet to the sink and let it hiss beneath the faucet. He scrubbed
it, wiped it lightly, and put it back on the burner for the lamb. This
was the moment that demanded the most concentration. The meat
needed to be charred on the outside without drying out on the inside; a few seconds made all the difference between a sublime and
a mediocre dish. Andrew took another sip of wine, put down his
glass, scooped up some coarse salt, studied the lamb spread out on
a tray, and dashed the salt over it with an experienced, theatrical
flair. Alone, he could play the role of the master chef to his heart's
content.

The skillet sputtered with the savory odor of browned meat,
conjuring up seemingly lost Sunday memories of Walter Cohen
standing by the large grill in their backyard, like a captain at the
helm of his ship, turning hot dogs, steaks, and hamburgers with
the intensity—surprising in such an unsensual, almost ascetic a
man—of someone engaged in a solemn ceremony whose rules are
known to him alone.

Andrew seldom thought of his father while cooking, but this
time the memory was strangely vivid. What could have evoked it?
The sweet, grassy smell of the searing lamb was so different from
the overpowering odor of the all-American beef Walter grilled so

proudly. It was hard, almost oxymoronic, to imagine Walter grill-
ing anything as exotic and subtle as Mediterranean marinated lamb
in their New Rochelle backyard.

The cubed lamb sizzled on the hot brassy surface of the skillet,
crisping at the edges and turning an appetizing amber. He and his
father had been so unlike each other, so different. The meat was beginning to smoke thickly; it was time to turn it before it blackened
and grew bitter. Deftly, Andrew flipped the chunks of lamb in the
pan. They were almost ready to be taken out and to make way for
the carrots. More images drifted through his mind, borne on the
savor of the meat like puffs of cloud on a spring breeze. Escaping
the confines of the New Rochelle yard, they changed texture and
hue, taking him to a vast sandy sea of yellows and grays. *Large,
crudely cut gemstones were embedded in a heavy breastplate of burnished gold, glowing in the desert sun like small, mysterious-looking,
celestial orbs.* Where was this place? Where was all this light coming from? The meat was done. Andrew, rudely awakened from
his daydream, quickly transferred the browned pieces to a platter
waiting by the stove. *The golden bells rang with a gentle, tranquiliz-
ing chime, a sound clearer and purer than any he had ever heard.* The
meat, still faintly sizzling, lay piled on its platter. Now the carrots
crackled in the skillet, frizzing in the hot oil while soaking up the
meat's flavor and scent. *The tinkle of bells heralded the arrival of the
priest in the sanctuary, alerting God and man to his presence. Golden
bells, pomegranate-shaped orbs of purple and scarlet. A golden bell and
a pomegranate, a golden bell and a pomegranate, upon the hem of the
robe round about.* A sweet scent wafted in his nostrils, inducing a
dreamy wakefulness. *Thin cakes of meal anointed with oil. A bullock and two rams.* The meat exuded its pink juices on the counter.
Excellent: that meant it was still tender inside. The sound of the
frying carrots grew louder, dulling his senses like static. He leaned
over the bowl and dipped two fingers in the warm bloody liquid to

check the seasoning before putting the meat into the oven. They were halfway to his mouth when, with a fascination that made no sense of what it saw, he found himself staring at them rubbing the lucent blood against his thumb. His right earlobe itched. Unthinkingly, he scratched it and smeared it with blood. From somewhere came a great tumult, the noise of a crowd—and in it, a small, still voice. *Flaxen tent flaps glimmered in the sunlight. Ribbons of indigo and scarlet, twined from fine linen, shone brightly against the drab desert.* Excited yet apprehensive, he disbelievingly bent and daubed the reddish liquid on the big toe of his right foot. *The bleats of animals about to be slaughtered mingled with the throng's singing and cries.* Where was it coming from? What language was it? Definitely not Latin, it wasn't ancient Greek, either. It was harsh-sounding, guttural, gritty with sand and splintered rock. Unknown sensations ran powerfully through him. *The tent flaps billowed in the desert breeze. Inside them, in a tenebrous light, the tent's golden fastenings glistened in blue loops like stars in a summer sky.*

There was an acrid smell of burning. The carrots! Startled, Andrew snapped out of his trance, frantically eyeing the smoking skillet. The strips at its center were nicely done, but the blackened ones at the edges would give the dish a harsh, carbonized taste. Whisking the skillet from the fire, he quickly fished the burned carrots from the bubbling oil. The desert was gone; gone the glitter of gold, the hypnotic gleam of the gemstones, the dreamlike tinkle of the bells. The white wall tiles of the stove's backsplash reflected his image in broken, Cubist planes. The last strains of sound receded. Some citrine-colored wine remained at the bottom of his glass. What had just happened? If not for the sticky semidried blood on his right thumb, earlobe, and big toe, he could have sworn it was nothing but an illusion. He emptied the glass and poured himself a bit more wine. The carrots needed to be removed from the oil before they got soggy, but he stood watching them shrivel darkly in the fatty fluid, absorbing more of it with each passing moment.

Four o'clock. Inside the lit oven, the meat and vegetables, well seasoned and garnished with raisins and crushed walnuts, were cradled peacefully in a heavy, fruit-and-floral-patterned ceramic pot purchased in Italy years ago. Beside it, the tarte tatin silently simmered beneath its topping of cinnamon, cardamom, brown sugar, and calvados. Andrew expertly moistened the couscous. In place of the butter, he preferred the expensive olive oil he kept for special occasions, which gave the grain a buoyant freshness. Before serving, he would steam it in a wicker steamer to make it warm and fluffy. The fresh greens were tossed but not dressed; he didn't want them to get soggy and overpowered by the vinaigrette. But while his hands were busy with the crispy, doughy semolina, his heart was no longer in it. He was going through the motions, but the ritual felt stale. The last of the wine he had poured had not been drunk. Something of his eerie vision, though it was mostly forgotten, still lingered. What could it have been? Fatigue and overstimulation, he supposed. Such things happened all the time. Usually, the conscious mind overlooked and repressed them. Waking and sleeping, after all, were a single continuum, not separate, discrete states. But what language had it been? He had never heard it before. Where had all those scenes come from? Some Turkish or Iranian movie he had seen? God only knows. He finished kneading the couscous, washed his hands thoroughly, wiped the counter clean, and piled the dishes in the sink. He still had to shower and change, and the table wasn't yet set. The guests were coming at seven.

2

March 22, 2001

The 27th of Adar, 5761

D o you remember how you surprised me that time, Andy, on our first anniversary?" Linda was curled up cozily on the couch, her feet beneath the white woolen wrap that usually lay, carefully folded, on an armrest. Winter or summer, her feet were always cold. "Early that morning you took the table out to a field in the middle of nowhere and set it with sterling silver and china and crystal, like in a fancy restaurant. There was even champagne in an ice bucket, all comme il faut. And white roses. We never cared for red. Everything was so beautiful! It was so romantic, so perfect. You made me happy, happier than I ever had dreamed I could be!"

Why had she suddenly remembered all this after twenty-five years? "Memories have their own laws. They're no more related to the events they originated in than the US dollar is to the gold bars, kept in the famous safes of Fort Knox, that once backed it and were its iconic symbol." No, something was wrong with that last sentence. Iconic symbol? Linda never used those words, never thought in them. *Those are my words! It's a dream, I'm dreaming!*

This realization, however, did not cause Andrew to awake, at least not at once. He clung to the pleasantness of the dream, loath to part with its sweet intimacy. When he opened his eyes at last, the bedroom was dark except for a narrow band of reddish light beneath the not fully lowered blinds. Ann Lee was lying on the far side of the bed, nestled in the ruffled sheets like a tiny, naked nestling. He looked away from her and shut his eyes again, trying unsuccessfully to revive his dream and reenter its warm, brightly lit space. That lovingly set table in the flowering meadow, bright in the afternoon light like an advertisement for promise! How happy Linda had been!

Yet something was nagging him, clouding the almost too bright glow of it. Their first anniversary? Rachel was eight months old. He was totally involved in finishing his dissertation. They were living in Brooklyn, in the little apartment in Park Slope from which they moved to their own house a year later. Why couldn't he remember their first anniversary? The wonderful table, the sense of bliss—had it really been then? Could it be that it never had happened? But it had to have! He couldn't have made it up! His dream had been there all along, like a secret room behind a hidden door. He needed only to find the door and open it to resolve what was nagging him—to resolve all the nagging questions there were.

He opened his eyes again. They were getting used to the darkness. The room no longer looked so strange. *No, it hadn't happened. Never.* There had been no table, no silver, no crystal. No roses, either. He had never courted Linda that romantically, not before their wedding and certainly not after it. The wedding itself had been perfectly ordinary. Back then, no one made much of such things. The ceremony was nondescript, almost cynical: an early morning visit to City Hall, a few comically mumbled lines with the famous "I do!" of movies and TV shows, a hurried breakfast afterward. He could at least have brought her a bouquet of roses. White or red, what did it matter? Even playing it for laughs would have been better than nothing. Forget the roses. Twenty-five cents' worth of miserable carnations would have done the trick, too. True, there was a party. On Steve and Marney's roof. Linda wore a white Indian gown that billowed charmingly—she was in her fifth month—over her belly. As parties went, it was a nice one. Still, it was only a party. They had never had a real wedding, of the kind that feeds the flame of nostalgia in years to come. None of their friends wanted a big, old-fashioned wedding back then, it felt so bourgeois, so old. And yet why does he feel so sad, after so many years and all that had happened between them? Was it guilt? Absolutely not! He had no reasons for guilt. She wasn't the only one who had suffered. They both had paid a heavy—a very heavy—price. It was too late to do anything about it, anyway.

His sadness deepened, feeling infinite. If the dam holding it back were to burst, nothing would stand in its way. He threw a worried glance at Ann Lee, as if fearful his inner monologue might wake her. *Please, let her sleep!* He really couldn't deal with her right now. A sharp, angular shoulder protruded from the satin sheet. A skinny little bird. *Please!* There was a salty, burning lump in his throat. He felt an involuntary tremor. *Breathe deep. Breathe deep. Whatever you do, don't wake her.*

3

April 6, 2001

The 13th of Nisan, 5761

Springtime. As it does every year, April is already driving the city to distraction with the overwhelming feeling of desire, lighting the flames of yellow daffodils, deep red tulips, and pinkish-white magnolias. With any luck, their heady display will last for a few weeks before being quenched by spring rains and May breezes, followed by the insufferable heat of a summer that seems to arrive earlier with each passing year.

Andrew was happy to skip the family Passover Seder. Linda's decision to have it at Cora's had given him the perfect excuse. It was always the same: the sweet Kiddush wine, the summer-camp songs, the strained discussions about freedom and memory. He needed a break from it, and he made up his mind to have dinner guests that night. There would be a colleague from the Comparative Culture Department and her husband; a painter who teaches in the MFA program at Hunter; the art critic for *The Public Sphere* and her female partner who wrote popular cookbooks under a pseudonym; the cultural attaché of the Canadian consulate (they had met at a party and exchanged cards); and a woman from out of town, a young urban anthropologist from Vancouver who was being hosted by the department.

He remembered the Seders of his childhood only dimly. Not that they weren't taken seriously—far from it. Ethel made all the heavy, sweet, overcooked East European dishes that were eaten once a year and had names that were as strange as they tasted, all concentrated in his memory in that single mysterious, preposterous phrase, *gefilte fish*. Walter wore a white robe, removed from mothballs and stiff with age, whose yellowed creases seemed ironed into it, and a high white skullcap sewn from the same fabric. It was weird to see him, the sober, practical father who always kept his two feet on the ground, dressed in an archaic outfit and mumbling ancient verses that sounded like prehistoric incantations. Yet searching for the *afikomen*, the hidden piece of matzo that ended the meal, had been fun. He and Matthew had teamed up for a change in their frantic search.

How long ago that had been! Although Linda had revived the tradition of the Seder, it was not like what he remembered. She invited friends and relatives, distributed songbooks, and handed out funny figurines shaped like frogs, lice, and other pests that symbolized the Ten Plagues. Still, Andrew felt a pang. Tomorrow night they would be sitting around the table, eating, laughing, singing, and reading long passages from the Haggadah that no one understood. How nice it would be! Should he call off his dinner and join them? No, it was too late. He couldn't cancel a dinner party at the last minute. Never mind. He would go to Linda's Seder

next year. What should he make, though? The lamb tagine stew
with couscous once again? No, something more springlike, more
festive. He would roast a whole leg of lamb, on the bone, served
medium rare. He would bring it to the table and carve it in front of
everyone, they'll love the dramatic effect.

4

April 7, 2001

The 15th of Nisan, 5761

Eleven p.m. The guests had gone home. The table was cleared
and the dishes were neatly stacked in the sink. The dinner had
gone more than well. The conversation had flowed, the wine was
superb, and the food earned the kudos of all.

But Andrew felt wrung out and depleted. He switched off the
lights and went to bed. Although it was early for him, he fell asleep
the minute he lay down, as though plunging into a deep crevasse.
His tired brain had only a second to think before switching itself
off, too. The last thing he saw was a round, thick-rimmed well
that broke loose from the earth and rolled slowly down a gentle
incline. Round and heavy like a pregnant belly, it sprayed water
in all directions, the drops glinting in the sunlight like little shards
of glass.

"What?" Andrew's eyes opened wide by themselves. He couldn't
believe the time on the alarm clock: 11:50, not even midnight! To
his surprise, he felt oddly wakeful, as fully rested as if he had slept
for twelve hours. Or could it be daytime already? There was light
outside. He got out of bed and went to the window: a full, incredibly large moon hung over the river, cloaked in a velvety halo and
gilding the fanlike ripples on the water. He opened the window. A

clear, cloudless spring night greeted him with its sounds. The air was unexpectedly warm and fragrant. Since when were there such balmy nights in early April? It was as if someone had imported a foreign climate and let it loose under the cover of darkness on Riverside Drive. The desert dryness felt more like Arizona than the East Coast.

Andrew, stirred, turned from the wondrous view back to the room, padding about in bare feet with the lights off. He hadn't felt so alert in ages, perhaps since his childhood. Every cell tingled with pleasure. The familiar room seemed new. He regarded it with amazement, running his fingers over its walls and objects as if touching their textured surfaces for the first time. Although the moon was gone from the window, the bright sky filled the apartment with light. He rested his elbows on the windowsill and leaned outside, studying the glyphs and cartouches sculpted on the cornices of the building nearly a century before. Light flickered on the river and a breeze blew through the branches of the budding trees. Leaving the window open, he sprawled out on the couch, still breathing the enchanted night. He didn't feel like eating, drinking, sleeping, reading, or talking to anyone—not even like making love. He wanted only to go on sitting there, surrendering to the intoxicating wakefulness that he felt in every part of him.

Time passed unnoticed. Could it already be morning? The pale dawn light was soft and dreamy. Perhaps he had dozed off for a while. Rising from the couch, he took off his pajamas, put on his tracksuit, quickly laced his sneakers, and hurried outside. Each minute was precious. He crossed the empty lobby and half ran to the park. Everything continued to feel special. Although not a soul was in sight, the street seemed vibrant with life. The sidewalk quivered beneath his feet. The last lights illuminated in the buildings across the river twinkled, going out one by one as the pallid dawn brightened. He followed a path in the park, breathing deeply in and out. The lampposts shone like candles in the haze. A white mist floated above the lawns. The breeze was soft and caressing. From afar came a sound of song. Who could be singing so early in the morning? Andrew sat excitedly on a bench facing the river, an electric field of anticipation crackling around him. The breeze was like a stream in which he was totally immersed. The singing grew closer, louder. This time he recognized it. The melody, the lilting, guttural tongue, the ancient, rocking rhythm—they had all but raised the roof at the bar mitzvah in Long Island in February. There were string and wind instruments now, too, like those he had heard that fine winter day near the university, in that wondrous procession, where he saw that beautiful white bull being led through the street.

A fierce blue sky broke sharply over the jagged ridges of the bare mountains. The desert wind was dry and warm. Brightly dressed women jangled tambourines; men in white played drums and violins, blew large horns, and piped on reed flutes. The singing kept growing stronger. So did the light, sevenfold like the days of Creation. More and more figures joined the procession, thousands, tens of thousands, myriads of them, flowing eastward like a mighty river. Andrew rose, carried away by the human current, his bare feet sinking into the dry, white sand. The stinging sensation of the thick, semidry blood caked on his right thumb, toe, and earlobe filled him with pride and an overflowing joy. *A ram's horn sounded a loud, prolonged, many-toned blast. Brooks and rivulets cascaded from the tops of the high mountains. The singing swelled and mounted, mounted and swelled sacramentally. A great peak loomed on the horizon, royally crowned by flames and smoke. The winding current surged toward it, sweeping up all in its way.*

A warm tongue was licking Andrew's hand. With a start, he roused himself. A strange woman was standing there, smiling with embarrassment. "Sparky!" she mock-childishly scolded her frisky puppy tugging at its leash. "You can't go licking every hand you see!"

Andrew stared at her, struggling to fathom where he was. Where had everything disappeared? Had it been only a dream? But how could that be? He hadn't been sleeping. He hadn't shut his eyes all night. The dog wagged its tail and gave Andrew a playful look, as if inviting him to romp with it. He shivered. It was cold, cold and damp. His back hurt from leaning against the hard bench and all his muscles ached. Locks of hair, wet with dew, stuck like cold leeches to his temples and forehead. His tracksuit was damp and clammy, as were his socks and sneakers. How long had he been sitting there? When had it become so damp and chilly? The exotic climate had withdrawn into itself, leaving behind an ordinary cold, clammy April morning. Now the woman was tugging at the dog, her movements growing agitated. She was afraid of Andrew. He tried his best to smile normally, but with no success. The muscles of his face were frozen, his teeth clamped in place.

After a while, the puppy relented and turned away. The woman followed, walking as fast as she could without breaking into a run. What time was it? Andrew glanced at his watchless wrist. Something strange was going on, something unclear. He felt weak. A profound fatigue seeped through him, making his limbs limp and his head swim. For a few more minutes, he remained seated. Then, with the last of his strength, he pushed off from the back of the bench, rose to his feet, stretched his aching body, and staggered toward the park exit.

5

An infinite ocean stretches to the horizon in all directions, so solid that its waves seemed frozen.

Suddenly, its boundless serenity is disturbed. The water begins to churn and seethe. White bubbles rise to the surface, breaking ominously. Something is happening deep down, something portentous.

A whale had risen from the ocean's depths. It is the Leviathan of Memory, an immense mass that bears no relation to time or individual memory, that isn't even the sum of all individual memories. Its huge body is poised to breach, stirring up the darkness below, reversing the flow of the hidden currents. Bubbles foam and swirl by the millions, striving to rejoin the air that was their original source. Each is a separate soul, the story of a life, the memory of a single person. The whale craves air, too. It needs to fill its lungs with a pure draft of reality before diving back down to its forsaken depths.

The waves mount. The water gurgles, gushes, and parts in two. Glistening in the sunlight, a smooth, white, giant form fills the visible universe with its powerful presence. The past becomes the present. All that was forgotten is again remembered. Those dead and buried come to life. The irretrievably lost is suddenly restored in its all-palpable existence. The moment seems to last forever. The whale's exposed body hovered over the face of the water. Time stops in its tracks, looking on in amazement. Yet this, too, shall pass; it wouldn't last long. That which had been is that which would be. The Leviathan of Memory would plunge back down. The raging sea would swallow it with a gulp and wipe away the great orifice that had yawned in its midst. The tumult shall subside. Motion shall revert to rest. The foamy ripples shall dissipate, spreading equally over the waters. All shall be quiet again. An infinite ocean shall stretch to the horizon in all directions.

6
April 8, 2001

The 15th of Nisan, 5761

It felt strange to be so sick in springtime. Andrew woke late. Although the apartment was warm and flooded with light like a greenhouse, his chills and sore throat were like a reversion to winter. It was all he could do to get out of bed, blinking in the bright light, his rumpled, sweaty pajamas hanging loosely on his limp frame. The lump in his throat hurt annoyingly. He felt stuffy and light-headed. He dismissed the thought of coffee in favor of herbal tea with honey. Was there any lemon in the refrigerator? Sickness triggered old reflexes, a childish, semi-instinctive desire for somebody—a woman, to be precise—to take care of him.

But his neediness was short-lived and soon yielded to its opposite. It was better in his state to be alone, to have the apartment to himself, to go about unwashed and unshaven, wrapped in old clothes, gagging on the cloying perfume of his own sweat, his scalp crawling with the not entirely unpleasant sensation of gritty unwashed hair, his mouth sour with the taste—enjoyable, too, in its way—of unbrushed teeth. There was something cozy and intimate in this unexpected bout of flu, something liberating. Even its chills, which made him feel half out of his body, were irresistible. It was good Ann Lee was out of town. He liked to look and be at his best with her. She wasn't the nurturing type.

But what was he going to do with himself? He could hardly go on sleeping all day long. He turned on his computer, went to its mailbox, and exited immediately. Too weak and groggy to answer his e-mails, he absentmindedly surfed the Web without remaining anywhere long. He even visited the repulsively titillating

Back to the Foreskin blog that Rachel had introduced him to a few months ago, curious to see how the circumcised author's pursuit of his anatomical holy grail was proceeding. But the close-ups of male organs made him cringe and he swiftly switched off the computer, padded to the couch in the living room, stretched out on it listlessly, and tried driving away the revolting visions of foreskins that, no matter how hard he shut his eyes, kept lurking under their lids in intense color and detail.

ONE THIRTY P.M. The delivery guy arrived with lunch. Andrew, coming to the door in his bathrobe, tipped him handsomely, as if in compensation for not belonging to a privileged class that could be sick at its leisure and sleep till noon. Not up to eating in the kitchen or transferring the food to bowls and dishes, he took the bag to the living room, emptied it onto the coffee table, and picked at the greasy plastic containers, sampling soup, meat, rice, and vegetables in no particular order. His eye fell on the remote control, and he switched on the TV. An animated film flashed hectically on the screen, its grotesque, pointy-headed creatures from outer space frantically chasing each other with laser guns. The antitheses of Mickey Mouse, Donald Duck, and Pluto, they were anything but cute or lovable. Who had left the TV on this channel? Rachel? Ann Lee? Now, its humor even more sinister, a new cartoon was starting in which a legless monster swooped down on its hapless victims and turned whoever looked at it into a pile of bones. Did children really like this stuff? It was another generation, a new world. Damn! Soy sauce was dripping on the rug. When was the last time he had eaten like this, in his pajamas, in front of the TV? Perhaps not for years.

His lunch made him sleepy and he stretched out on the couch, knees curled semi-fetally beneath him while the TV blared high-pitched, rapid-fire dialogue. Though he yearned for some quiet, he felt too weak to get up and turn it off. The last day and night's vivid daydreams and visions continued to haunt him, but he couldn't think clearly about them. Never mind. Perhaps tomorrow. He shut his eyes and let himself surrender to his exhaustion, trying to picture the thick fluids that were flooding his forehead and draining into his sinuses and skull cavity. They made him think of the ornamental Lava Lamps, popular in the seventies, in which fat colorful bubbles reproduced the same random forms in an oily, phosphorescent, unnaturally slow-circulating liquid. His temperature must be going up. He should take a Tylenol.

The high-pitched voices were still arguing. What a racket! Early morning. Half-empty bowls stand on the table beside cartons of milk and boxes of breakfast cereal. An orange light shines through the kitchen window, glancing dazzlingly off the television screen. Although it is hard to make out what is happening on it, he recognizes the voices: Ernie and Bert. Big Bird. The Transylvanian Count counting to ten in his funny Romanian accent. Alison's fruity laughter. Linda is packing sandwiches in their lunch boxes. *Let's go, Rachel, it's late. Time for school.*

The sound was getting to be unbearable. Andrew forced himself to sit up and turn off the TV. What now? Hefty and inviting, the Sunday *Times* had been waiting since morning. He placed it in front of him and took it apart, discarding the Business, Sports, and Classified pages while reserving the Book Review, Arts and Leisure, and Metro sections under a pillow. Glancing at the news, he decided to start with it. Its broadsheet format in his raised hands, he lay on his back and laboriously began to read. Yet he couldn't focus on the wavering lines or combine their letters into words and sentences. No problem. He would shut his eyes for a few minutes. *Hey, Bert, are you sleeping? Yes, Ernie, I'm asleep. But I can't fall asleep, Bert. Then count sheep, Ernie.*

7

Andrew awoke bathed in sweat and assailed by the light. The sun was in the west, turning the windows of the living room into four giant spotlights. Something was bothering him—something urgent, something disturbing. He had forgotten something important. He had to remember, now. Oh, God, yes! Alison's performance! At her ballet school. Linda had phoned to remind him of it. When was it? What day was today? More pungent sweat poured off him as his anxiety released a surge of adrenaline. How could he have forgotten that? Quick, the phone! He had to listen to Linda's message.

But his body, as though chained to the couch by thousands of cobwebs, refused to get up. His hands and feet felt immobilized, as if shackled in irons. The wave of anxiety washed over him and receded. The light assaulting his eyes, lining their lids a fiery red. What time was it? He couldn't find his watch. When was the performance? It was the *Nutcracker*, Alison was a snowflake, with a shiny white leotard and silver spangles in her hair. Why the *Nutcracker* now? It was April, not midwinter. But Linda had left a message. He couldn't have made it up, he simply could not have! Linda had called him, he could swear to it. What time was it? There was a tiny digital clock on the cable box beneath the TV that he could see if he turned to the left. Could he be dreaming, is that possible? Yes, it was a dream. There was no message from Linda, there was no performance, Alison hasn't done ballet in years. How could he have dreamt it all?

He felt pressure in his bladder. Sweat dripped onto the collar of his pajama top. He had to get up. Craning his neck, he made out the digits on the cable box: 4:20. It was a dream: what a relief! Although the sticky webs of sleep had dissolved, he still felt too exhausted to rise from the couch. He looked around him. What an unholy mess! The news section of the *Times* was spread out on his chest like a dead albatross, its severed limbs scattered over the rest of the couch. The coffee table was splotched with greasy food. Plastic and paper bags lay on the rug. His throat was sore and his eyelids felt inflamed and swollen. Forcing himself to sit, he surveyed the disorder with disgust. What luck it had been a dream! He could have sworn there was a message. Just look at all that soy sauce, what a waste! Why did they always send twice the amount anyone could eat?

The tea soothed his throat without calming him. Something was still bothering him, a void he couldn't explain. He needed to talk to someone. Linda! But that was ridiculous. How could he call her just like that? His fingers knew her Brooklyn number by heart. There was a recorded announcement on her voice mail. "Hi, you've reached Linda and George." Alison's muffled laughter could be heard in the background. "We aren't home now." Alison gaily completed the announcement: "Please leave a message and we'll get back to you at the first opportunity." Feeling weak, he gripped the receiver. A long beep was followed by the heavy silence of the listening device. Andrew hesitated with the receiver to his ear before hanging up carefully, as though afraid to wake someone. Suppose, he thought with alarm, they had a caller identification service. At once, he realized how childish the fear was. His head is not working right, he should take two more Tylenols and get back into bed.

He picked up the receiver again and automatically dialed Rachel's number in Princeton. Even though it was new, he knew her number by heart, too. The phone rang. No one answered. He suddenly missed her as badly as if he hadn't seen her in years—missed her as one misses a mother more than a daughter. If only he could hold her cool hand in his own, everything would be all right. He let the telephone keep ringing, lulled by its hypnotic trills.

"Hi, Dad, is that you?" Rachel sounded as close as if she were sitting next to him.

He had almost forgotten that the phone was still ringing and sat up with a start, trying to sound normal. "Hi, sweetie, how are you?" For a moment, bemused by his casual tone and his need to pretend that nothing was wrong, he thought he was about to deny he was sick. Rachel, though clearly glad to hear his voice, sounded puzzled. Andrew wasn't the type for small talk and never called her just to chat. "What's up, Dad?" she asked. "Is everything okay?"

In the same ironic, nonchalant tone, which he clung to without knowing why, he told her he was running a high fever and hadn't been out all day. "Poor little Dad!" she teased back. "If I were in the city, I'd make you chicken soup." Andrew smiled. Chicken soup was their private joke, a sardonic code word for their family situation. Not only was there no longer anyone to make it, there never had been one. Linda hadn't inherited her mother's cooking skills. She never liked being in the kitchen and spent less and less time there as her career progressed. And when she did make something for a weekend meal or special occasion, it was usually some closely followed Thai or Italian recipe, taken from a best-selling cookbook. It was the very opposite of Andrew's adventurous, creative approach to food. Rachel, in her typical perfectionist style, made it her business to master the recipe of Cora's famous chicken soup, experiment with ways of improving it, proudly bring it to perfection, and then proceed to abandon it and never cook it again. "It's an empty gesture, a smile without a cat," she once told Andrew. "We never had it when I needed it and now it's too late. And anyway, what's so special about chicken soup? It's just another nostalgic myth. For a comfort food, give me an organic vegetable curry with noodles."

"Okay, sweetheart, see you soon." Andrew hung up, an uncharacteristically hesitant hand still on the receiver. The conversation had left him with a bitter, medicinal taste. Something he couldn't put a finger on had been left unsaid. If it weren't ridiculous, he would call Rachel back. But what did he expect of her? To drop everything and come running? To actually make him chicken soup and serve him fresh squeezed orange juice? That wasn't how things worked, it just wasn't. She was a grown, busy woman. She had her life and so did he.

He should take those damn Tylenols. He let go of the receiver, strode resolutely to the bathroom, opened the medicine cabinet, took out a plastic bottle, shook two pills from it, swallowed them without water, replaced the bottle in the cabinet, and shut it. Finding a heavy old winter bathrobe in the closet, he put it on and returned to the couch. He switched the television back on, switched it off again, dropped the remote control on the rug, and stretched out with his feet tucked under a blanket and his head propped on the large pillow.

He shut his eyes. The liquid in the glass container of the Lava Lamp swished slowly behind his forehead, bearing down on his eyeballs. The doors of the train shut on the platform to his right and its locomotive started to move, picking up speed as its lit windows flashed by him. Now the train on the platform to his left shut its doors, too, and shot off in the opposite direction. *Mom, Mom, where are you? The doors are closing!*

8
April 9, 2001

The 16th of Nisan, 5761

Ten a.m. The espresso machine hummed. The front page of the newspaper was spread out on the kitchen counter beside

a jar of jam, a butter dish, and the remains of a croissant. Andrew
sat at his desk, listening to the messages that had accumulated the
day before. Fourteen hours of deep, dream-fraught, nonstop sleep
had cured him of whatever ailed him, leaving only a slight weakness, the only sign of yesterday's collapse. It had been just a cold, a
twenty-four-hour spring virus.

He glanced at his watch. He had a free morning. He had already
checked his e-mail, answering some and deleting others. Ann Lee
was due back that afternoon and there were some things he might
as well take care of before that. Making room for them on his desk,
he started with the easier ones: signing off on several revised student grades, approving the disqualification of a term paper reasonably suspected of plagiarism, and drawing up a list of guest
lecturers for next year's departmental seminar. The more the desk
was cleared, the more clearheaded he felt.

His main chore was giving final grades in the introductory survey course and faxing them to the secretaries in the office. Generally, the term papers were read by his teaching assistants, who
passed him their evaluations along with some samples to help set a
grading curve and any papers that they didn't trust themselves to
judge. Andrew sifted through these. Most consisted of page after
page of shopworn banalities and tautologies. What was it about the
younger generation that made it so tentative and unsure of itself?
He made his decisions quickly, scrawling a grade at the bottom
of the last page with his famous fountain pen. The pile of papers
shrank. He glanced again at this watch: it had taken him an hour
and a quarter. Not bad. Two or three more papers and he would
have put in a good morning's work.

The most unusual of the submissions awaited him at the bottom of the pile, as if having lain there in ambush all morning. He
sized it up immediately. There was one like it nearly every semester: an original work, sometimes brilliant and sometimes absurd,

that stood out amid the repetitive, astonishingly predictable mo-
notony of rehashed clichés from Wolf, Said, Derrida, and Fou-
cault. He could also generally count on at least one Communist,
an unshaven young man with a head of black curls who smoked
unfiltered cigarettes and discussed, as if living in a Marxist nature
reserve, mass production, surplus value, and commodity fetishism.
The same arguments, the same grievances, over and over in an
endless feedback loop . . . Yet what right had anyone to complain?
This was how he and his contemporaries had taught their students
to think. They had brought the politicization of the social sciences,
the liberal arts, and the entire academy down on themselves.

The odd essay out this time was written on thin stationery with
a ballpoint pen, in large, round, elementary-school cursive letters
that seemed engraved in the onionskin paper. No name appeared
on it, though he searched for one everywhere. *Who the hell can he
be?* Andrew wondered, sure for some reason that the writer was
male. Taken aback by the unease that accompanied his curiosity,
he held the strange-looking work up to the light as if hoping to discover a cryptogram that might solve the mystery. Was it the work
of some religious fanatic? A recent immigrant? A psychopath? Its
pompous title had a seventeenth-century ring: *A Treatise on the
Constructions of Consciousness and the Reality Constructed.*

Andrew smiled. So that was it! He was a first-year philosophy
major who had read Spinoza and decided to write his own *Tracta-
tus Theologico-Politicus.* Again he looked in vain for the author's
name. An anonymous term paper, how bizarre! Picking up its first
page, he began to read, his lips curling in a smile of sympathy.

*The idea that consciousness constructs reality has become a com-
monplace of contemporary discourse, a lifeless metaphor, a banality
that has lost its power to clear new ground or serve as an intellectual
trigger. It behooves us, therefore, to reopen the discussion of this*

highly charged concept and investigate the infinite possibilities con-
tained in it. Its everyday (let alone vulgar) interpretation leaves it
in the psychologically subjective realm: by constructing our psycho-
logical reality, our consciousness affects not only our behavior but
the ways in which we perceive the real world and make narratives
of it for ourselves and others. The processes of socialization and the
social construction of reality that we engage in from infancy deter-
mine how we shape our personal and collective histories. Against
this, the first part of the thesis, it would be pointless to argue or look
for refutations; it has exhausted itself intellectually and become a
cliché that no longer contributes to the conversation. The discussion
only becomes interesting when we proceed further and venture to
explore the possibility that consciousness constructs not only human
but trans-human, so-called objective (a term that is taboo in the
current intellectual climate), reality as well. Can it be (it being our
right, and thus our duty, to pose the question) that our conscious-
ness and its underlying cultural assumptions determine not only
our perceptions of the world and the categories to which our brains
assign our sense impressions, but things in themselves—that is,
the referents that cast their semiotic shadows on our consciousness?

Semiotic shadows? Andrew's head spun. *Things in themselves?* For
a moment he feared the distress in his frontal lobes was a sign he was
getting sick again. His eyes were smarting, as if he had been reading
too long. Shutting them to let them rest, he gently massaged his eyelids. Although the essay was tedious, puerile, awkwardly phrased,
and overly dense, there was something interesting, even intriguing,
about it. He opened his eyes and read more:

Modern Western civilization has excelled in analyzing one side of
the equation: that which describes how human consciousness per-
ceives the world. It has, however, dismissed (perhaps in the hope of

making it disappear) the other side—how this consciousness cre-
ates and influences the world—by disparagingly referring to it as
"mysticism," "magic," or "shamanism." Yet other cultures have
explored their frames of reference no less deeply than has our own.
Their researchers, known to us as "magicians," have exercised
their consciousness in order to create new existents (in the actual,
noumenal, not just the phenomenological, world). These existents,
it needs to be stressed, have an ontological and not just an episte-
mological status, a real and not just a psychological dimension.

Aha, cultural relativism! Andrew put the essay down and permitted himself another, not entirely convincing smile at having
theoretically placed it. Half-conscious of a twinge of disappointment, he reached into a drawer for some stationery of his own that
bore his personal letterhead underneath the emblem of the university and wrote in as polite, even friendly, a manner as he could:

Dear Anonymous,
    Your paper is highly interesting and has no little poetic power
that stimulates the intellectual imagination, which is something
that I greatly value and encourage in my students. At the same
time, it belongs to no genre taught within the framework of the
course. I'm sorry to say, therefore, that I can't give it a grade in
its present form, there being no uniform standard of evaluation
that can be applied to it. Since I do recognize your seriousness,
however, you have my permission, should you wish to be given a
final grade, to submit another paper or rewrite this one to make
it conform more to the subject matter of the course. Before doing
so, I would recommend that you consult the available academic
guidelines to scholarly writing, as well as some of the papers sub-
mitted by your classmates. These will give you an idea of the kind
of content and style of presentation expected of you. If you would

*like, I would be happy to meet with you during my office hours to
advise you as best I can. As I say, I respect your creativity and
wish to see you channel it in a way that will meet with the appreciation it deserves.*

Sincerely,
Andrew P. Cohen

Andrew reread what he had written. Its almost effortlessly
achieved tone of firm yet not patronizing authority should have
pleased him. Instead, though, he had a vague sense of a missed
opportunity—and of something else. Could it be guilt? But what
was there to feel guilty about? Neatly arranging the thin pages,
he clipped his note to the first of them, pausing to regard it while
fingering its margins, and slipped them into his leather briefcase,
together with the other term papers, with yet another pale, disconcerted smile.

9

April 23, 2001

The 30th of Nisan, 5761

Nine a.m. Spring break was over. Andrew was glad to return
to the academic whirl and be back in contact with the world.
Lathering himself before shaving, he whistled gaily. Ann Lee was
still sleeping soundly like a teenager. The razor glided over his
cheek, skimming off its bristles and leaving fresh trails of bare skin
in the clouds of white foam on his face.

An unpleasant memory came to mind: the image of a slim young
woman with large, firm breasts and a smooth, shiny, closely shaved
skull, sitting stark naked in front of a mirror, her faced covered in a

foamy white coat of shaving cream, holding a large, old-fashioned barber's razor blade in her hand. It was a black-and-white photograph hanging on the door of a student at Berkeley, a sadistically seductive girl who had baited him mercilessly during his first months on the West Coast, exploiting his natural delicacy and the feminist mores of the times to bring him repeatedly to the verge of consummation, only to impose a sudden change in the rules of the game at the last moment. She had made him feel ashamed to desire her, ashamed to be a heterosexual male. How many years ago had that been? How many women ago? The razor glided effortlessly down his cheek, descended to his throat, and finished up under his chin. A nice, smooth, clean job. *What if he were to shave the rest of his head, his eyebrows, too? What if he were to shave his whole body, even his pubic hair and armpits?* The image of the sleek, ageless hermaphrodite he would have become made him shudder. Yet the strange thought of so much naked, white, sensitive skin exposed to daylight for the first time in years was also somehow pleasurable.

A ridiculous fantasy! He had better get on with it. He rinsed the last lather from his face and leaned over the sink to inspect himself in the mirror, stretching the skin to make sure no stray hairs were hiding under his lip or chin while regarding, with a small smile of satisfaction, the handsome man staring back at him. Although he did not look exceptionally young, his fifty-two years had preserved his golden features, the clean Matisse-like contours of the cheeks and chin that were the stock-in-trade of many a plastic surgeon. His fingers probed the corners of his eyes, searching for hidden crow's-feet, and lingered by his forehead to brush back a thick lock of hair. There was a small, nearly invisible cut near his right ear. He touched it with a reassuring fingertip and gently took hold of the earlobe with his thumb and forefinger. Tantalizing traces of memory breached the surface of his mind and dove back down like clear-finned flying fish. His hand slid over his still reasonably trim belly and on to the love handle of his hip, which passed muster, too. But though the middle-aged man facing the mirror was in good shape, never again would he have a boy's smooth skin—not in this incarnation, anyway. If only one could shed one's epidermis like a snake and let the fat trickle slowly out like warm drops of urine— have muscles that once again were hard, strong, and supple—jump into a cleansing pool and emerge new, fresh, and purified!

An itch beneath his right nostril caused Andrew to peer into the mirror again. An odd, reddish-white rash had appeared on his freshly shaven skin. He ran a finger over it. Could it be an allergic reaction to something? Spring was one big allergy, especially if you lived near the park. It was nothing. It would go away by itself.

He surveyed his bottles of shaving lotion and chose one that Rachel jokingly liked to call "Dad's English squire fantasy" because it smelled, she said, like an old stable. He poured a bit of the clear green liquid into the hollow of his right palm and rubbed it into his face and neck. The alcohol stung refreshingly, its scent of raw leather, moss, and cedar wood dilating his nostrils. He glanced at his watch: twenty past nine. He'd buy his second cup of coffee at Starbucks, by the entrance to the subway. The meeting was scheduled for 10:30. At two he had a class, the first of the week.

10

April 23, 2001

The 30th of Nisan, 5761

Ten a.m. Andrew, his battered but elegant briefcase in one hand and a paper cup of fine-smelling coffee in the other, descended the subway stairs while humming a bar of an unidentifiable aria. He was in the habit of buying the morning's second cup of coffee, a small cappuccino lightly sprinkled with cinnamon, at the Starbucks on Broadway and 110th Street. He liked the good-natured bustle of the place, its smell of freshly ground beans, and the little drama enacted each time its scalded milk was poured frothing into a pitcher. What could be more New Yorky than heading into the subway with a paper cup of coffee in hand?

Andrew liked the subway, too, perhaps because he almost never had to travel in the hellish rush hours that not unjustifiably gave the New York mass transit system its bad name. He liked the mystery of its dark, Tolkienesque tunnels, the cleanly styled, gleaming aluminum cars that sped through them, and the steady, meditative rhythm of the ride itself. Swiping his MetroCard, he pushed his way through the turnstile. The platform was almost empty, as was the train that soon arrived. He settled into his seat, carefully balancing his coffee on his knees while looking in his briefcase for a book. He always read on the subway—books, magazines, or the inner pages of the *Times*. Reading was part of the subway experience, a Pavlovian reflex.

His freshly shaved face itched and smarted. The distress this caused him seemed greater than was called for. Nervously, he felt his face. The reddish-white rash had spread over his right cheek, causing him to think, with an atypical hypochondria that was not like him, of rare skin diseases like psoriasis, leprosy, or scabies. Across from him was an advertisement for Dr. Jonathan Zizmor, "New York's dermatologist" or "Doctor Z.," as it referred to him. It featured the usual "Before" and "After" photographs, the first of tormented faces looking mournfully at the camera, disfigured by their fungal blotches and pussy pimples, the second of their healed doppelgängers, their newborn skin rejuvenated and their eyes shining in newfound vitality. At the bottom were fervent appreciations in large block letters, punctuated with multiple exclamation points. THANK YOU, DOCTOR Z.! THANK YOU FOR SAVING MY FACE!! THANK YOU FOR CHANGING MY LIFE!!!

A bird writhed in the priest's hand. A shining thread of scarlet blood dripped into a clay bowl, forming delicate red cloudlets in the living waters. Andrew shut his eyes hard and then opened them wide, blinking in the neon light of the subway car while groping blindly in his briefcase for the binding of a book. He felt the need not only to read but, even more urgently, to take refuge in the printed page from the brutally invasive images assailing his consciousness. Damn! Where had he put it? He lifted the briefcase and peered inside. The book wasn't there: he had left it at home, on his desk. Though his disappointment was out of all proportion, like a child's who has lost a piece of candy, he mastered it at once. One had to forgive oneself one's little oversights. Fumbling some more in his briefcase, he came up with a sheaf of thin pages. The term paper! He took it out and stared at it, still puzzled by its handwriting, its dense blue letters a maze of hatchings and incisions. Reminded of the vague guilt he had felt when stuffing it into his briefcase as if to make it disappear there, he turned it in his hands, separated its pages, and read a few lines. Why, lurking all along in the back of his consciousness, had it made him feel so uncomfortable? It was simply a crude intellectual provocation—and a childish one, too. He began to reread it, sounding its circuitous sentences to himself as if in the hope of making more sense of them.

The modern, Western, scientific paradigm (or, more exactly, model) is unique in insisting that the relationship between consciousness and reality is a one-way street. This being the case, is it not our philosophical duty to take time out to reexamine our post-Cartesian arrogance with its patronizing, primitive modernism that heedlessly denies the existence of any dimension of reality not in accordance with our narrow view of the world—a view that is more often ideological than theoretical, not to mention empirical?

Andrew put down the pages, stroked his forehead, and massaged his smarting eyes at length. The morning had lost all its freshness, yielding to a brackish, stinging fatigue. He stared into the darkness racing past the car's long window. The rumble of the wheels on the tracks grew louder as the train traveled faster. Turning more pages, his eyes fell on another passage.

What this amounts to is the claim that all the historians, philosophers, scientists, and other meaning-makers of premodern times were either liars, fools, or hallucinators. The first possibility calls for absurd conspiracy theories and needn't be taken seriously. Would it not be wildly irresponsible of us to assume that entire cultures, with their educated elites, their merchant classes, their craftsmen, and their rank and file deliberately spent all their time propagating falsehoods?

The second possibility, according to which our predecessors were superstitious dolts, is the spoken or unspoken starting point of most contemporary investigations of culture and in fact the basis of all modern thought.

The next sentence was incomprehensible. Andrew briefly struggled to decipher it and skipped to the sentence after it.

Not only do we have no reason to believe that the academic establishments of civilizations prior to our own were hallucinating, or composed of fools or madmen (just as, returning to Possibility 1, there is no reason to think that they consisted of inveterate liars), such an argument is diametrically opposed to the cultural relativism that is upheld today. There are those who will rush to protest that the experiences and sense impressions of our predecessors (and of other non-Western cultures that still exist) were mediated by the prism of the ingrained cultural attitudes of their time and place. Yet this claim, too, as tempting as it may be, must be rejected. We can hardly believe that entire populations, generation after generation, accepted as true and reliable descriptions and analyses that contradicted their everyday experience, which included sensory data and not just ideas and concepts. We are thus called upon to take seriously the possibility, even if it does not accord with our own scientific views and prejudices, that the scholars, historians, clergy, etc., of the past were neither liars nor fools, and that the populations that accepted their views of the world were far from being the blindly believing dupes that we find it convenient to picture them as. We must honestly confront the possibility that events and phenomena that strike us as supernatural and therefore impossible actually occurred in the world and not just in the confused minds of those who lived before us, and that the descriptions of them that have come down to us are as accurate and trustworthy as those that will come down to our successors from us.

It was totally preposterous. Andrew found himself seething at this brash, nameless young man who had the impudence to make demands on his valuable time with such gobbledygook. America had fallen on intellectually hard times. The smug, pompous language, the baseless assumptions, the sweeping, wild-eyed generalizations! And all this apart from the flagrant violations of academic style: where were the footnotes, the bibliography, the political and historical context? Who on earth still handed in handwritten papers?

The rash on his cheek was aflame. His face burned like a brush-fire. He should throw the essay in the nearest trash bin. Instead, however, he turned a few more pages, smoothing them out as though he had already crumpled them with an eye to discarding them, and went on reading.

If we challenge (as we are doing) the arbitrary post-Cartesian distinction between subject and object, the thinker and the thought, we must seriously face up to the possibility that consciousness and the world are parts of a single system, ruled by the same laws, of which our limited minds perceive only a part. The world and the laws of nature do not just construct consciousness; consciousness constructs them, too. Wherever consciousness allows miracles to happen, they will happen—happen in reality and not simply in credulous minds—exactly as they were described on the basis of personal experience or firsthand knowledge by the serious, trained historians of the period they occurred in! Their actual, ontological existence legitimates their existence in consciousness. The stronger the epistemological status of a given phenomenon, the greater the belief in it becomes and the more basis it has in reality. And vice versa: the more a belief's epistemological status weakens, the weaker is its ontological status, until it vanishes completely or lingers on as the ghost of itself. The reason it is possible today to accurately foresee natural phenomena like hurricanes and earthquakes is not just, as is generally thought, our improved predictive technology. It is also the fact that the more faith we have in this technology, the more pronounced are the laws of nature it relies on. Natural forces were wilder in times and places when they were thought to be arbitrary and unpredictable, agents of God's will and wrath; it is our belief that nature has clear, rational, quantifiable laws on which predictions can be based that creates a reality in which nature behaves according to such laws. Although the consciousness of plants and animals is also a determinant of the real world, human consciousness, being consciousness's strongest and most concentrated manifestation, affects the world, nature, and the laws of nature more. There is, of course, a "snowball effect" here, too: the stronger grow the laws of nature, the more convinced human consciousness is of their existence; the more convinced it is, the stronger they grow. This also holds true for miracles: they occurred as long as human beings believed in them. No less than rain and snow, day and night, they were natural, not psychological phenomena. The earth began to orbit the sun only when it was collectively thought to do so; before the Copernican revolution, it was indeed a stationary mass. The Nile really turned to blood at the time of the Ten Plagues and the Red Sea really split in two. (No, it was not the result of an earthquake or of mass autosuggestion!) Houses in England are actually haunted by the ghosts of those who died unnatural deaths in them, and these will continue to return to the scene of the crime as long as they are believed in. The Brahmins of India remember their previous incarnations as clearly as we remember our own childhood because they really lived them . . .

It's actually interesting, Andrew thought, feeling calmer. *Infantile, intellectually irresponsible, and of no relevance to anything—but still interesting.* What should he do with it, though? Give it an F? Ask whoever wrote it to come see him? There was no way of grading such a work. He had a sudden urge to meet its anonymous author, even though this would surely be as pointless as was such a textual escapade itself, which he had let himself be caught up in. It had been happening to him too much lately. He was feeling too vulnerable. Something in him had let down its guard. He reassembled the pages, clipped his note to them again, and returned them to his briefcase. Would the student, he wondered, get in touch with him? But even if he would agree to rewrite the paper, how, in all seriousness, could this be done?

The train pulled into Andrew's station. He had better do something about his rash. How could he walk around with something like that on his face? He needed to see a pharmacist or a doctor.

11

April 27, 2001

The 4th of Iyar, 5761

Four p.m. Andrew hesitated slightly before opening the door to his apartment and paused for a second in the doorway as if irrationally afraid of what he might see. The apartment was bathed in an afternoon light that colored it a fruity orange. Spring had arrived; the days were getting longer. All was spick-and-span. Nothing was left of last night's horrendous drama.

And yet what, really, had it amounted to? Nothing at all except for Ann Lee's having gone off early in the morning without making herself coffee, saying good-bye, or leaving one of her adorable notes signed "Me," and for the bottom sheet permanently stained with blood. Andrew took off his shoes and placed them in their corner, aligning them with his toes, and waited a moment before entering the bedroom. The bed was neatly made, its fresh, cool, white sheets looking stiffly starched. The white bathroom tiles gleamed. His fear of encountering the snarled pile of soiled bedding that had lain there the night before like a heavy, menacing corpse in its shrouds was baseless.

The memory of it came wrapped in such nightmarish images that it was hard to believe it had all actually happened. Something terrifying had woken him in the middle of the night, jolting him out of a deep sleep. There was a scary creature in the bed! Some poisonous, crawling thing—a viper that killed with a glance, a barbed armadillo, its teeth rusty with blood—was wriggling next to him, rubbing its scales against his bare skin. He retracted his hand convulsively, dealing himself and the tangled sheets a blow. But there was nothing there. The bed was empty except for Ann Lee sleeping on its far side. He sat up and looked around with dazed eyes, still unsure it had been only a dream. Yet although his heart kept pounding like the twitching of a beheaded animal, his mind, its bad dream over, was already sinking back into sleep. His head fell onto the pillow and his eyelids fluttered in preparation for the next round of nocturnal imagery.

Just then, however, a new wave of panic swept over him, less extreme but more penetrating than the first. Jarring him into full wakefulness, it forced him to raise his head, open his eyes groggily, and look around. The room was not wholly dark. The lurid light of the streetlamps shone through the window, whose blinds they had forgotten to lower, painting Ann Lee's curled-up body an eerie pink. On any other night, he would have reached out to gather her slumbering, birdlike form to him. Now, though, under his indifferent gaze that descended the curved stairway of her spine to cast a cold eye on her bare buttocks and sharply boned pelvis, her familiar nude form seemed an alien presence. How strange: he was not in the least attracted to it. Quite the opposite: something about it repelled him—and the more he stared at it, the more irrationally, unaccountably profound his revulsion became, heightening the dread he had felt since waking. He turned his back to her and tried settling back into the crumpled pillow. She must be cold. He should cover her, pull the blanket over her slim shoulders. Yet all that was reflected back to him from her side of the bed was his own chill anxiety. He shivered. What was happening to him?

He reached behind him, groping in the tangled sheets for the corner of the blanket. His fingers, making their way across the bed's rumpled surface, recoiled as though bitten by a snake. Something disgusting, something warm and wet, was sticking to them. His uncontrollable cry of fear as he jerked his hand away woke Ann Lee from her sleep. Rising on all fours, she stared in alarm at the dark puddle forming on the sheet beneath her. Andrew leaned to turn on the lamp on the night table, but quicker than him, she had already jumped out of bed and run like a pathetically naked, frightened little girl to the light switch on the wall. The violent glare that filled the room brought to mind a Hollywood murder scene. Ann Lee stood in one corner, pale and thin, her small hands covering her gaping mouth, regarding the horrifying sheet that pullulated like a sacrificed bird with that bright shade of red called "pigeon blood" by interior designers and jewelers.

Andrew had leaped out of bed, too. Standing naked at the other end of the room, he tried unsuccessfully to turn his eyes from the gruesome stain to Ann Lee. Although he knew he should run to her and break the evil spell by taking her comfortingly in his arms, his body refused to budge. Agonizingly long seconds passed. Ann Lee was the first to recover. She ran to the bed, furiously stripped its soiled sheets, rolled them into a lumpy bundle in which the bloodstains were swallowed up, dragged it to the bathroom, and slammed the door behind her, catching sight as she did of Andrew, transfixed, staring guiltily at a splotch on the bare mattress. She stayed there a long time, running water and flushing the toilet over and over to drown out her spasmodic sobs of humiliation, each of which cut like a lash into Andrew's unprotected goose flesh. Hurriedly, he remade the bed with fresh sheets. He should knock gently on the bathroom door, go to her, persuade her to come out. Nothing would be simpler than to make a joke of it all, an amusing incident. Yet his body refused to listen to his mind's advice.

He finished making the bed, spread a blanket over it, and walked aimlessly about the apartment, waiting for the bathroom door to open and Ann Lee to come out. Not until the lights went out in the bedroom did he quietly reenter it. Ann Lee's small, trembling body was huddled under the blanket like a wounded animal. Instead of lying down next to her, though, he walked wordlessly to the bathroom and shut the door. It was all he could do to keep from locking it.

The usually refreshing coolness of the floor tiles, colored by the streetlamps the same sickly pink that had bathed Ann Lee's body, was no help. His bare foot touched something that filled him with new horror. It was the bloody bundle of sheets, which lay on the floor like a frightening white mummy, its hidden stain the beating heart of a monster come to life. He felt a volcanic eruption of anger and repugnance. She was a spoiled, self-indulgent child! An unclean, polluted thing! Right after which, however, came a rush of astonished shame at himself, at his strange response. What did he want from the poor girl? It wasn't her fault. She had done nothing wrong. What had come over him to make him so hostile? He stood facing the mirror, leaning on the sink. He had to get a grip on himself, exorcise the demons, turn on the light.

Andrew straightened up and forced himself to press the light switch. The sight made him gasp. The entire face of the mirror was splattered with blood, its glass a living integument lanced by thousands of needles. How hideous! Feeling trapped in a horror movie, he turned the light off and fought back the scream that was about to burst from him. He was dreaming, that was all! It was a nightmare. He took a deep breath and made himself turn the light back on. To his relief, the blood spots were gone. Another breath. It had been a hallucination, nothing more, it was all in his imagination.

But it wouldn't go away. While the blood was gone, its frightful, abhorrent presence lingered on, as if the whole room were contaminated by it. He scrutinized the walls, the floor, the ceiling. There was no trace of blood on them. He turned back to the mirror; his red-eyed, bedraggled reflection stared emptily back at him. Gray bristles surrounded the ugly rash on his face, forming a single coat of hair that covered his face, throat, chest, and stomach. He could feel the frightening, defiling presence of blood, it was there, very close to him. His gaze dropped to the bottom of the mirror. An instant wave of nausea, as if he had known what he would see even before his battered nerves could transmit it to his brain, overcame him. His testicles, pubic hair, and penis were caked with a ring of dark, rusty brown dried blood.

He felt a new surge of fury, disgust, and panic. He had to wash himself, to scrub his polluted flesh with soap and scalding hot water. The voice of reason, echoing in the empty chamber of his mind, was hollow and unconvincing. Why on earth should he feel this way? What had happened, for goodness' sake? She had gotten her period, that was all. He wasn't born yesterday. She was simply menstruating—surprisingly heavily, it was true, and not, if he recalled correctly, at her usual time, but it was all a minor mishap. Why feel so angry, then? Nor could he possibly shower while she was lying there listening to his every movement. Nothing escaped her. She had the intuition and keen senses of a wild animal. She would hear the running water; there was no chance that she wouldn't: he couldn't do it to her. Should he wet a washcloth and wipe away the blood from his privates? Just thinking of the damp, bloodied rag made him feel sick. Absolutely not!

He opened the faucets and washed his hands with hot, almost boiling water, holding them under it for as long as he could before drying them thoroughly. He hung the towel back on its rack, then grabbed it, flung it on the heap of sheets in the corner, and tiptoed into the bedroom, pretending he was trying not to wake her even though it was obvious that she wasn't asleep and that he knew it, and she knew that he knew. If only he could stretch out by himself on the living-room couch! Yet as queasy as the thought of lying next to her made him, it would be madness to give in to such an urge. The wretched creature would be wounded to the core.

The dried blood on his loins stung like a burn. He groped in the dark for his pajama pants, put them on, lifted the blanket, and slipped silently between the fresh sheets, whose ironed crispness failed to make him feel better. Turning cautiously on his side, he lay with his back to Ann Lee, a stranger in his own bed, waiting for her breathing to become slow and regular. What a ghastly night. Why wasn't she falling asleep? What in the name of God was keeping her awake?

12

A young, fiery red, sweat-slathered stallion gallops freely down a gray asphalt road. Bronzed village boys, young colts themselves, chase after it, but it's too fast for them. At the sight of it, an old, black Mercedes screeches to a frightened halt in the middle of the road. The horse's hard hooves stamp the asphalt that is softened by the heat and sink into it time and again, leaving their imprint in it. The unbridled power of its muscular, bloodred body! It's as wild as can be, an unbroken mustang. Quick, rhythmic, violent movements. Bare, rounded hills. Dry ravines. Far-off minarets appear and vanish in the purple haze like mirages. The road runs south to Bethlehem. How do I know it's Bethlehem? Some things don't need to be explained. You know them and that's enough. Things fall apart; the center cannot hold. A memory? A fantasy? It's too real to be a dream.

13
April 30, 2001

The 7th of Iyar, 5761

Nine thirty a.m. The fast train to Washington, DC, pulled into the station on time and the loudspeaker announced boarding. The empty car, whose light-blue upholstery and nicely styled plastic panels made him think of jet travel and uniformed stewardesses, looked clean and welcoming. He found an empty row, settled into the window seat, and took the latest issue of *Daedalus* from his briefcase. In it was a much-discussed article on foundational myths that he was eager to read. He looked forward to the cozy two-hour ride with its lulling, almost imperceptible cadence of wheels on rails and the April sunlight gentled by the passage through double windows. Although his on-the-spot acceptance of an invitation to a conference at the University of Pennsylvania in Philadelphia had surprised even himself, it was the perfect chance to get some rest. That was something he needed more than ever.

The need for peace and quiet may have explained his overreaction when, his eyes on the magazine's table of contents, a broad male body sinking into the seat next to him invaded his private space. Stifling a muttered protest, he turned automatically and not very courteously toward the window. He was still searching for the article when the newcomer said in a voice that, if not exceeding the publicly permitted level of decibels, came close to doing so, "I see you're interested in culture."

Andrew's fingers froze halfway through turning a page. Flabbergasted, he looked up to regard the intruder. A huge baby face was smiling at him sociably. The man's broad, conservative tie was loosened, baring a patch of pinkish-white neck, and his off-the-rack suit jacket hung limply on a bulky, flabby frame. "That gives us something in common!" he boomed in the hearty tone one expects of traveling salesmen and weather forecasters. "I'm interested in it, too. Pleased to meet you: Herman Lindenbaum!" His plump hand, though unexpectedly dry, was repellent to the touch. Andrew squirmed in his no-longer-comfortable seat. *Herman?* Who still went around with such a name? The man's outward manners concealed a flagrant lack of boundaries such as Andrew had not encountered in a long while. "You're a college teacher, I presume?" he asked. Andrew nodded, murmuring a few vague syllables of qualified assent. For a moment, before realizing how ridiculous it would be, he was about to say, "Professor. University. NYU." Instead he chose silence, hoping to bring the unwelcome exchange to an end.

But the crass stranger persisted. "I could have been a university prof myself. I went to Harvard." His Jewish accent made "Harvard" sound like the name of a neighborhood in Brooklyn. "I graduated summa cum laude. My senior thesis won a big national award. You must have heard of the Stuart Ratner Prize."

Andrew murmured something indistinct again, making a last-ditch effort, though it was clearly in a losing cause, not to be drawn into conversation with this annoyingly collegial flaunter of dubious and irrelevant academic credentials. "But I chose another path in life," the man went on. "I'm a lawyer. I represent big corporations against the environmentalists. Not that I don't care about the environment, mind you. I'm very ambivalent about the whole thing—very."

Andrew pursed his lips, refusing to say a word. He hadn't fallen into a trap like this in ages. It was beyond him how he had let this person encroach on him and gain his attention. "To tell you the truth, though," Herman said with a mysterious glint of satisfaction, "my little secret is that I'm an artist." With a dramatic flair

suitable to a Grade B Hollywood movie, he produced from his
jacket pocket a stack of half a dozen black-framed slides, the claustrophobic reductions of as many uninspired, overly busy, abstract
oil paintings. Andrew stared at them blankly, overwhelmed by
their abundance of detail. The man paused to gauge the impression made by them and continued: "I write poetry, too, though I
haven't published any yet. You see, I have a big ego and can't take
criticism. You're Jewish, aren't you?"

This question caught Andrew unprepared. He had never been
asked if he was Jewish before, perhaps because a Cohen could
hardly be anything else. With a bob of his head that fell short of
being a nod, he stammered "Yes" more hesitantly than seemed
called for even by so gross a question.

"So am I," declared the man triumphantly. Unfazed by Andrew's unforthcoming mien, he had the air of a bridge partner
playing a trump card kept up his sleeve. "I was a yeshiva boy until
I ate from the forbidden fruit and lost my faith." He gave Andrew
a long wink, followed by an ostensibly cynical snicker.

An ex-yeshiva student! That explained things, thought Andrew
without knowing exactly why it did.

Herman Lindenbaum pursued his monologue:

"Seeing as we're both Jewish and men of culture, I'm sure you'll
be interested in what I have to tell you. You see, I had this problem, a real phobia, a terrible fear of water. It was totally irrational and had no obvious cause. I went for therapy, for psychiatric
treatment—nothing helped. It just got worse. I had to stop washing. I cleaned myself with a washcloth dipped in alcohol. I shaved
with a dry razor. I have sensitive skin, very sensitive, and I developed acne and rashes all over."

Although Andrew edged closer to the window, the more intimate the details of Herman's story became, the nearer to him the
man kept moving. The proximity of his fat, pallid, unwashed body

was abhorrent, nauseating. Nor, to judge from the smell of him, had he completely gotten over his phobia. Yet at the same time, Andrew was taken aback by his own malice. The pressure of the metal window frame against his arm served to remind him to show some consideration. Shutting the magazine that he had kept open until then as a symbol of passive resistance, he folded it resignedly and turned to his traveling companion.

Herman, evidently not as oblivious of others as he had initially appeared, took note of this and plunged deeper into his story, the details of which piqued Andrew's curiosity while in no way lessening his unease. "In the end, after trying everything, from psychoanalysis to hypnosis to behavioral psychology, I went to see a well-known psychiatrist who was recommended to me, a Jew named Weisberg. Professor Stuart Weisberg of Miami. It's funny how they're all Jews, isn't it?" A knowing glitter in his eyes and his oily *s*'s hissed through small teeth, Herman was increasingly resembling an anti-Semitic caricature himself. "I'm sure you must have heard of him. He's developed his own technique, he's written books about it." Andrew shook his head, trying not to seem too interested. "He works with hypnosis, too, but he doesn't limit it to your present incarnation. He permits and even encourages his patients to go back in time to their previous lives and look there for the source of their problem. Needless to say, I'm a rational man with a scientific outlook just like you" (Andrew felt a burst of indignation at this comparison), "but I eventually let myself be talked into it. What did I have to lose? I decided to go with an open mind to Miami."

The renowned rationalist's departure for Miami was related as portentously as if he had been a bemedaled general operatically surrendering his decorated sword to an enemy commander. "It's a very expensive treatment, but I could afford it. I've got a highly successful practice with eight people working under me. I live in a luxury apartment in Midtown Manhattan with a view of both rivers." Herman smiled with apologetic superiority. "It works by stages. Dr. Weisberg put me in a hypnotic state and began taking me back in time, first to my adolescence and then to my childhood and infancy. That's when it happened. There was something beyond infancy. I was visualizing other scenes from other lives. It began with a name: *Yossil-Chaim*. I had no idea where it came from. It was as if someone had whispered it in my ear, a nearby voice that didn't bother to explain. It happened a few times. I knew the name, of course: it was a common enough Jewish one. It just never occurred in my family. Then came another whisper: *Zuritsh*. It was in a different voice that belonged to someone else. And there was a third one, with an entirely different way of speaking. It whispered a date: October 3, 1941.

"I didn't recognize any of these voices. I had never heard them before. But the names kept repeating themselves. So did the date. And then I began picturing scenes. A deep, deep green, almost black forest. A small house—a log cabin, really—with little windows. Goats. Chickens. Children. Lots of them. Mostly girls, all ages, with long braids and flowing dresses. They were talking in Yiddish. I know Yiddish from home, but this was a different dialect, in an accent I wasn't familiar with. One of the children was me: a small, skinny boy of eleven or twelve with *peyes* curled around his ears, close to bar mitzvah age. Although I don't know if I was an only son, I can't remember having any brothers. It's hard to explain. It was spooky, like an out-of-body experience."

Herman took a quick, wheezing, asthmatic breath, wet his lips, and continued:

"It started early in the morning, before sunrise. We heard dogs barking. It was close by, very frightening. Suddenly, we were surrounded by dogs. Our house stood by itself, apart from the other houses in the village, almost in the forest. The Germans came with local collaborators. Our parents were already awake, but we children were still asleep. The soldiers yanked us from our beds by the legs like chickens from a coop. My little sister Rayzl was screaming with terror. She was two or three. There was a dog as tall as she was, maybe taller. No one dared run to pick her up. We were all petrified."

Herman took a few quick gulps of air. The longer his story, the shorter of breath he was becoming. "I don't want to tell you what I saw. I could tell you things that would keep you from sleeping at night. I saw my mother raped over and over . . . five, six, seven men, in the middle of the room, with all the children standing there. They hiked her dress above her waist. She had long, white legs. I had never, you know, seen a bare inch of a woman's body. They—we—were very religious. My father was dragged to the yard like a bull to slaughter. They finished him off with clubs and axes. My big sister was raped, too. She was sixteen, maybe seventeen, a virgin—she had never been alone with a strange man in one room. They saved the little ones for last. A soldier grabbed me by the collar, lifted me like a puppy, and dragged me to the water barrel. There were no pipes or faucets in the house; the drinking water came from a barrel that was refilled every few days. The soldier's big, hard hand on my neck was like a vise. It was thin and frail, my neck. He lifted me up, showing me to everyone as if I were a rabbit in a magic trick, and then lowered me into the water and kept me there until I was choking."

Herman's short, wheezing breaths came faster and faster, in time to his grisly story. "Each time, a second or two before I drowned, he pulled me out of the barrel, showed me to everyone as if it were a big joke, gave me a while to catch my breath, and plunged me back in. The soldiers and collaborators stood there laughing as

though at a circus act. I don't know how long it went on. It was
awful. Can you imagine how terrifying it is to feel that you're
drowning, again and again and again? In the end, they grew tired
of it. They told him to get it over with: they had to move on, there
were other Jews to take care of. He gripped me even harder and
forced me down to the bottom of the barrel. I saw myself from
above, as though I were floating in air. The child's little body kept
jerking. My feet were kicking in all directions. They wet his pants.
So did he, because he couldn't control his bladder. After a while, I
can't say exactly how long, no more bubbles rose to the surface. My
body stopped twitching and grew very heavy. The soldier pulled
me from the water, shook me a few times, and tossed me on the
ground like a fisherman sorting fish. By then I was far away. I saw
it all as though I were looking through the wrong end of a telescope."

Herman paused, leaving his story unfinished. Pleased with its
impact, he regarded Andrew with a toxic, tortured, obsessive satisfaction. Andrew said nothing. He licked his dry lips, awaiting
the denouement. "After all this, I went to see the Holocaust Museum in Washington. The new one—have you been there? You
should go. They have an archive with computerized lists of millions of Jews. An archivist logged on for me and typed in Zuritsh.
There are different ways of spelling it and it took him a long time,
but in the end it turned out that there really was such a place, on
the Polish-Lithuanian border, and that there was a Jewish family
there that lived on the edge of a forest and was killed by a unit
of German *Einsatzgruppen* and local collaborators on October 3,
1941. Guess how they called the young boy, who was eleven when
he was killed. That's right: Yosef Chaim. Yossil-Chaim!" Herman
fell silent again, equal amounts of horror and pride in the smug,
tormented eyes that were turned on Andrew.

He's mad! The realization dawned on Andrew all at once. A mentally ill, pathological liar! All the symptoms were there: the lack of boundaries, the autistic single-mindedness, the low self-esteem of someone wanting to be someone else, the insufferable appearance of the man . . . Andrew knew that his defenses were rejecting a story that, however improbable, could not be dismissed out of hand, but his anger and loathing silenced the voice of intellectual probity. He refused—quite simply refused—to be impressed or shocked, much less feel the slightest sympathy. Herman's neediness was more than he could bear. All he wanted was to rise from his seat, step over the fat thighs pressed against him that were barring his way, and escape—where didn't matter. Yet a sense of lassitude, combined for some reason with a feeling of guilt, kept him glued to his place, seemingly stuck with this haranguing stranger forever.

14

Eleven twenty. The train pulled into Philadelphia. The loudspeaker system came alive, spewing a torrent of pointless information into the car. Herman extricated his fat frame from the confines of its seat and stood in the aisle, waiting like a good friend for Andrew, who took his time gathering his belongings in the hope that the man would give up and go his way. But Herman had endless patience. He descended the steps to the platform alongside Andrew and handed him his business card. "It's been a pleasure! Do you have a card? I'd love to meet again and talk some more. Maybe I'll even show you a poem or two, who knows?"

His smile held out the promise of a poetry reading. Andrew's nonchalant shrug implied regret at having left his calling cards at home while falling short of being an outright lie. "Which way are you heading?" Herman asked with genial forbearance. "If it's downtown, I'd be happy to share a cab. Where do you have to be?"

A frantic mixture of hand signals and muddled syllables somehow convinced Herman that Andrew had no idea where he had to be. He smiled again, this time indulgently at such professorial absentmindedness. He gave Andrew a hearty handshake and wished him a good day, repeating how much he had enjoyed their conversation and was looking forward to more. Andrew, watching his broad back recede, couldn't believe he was rid of him. What made him shrink with something like dread from someone who wasn't the least bit violent or dangerous? Quickly, he hurried toward an exit at the other end of the platform, embarrassed by the instinct to turn around and make sure he wasn't being followed.

Herman's business card was still clenched in his fist. It took a few minutes to feel safe again and out of the man's field of vision. Tearing the card into pieces without bothering to read it, Andrew tossed them into a trash can behind a column while hysterically fantasizing that Herman might find them there. He felt sick. What was wrong with him? Hunger? Fatigue? Overwork? There was no hope of calming down before he found a men's room in which to wash away the man's revoltingly sticky handshake with soap and water. Perhaps these would also cleanse his mind of the morbid scenes Herman has planted in it, horror scenes that went on flashing mechanically on and off in it, dancing jerkily as if shot with an exasperatingly old, slow camera.

15
May 1, 2001

The 8th of Iyar, 5761

Two thirty p.m. The gym locker room was humming as usual. The metal doors of the showers opened and banged shut noisily. Men with towels wrapped around their waists stood before the large mirrors, shaving, smearing themselves with creams and lotions, and combing their wet hair with a grotesque painstakingness. The door of the sauna kept opening and closing, filling the room with moist, hot steam. An elderly man with sparse gray hair and a potbelly stood stark naked on a physician's scale, sliding its metal weights back and forth in the hope of getting them to correspond to the poundage recommended by his doctor. Andrew, leaning heavily on a granite washstand, looked wonderingly at his reflection's thick growth of white bristles. The rash on his right cheek that had refused to go away shone through them like an exotic red flower. The dermatologist he was referred to had advised him not to shave for several weeks. "These little pustules can turn nasty. At your age, I wouldn't take any risks. You have tenure, don't you? Great! Now you can show up for work with a beard!"

Andrew had let this pass in silence, without even the amused smile of complicity that such quips called for. The whiteness of his beard startled him. And yet why expect it to be dark like his eyebrows rather than white like the hair of his head? It made him look old, like an old, traditional Jew. How much longer would it go on? A few more weeks, he supposed. He had to remember to apply the prescribed cream twice a day, once today after working out and showering.

The door of the sauna swung open to reveal two or three naked men no younger than himself, their far from perfect bodies bright in the steamy mist. His energy felt low. It had been low for a while. Should he take vitamins? Eat differently? Drink less coffee and forgo his regular nightcap? Resisting the temptation to give in to how he felt, rest for a few minutes in the sauna, shower, and go home, he pushed against the washstand in an effort to tear himself loose from the mirror and go to the gym on the next floor. Yes, he looked like an old Jew with a white beard and bottomless eyes. All that was missing was a large black velvet yarmulke.

A fresh billow of steam from the sauna fogged the mirror, blurring his face behind a dreamlike haze. Squinting, he studied the pearly glass. The familiar yet strange reflection looking back with a penetrating, all-knowing look had something haunted, even spiritual about it, a divine imprint as airily elusive as a wind upon the water. *A long, silken, silvery white beard shimmered as if its strands were alive; long earlocks curled down the angular cheeks; a black phylactery stood out on the high, wisely wrinkled forehead, the hair above which was trimmed to make room for its artfully worked leather cube. From afar came a primal, profound, bowel-piercing lament. In the cavity at the back of his head where skull met neck, the black cube's leather straps were tied in an intricate, hierophantic, transcendentally mysterious knot. Hanging down on either side of his neck like black snakes, they crawled out of sight at the bottom of the mirror.*

Where were these visions coming from? Was he going mad? Andrew reached out apprehensively and wiped the mirror clean. The long beard disappeared, and with it the earlocks, the leather cube, and the straps. Apart from its tormented look, bloodshot eyes, and coronet of bristles, the face peering back at him from the droplets beading the glass was again recognizably his own.

What time was it? Already three o'clock. It was late. He had better start working out. Turning away from the mirror, he headed reluctantly for the locker room's exit. The shabbily naked bodies around him were more irksome than usual. How could such neglected-looking men go around with nothing on? The old Jews taken to the gas chambers must have looked like that: naked, ugly, stripped of their clothes and their dignity. *What would have happened had we remained there, in Eastern Europe?* We would have been lined up naked just like them, pressed against each other skin to skin, flesh to flesh, helplessly waiting our turn to run to the edge of a mass grave in a forest, to a gas chamber, to the ovens. A sickening smell of burned flesh, a stench of singed hair and charred bones. Raucous, hate-filled voices shouting orders in a hard, savage German. Naked men run in terror, lashed by a rain of whips and clubs. They keep their heads down, trying to protect their faces from the blows, hands spasmodically pawing skinny loins. Ferocious dogs bark, a machine gun rattles mercilessly: darkest dread. Little Rayzl screams, her fear-crazed eyes fixed on the slavering jaws of a growling German shepherd. How awful to see your own daughter screaming like that and not dare do anything. To be paralyzed with fear, your hands and feet unwilling to run to her and pick her up. *The girls!* What would have happened to the girls? Who would we have given them to? Friends? Colleagues from work? Rachel's first nanny who loved her so much— the always laughing, good-natured Ramola from Trinidad? And what about Angie. He would trust her blindly. But she was black and they were white—how could she pretend they were hers? How would he even approach her? "You're the only person in the world I can count on. Please, please, take care of my little girls! Don't let anything bad happen to them!"

Andrew's chest froze in anguish, unable to breathe. Suppose there are informers? You had to watch out for them. There are people who will sell us to the Germans for a hundred dollars, for a few bottles of whiskey or a good meal, for nothing at all, just for the hell of it. Whole families were turned in to the Gestapo for half a pound of salt! How much was given to whoever informed on Anne Frank? It couldn't have been much. That insolently fawning doorman of ours, he's just the type to do it. Or our super, that Serbian (or was it Croatian?) hoodlum with his black Mercedes, his narrow eyes in which violence dozed, and the horde of square-headed, broad-shouldered cousins and nephews that he employed. He would have to be bribed all the time—and even then there was no being sure he would keep his promise and not hand us over on a moment's whim. There would be nothing to depend on—not the law, not morality, not physical strength. Nothing! Absolute helplessness. What will we do when our money runs out? When there's nothing left for bribes? There must have been women and girls who had to sleep with their rescuers and pay them with their bodies not to turn their families in.

Enough! Stop it! He had to put an end to these poisonous fantasies. He had to go to the next floor. Sergeant Andrew, his trainer, had been waiting for fifteen minutes.

16

Four p.m. A pair of familiar faces is on television. The twins are gratified—in fact, overjoyed. The prize they have won means a beautiful new life of pure love. And who are they going to look like? Brad Pitt! They're going to look like Brad! There's something oddly, disarmingly moving in their sincerity. They have the touching honesty of those with nothing to lose. In their hands they hold a color photograph of America's handsomest man, a blond,

blue-eyed dream boy such as only a genius could sculpt. Next to
his radiant image, their pitiful faces look even more monstrous.
One might be regarding two different species—a pair of hyenas
and a graceful gazelle, or a royal peacock in the company of two
misshapen dodos. And yet victoriously verbalizing their absurd
fantasy has been liberating. For a brief moment, their ear-to-ear,
doppelgänger grins grace their ugliness with a new optimism. For
a moment, it seems to them—to us all—that their past is behind
them, that they've been redeemed, that they're already Brad Pitt.

Naturally, their work is cut out for them. So much needs to be
changed. The nose goes without saying. It's the most conspicuous
thing. But the cheekbones, too, have to be redone, restructured at
the top to give them the same fabulous, indescribable sweep that
is part of Brad Pitt's perfection. The chin must be shortened and
strengthened. The teeth can't be left as they are, either: no small
investment in them is necessary. And the sooner that oily, matted
hair is gotten rid of, the better! Not to mention the acne, which
can hardly be allowed to remain. Plastic surgery won't be enough.
They'll have to be completely redone. Ironically, Brad's blue eyes
are the easiest part. There are now contact lenses in every conceiv-
able color.

Andrew wondered what Dr. Mengele would have said about
that. He had worked so hard to make brown Jewish eyes blue, injecting their eyeballs with chemicals and toxins to Aryanize them.
Dr. Mengele? What made him think of Mengele? Where were all
these gruesome thoughts coming from? What was the matter with
him today?

Four twenty. Perfectly synchronized, the large clocks hanging
on the walls merged their hour and minute hands. Andrew, with
a slightly dissatisfied sigh of relief, slowed his pace on the tread-
mill to a brisk walk, and then to the easy stride that would relax

his strenuously exercised leg muscles. Although he had persisted
for ten minutes less than usual today, who, he thought wryly, was
counting? Everyone had his off days. Perhaps he should eat one of
the suspicious-looking, overpriced "energy bars" sold at the gym's
cafeteria. The final results on the digital screen had left much to
be desired: too few calories had been sacrificed on the altar of the
Religion of Health and his average heartbeat was far from optimal.
And why was he sweating so much and feeling heartburn? Should
he see a cardiologist? Men his age died of heart attacks all the time.
As silly as such hypochondriac anxiety was, he should call for an
appointment.

  He glanced again at his watch: 4:25. Lingering idly by the stilled
machine had left him with little time. He would skip the usual chin-
ups and arm, back, and stomach exercises and head back down to
the locker room. You had to know when to cut your losses and call
it quits. You can't climb Mount Everest every day.

17

A fresh stack of white towels, still warm from the dryer, greeted
Andrew at the entrance to the locker room. Their almost too
immaculate whiteness soothed the sour, guilty feeling that had accompanied him as he descended, with an unearned athletic gait,
to the floor below. He took a towel from the elegantly arranged
stack, stopped for a quick sip of cold water, and had turned to go
to his locker when something brought him to a halt. Standing on
the slate floor of the locker area with his back to him was a wonderfully well-built Latino youth, a bronzed, muscular Adonis.
Draped nonchalantly around his waist, his white towel played up
the rich copper of his skin. The sensual gleam of his rare, dazzling

beauty was almost spiritually intense. Visually, it affected Andrew like a slap. He stood without moving, mesmerized by the superb body that was unblemished from head to toe. So, suntanned and sand-warmed, must have looked the living Apollo, Ganymede, and Paris, not at all like their white, empty-eyed marble icons, the work of Greek and Roman sculptors who painted them with colors that the years washed away, leaving only a bright, abstract starkness that came to be identified with the classical ideal of beauty.

Although his voyeuristic absorption could not have lasted more than half a minute, it seemed to Andrew an uncomfortably long time. The young man stretched, flexed his muscles, and joined his hands behind his neck in a lazy movement suggestive of a predatory big cat. With the theatrical air of someone accustomed to being stared at, he raised a foot, planted it on a wooden bench, and bent toward it—whether to continue his stretches, or admire himself better from a different angle, wasn't clear. Almost unwillingly, Andrew's gaze fell on his sturdy hip and the delicate curve of his calf, circled his thin ankle, and dropped to his arched foot on the waxed bench. The vitality, the perfection of his young body! Only rarely did one encounter such pure beauty in the raw. It wasn't to be found in slick magazines, ads, or fashion pages.

The gorgeous young man straightened up. Something in the way he moved, as though for a camera, strengthened Andrew's impression that he knew he was being watched. This was confirmed a moment later when his back muscles undulated in a half turn that became a full pivot that left them facing each other. Two large, golden, catlike eyes looked straight at Andrew with menacing amusement, forcing him, as if caught doing something wrong, to lower his gaze until it was level with the youth's stomach. Flat and muscular, the center of which was tattooed with a large, sinuously rayed sun whose bright radiance seemed to illuminate the room.

Warm reds, browns, and oranges encircled the navel. Objects of
Platonic desire, a parade of classical images marched through Andrew's mind as though from the bronze gates of an ancient city,
led by the fiery chariot of Helios, which streaked across the sky
harnessed to four noble steeds whose hooves wildly pounded the
blue ether.

The beautiful youth matched Andrew's stare with his own. His
stomach muscles rippled, echoing his hint of a smile and causing
the serpentine rays of the sun to splay over his bare skin. Provocatively, with a coquettishness that could only be called feminine,
he undid his white towel and retied it around his sharply defined
pelvis, allowing Andrew a quick, thrilling glimpse. Though this
lasted a mere second, Andrew flushed, his heart racing. His gaze,
recoiling from the unveiled pit of Eros as though from an electric shock, once more met the young man's, in which was now a
captivating challenge. The eyes, suddenly more brown than gold,
flashed a warning that (ah, how wonderful, how terrible, the
thought of it!) was at the same time an impish invitation. For a
second or two, their glances remained locked. Andrew, frantically
adopting a neutral expression suitable for a chance encounter, was
the first to look away. Nothing had happened! Nothing had passed
between them! Nothing, nothing at all.

He turned back to the corridor leading to the showers, leaving
his belongings in his locker. Stripping off his sweaty gym clothes,
he threw them in a corner instead of arranging them in their usual
neat pile and hurriedly locked himself in a shower stall. The young
man's eyes, which still bored into his bare flesh, now seemed to
have been more black than brown. For a long time he stood beneath the hot water, his mind an irritating cacophony of voices
and thoughts. Though he knew very well why he was taking so
long, he couldn't help but marvel at himself. It was impossible to

get dressed without going to his locker. What if the youth were waiting for him there?

Ridiculous! Why should he be? Nothing had happened between them! Still, he was wasting precious time. He had to get back there before the youth disappeared! Not, of course, that he was attracted to men—and you couldn't call this an attraction, either. Absolutely not! It was a moment of confusion, a temporary loss of coordinates, nothing more.

Andrew shut the faucets, emerged from the shower stall, and set about drying himself—more slowly than usual, so it seemed. Or was it more quickly? Throwing back his shoulders, he took a deep breath and headed for the locker. Suppose he was there? Why was his heart beating so fast? He breathed deeply again, leaving the air trapped in his lungs, and turned to the slate floor of the locker area, desperately trying to convince himself that it was all absurd, a molehill turned into a mountain.

The locker area was deserted. Where was the young Greek god? Gone! Nothing remained of him. Who knew if he had ever been there? Andrew stood there, stunned, for a moment. Was he relieved or bitterly disappointed? He couldn't tell.

And yet why feel disappointment? He hadn't really been hoping that the young man would be there. He made himself go to his locker, took out his clothes, and dressed with an affected everyday nonchalance. Was there a man who hadn't thought once or twice in the course of his sexual experience that . . . no, not that he was homosexual . . . but that he might be turned on by men, too? The categories of gender behavior were among the most easily challenged. He had taught countless classes of students to question conventional versions of them and analyze them as social constructs.

Enough with this pseudo-academic verbiage! He had had a long, hard day. He pulled on his pants, tucked his buttoned shirt into them, and fastened his belt. The warm, dry, sobering clothes restored him to reality. He had no plans for the evening. Would Ann Lee be coming over? The thought of it made him uncomfortable. Recently, there had been too much of that. He found himself less and less looking forward to spending time with her. On second thought, there was no dilemma, she was busy tonight. Yet the open relief this made him feel was enough to cloud whatever peace of mind he had left. Something was not right. Something had stopped flowing between them. Their conversations had grown shorter, more practical. Their sex life, too, was suddenly a sad, embarrassing shadow of itself. What had happened to their remarkable physical and mental chemistry? Where had it gone, that mutual magnetism that was too strong to be put into words? There had been a time when, at some seminar or conference, or in the middle of a cocktail party or dinner with university donors, a hot rush of desire for her would startle him with its urgency. Once, while lecturing to a packed auditorium, he had even had to turn to the blackboard and find some excuse to remain with his back to the class until the physical excitement produced by the thought of her had passed. Where had all that gone to? It now seemed part of another life.

The beautiful youth had disappeared without a trace. Suppose he had given him an open, explicit, come-on? Andrew would have gone with him, gone wherever he chose to lead him.

18
May 4, 2001

The 11th of Iyar, 5761

Eleven thirty a.m. The classrooms are deserted. The approaching weekend felt in the hallways. The spring semester has ended all at once. It was too quick, the spring, too unsettled and unsatisfying. Mature foliage hurried to take its place on the branches, pushing aside the bright green plumage of new leaves. The pink, white, and yellow blossoms fell too fast, impatient to get it over with. The tulips and daffodils, too, more artificial-looking every year, flowered and wilted prematurely, their petals going overnight from a freshly budding virginity to a final decadence in which they resembled the gaping loose genitals of old animals.

As though at the wave of a magic wand, the corridors of the university have emptied out on the first day of the summer vacation. The lively commotion of the semester's end has vanished abruptly. The term papers have been submitted, the exams marked, the final grades handed in to the departmental secretaries. Now, at this very moment, the students are heading for faraway summer destinations, avid to replenish their future fund of youthful memories with new bathing suits, snorkeling masks, large quantities of bad beer, and summer romances. The teaching staff, too, hears the tick of the great clock. Another year of research has gone by with its conferences, publications, prizes, and grants; another milestone has been passed on the road to tenure; another graduating class has soaked up what was required of it and gone out into the world. The empty corridors are filled with a solemn yearning. Time lingers on in them by itself, smiling and contented, savoring a few last minutes before packing up and moving on, too.

Andrew sat in the cafeteria, the day's third cup of coffee (it was about time he woke up!) slowly getting cold on the table. He had forgotten to finish it. His bleary, reddish eyes stared absently into space. Tiny motes of dust swirled like feathers in the diagonal shafts of light pouring through the high windows. With one hand, he automatically stroked the bristles on his cheeks. His rash was almost gone. In a few more days, he could shave and look himself again. Naturally, Ann Lee, little devil that she was, hadn't missed the chance to call him "Grandpa." Soon riders on the subway would have started giving him their seats, deferring to an old age that left him uncertain if it was real or imaginary. He smiled tentatively to himself. He wasn't complaining. It had its enjoyable side. There was something comforting about his new beard. It gave him, so it seemed, an Old World venerability, the look of a tribal elder or Hasidic rabbi.

He raised the cup to his lips, took a sip, and made a face. The coffee, the tang of its bitterness gone, was cold and undrinkable. He had already been to the office to check that all was in order. All the term papers had been returned to their authors—all except for one oddly handwritten one that was still waiting in its box, a strange fledgling in an abandoned nest. Whose work could it be? Who had written it? Why hadn't he come to pick it up? Andrew was loath to concede that he felt let down. Why should he care? Yet there had been something annoying about Ms. Harty today, something insidious in the way she had said with a sly, last-second smile, "You do know, Professor, that the final date for filing for an extension passed a week ago, don't you?" And what exactly had Bernie meant by "We have to face up to there being other forces at work behind the scenes. It's not entirely up to us, if at all . . ."? Forces behind the scenes? Nonsense. What could they be? He should take Bernie out to lunch sometime and feel him out.

The stimulating sight of bared flesh brought Andrew back to earth. The young student sitting at the next table with her back to him had suddenly leaned forward over the book she was reading. Something, a footnote or diagram, had called for closer examination. Her blouse lifted, revealing a curvaceous waist and a white lower back on which a shockingly graphic blue tattoo made her pale skin look even more exposed. Its effect was giddying. Yet the impulse he felt was not an ordinary sexual one. It was more primitive, a child's instinct to peek that took him back to prepuberty. Half-unthinkingly, he leaned forward himself to scan the intricate, attractive tattoo, his eyes drawn to two winning dimples on either side of it. From there, they continued downward to where the sensuous delta of the young woman's buttocks disappeared in the dim recesses of her pants.

His change of posture stretched Andrew's shirt over his stomach, opening slant-eyed spaces between the buttons. It wasn't the first time he had noticed this happening, especially when the shirt was close fitting. Although the knowledge that he was putting on weight worried him, it also gave him a not unpleasant feeling of intimacy with his declining body, one that the elderly possess.

Enough of this melodramatic posturing! He should be exercising more regularly. His eyes traveled back up to the tattoo, which seemed to float above the creamy skin. What did she look like from in front? Should he find some excuse to get up and see? Of course not. What an objectionable idea! He suddenly felt that the student's youth formed an impassable gulf between them. Sex with her would be not only obscene and incestuous but quite simply impossible, a biological contradiction in terms. It was as if their ages had placed them on two different sides of an invisible barrier, like members of separate species that were incapable of mating.

What time was it? Eleven forty-five. His class began in half an hour. Pushing against the table, Andrew rose heavily from his chair and headed for the exit. No, he would not turn around to look at her face. Absolutely not. He would throw his cold coffee in the trash bin and go straight to the elevator. And the term paper in its box? Sooner or later, someone would come for it.

He walked down the empty corridor as though at gunpoint, mindless of where he was going or had come from. The bittersweet stir of the semester's end had left him cold. Nothing was concluded; no closure had been reached; there was no feeling of catharsis. No equation of time, memory, and longing had been solved. The corridors were empty. The floors were littered with papers and empty cups. The cleaning staff had yet to arrive.

END OF BOOK FOUR

[Mishna, Treatise Yoma, Chapter 3, Mishna 6] They brought him to the Parwah Chamber——which was on holy ground. They spread a sheet of byssus [linen] between him and the people. He sanctified his hands and his feet and stripped. Rabbi Meir said: He stripped, sanctified his hands and his feet. He went down and immersed himself, came up and dried himself. Afterward they brought him white garments. He put them on and sanctified his hands and his feet.

[Mishna, Treatise Yoma, Chapter 3, Mishna 7] In the morning he put on Pelusium [Egyptian] linen worth twelve minas, in the afternoon Indian linen worth eight hundred zuz. These are the words of Rabbi Meir. The sages say: In the morning he put on [garments] worth eighteen minas and in the afternoon [garments] worth twelve minas, altogether thirty minas. All that at the charge of the community, and if he wanted to spend more of his own, he could do so.

The High Priest was brought to the ablution pool. A sheet was spread before him again. He washed his hands and feet, bathed, and dried himself, after which the superior signaled Obadiah to bring him white garments. These were made of the finest, most expensive pile, and Obadiah held them as if holding a newborn baby, for never had he touched anything so light or precious in his life. It was thinner than thin and stirred in his hands like a living creature. The High Priest took the garments with a twinkle of acknowledgment, as if wishing to thank him but too rushed to speak. Obadiah felt a pang of contrition: here he was, a simple priest, being treated by the High Priest like a brother! But he did not have long to think about it, for the time had come for the High Priest's confession.

[Babylonian Talmud, Treatise Yoma, Folio 35a] What does [the name] Parwah mean? Rav Joseph said: Parwah was [the name of] a [Persian] magician. Commentators: The Persian magus [sorcerer] Parwah had dug a tunnel under the ground of the Sanctuary, so that he might be able to watch the High Priest at the service of the Day of Atonement. The priests, noticing the digging, found the intruder and killed him, as it is written [Numbers, Chapter 3, Verse 38]: [. . .] *and Aaron and his sons, keeping the charge of the sanctuary, even the charge for the children of Israel; and the stranger that drew nigh was to be put to death.*

[Babylonian Talmud, Treatise Yoma, Folio 35b] They told about Rabbi Ishmael ben Phabi that his mother made him a tunic worth one hundred minas that he put on to officiate at a service and then handed it over to the community. They told about Rabbi Eleazar Ben Harsum that his mother made him a tunic worth twenty thousand minas and his brethren, the priests, would not suffer him to put it on because he looked like one naked. But how could it be transparent, did not a Master say the thread [of the priestly garments] was six times twisted?—— Abaye said: [It was visible] even as wine shines through a [glass] cup.

The Gate of Rebirth:

On the other hand, the cleaving of a soul to a soul takes place not at birth but in the course of a lifetime. It may happen then that the Vital Soul of even a biblical patriarch cleaves to another soul. All depends on the merit that the possessor of such a soul has accumulated, since there are deeds that have the power to attract the greatest of souls. It may even happen that a Vital Soul is cleaved to by a Vital Soul and then cleaved to again by an even greater one. The first of the two cleaving souls may act as the Intellectual Soul of the Vital Soul that it assists, the second as its Spiritual Soul.

[Leviticus, Chapter 16, Verses 5—6] And he shall take of the congregation of the children of Israel two he-goats for a sin-offering, and one ram for a burnt-offering. And Aaron shall present the bullock of the sin-offering, which is for himself, and make atonement for himself, and for his house.

[Mishna, Treatise Yoma, Chapter 3, Mishna 8] He came to his bullock and his bullock was standing between the hall and the altar, its head to the south and its face to the west. And the priest stood in the east with his face to the west. And he pressed both his hands upon it and made confession. And thus he would say: O Lord! I have done wrong, I have transgressed, I have sinned before thee, I and my house. O Lord! Forgive the wrong-doings, the transgressions, the sins which I have committed and transgressed and sinned before thee, I and my house, as it is written in the Torah of Moses thy servant: for on this day shall atonement be made for you [to cleanse you; from all your sins shall ye be clean before the Lord]. And they answered after him: Blessed be the name of his glorious kingdom forever and ever!

Donning his white garments, the High Priest hurried to the bull of the sin-offering with Obadiah and the other acolytes on his heels. The bull stood between the altar and the Sacred Hall with its body to the south and its face turned to the west. The High Priest placed his hands on its head and prayed, uttering the unutterable name of God that must not even be written in full:

"I beseech Thee, O LORD! I have sinned, transgressed, and offended before Thee, I and my house. I beseech Thee, O LORD! Atone for my and my house's sins, transgressions, and offenses! As is written in Thy Torah: 'For on that day shall He make an atonement for you to cleanse you, that ye may be clean from all your sins before the Lord.'"

When they heard the great and terrible Name of God uttered by the High Priest in sanctity and holiness, the priests and the Israelites in the Gallery bowed to the ground, every one of them, and cried in one voice:

"Blessed be the name of his glorious Kingship forever and ever!"

And the High Priest proclaimed to them, concluding his prayer:

"Be ye cleansed!"

[Babylonian Talmud, Treatise Yoma, Folio 20b] There is a teaching in accord with Rab: What does Gebini the Temple crier call out: Arise, ye priests for your service, Levites for your platform, Israel for your post! And his voice was audible for three parasangs. It happened that King Agrippa, who came along traveling, heard his voice from three parasangs, and as he came home, he sent gifts to him. Nevertheless, the High Priest is more excellent than even he, for the Master said: It has happened already that when he prayed "O LORD" that his voice was heard in Jericho.

[Babylonian Talmud, Treatise Kiddushin, Folio 71a] Rab Judah said in Rab's name: The forty-two-lettered Name is entrusted only to him who is pious, meek, middle-aged, free from bad temper, sober, and not insistent on his rights. And he who knows it is heedful thereof, and observes it in purity, is beloved above and popular below, feared by men, and inherits two worlds, this world and the world to come.

[Babylonian Talmud, Treatise Kiddushin, Folio 71a] Our Rabbis taught: At first [God's] twelve-lettered Name used to be entrusted to all people. When unruly men increased, it was confided to the pious of the priesthood, and these "swallowed it" [i.e., pronounced it indistinctly or inaudibly] during the chanting of their fellow priests. It was taught: Rabbi Tarfon said: "I once ascended the dais after my mother's brother, and inclined my ear to the High Priest, and heard him swallowing the Name during the chanting of his fellow priests."

[Leviticus, Chapter 16, Verses 7—10] And he shall take the two goats, and set them before the LORD at the door of the tent of meeting. And Aaron shall cast lots upon the two goats: one lot for the LORD, and the other lot for Azazel. And Aaron shall present the goat upon which the lot fell for the LORD, and offer him for a sin-offering. But the goat, on which the lot fell for Azazel, shall be set alive before the LORD, to make atonement over him, to send him away for Azazel into the wilderness.

[Mishna, Treatise Yoma, Chapter 3, Mishna 9] He then went back to the east of the Temple Court, to the north of the altar, the deputy High Priest at his right and the head of the family [ministering that week] at his left. There were two he-goats and an urn containing two lots. He bound a thread of crimson wool on the head of the he-goat which was to be sent away, and [meantime] he placed it [at the gate] whence it was to be sent away; and the he-goat that was to be slaughtered, at the place of the slaughtering. They [the lots] were of box-wood. Ben Gamala made them of gold and therefore he was praised. King Monobaz had all the handles of all the vessels used on the day of atonement made of gold. His mother, Helena, had a golden candlestick made over the door of the shrine. She also had a golden tablet made, on which the portion touching the suspected adulteress was inscribed. Nicanor experienced miracles with his gates and his memory was therefore praised.

The Superior took the High Priest by his right hand. The day's managing priest took him by his left hand and he was led to the east of the Gallery, where stood two he-goats of similar height and appearance. Beside them was a golden box with two lots. On one lot was written "For the LORD" and on the other "For Azazel." The High Priest shuffled the lots and took one in each hand. "For the LORD" was in his right hand. The Superior told him, "My liege the High Priest, raise your right arm." He raised his arm and the people rejoiced, for it was a good omen. Now they knew which goat was to be slaughtered and which to be driven into the wilderness. He tied each lot to its goat and proclaimed, "This goat is for the LORD!" And the people replied:

"Blessed be the name of his glorious Kingship forever and ever!"

[Babylonian Talmud, Treatise Yoma Folio 38a] NICANOR EXPERIENCED MIRACLES WITH HIS DOORS: Our Rabbis taught: What miracles happened to his doors? It was reported that when Nicanor had gone to fetch doors from Alexandria of Egypt, on his return a gale arose in the sea to drown him. Thereupon they took one of his doors and cast it into the sea and yet the sea would not stop its rage. When, thereupon, they prepared to cast the other into the sea, he rose and clung to it, saying: "Cast me in with it!" [They did so, and] the sea stopped immediately its raging. He was deeply grieved about the other [door]. As he arrived at the harbor of Acre, it broke through and came up from under the sides of the boat.——Others say: A monster of the sea swallowed it and spat it out on the dry land. [. . .] Therefore all the gates in the Sanctuary were changed for golden ones with the exception of the Nicanor gates because of the miracles wrought with them. But some say: Because the bronze of which they were made had a golden hue. Rabbi Eliezer Bar Jacob said: It was Corinthian bronze, which shone like gold.

[Leviticus, Chapter 16, Verse 11] *And Aaron shall present the bullock of the sin-offering, which is for himself, and shall make atonement for himself, and for his house, and shall kill the bullock of the sin-offering which is for himself.*

[Mishna, Treatise Yoma, Chapter 4, Mishna 2] He came to his bullock a second time, pressed his two hands upon it, and made confession. And thus he would say: O Lord, I have dealt wrongfully, I have transgressed, I have sinned before thee, I and my house, and the children of Aaron, thy holy people, O Lord, pray forgive the wrongdoings, the transgressions, and the sins which I have committed, transgressed, and sinned before thee, I and my house, and the children of Aaron, thy holy people. As it is written in the Torah of Moses, thy servant: For on this day atonement be made for you, to cleanse you; from all the sins shall ye be clean before the Lord. And they responded: Blessed be the name of his glorious kingdom forever and ever.

The High Priest did not tarry there, for it was already time to slaughter the bull of the sin-offering. He tied a scarlet band to the scapegoat and led it to the place of its dispatch. Then he led the goat that was to be slaughtered to the place of its sacrifice and hurried back to the bull with his attendants on his heels. He placed his hands on the bull and prayed:

"I beseech Thee, O LORD! I have sinned, transgressed, and offended before Thee, I and my house and the House of Aaron, Thy holy priests. I beseech Thee, O LORD! Atone for my sins, and for the sins of my house, and for the sins of the house of Aaron. Atone for our sins, transgressions, and offenses! As is written in Thy Torah: 'For on the day shall He make an atonement for you to cleanse you, that ye may be clean from all your sins before the Lord.'"

Once again, hearing the great and terrible Name of God uttered by the High Priest in sanctity and holiness, the priests and the Israelites in the Gallery bowed to the ground, every one of them, and cried in one voice:

"Blessed be the Name of his glorious Kingship forever and ever!"

[Babylonian Talmud, Treatise Sukkah, Folio 55b] Rabbi Eleazar stated: To what do those seventy bullocks [that were offered during the seven days of the inauguration of the Temple] correspond? They represent the seventy nations of the world. To what does the single bullock [of the Eighth Day] correspond? It represents the unique nation [of Israel]. This may be compared to a mortal king who said to his servants, "Prepare for me a great banquet"; but on the last day he said to his beloved friend, "Prepare for me a simple meal that I may derive some pleasure from you." Rabbi Johanan observed: Woe to the idolaters, for they had a loss and do not know what they have lost. When the Temple was in existence the altar atoned for them, too, but now who shall atone for them?

The Gate of Rebirth:

The act of cleaving takes place for two reasons. One is that it may assist a Vital Soul to perfect and purify itself until it can rise in the World to Come to the station of the cleaving soul. But the cleaving soul also benefits, since by assisting another soul to do good and perfect itself, it, too, does good. This is the hidden meaning of the saying of the Sages, "Great are the righteous, for they bear issue even after death."

[Numbers, Chapter 18, Verses 1, 7] And the LORD said unto Aaron, Thou and thy sons and thy father's house with thee shall bear the iniquity of the sanctuary: and thou and thy sons with thee shall bear the iniquity of your priesthood. [. . .] Therefore thou and thy sons with thee shall keep your priest's office for every thing of the altar, and within the veil; and ye shall serve: I have given your priest's office unto you as a service of gift: and the stranger that cometh nigh shall be put to death.

[Mishna, Treatise Yoma, Chapter 4, Mishna 3] He slaughtered it [the bullock] and received its blood in a bowl. And he gave it to the one who should stir it up on the fourth terrace within the sanctuary lest it congeal.

[Mishna, Treatise Yoma, Chapter 2, Mishnayot 1—4] Originally, whoever wanted to remove the ashes from the altar would do it. And when there were many, they would run up the ramp, and whoever got to within four cubits [of the altar] first would win [the task of removing the ashes]. If two tied, the assigner [of tasks] would tell [all of] them: "Stick out your fingers [for the procedure to assign the task]." And what would they stick out? Either one or two

The High Priest prepared to slaughter the bull. The superior signaled Obadiah to assist him. Obadiah felt both fear and pride. The honor was a great one, coveted by all. Many would have paid a stiff price for it. He had no idea why he, one of thousands of priests and the youngest in his family, had been chosen. Before he had time to wonder, however, the knife was poised above the bull in the High Priest's hand. Obadiah was given a stoup and pushed toward the altar. As the High Priest lowered the knife to the bull's throat, its handle clinked against the stoup. Alarmed, Obadiah glanced at the High Priest, who glanced back with a smile of reassurance. He slit the bull's throat, took the stoup from Obadiah, and handed him the knife to finish the cut. Obadiah stood there uncertainly, the knife in mid-air. His heart was full to overflowing. Another moment and the sacrifice would have had to be declared unfit. Then none would be atoned for.

[Babylonian Talmud, Treatise Yoma, Folio 24b] There is the teaching in accord with Rab: These are the services for the performance of which a common man [who is not of the priestly clans] incurs penalty of death: the sprinkling of the blood, both within [the Temple] and within the Holy of Holies: and he who sprinkles the blood of a bird offered as a sin-offering; and he who wrings out the blood, and who smokes the bird offered up as a burnt-offering; and he who makes the libation of three logs, of water or of wine. There is a teaching in accord with Levi: The services for the performance of which a common man incurs penalty of death are: the removal of the ashes, the seven sprinklings within [the Holy of Holies] and he who offers up on the altar a sacrifice whether fit or unfit.

[fingers], and they would not stick out their thumb in the Temple. Once, two were even as they ran up the ramp, and one pushed the other, and he fell and his leg broke. And when the court saw that this practice leads to danger, they decreed that the ashes would not be removed from the altar except by lottery. There were four lotteries there, and this was the first lottery. The second lottery [decided] who would slaughter [the daily sacrifice], who would throw the blood [onto the altar], who would remove the ashes from the inner altar, who would remove the ashes from the candelabra, and who would bring the limbs to the ramp: the head and the [left] hind-leg, the two fore-legs, the tail and the [right] hind-leg, the chest and the throat, the two sides, the innards, the flour [for the accompanying meal-offering], the pan-cakes, and the wine offerings. Thirteen priests were chosen in this [lottery]. In the third lottery, new priests [who had never offered the incense] came and drew lots. The fourth [lottery] consisted of new priests and experienced priests [to determine] who would take the limbs from the ramp to the altar.

[Leviticus, Chapter 16, Verses 12—13] And he shall take a censer full of coals of fire from off the altar before the LORD, and his hands full of sweet incense beaten small, and bring it within the veil. And he shall put the incense upon the fire before the LORD, that the cloud of the incense may cover the ark-cover that is upon the testimony, that he die not.

[Babylonian Talmud, Treatise Kerithoth, Folio 6a] Our Rabbis have taught: The compound of incense consisted of balm, onycha, galbanum, and frankincense, each in the quantity of seventy manehs; of myrrh, cassia, spikenard, and saffron, each sixteen manehs by weight; of costus twelve, of aromatic rind three, and of cinnamon nine manehs; of lye obtained from leek, nine kabs; of Cyprus wine, three se'ahs and three kabs, though if Cyprus wine is not available, old white wine may be used instead; of salt of Sodom the fourth of a kab, and of ma'aleh 'ashan a minute quantity. Rabbi Nathan says: Also of Jordan resin a minute quantity. If, however, honey is added, the incense is rendered unfit; while if one omits one of the ingredients, he is liable to the penalty of death.

[Mishna, Treatise Yoma, Chapter 4, Mishna 3] Rabbi Simeon son of Gamaliel said: Balm is nothing but a resin which exudes from the wood of the balsam tree; the lye obtained from leek was rubbed over the onycha in order to render it beautiful, and in the Cyprus wine the onycha was steeped that its odor might be intensified. In fact, urine might well serve this purpose, but urine may not be brought within the precincts of the Temple. This supports Rabbi Jose son of Rabbi Hanina, who says: It is holy and it shall be holy unto you, implies that all work in connection therewith must be performed within the sacred precincts.

[Rashi, Numbers, Chapter 16, Verse 6]: *This do; take you censors.* As for you, marital intercourse most pleasing, so is incense to the Lord.

The Superior coughed loudly. Obadiah half came to his senses and severed the bull's neck, his hands working as if unconnected to his brain. The High Priest gathered the blood in the stoup. He passed it to Obadiah, who stirred it to keep it from congealing, and strode quickly to the burning logs on the altar to take coals for the burning of the incense, his acolytes running before and behind him. Their hearts were all aflutter, for the time had come for the High Priest to enter the Holy of Holies and burn the incense.

Obadiah stood on the top flight of the stairs leading from the outer altar to the Sacred Hall. The gold stoup was heavy and the smell of the still warm blood assailed his nostrils. He stirred it and thought without knowing what he was thinking. His mind was awhirl. "Who do you think you are? Who do you think you are?" he kept saying to himself. This only increased his agitation, for what he said was not what his heart was telling him.

[Babylonian Talmud, Treatise Kerithoth, Folio 6b] Our Rabbis have taught: Twice in the course of the year is the incense put back into the mortar. During the summer it is scattered, so that it does not rot away; during the winter it is heaped together, so that its fragrance may not escape. While it is being beaten, he who beats it calls out loud: "Pound well, well pound." These are the words of Abba Jose ben Johanan. The three remaining manehs of it are those that the high priest separates with his bare hands on the Day of Atonement. They are put back in the mortar on the eve of the Day of Atonement and pounded very thoroughly, so that the incense is of the very finest. [...] The Master said: "While it is being beaten, he who beats it calls out loud: 'Pound well, well pound.' [...] for Rabbi Johanan said: Just as speech is harmful to wine, so it is beneficial to spices."

BOOK
FIVE

1

May 10, 2001

The 17th of Iyar, 5761

Over in the meadow,
In the sand, in the sun,
Lived an old mother turtle
And her little turtle one.
"Dig," said the mother.
"I dig," said the one. And they dug all day
In the sand, in the sun.

A small girl's voice chimed sweetly in the room. She was singing right next to him, into his ear, enunciating each syllable with a touchingly childish precision. Andrew shut his eyes tight, refusing to wake up. He recognized the song immediately. It made his heart beat faster. It was "Over in the Meadow," a haunting old nursery rhyme that Linda had sung with Rachel when putting her to sleep, rocking her in her lap while leafing through its illustrated book. Linda had had a beautiful voice, clear, pure, and amazingly rich. He even remembered the book. It had old-fashioned, curiously exact drawings of turtles, foxes, robins, and bees. But why this dream? From where had the distant memory of this song surfaced? How many years had it been since he last heard it?

Over in the meadow,
Where the tall grasses grew,
Lived an old mother fox
And her little foxes two.
"Run," said the mother.
"We run," said the two.
So they ran and were glad
Where the tall grasses grew.

The ghostly voice was singing again. Andrew shivered. It wasn't a dream! How was that possible? Who could be singing at this hour? He was totally awake now, gripped by anxiety, though his eyes remained tightly shut. Where was the voice coming from? Could it be the next-door apartment? But the walls weren't made out of paper. She was singing on and on. Her sweet voice sent a chill through him. He didn't want it to stop. If only it didn't. If only it would go on forever.

Over in the meadow,
In a nest in a tree,
Lived an old mother robin
And her little robins three.
"Sing," said the mother.
"We sing," said the three.
So they sang and were glad
In the nest in the tree.

It was the voice of a siren, a little urban siren. *I would go to the far ends of the earth for a voice like that.* But it was already fading, already beginning to vanish, leaving behind a transparent wake, the shadow of a shadow, an echo of an echo. He mustn't open his eyes. He mustn't open them now! What was he more afraid of? That she wouldn't be there if he did or that she would be? He mustn't! Maybe she would sing it again. The sweetness of that voice. You could drown in it. You could dissolve in your own tears and drown from so much longing and sorrow. Was it a dream? A hallucination? He didn't care. He just wanted her to sing some more. Why wasn't she singing?

2

May 11, 2001

The 18th of Iyar, 5761

Nine a.m. The spring semester had officially ended the day before. Summer vacation had begun. It was already unseasonably hot. The wind had stripped the last tender buds of May from the branches and a blazing sky stared cruelly down, melting the hazy, golden outline of the horizon.

Yet the apartment felt fresh and cool. The tiles of the bathroom walls released the pleasant chill stored up in them during the night, evoking a dim, bittersweet memory of a once boundless purity. Bare-chested, a towel around his waist, Andrew stood facing the mirror, a new razor blade on the marble counter of the sink, carefully lathering three weeks' growth of beard. It wasn't a day for whistling or cheerfully humming snatches of nameless arias. As much as being clean-shaven again was a cause for renewed optimism, he felt tense and on edge. He had mixed feelings about parting with the soft white bristles that had hidden him from the world, enabling him to commune with himself for a while. Had it not been so absurd, he would have said he was afraid to confront the person they concealed. And shaving was far from simple. The new blade, though sharp, traversed the matted hair with difficulty and had to be rinsed after each stroke.

In the end, however, the bristles' stubborn resistance yielded to the forces of circumstance and fashion. One by one, broad swathes of pale, soft skin appeared on Andrew's face like harvested fields. They resembled the white skin beneath his wedding ring when he had removed it after his divorce. His finger had looked naked and vulnerable, like a deep-sea creature forced to the surface. Although the white patch disappeared within a few weeks, it was hard to get over this last sign of a covenant, stamped in his flesh, that gradually faded as his skin adjusted to the air and light.

He was almost done. Rinsing the last of the lather, he leaned over the sink for a better look at his old-new face. The rash on the cheeks had vanished without a trace. The skin was smooth—if anything, too smooth. Without its beard, the naked line of his lips looked exaggerated, almost feminine. In the past three weeks, he had grown heavier. Was that what he had been afraid of discovering? All those years of lavish, guilt-free eating were finally taking their toll. Not that he was getting fat, far from it. He had simply put on a bit of weight. He needed to cut down on the carbs and stop cutting corners at the gym. Quickly, involuntarily, his right hand slid down to his waist, lightly fingered its fold of flesh, and returned to the marble counter. Although the man staring back from the mirror was still handsome and well kept for his age, his Peter Pan, golden-boy look had vanished almost entirely. His chin was rounder, his cheeks plumper. Even his hair had lost its exotic sheen and was now an ordinary, everyday gray.

Andrew reached for the faucet, turned up the hot water, and rinsed his face slowly as if removing a mud mask. He felt no cathartic relief. The chill of the tiles was gone, yielding to the unexpected heat. He would have to ask the super to get the air conditioners out of storage if he hoped to get any work done today. Who would believe it: air-conditioning in May! Andrew hated air conditioners, especially the one that took up half the living-room window and spoiled the perfect symmetry of the view.

He straightened up and peered blankly at the mirror, forgetting to dry his face. Large beads of water, as warm and heavy as tears, dropped from his cheeks and chin to the sink. What had happened to his wedding ring? Where had he put it? He last remembered seeing it tucked away in a little box in the top drawer of the living-room chest. It must still be there. You didn't throw away a wedding ring. Or did you? The antique shops were full of them: old gold rings, smooth or engraved, inset with diamonds or festooned with sapphires, inscribed with the names of those long gone. It wasn't worth melting them down. The metal had little value. People obviously bought them, perhaps even wore them as wedding rings themselves. Ghost rings. How bizarre: the living wearing the dead. Jesus, it was muggy! A burning lump of sorrow pressed on his heart and chest. If only it could be washed away by clear, living water. A dive into a cold, pristine pond.

The bittersweet memory was working its way toward the surface of his damp skin. His first swim with a wedding ring. Lake Placid, August 1976. It was the closest thing to a honeymoon that he and Linda—loath to do the conventional, middle-class thing—had permitted themselves. The lake was huge, deep, ice-cold even in summer. Curled anxiously, his finger was conscious of its thin gold band. It gave new meaning to the water, now a transparent, semisolid expanse, the clearest matter he had ever seen. He was constantly afraid it would slip from his finger and disappear into the long fingers of eelgrass stretching toward him from the deep. Large water birds skimmed the surface, quacking to each other with wild glee. Linda was swimming gracefully. The cold water rocked her body, which was heavy with child, cradling her in its clear lap. Her wedding ring didn't worry her. She was used to rings. She wore this one on her finger as lightly as if it were a part of her, an extension of her body.

Where, damn it, was all this taking him? Nowhere! In the end it would all disappear—the angry words, the insults, the memories, the longing—all swept away by the waves. And yet, deep down, it hurt.

3

May 18, 2001

———————

The 25th of Iyar, 5761

Ten a.m. Andrew, naked except for the damp towel still wrapped around his waist, went to his desk. He drank his coffee quickly, afraid to put off the start of the day's work. At the height of a flourishing career, after years in which writing had come so easily, it had suddenly turned into an exhausting, menacing chore, one whose outcome was uncertain. Even drinking his coffee had lost its cozy, meditative quality. He was too tightly wound to enjoy it. The morning's *Times* still lay on the mat outside the front door; he would look at it at lunchtime. He had stopped leafing through it on mornings set aside for work, loath to cloud the clarity of mind that came from proximity to the workings of the sleeping unconscious. The mail could wait, too, including the special-delivery envelope that had arrived from the department yesterday. This wasn't the time for it. He no longer even liked starting the day with music; it made him feel nervous, impatient. A tinge of anxiety, growing as his coffee cup emptied, colored the creativity he now had to make a daily effort to arouse. Yes, work had become a burden. It had taken a while to admit it to himself—

and to himself alone. Despite the pressure to publish as much as possible now that the semester and its duties were over and the fact that he had time to spare before his new appointment and its heavy demands took effect on September 1, 2001, he had been trying for weeks, morning after morning—trying and trying without success—to finish a small article that in better days would have been in page proofs long ago. Music. That would wake him up. Gershwin's *Rhapsody in Blue*, of course! What could be more inspiring?

These dreadful mornings had all started out well. Clear, blue, early spring hours had seemed to promise a breakthrough, a burst of productive inspiration. The article, too, had shown every sign of being a good and elegant one. "Woody Warhol and Andy Allen: Representative Antitheses or the Antithesis of Representation" (a working title) took an elusively sophisticated position that was hard to pigeonhole. Rather than treat the crisis in representational art as a springboard for the standard elegy on a forever-lost golden age of symbolic absoluteness, "Woody Warhol and Andy Allen" had begun by examining, using a theoretical model based on a priori aesthetic assumptions, the physical resemblance between New York City's two great cultural heroes. This visual perspective, it argued, in which both the eye of the observer and the vanishing point it was drawn to kept changing with the descriptive framework and its representational conventions, repeatedly reversed the subject-object relationship like two crisscrossing trapeze artists. The free, inter-contextual flow of the article's prose was in keeping with its parodic, fetishistic dimension. In short, it was a gem of a piece, its jewel-like concentration an example of city culture at its best. He just had to finish it and send it off.

To work! His open laptop lay on the table like a faithful pet eager to do its owner's bidding. Andrew switched it on with a casual flick. If anything, it was a bit too casual, as if he were trying to fool it—or himself, or his Muse, or somebody—into thinking he had what it took. The computer came to life with a merry whir, emitting playful sounds of efficiency, perhaps in collaboration with Andrew's facade of self-confidence, perhaps in mockery of his pretense of being up to the job. It flashed little icons, sent letters and numbers dancing across the screen, and displayed vertical and horizontal application bands. All systems were go. To work! He just had to fight back the urge to check his e-mail. More than one day of work had been lost that way: a message here, a reply there, an urgent matter to take care of—and before he knew it, an entire morning had gone up in smoke. He would check his mailbox at noon, after finishing the morning's quota of words.

Ten thirty. The room was terribly hot. The air had gotten muggier. Midsummer in May! Where on earth had the transitional seasons gone? His naked body was dotted with small, sticky beads of sweat. He unknotted the towel, still damp from the shower, tossed it onto a chair behind him, and went on working in the nude. Andrew liked to write that way. His deliciously private secret, from which he derived a brazen, almost anarchistic satisfaction, was that he had written several of the major pieces that had won him his reputation and academic standing in his birthday suit. His bare buttocks settling with a sensual intimacy into the burnished bottom of his chair, he took a deep breath of humid air and turned his attention to the screen, searching for where he had stopped the day before—or more precisely, two days ago.

"The object [writes Warhol] signifies itself as object and its representation brands it and establishes the context for its existence." From here it is but a short step to the figure that steps out of its two-dimensional world as defined by others and off the flickering screen, as in Woody Allen's The Purple Rose of Cairo. *Could one conceive of a more perfect, better-orchestrated visual image for*

how art and theory break free of the conceptual realm and flood the
"real world," the world of objects, spontaneously annulling the gap
between reality and representation, between . . .

The sentence had broken off in the middle. He could almost
hear its faint pop, like a burned-out electric bulb's. Where was the
problem? Only the three last words were missing, no more—and
they weren't crucial, either. He needed them more for rhythm and
balance than for content. Just write them, for fuck's sake! Finish
the sentence and move on to the next one! But the small, still mental voice that dictated his sentences had fallen silent. And the silence was oppressive, disenabling. It weighed on him like a blanket
of lead, like one of those apron-shaped X-ray shields that made
you feel deathly feeble.

What was wrong with him? The letters wriggled on the screen
like little insects. What, really, was the matter? Was it his doubts
whether, apart from a single scene in *The Purple Rose of Cairo* and
a certain physical similarity between the two men, they had anything to do with each other? Was it all just intellectual smoke and
mirrors, an infatuation with the sound of his own words? Andrew
stared dully at the screen. The unfinished sentence seemed as
senseless and indecipherable as hieroglyphics. He searched for his
reading glasses and found them perched on his nose. A moment of
comic relief! Yes, a lighter touch, that's what was needed! He didn't
need to sound so serious. Removing the glasses, he studied the
screen again. No, it was unreadable, simply unreadable!

Andrew jumped up as though to fetch or look for something.
For a moment—he had forgotten he was naked—he stood there,
embarrassed, before sitting down again in the chair that was by
now warm and damp from his body. What now? The tinge of anxiety that routinely accompanied his mornings was growing, turning into a full-blown panic. What was he to do, how was he to go

on? He jumped up again, more abruptly than the first time, as if the seat beneath him were on fire. But what had he gotten up for, what was it he wanted? He wanted . . . ah, yes, of course: to go to the bathroom. He took the towel from its chair, its wet fabric, unpleasantly reminiscent of the sea, making him shiver, and crossed the living room quickly to the bathroom. Leaning over the toilet bowl, he hiked up the towel and managed with difficulty to squeeze out a few drops of urine. He let the towel drop back to his knees, washed his hands thoroughly at the sink as though to purge them of their paralyzing writer's block, dried them well, rearranged the towel around his waist, and returned to his desk. This time, buoyed by the bright sunlight already bathing the bedroom, he was determined to stay seated.

But the damp, prickly towel, pressed between him and the seat, forced him to his feet again. It was revolting, like sitting on some dead sea creature. And what was this business of sitting naked, anyway? What was he, some kind of Calvin Klein model? It was nothing but a dumb affectation. He had to get dressed at once! And how was he to work with all that music? What a racket! He went to the stereo, savagely turned it off, and strode back into the sunlit hothouse of the bedroom with its south-facing window, whose blinds he had forgotten to shut. Tearing off the damp towel, he tossed it disgustedly on the floor and went to the closet while resisting the clutches of a strange urge to crawl back between the rumpled sheets on the bed like a sick, old animal to its den and let them soak up his sweat while the warm spring light rocked him to sleep. His reflection in the full-length mirror by the closet was mocking, malicious. He halted before approaching it with hesitant steps and staring at its uncomplimentary image of a pale, hairy body speckled with small birthmarks. Its shoulders were slumped, its chest sunken. Its waist was beginning to spread. With its shrunken penis, dangling slightly to one side and half-hidden by its thinning pubic hair, it looked flabby and almost like a woman's. Yes, he was run-down, not his old, solid self. He had to exercise more and lay off the white bread. But enough standing there like an idiot! Get dressed, right away!

His drying perspiration stung his skin. Should he take another shower? No, not now. Andrew picked up the towel from the floor, wiped himself quickly, and hung it to dry on the hook over the bathroom door. It was too wet and sweaty for the hamper. The warm sunlight soothed him a bit. He opened the closet and surveyed his clothes. Clean and neatly folded and in their proper place, they restored a sense of control and sobriety. What should he wear? Definitely not a grandiose-looking dressing gown or one of his old tie-dyed T-shirts. He needed something serious to put him in a proper, businesslike frame of mind. Picking out a pair of comfortable, loose-fitting linen pants, he looked for something to go with them among the crisply ironed shirts delivered two days ago by the laundry—something purposeful, not too heavy and not too light, conducive to the creative mood he was looking for. Linen again? No, it was too early in the year for that, too strong a statement. White cotton: that was simple, springlike, and nice. And that brown belt would go well with it. Plus a tie? But how could he think of a tie! That would be making a joke of it. He had a long, hard day's work ahead of him. With a bit of luck, he could finish by the end of the week.

4

Eleven thirty. Andrew returned to his desk neatly dressed and combed, carrying his second cup of coffee. Passing the mirror on his way from the bedroom, he was more satisfied by what he saw. It had been a bad moment, no more. It was too soon to check his e-mail. Perhaps in an hour, depending on how much he got done. He sipped some coffee. His glasses were at hand. To work!

Andrew scrolled upward to the start of the article. When had he written its first sentences? That was easily checked. He simply had to look for the date on which the document was opened. But what did it matter? He had to stop this compulsive browsing! And he didn't need an exact word count, either, even though it was encouraging to know that he had already written several thousand. They were a good base to build on; he wasn't starting from scratch. It would be a nice little article. He had published dozens like it during his productive career—it *was* productive, no one could deny that—many longer and more complicated than this one. Still, it would be better to go back to the beginning and work up momentum. What had he done with his glasses? The title was fine, as was the opening paragraph. The sentences were well turned. You couldn't say they didn't have style. Should he have some more coffee to perk up a bit? No, wait, he still had some in his cup that was warm. Page two. The quotations were fine. It was a good piece. What was new in the world? A world war could have broken out and he . . . should he log on for a second to the *Times* website? No, stay concentrated! Page three. There was a disturbing flicker on the screen. It was hard to focus on the text. Should he print it? That meant increasing the spacing between lines to leave room for written corrections. Yes, it was a good idea.

Andrew looked for the printer jack, plugged it into the computer, switched on the power, doubled the line spacing (he now had twenty-three pages instead of eleven), and gave the print command. Leaning back in his chair, he waited with an odd pleasure for the machine to start working. A few seconds went by. Nothing happened. Then, something began to clatter and click. Springs unwound, cogwheels turned. The printer shuddered on the desktop, coughed, fell still, and shuddered again. Something muttered and murmured inside it. The top page of the stack of white printing paper was snatched from its place and fed into the printer's plastic mouth. Andrew watched with childish enjoyment. The mechanical workings were calming; they made him feel an illogical contentment. Out came a handsome, printed white page, gradually covered with orderly, symmetrical lines of characters on which he could meditate without feeling responsible for them. In a curious way, he would have liked to be a part of the process, to spend the rest of his life staring idly at the pulsating machine as it greedily swallowed the virgin-white pages and lustfully spat them out as printed matter.

His odd pleasure lasted only a few seconds. By the third page it was spoiled by a feeling of guilt. Didn't he already have a hard copy of the article somewhere? Every page of newsprint, so they said, was half a tree, half a cell in the afflicted body of a disappearing rain forest. But this wasn't the real reason for his discomfort. The rain forests, with all due respect, were far, far away. More to the point was his awareness that procrastinating with the printer instead of facing up to the impasse he had been floundering in for weeks as though he were drowning in a warm mud bath was just more avoidance. Hurriedly, as if the appearance of being organized could silence the inner voice telling him it was all a pitiful pretext, a cowardly evasion of the call of duty, he gathered up the pages that still seemed to vibrate from the machine and arranged them neatly. Yet the hope that they might serve as a source of inspiration was crushed the moment the printer stopped its chattering. The familiar anxiety was back. He sat down again, pushed the laptop aside, and laid the printed pages in their place.

It wasn't going to be a productive day. He might as well go back to bed or look after other business. Still, he wasn't ready to give up. What kind of poisoned sleep could he expect to have? Should he try a change of place? Lately, it had been hard to concentrate at

home. How about the Hungarian Pastry Shop? Its pleasant bustle
had been the setting for more than one original idea and successful
article in the past. The thought of his favorite café instilled new
hope in him. Buoyed, he unplugged the laptop and the printer. Although ordinarily he would have switched the computer off before taking it anywhere, waiting patiently while it parked its icons
and shut down, there was no time to waste today. Snapping its lid
shut with a vigor that caused him to feel strong and determined,
he slipped it into its leather briefcase and strode to the door. He
took his wallet from the metal bowl on the table, extracted a few
bills, stuck them in a pocket—the wallet would have bulged there
unbecomingly—and took his keys. Remembering his sunglasses,
he put them on for the first time that year (after all, spring has
sprung!) and left the apartment at a rapid pace that was almost a
run. With some luck and perseverance, he could finish a first draft
today. Most of the piece was already written. He had to reconnect
with his creative self. That was all he needed to do.

5

Andrew was greeted by a fine spring day. The sun shone
brightly, optimistically, glinting off the buildings at a sharp
angle to the blue sky. What had happened to the morning's oppressive mugginess? The thick, fresh foliage of the trees erased
the gray vestiges of the long, sullen winter and made the city look
young again. He walked briskly up Broadway, half-unwillingly
glancing at the deserted bench on which he had hoped to spot the
fat homeless man, who should have been back by now. He wasn't
there. Although his huge figure's absence was like a missing tooth
marring a perfect smile, Andrew was not about to let it be an omen
spoiling the rare mood that had descended on him out of the blue.

He would turn up in the end; everyone did. Looking away from
the empty bench. Andrew set out with long strides along 110th
Street, carried merrily like a little skiff by an unexpected wave of
urban euphoria. It wasn't just the weather. The street had a festive
atmosphere. What could it be? Of course: graduation day at Columbia! He had been living in another world. Young, attractive,
and brimful with hope, the graduates strolled festively along the
wide sidewalks of the Upper West Side. Forever gay and carefree
in the heady spring light, their gowns and mortarboards like carnival costumes, they would one day long for these streets without
knowing why or for what. But enough of poetic nostalgia! He had
reached the Hungarian Pastry Shop.

The café was packed. The graduates, laughing, stood by the
display window of cakes, their solemn, powder-blue robes unable
to hide their youthful excitement. Some, surrounded by parents,
grandparents, and younger brothers and sisters, were already
seated, their mortarboards on their knees, carefully protected from
the crumbs and coffee drippings. Surveying the scene with the
expert eye of an urban marksman, Andrew spotted a small table
in a corner that was being vacated. An empty table on a day like
this was surely an auspicious sign! He hurried over to it, placed
his computer case on a chair, and laid his sunglasses on top of it as
a double proof of possession before going to the counter to order
his coffee. A semi-familiar face caught his attention on his way
back to the coffee counter. Seated at one of the front tables was
that man—it took Andrew a second or two to locate him in his
memory—the Israeli man, with the two dogs, the one that taught
Hebrew at Alison's Sunday school in Brooklyn. He was hunched
over his laptop, hitting the keyboard fervently. What was he writing there, with such passion? Funny, he didn't strike Andrew as
the bookish, intellectual type who could be so absorbed in writing. Joining a line of students, Andrew decided to ask for a cap-

puccino instead of a latte and even to indulge in a pastry, tempted
by a heaping tray of fresh croissants carried in from the kitchen
in the muscular arms of a kitchen worker. Never mind: one only
lived once! He would go to the gym that afternoon and work off
the extra calories. Whistling an unidentified tune, he took a seat
facing the large window, through which the day looked finer than
ever, opened the laptop, and hit a key to activate it. The cappuccino arrived with its croissant, along with little bowls of butter and
jam. Andrew graciously thanked the young waitress, who smiled
at him sweetly while arranging the table, then turned to his computer, eager to get to work. Yet instead of opening the document
he had been working on, he found himself creating a new one, at
the top of which, without thinking or knowing what he was doing,
he typed the short line, as though it were the epigraph of an essay
of uncertain contents: "Short views, for God's sake, short views."
Beneath this, he wrote in italics: *Saul Bellow, Mr. Sammler's Planet.*
He hit the Enter key twice to increase the space before the text
that would follow, took his hands off the keyboard, leaned back in
his chair, and stared at the screen as though waiting for it to write
something on its own—something whose swift, even lines, one
after another, would reveal a transcendent truth, long felt by him,
that he had been unable to find the words for.

Ten seconds went by. Ten. Twenty. Thirty. Nothing happened.
The odd motto remained by itself at the top of the page. Forty
seconds. Fifty. A minute. Nothing: not an idea, not an association,
not the shadow of a thought. A total, complete void. A free fall
into a deep, bottomless pit. The romantic impulse that had brought
him here had melted like wax wings in the sun. Andrew glanced
blindly around him. He felt as crushed as if dropped from a great
height onto the chair he was sitting on. The festive feeling of com-
mencement day was gone, its place taken by a sour sorrow, a bitter,
inconsolable fatigue. What should he do now? Mechanically, he

saved the abortive document and looked around once more, head spinning from the colorful scene that revolved around him like a diabolical carousel. He was falling, falling into an abyss.

The smell of something freshly baked brought him out of his trance. His croissant! With a wolfishness that wasn't like him, he tore it open along its length, spread it with gobs of butter, and emptied the jam bowl onto it. It was good, fantastically good. The rush of sugar in his bloodstream made him dizzy. The jam—cheap preserves, with artificial red coloring—got all over his fingers and lips. Fantastic! Two or three large bites and it was gone. He had had no idea how hungry he had been. And still was. Famished. The croissant had only made his hunger worse. He had to force himself to be sensible and not order another. Although he licked his lips clean, his fingers remained sticky. He mustn't get the keyboard dirty. Rising abruptly, he hurried to the men's room, elbowing his way past the customers crowding the tables and aisles. There was more of a line than usual and he had a long wait. His sticky fingers were beginning to itch annoyingly. Jiggling his right foot impatiently, he awaited his turn for the café's only sink.

6

The cool dampness of the men's room made Andrew feel a little better. He took his time washing his sticky hands before leaning over the little sink and splashing cold water on his face. Drying himself well with paper toweling torn from a cardboard cylinder, he checked the mirror to make sure that none of it was plastered to his face. People here knew him after all. He wasn't just anyone.

He tossed the wet paper into the trash, conscious of the waiting line outside. Just as he was about to leave, however, his attention was caught by graffiti on the door. He had never seen it there before. Might it have been scrawled today, in honor of graduation? He felt that it spoke to him, its heavy block letters standing out from the scrawls around it:

KNOWLEDGE IS NOT A COMMODITY!

SOCRATES' TUITION FEES = $0.

COLUMBIA'S TUITION FEES = $28,000 PER SEMESTER

AN ACADEMIC DEGREE IS THE SUREST ROUTE TO A JOB

90% OF AMERICANS HATE THEIR JOB

QUIT SCHOOL, START TO LIVE

Andrew stared at the writing, surprised by the effect it had. Although its childish naïveté should have made him smile with fatherly indulgence, he felt a sour bitterness that caused him to swallow hard and make a face. Knowledge *was* a commodity. It determined your worth. You were measured by the number of your publications, your titles and degrees. You were as proud of them as was a warrior of the scalps he took. You trod the dry, cruel ground of a gladiator's arena. At sixty no less than at twenty, you were a slave of the system. You danced to the tune of the administration, of the rich donors who funded a new library or wing of the law school. Knowledge was budgeted. Learning was quantified. Everything was calculated by its exchange rate, by the years until the next centenary celebration, the next public relations hoopla. The slightest hesitation, the smallest slip, and you were out. The academic establishment would let you know it. Nothing dramatic, of course. You weren't excommunicated like Spinoza, even though, ironically, it might have helped your reputation if you were. No, you were ostracized quietly, humiliatingly, ground down step by step, slowly obliterated until nothing was left of you. It was all lies, perfectly useless nonsense. *The truth is written with an iron pen on the tablet of the heart, with the point of a diamond.*

Andrew gave a start. Someone was knocking impatiently on the door. He looked around him in a fright: where had these strange words come from? Had he really said them out loud? It had been like talking in his sleep. Suppose someone had been listening? He was letting himself be helplessly transparent. Anyone standing by the door could look right through him. Whoever was within earshot would know he was deranged.

There was another knock, louder and more insistent. Andrew flushed the toilet, as though to drown out the inner voice. For no reason, he washed his hands again at the sink, wiped them, unbolted the door, and stepped back into the crowded, brightly arrayed Hungarian Pastry Shop. The place was hopping. It seemed to have filled up even more in the few minutes he had been in the men's room. He made his way through the crowd to his table, sank into his seat, and reached automatically for the empty coffee cup that was still by his computer, whose battery, he feared unreasonably, might be about to run out. Stinging butterflies roamed his stomach, scraping his insides abrasively. He put down the cold cup, rested his fingers on the keyboard, and kept them lifelessly there while staring blankly at the white screen. By now it was clear that he wouldn't write a word today, that nothing would be accomplished. Another wasted day, a day like yesterday and the day before! He might as well pack up and go to the gym, where he could at least make up for his feebleness of mind by strengthening his body. Who was to say? Perhaps his mental state came from neglecting his physical one. There was no point in simply taking up space on a busy day like this. And yet he went on sitting there, unable to stop the pointless punishment inflicted by the celebration around him. His despair made him nervous and hypersensitive, drawing him against his will into a conversation between two young men at the next table. Both unshaven, they had the self-satisfied look of wannabe revolutionaries cultivated by students in philosophy and

film departments. A pack of cigarettes and a heavy, silver Zippo
lighter lay ostentatiously on their table, even though smoking had
been prohibited in cafés and restaurants for years. One had tattooed on his arm, the scrawny limb of an urban intellectual, a menacing assault rifle. Was he a member of the Special Forces? Of a
secret militia? The second, with black, shoulder-length curls and
silver rings inlaid with turquoise, had a vaguely South American
accent, from what country Andrew couldn't tell, though the more
the two talked, the more he sounded like an ordinary New Yorker.
They were conversing with a half-bantering earnestness, throwing around big words in a youthfully ironic tone while pointing
repeatedly to a thin brochure that lay on the table between them.
Clearly, they were having a good time, enjoying their erudite conversation as much as the slightly younger graduates were enjoying
their cakes, which looked better than they tasted. Why did he feel
such contempt for them? What had happened to that tolerant, all-
knowing smile of his, the smile of someone who had been there
himself and could look back without anger? *Non, je ne regrette
rien!* Edith Piaf's charcoal voice was the perfect sound track for
the dramas of one's youth. What did a young person have to regret? Nothing! The regrets came later, when it was already too
late. When had the magic vanished? Why? Over the years he had
only grown more intellectually mature. Knowledge as a commodity, knowledge as a career! You only noticed it once the first cracks
appeared in the retaining walls of your complacency. What noise!
It was unbearable. Home, to bed! The gym was the last thing he
was up to. He was exhausted. He had to rest. Perhaps tomorrow.

Stifling a resigned sigh, Andrew switched off the laptop, gathered his things, and glanced up from the grayish-brown table-
top. The front window of the Hungarian Pastry Shop gleamed
in the afternoon light, which turned it into a magical planetarium
in which a blue, vitreous moon hung beside little glass stars like

props in a children's play. A very pretty, ethereal young woman in her last months of pregnancy was leaning on the counter and talking to the help. Proud, she glowed like a celestial body against the stars and bright spheres in the window as though at the center of her own enchanted solar system. In the light pouring in from outside, she could have been a Renaissance painting, her thin summer dress forming a soft halo around the deep curve of her hip and high belly with its entrancingly prominent navel. Her high, patrician forehead beneath the ribbon pulling back her hair had an otherworldly radiance. It was as though a portal had been opened through which this Madonna of the Coffeehouse projected a different age, a luminous time full of longing, into the dim, crowded interior of the café.

Andrew stared at her in wonder, feeling a strange absolution. Thinking of Linda's pregnancies, he couldn't help but smile. How comical they seemed when compared to the magazine-like perfection of the young woman by the counter. Even Linda had laughed at her ordinariness. She had been a textbook case: her morning sickness, her insomnia, her lower back pains, even her perfectly banal craving for sour pickles and exotic foods. Her face puffed and her ankles swelled until she could barely walk. By the third month, even before she started to actually gain weight, her body had adopted the pregnancy posture, with her back arched and her hands half crossed on her abdomen. Yet these months, especially the first time, were remembered by him as good ones. Perhaps they had even been happy ones. There had been tender, intimate moments, punctuated by memories that became the funny anecdotes recounted at holiday dinners. "Do you remember that time in the middle of the night when she had to have, just *had* to have, a slice of pizza? And with anchovies! She always hated anchovies. The thought of them made her sick!" He had run from one pizzeria about to close for the night to another. In the end, an elderly Italian who was saving his last slice of pizza with anchovies for his own midnight snack took pity on him and smilingly let him, the future father, have it. Everyone knew the story and could even supply its punch line. "And so you finally brought it home—and when you did, she was in such a deep sleep that you couldn't wake her for love or anchovies!"

It evoked a bittersweet smile. Where had it all gone? What had happened to all the memories of their intimate, shared past? He still remembered the course they took before Rachel's birth with the breathing exercises practiced by all the young mothers with a religious devotion, as if no child could be born without them. The fathers, ties loosened after a day at the office, had joked awkwardly to hide their discomfort. The two of them shone, Linda gay and laughing, Andrew the charming egalitarian husband hugging her from behind on the floor, her back propped against his bare legs, her head nestled in the crook of his neck while they breathed rhythmically together. The men grumbled. The women regarded Linda with curious "What does he see in her?" looks. But the two of them, not without pride, floated above all the subliminal, prepartum currents. Young and beautiful, their future ahead of them, they enjoyed playing the perfect couple. Andrew winced, carried away on a wave of poisoned nostalgia. The promise had remained unfulfilled. Whatever it was, they failed; they had lost it and could never get it back.

The second pregnancy was less, much less, idyllic. He would never forget Linda's face after giving birth to Alison. Pale and anguished, she was unrecognizable: a gray, limp-limbed woman holding a crimson-faced baby that looked more like her granddaughter. She was almost forty and had been in labor for twelve hours. It wasn't fair to remember her that way. But although he had often tried to erase the scene from his mind, it kept coming back with its aversion and guilt. They had tried, honestly tried, to breathe life back into their relationship. The baby had been so sweet and innocent: the cowlicks of milk dribbling down her round cheek when she fell asleep after nursing, the first flashes of self-awareness, the first smiles, the first teeth. She was only a year old when he left home. The thought of it caused his upper lip to tremble. The tremors went to his nose, traveled up it, and reached the blocked tear ducts of his eyes. Trying to shake off the black mood he was settling back into, he glanced at the counter, where he hoped to see his bright Madonna again. But she was gone. The window was just a window, its stars and constellations orbiting in empty space.

Andrew stifled another sigh, took the check from the table, and went to the counter to pay. Home! He needed to rest. Maybe this evening he would feel more inspired. Or clearheaded. Or something.

7

June 1, 2001

The 10th of Sivan, 5761

Linda stands barefoot on the stone floor, pilloried at a crude stake. The coarse rope around her waist makes her exposed breasts look heavy and vulnerable. Large, milky tears drip slowly from her enlarged nipples into a pool, forming little gray storm clouds in the turbid water. A frenzied crowd of leprous, one-eyed, disfigured invalids surrounds her. Mouths with rotted teeth like the broken columns of ruined temples sound jagged, bestial cries, wild screams and laughs. I stand in the crowd, paralyzed with fear. Linda looks at me imploringly, but I'm rooted to the spot. A single word from me can save her! An abyss of regret. Who cares who the father is? Is there the slightest doubt whose child it is? The last of the bitter waters dribble from the corners of her mouth, leaving black trails of ashes. I want to run to her, to wrap my jacket around her and protect her from the lewd, greedy stares of the riffraff besieging her. I want to get her out of here and bring her home but I can't move. It's too late. All is lost. It's all my fault.

8

June 1, 2001

The 10th of Sivan, 5761

Two forty-five a.m. A fierce, burning sensation in the pit of his groin violently shook Andrew from his sleep, searing his bladder like burning coals and sending him, doubled over, to the bathroom. Shutting the door without turning on the light so as not to awaken Ann Lee, he groped his way in the dark to the toilet, lifted the seat, and leaned over it, the stabbing pain causing him to choke back a frightened gasp. But though he felt unable to hold his urine in a second longer, it took its time, pressing on his tormented bladder while refusing to flow and grant relief. He sought to summon nameless muscles he always had taken for granted. He squeezed, bent, straightened up, leaned forward again with his hands on the wall in front of him—nothing came. Something was blocking it, holding it up. Only when he arched his body against the wall behind him did a sudden, irregular jet of liquid slash its way through him as if laced with slivers of glass.

Andrew sprang forward, trying not to undershoot the toilet bowl. The flow of urine stopped and started again, dividing into two: a current that arched into the bowl and another, weaker one that dribbled in large, warm drops onto his pajama pants and bare feet. Their sting fully woke him from his painful semi-sleep. Though fully aware now of his state, he wanted only to tear off his stained pajamas and cleanse himself of the surprisingly warm urine that might be a sign of some terrible disease. For a moment, he stopped its flow by half-involuntarily contracting the muscles hiding behind his pubic hair. The burning sensation resumed— not as strongly as before, but enough to reactivate his panic. He pulled off his pants, bent to wipe his feet with them, rolled them into a ball, and flung them in the sink. Dry, he felt more in charge, as ludicrous as it was to be standing there like a baby waiting to be diapered. Never mind. It was too dark to see and Ann Lee was a heavy sleeper.

The thought of Ann Lee entering the bathroom, turning on the light, and literally catching him with his pants down was almost as humiliating as the thought of her smelling the laundry hamper in the morning. What should he do? A new pain in his bladder sent him staggering back to the toilet, whose open mouth was like a crow of derision in the darkness. More urine spurted out an instant before he could aim it at the toilet bowl, cauterizing his penis in hot, sporadic bursts and spraying him again, this time on the thighs and knees. It took more effort than before to make it stop. For a moment, he stood helplessly in the dark; then, lowering the toilet seat carefully to keep it from banging, he crouched on it quickly and hunched forward to pee in the bowl. His urine dripped slowly, hitting the water with a soft tinkle that he feared could be heard throughout the apartment. Eyes shut, shivering from the cold seat despite the warm night, he concentrated on its slow, painful release.

A vague memory nagged at him like a stubborn mosquito. It was of something recent, something unimportant but unpleasant . . . but what? Why was it trying to surface now, in the middle of the night? His urine kept dripping drop by drop, sometimes more and sometimes less quickly. The disconcerting something was looming into sight like a strange, outlandish geological formation. Yes, he remembered. It was the saggy, wrinkled skin hanging from the belly of the old man urinating yesterday at Equinox.

Andrew had seen him once or twice in the past. It was hard to overlook him: an aging, ridiculous-looking fellow whose hair, cut like a teenager's, was dyed a monstrous yellow. He was a regular on the gym's first floor, where he lifted weights with the votive dedication of a priest at the altar. Although he looked reasonably strong and his posture was erect—it might be stiff from age, but nonetheless—the problem was his skin: totally decrepit, it hung in loose folds from firm muscles like an old sack. This was most pronounced around the abdomen, where it made Andrew think of a tattered curtain, suspended from the rib cage as though in an amateur theater production. Worse yet, the man perversely insisted on wearing odd, feminine crop-tops that exposed his stomach grotesquely. He was preposterous, in a narcissistic world of his own, a walking oxymoron strutting about the locker room like an old, tragicomic rooster with his comb of yellow hair and his shamelessly Semitic hook nose. Just as unreal was the way he peed. Its upsetting memory passed before Andrew's sleepy eyes. The misshapen, youthfully geriatric body had been propped against a wall with its left shoulder flattened against it. His face was hidden by the right arm, pelvis thrust forward; the shrunken penis, aimed at the toilet bowl, held carefully in the left hand. Laughable, defenseless, and touching, the man had stood for a long time, his sheltering arm like a bird's wing, groaning by the white wall like an old Jew at prayer. He was surrendering to his own decrepitude, to the perverse enjoyment of feeling his thin liquid waste make its frightfully slow exit from what was once his very manhood.

Andrew could feel the trickle of urine subsiding. The burning stopped, yielding to a dull after-pain. What was he supposed to do

with such a memory? How should he think of it? It was best to forget it and go back to sleep. Flush the toilet quietly, mop up the last
drops with a towel, return to the bedroom, put on clean pajamas,
and slip noiselessly back into the double bed. And the wet pants?
He couldn't very well leave them in the sink. He would throw them
in the hamper after all—they weren't that wet. Could it be prostate
cancer? What an idea! Since when was he such a hypochondriac?
Still, it was time he saw a doctor for a checkup: heart, digestive
system, liver functions, kidneys, yes, prostate, too. At his age, one
mustn't put such things off.

9

June 6, 2001

The 15th of Sivan, 5761

Four ten p.m. His appointment had been for 3:15. Something
urgent, apparently, was holding Dr. Gutman up. Andrew
grumbled with what seemed to him legitimate annoyance and
went back to reading an article about the dangers of abdominal
fat in men. There were, it said, two types of weight gainers, the
"Apples" and the "Pears." The Apples, who put on weight at the
midsection, were subject to illnesses caused by the hormonal se-
cretions of abdominal fat cells. The Pears expanded farther down,
in the pelvis and thighs, which was apparently less unhealthy.

But why was he reading this when he had brought a book with
him? Such articles drew you in; there was something addictive
about them. Whole alternate universes lay concealed in hospitals
and doctors' offices, waiting in ambush for everyday life; other
worlds in which everything revolved around bodies, diseases, and
death. When we're there—that is, here—we think that's all life

is really about and that our daily existence, with all its trivial en-
joyments and lofty ambitions, is nothing but an empty dream, a
foolish illusion for the indulgence in which we'll pay dearly.

The office's location on 65th and Madison should have made
seeing a cardiologist less onerous—it was four blocks from Barney's and two blocks from the Belgian chocolate shop and the
MoMA design store. And yet the East Side made Andrew feel
intimidated. He wasn't used to feeling threatened, especially not
by material status symbols like polished marble counters, thick,
emerald-colored glass dividers, and heavy cherrywood doors with
brass handles that once, no doubt, had graced some mansion torn
down to make way for a skyscraper.

What was taking so long? It was already 4:20. What a waste of
time! He should never have pressured Dr. Nesselson for a referral to
a cardiologist. There had been no need to insist on it. Was the fat,
bored-looking man across from him waiting for Gutman, too? The
man sat perfectly still, not reading or even reaching for his cell phone
or PalmPilot, sprawled in a chair too small for his broad, spreading
bottom, blinking with lifeless eyes at the cold, bright neon ceiling
light. Was he a Pear? He looked like one, even though "a pear" was
far too luscious a term for him. And what about the thin, nervous
man facing him? There was something odd about him, too. Did he
dye his hair? No, he plucked his eyebrows! Two grotesque black arcs
ran above his eyelids, framing his darting, roach-like eyes and making him look like the villain in an old movie.

Was hostility toward other patients an integral part of the
waiting-room experience? A defense mechanism meant to protect
one's boundaries from invasion by the Other? Someone must have
written about it; he couldn't imagine that no one had. In general,
one was always on the defensive. Frightened middle-aged men
told pointless jokes and hid behind salacious descriptions of occult
medical procedures. *It's like having an umbrella shoved up your ass*

and opened! Wasn't that the ultimate male fear, having to go down bare-assed on all fours while awaiting the inevitable penetration? The doors of the clinic opened and shut. Young nurses and interns came and went. Modernity's most humiliating rite of passage was the colonoscopy, marking the transition from being a virile male to a harmless old man who stayed behind in the tent to do housework, chat with the women, and beg for sweets like a baby while the potent young warriors went hunting for game and scalps.

Four thirty. There was no choice but to wait patiently. Andrew put down the magazine and leafed through a pile of medical notices on the low table beside him: "Cancer of the Large Intestine: Early Detection," "Arteriosclerosis: Causes and Prevention," "Cancer of the Prostate: Facts and Explanations." Dr. Nesselson had ruled out a prostate problem; there was no symptomatic indication of one, he had said, calming Andrew's fears. He had interviewed Andrew at length, asking for a detailed account of his pain and his difficulty urinating, and had even inquired whether he had had sex earlier that evening. (As a matter of fact, he had—for the first time in a while, to tell the truth.) Andrew had felt uncomfortable. The doctor's penetrating gaze had torn aside a curtain of propriety drawn over his expanding, deteriorating body and Ann Lee's young, compact one. Their sex life had lost its ecstatic dimension and had become mechanical, uninspired. Not that the doctor had been in the least interested in any of that. Andrew was projecting his own anxieties onto him. But Nesselson did suspect that the problem might be dried semen in Andrew's urethra. He recommended urinating immediately after sexual intercourse. Although it was probably, he said, a one-time occurrence, Andrew should contact him if it happened again.

The fat man emitted a quick, dry cough and relapsed into stony silence. The roach man kept fidgeting in his chair, his nervousness crackling around him like a field of static electricity. Andrew pulled out a brochure on prostate cancer and began reading at random.

In the course of the rectal examination, the doctor checks for an enlargement of the prostate—a common phenomenon among older men. This examination can serve as an early-detection procedure for cancer of the prostate and intestine.

Dr. Nesselson had not bothered with such an examination, no doubt for good reasons. One thing he said had stayed in Andrew's memory. "I'd rather not detect prostate cancer early because then I have to start treating it—and the damage caused by treatments and operations can be much worse than the cancer itself, which is generally a friendly one." What a devilish paradox: a friendly cancer! Yet the formulation was reassuring. He went on scanning the brochure with an almost compulsive pleasure, as though picking at a sore.

The problem of erectile dysfunction after a radical operation for prostate cancer is a common one. Approximately half of those operated on suffer from it significantly. One way of minimizing its occurrence is by nerve-sparing surgery. Recovery of sexual potency can take from 6 to 24 months. This period should be utilized for physical and drug therapy to preserve the function of the cavernous nerves of the penis, which play an erectile role. Among the many factors that may lead to impotence in the aftermath of a prostatectomy is how radical the operation is, that is, how much of the prostate and its surroundings have been removed and how many of the nerve clusters and blood vessels responsible for an erection are preserved. The factors influencing a full recovery of erectile function are: youth, pre-surgical sexual potency, and damage to nerve clusters and blood vessels. The younger one is, the greater the normality of previous sexual functioning, and the less damage there is to nerve clusters and blood vessels, the greater are the chances of preserving potency. Unfortunately, the surgical need to clear away as much potentially cancerous tissue as possible can lead to such damage, and post-radical prostatectomy rates of impotence range from 25% to 89%. In cases of successful nerve-sparing surgery, erectile and orgasmic function can be gradually recovered, but often the orgasm is not accompanied by ejaculation. The operating urologist will explain this to the patient in order to minimize the psychological difficulty of adjusting to a dry orgasm.

Andrew imagined the surgically removed nerves, a snarled, wriggling mass of enfeebled worms. A pale, swollen sac lay on a nickel operating table, its sick, bluish blood vessels hanging loose like tails or antennae. He shut the brochure and returned it quickly to the pile. But the excised gland went on twitching before his eyes, straining to eject semen. The harder he tried banishing dry orgasms from his mind, the more stubbornly they remained there, smarting like a fresh wound. A 25 to 89 percent rate of impotence after radical surgery: what meaningless numbers! What could anyone learn from such a statistical spread? It was antiscience, not science! What was the goddamn time? How could patients be kept waiting so long, with no explanation or word of apology? Where the hell was Dr. Gutman? The minute they classed you as a patient, your time lost all value. You would think you had nothing better to do with your life!

10

Success, so it seemed, had not spoiled Dr. Gutman. He had an appealing modesty, a warm handshake, and a pleasantly singsong voice like a kind grandfather's that quivered at times with a slight stammer. For a moment, Andrew let his hand rest in the doctor's as though drawing strength and sustenance from it. Dr. Gutman was unmistakably Jewish-looking with soft eyes that blinked behind thick-lensed bifocals, a case of early-onset baldness, and smooth-shaven cheeks squarely meeting prominent sideburns from which Andrew could imagine a heavy beard descending. The doctor's hands were soft, too, their long fingers resting on Andrew's wrist while taking his pulse with a reassuring competence. Andrew, eager to cooperate and please, dutifully answered the doctor's questions like a kid in grade school. Although taken aback by his feeling of dependence, his awareness of it didn't lessen, as it might have done in the past.

Dr. Gutman refused to be rushed by the lengthening queue in the waiting room. His reputation for thoroughness, which had crossed Central Park from east to west, was the reason Andrew was here. Gutman took his time, asking detailed questions and listening patiently to the answers like an old-fashioned family doctor. Andrew's family's medical history? There were no special illnesses. Cancer, heart disease, strokes? No, there was nothing worth mentioning apart from Ethel's Alzheimer's. Andrew's eating habits? They were healthy, although lately, it was true, he had gone a bit overboard on the carbohydrates. "Yes, we need to watch out. At our age it's easier to put on excess weight than take it off." (*Our* age? Could the two of them be the same age?) Exercise? On a regular basis, more or less. Lately, a bit less. "Yes, one has to keep it up! At our age it's easy to fall out of shape and hard to get back into it." Alcohol? His consumption was average. Average? A drink or two a day, sometimes three. Dr. Gutman's eyes widened behind their bifocals. "Two or three?" Well, generally no more than two. *At our age, at our age* . . . How old was he? He seemed so elderly, organized, and responsible.

Andrew watched as the doctor let go of his wrist and consulted his notes. He studied his face, hair, and skin. No, Dr. Gutman was not as old as he had seemed at first glance. Examined closely, he appeared to be forty-plus. The baldness, the bifocals, the expensive, conservative clothes (those of someone traveling first class or occupying an executive suite: striped shirt, gray suit, red tie with matching suspenders)—all were as misleading as was his quiet, gentle air of authority. Breathe deep. Deep. Why should it matter how old the doctor was? They weren't in competition, were they? "Did you know you have a murmur?" The question tore Andrew from his thoughts. Dr. Gutman's soft, owl-like eyes peered at him through their bifocals. No, Andrew had not known. "It's nothing serious. There's no need to worry about it." The doctor's kind, grandfatherly manner. The word "murmur" coming from his mouth sounded like the silent flutter of a dove's wings.

11

Gentle Dr. Gutman was accustomed to dealing with the anxieties of heart patients. As soon as the intake was over, he switched to small talk, asking Andrew about his work while wrapping a scratchy blood-pressure band around his arm. Andrew answered as best he could, grateful for the doctor's excellent bedside manner but exhausted by the role he felt he had to play and the nagging sensation that he was misrepresenting himself, pretending to be a reputable professional every bit the doctor's equal when he was in fact just a patient awaiting good or bad news from an omnipotent authority. When left alone in the examination room to pedal an exercise bike for fifteen minutes, he felt relieved.

To his surprise, his heart sped up and he began to sweat sooner than he had expected. He pedaled clumsily, as if unused to riding a bike. Why was he perspiring so much? He was a seasoned cyclist and used the bike regularly at the gym. Yet sweating felt healthy there, part of the regimen, whereas here it seemed a symptom of illness. His brow and neck were soaking wet. And only five minutes had gone by—he still had ten to go. Why had he insisted on this examination? He had had to pressure Dr. Nesselson for the referral. All he needed now was an attack of hypochondriac hysteria! A hideous image kept running through his mind. It came from a photograph he had seen in a book about the social construction of death. A swollen dead human body lay like a monstrous beach ball in a puddle of sewage in Calcutta. Tautly stretched skin shone with a blinding, inhuman white light. According to the book, the body had undergone a chemical process similar to bleaching, making it lose all its pigment. Fellow beggars had stripped it bare and left it to rot by the roadside, abandoning it to the sun, the rain, and the teeth of rats and pariah dogs. A senseless life, a meaningless death. *And the carcasses of men fall as dung upon the open field, and as the handful after the harvestman, which none gathereth.* The sweat dripped down his chest and stomach, lathering his abdomen. The fat cells there were secreting toxic hormones, slowly poisoning his body. Cancer, diabetes, heart disease, erectile dysfunction. A diseased organ lying on an examination table, glistening like a dead animal, blue veins sticking out like lifeless antennae. Five more minutes! He couldn't stop now, he had to keep going. He had to keep his heartbeat steady, in the right cardiovascular zone. When had he last cycled in the park? Spring was over. It was so much easier to pedal on a moving bike. He felt he was carrying the whole earth on his shoulders, the shoulders of a puny, defeated Atlas. Enough histrionics! Five more minutes and he was done . . .

The stiff, semitransparent paper on the examination cot chafed beneath him when he lay down, sweaty and exhausted, his naked flesh pale in the cold glare of the overhead light. The sound reminded Andrew of another, long-forgotten one: the crinkle of the parchment paper that his mother had used to line her baking sheets to keep her cookies from sticking. Lying in his underpants, covered in goose bumps, he let childhood memories come and go. He wasn't feeling nostalgic. He felt far too depleted for that. He was just a conduit for senseless, arbitrary impressions that passed through him as though on their way to somewhere else. The last vestiges of his autonomy gone, he lapsed into the anonymous existence of a helpless medical patient and settled against the hard surface beneath him.

Long, irritating minutes of waiting went by before a young, not unattractive nurse stepped into the room, her arms loaded with electric cables that made him think of the torture chambers of a mad scientist in an old horror movie. With a curt professional hello, she proceeded to wire him all over, taping the cables' ends to his naked body. Her brusqueness, he imagined, came from an aversion to his sweaty, aging body. The cold in the room was unbearable, turning his sweat to ice. It was a hot day; the air-conditioning must be on full blast. He felt ashamed to complain or ask to have it turned down. It would be unseemly, unmanly. He lay in silence, shivering with cold, ignoring as best he could the obvious ineptitude that was keeping the nurse from getting the tape to stick. When he was told in an impatient, accusing tone that she would have to shave parts of him that were too hairy, he almost rebelled. How absurd! He wasn't as hairy as all that. Nevertheless, he shut his eyes fatalistically and let the razor hastily shave off several patches of thin, grayish hair from his chest.

These smooth patches were still itching several hours later when Andrew flung his overweight, weak, sweaty self into a taxi and asked in a voice verging on a whine to be taken to West 110th Street. Shopping, visiting a gallery, and sampling Belgian chocolates were the furthest things from his mind. All he wanted was a hot shower and bed. Needless to say, there was nothing wrong with him. The cardiologist, who returned to announce this when the stress test was complete, sounded sanguine. There was not the slightest reason for anxiety. And yet Andrew felt no relief. The white, bloated stomach of the Indian corpse threatened to burst at any moment, spraying its sickening effluvia in all directions. The soft whisper of the recently discovered heart murmur fluttered in an inner cavity of his ear, trapped there like a frantic butterfly. Home! A hot shower! To bed! To sleep!

The taxi lurched uptown, accelerating madly with every green light and braking suddenly before every red one. Andrew leaned against the headrest and shut his eyes, trying to overlook his ridiculous feeling of guilt for sweating up the sticky fake leather seat. The taxi's constant stops and starts made him nauseous. Even though he couldn't wait to get home, he asked the driver to let him off on Broadway and 109th Street, desperate to put an end to this nightmare on wheels. The two-block walk would help him shake off the mad ride. A long line of customers stretched in front of the ice-cream stand on the corner. A pretty young mother leaned over a baby carriage, sharing her ice cream with a round-faced baby who looked at her with bright eyes and smiled with a vanilla-smeared mouth. A spoon for Mommy, a spoon for baby. Bliss. Perfect bliss. A large white drop trickled onto the infant's chin. The mother wiped it with her hand and licked her finger clean, naturally, instinctively, without the least feeling of revulsion. Linda had shared the girls' food the same way, with a primal instinct, sharing their saliva with spoons of applesauce or macaroni and cheese, or testing with her mouth the nipples of their bottles, even when there was no need for it. Although he had bottle-fed his daughters many times, he had never allowed himself to do such a thing. The thought of it disgusted him. For all his passionate love for Rachel, he couldn't stand the slightest oral contact with her spittle, even on a finger. Once, when she was a year or a year and a half old, she had stuck a thumb wet with saliva and salty snot into his mouth. He had run to the sink, spat out what he could, and rinsed his mouth again and again, feeling guilty even then but unable to get over his disgust. A spoon for baby, a spoon for Mommy. The little mouth clamped down eagerly on the spoon. Vanilla ice cream with chocolate syrup. A little, flat plastic spoon. A baby girl eating ice cream. What was there to cry about? Get a grip on yourself, get a grip! Breathe deep! Stop that upper lip from quivering!

Dry, sterile sobs, like the little, frantic, dry orgasm sneezes of a prostateless penis, racked his body. Home, hurry!

12
June 6, 2001

The 15th of Sivan, 5761

Five forty-five p.m. Glancing at his watch, Andrew was startled to see how late it was. Although Ann Lee was due to arrive in half an hour, dressed and ready to go, he felt an urgent need to call off their evening. He was not up to being with her—with anyone, for that matter, but most of all, with her. He was simply feeling too frazzled. The slightest friction with reality had become painful. He couldn't possibly be her date tonight, couldn't charm or entertain her for the life of him. He had to call her right away, before she left home. Yet he shrank from talking to her. Better to leave her a light, friendly message than get involved in long, complicated explanations that made no sense even to himself.

To his relief, he was answered by Ann Lee's voice mail. "Hi, it's me," it said, greeting him with the youthful high spirits that once had aroused him and made him desire her, "but if you've dialed me, you already know it's me, don't you?" He waited for the beep and took a deep breath, hoping to strike a casual note that would take the sting out of his sudden cancellation. "Hi, sweetie, it's me. I'm

awfully sorry, but I have to call it off for tonight. I'm not myself today, I'll just bore you. Let's talk tomorrow, okay?" The obligatory
"Love you" at the end took a second too long to get said—a second in which the message time ended sooner than anticipated. The
shock of the flat, penetrating tone that signaled its end was mixed
with something else, unclear: a bitter, sterile feeling of loneliness that
brought to mind again the white, bloated corpse in the Indian street.
Should he call back? She was supersensitive. Nothing escaped her,
not even the smallest detail. But to do so just because of that damn
"Love you"? Wouldn't it seem hysterical and suspicious?

The loud ring of the telephone, its receiver still pressed against
his ear, spared him more absurd indecision. Startled, he held the
phone at arm's length, staring blankly at it for a second before re-
covering, pressing the incoming call button, and returning it to
his ear. "Hi, Andrew, it's me," said Ann Lee. "I was in the shower
and heard the phone." Her clear, laughing voice rang like a bell,
forcing him to distance the receiver again. What should he say?
She had caught him off guard. His hastily blurted "Hi, sweetheart,
how are you?" sounded nothing like the tone he had had in mind.

"Is everything all right?" Ann Lee asked. "Is anything wrong?"

Andrew hesitated. Although the sound of her buoyed him a bit,
the thought of an evening of make-believe was intolerable. And
what about the message he had left? How could he explain it if he
now pretended that everything was fine? He had to stick to his
original story. "It's nothing, really. I just feel a bit tired. Maybe it's
a cold or some allergy. It must be an allergy! I just left you a message. Didn't you get it?"

"Yes, I did." Ann Lee did not sound particularly concerned. "It
was cut off in the middle. My phone keeps doing that. I suppose I
should find myself some young guy who knows how to fix these
things, shouldn't I?"

Her constant teasing was getting to be tiresome. Andrew forced himself to smile. "I suppose I'm old enough to remember *my* phone being installed by Alexander Bell himself."

What had happened to them? This stale repartee! Where had the natural enchantment, the flow between them, gone?

"So what was the rest of the message?" Ann Lee asked, taking him by surprise again. Damn! This was the conversation he hadn't wanted to have.

"Nothing. There's no point in your wasting an evening, is there? You must have lots to do, and I'm sure that . . ."

Bad! Andrew knew how bad that sounded. Yet his voice, plaintive and unworthy of him, carried him along like an unstoppable mud slide.

"But we don't have to go anywhere." Her still cheery manner was unfazed. "We can spend the evening at your place. I'll stop at Kim's and pick out a video. How about *Breakfast at Tiffany's* or *My Fair Lady*? Some Audrey Hepburn is just what the doctor ordered! We'll order something in and stay home. What do you say?"

Andrew permitted himself a doubtful smile. It sounded too nice and domestic to say no. "Okay, sweetheart. If you'll promise me not to mind having to amuse a cranky, self-centered old man . . ."

Ann Lee sounded glad. "I'm used to that. See you soon."

Her cheerfulness restored the warm feeling that the prospect of seeing her had always given him. Yet he couldn't say he felt better. Something troubled him the minute he hung up. The warm feeling vanished, leaving him more irritable than before. What had he gotten himself into? He had called her to cancel the evening, hadn't he? And yet why, really, shouldn't she come? A movie, dinner, perhaps a glass of wine—what was wrong with that? No, he wasn't up to it, not tonight. He wanted to be alone, to be left to himself, damn it all!

Andrew was taken aback by his belligerence. What did he want from her? Why was he avoiding her? He knew the answer. He had known it all along. He just hadn't wanted to hear what an inner voice was whispering. *He didn't want to sleep with her.* He wasn't capable of it tonight. It was that simple and insulting, but it was true. He didn't want her seeing him the way he was, with all those bare, shaved patches on his chest, *all right?* He had to call her back right away, before she left home and it was too late.

He reached for the phone and pressed the redial button. Ann Lee answered at once, her voice different now, guarded. She knew, she knew everything! He had to talk fast, be firm, get it over with. "I know, sweetie, it sounds lovely, but why don't we put it off till tomorrow? I'll be lousy company tonight."

There was no answer. Her injured silence crackled on the line like an electrical interference. A second passed. Another. He had to say something. He had to fill the void before it swallowed them both like a black hole. "All right," said Ann Lee. "If that's what you want. I thought it would be nice to be together, but never mind. Whatever you say. Good night."

"Good night."

She was hurt. It thickened and disfigured her voice, making her sound older, almost his age. What now? What should he do? Call again and apologize? Tell her to come after all? He stared at the phone in his hand. It broadcast the end of the abruptly broken-off conversation like some cold, dark matter. No, he couldn't do that. It would be crazy. He had wanted to be alone, hadn't he? Well, now he was. *When you want to go, go. When you want to stay, stay. Just don't waver.* As if he had a need for three-penny Zen philosophy!

The phone suddenly rang. There was a digital message. "If you wish to make another call, please hang up and dial again. Thank you."

13
June 7, 2001

The 16th of Sivan, 5761

Linda's legs are spread-eagled, her ankles in metal stirrups attached to the two sides of the operating table, her naked body a greenish hue beneath the brutal spotlights of the delivery room. A bright metal sheet beneath her gleams like a carnival mirror, magnifying her torn vagina and gaping anus. I look away from the ugliness of it as if she were a strange woman rather than my wife. She screams. Her voice is inhuman, a savage's. "He'll die! My baby will die! Andy, do something! Something terrible has happened to the baby. Half its flesh is gone from its bones. It's being eaten by bubbling acid. How did this happen? My God, he'll die! Do something, he's burning up! Andy, help him! Please! Please don't let him die!"

14
June 7, 2001

The 16th of Sivan, 5761

Six thirty p.m. The kingdom of day was slowly fading. With their pedestrians gone, the avenues reverted to their clear geometric lines. The soft afternoon light lengthened the shadows of the skyscrapers, sending them ever eastward. But in the magnificent ballroom of Cipriani 42nd Street, across the street from Grand Central Station, the kingdom of night, bold and seductive, was in full reign with its bewitching artifice of eternal evening, its myste-rious dance of twilight silhouettes. Dark scarlet curtains hung on the Venetian stained-glass windows that never opened and looked out on nothing. The mosaic walls and gold and silver fluting of the marble columns gleamed in a dimness cloyingly perfumed with the sickly sweet incense-like smell of rotting fruit and the exotic scents of expensive, ponderous flower arrangements that sat in the center of the tables like tropical birds of prey.

Andrew glanced at his watch. How odd. Hadn't the invitation been for 6:30? He groped for it in his pocket: it was the right date, the right place, the right time. Where was everyone? He was about to return to the lobby and ask the doorman if there had been some last-minute change when something strange caught his eye. Fasci-nated by it, he was drawn, step by timid step, to the center of the large room. The long, thin, shockingly white neck of a large water bird—a swan? a heron? an albino flamingo? God only knew—hung lifelessly over the edge of a large table. Forlornly dangling from it, the half-open beak of its little, glassy-eyed head practically touched the waxed black marble floor. Someone had created an entire still life around it. An antique crystal decanter half-filled with amber wine stood in the center of the table, surrounded by an artful arrangement of red, yellow, and green apples in various stages of overripeness. Crystal goblets, some perfect, some cracked, stood amid the rotting fruit. The half-wilted petals of French tulips, fallen or placed by the skillful hand of a decorator, floated in several of them. Three small quail, their little feet tied with a brown drawstring, rested in the lap of a large pheasant whose colorful plumage gleamed in the dusky light like contraband gems, completing the composition.

Andrew stared, mesmerized, at the tableau of living death. Its exquisite eye for detail filled him with a mixture of admiration and abhorrence: the grotesqueness of it! Were the birds real? Did city law even allow it? He supposed it must. After all, poultry was

eaten, wasn't it? It took talent, daring, and a total lack of inhi-
bition to create such an arrangement. All of New York was like
that now, youthful and without boundaries. This was no city for
men over forty. Still, it was an odd choice of theme: *vanitas vani-
tatum omnia vanitas!* vanity of vanities, all is vanity, the aesthetics
of decay, decomposition, and dissolution. It didn't fit the season
of the year, nor was it appropriate for the occasion. In fact, the
whole event was rather odd: "The Friends of the Douglas-Sallon
Museum of Romantic Continental Art Invite You to Its Official
Reopening." The Douglas-Sallon Museum was a small, ephem-
eral institution with decadent taste that specialized in huge, bom-
bastic, early nineteenth-century oil paintings by unknown artists
who gave the romantic movement a bad name. Occupying three
incredibly expensive floors in the heart of New York's swankiest
neighborhood, its directors, rumor had it, were fronting for some
shady Russian oligarchs engaged in nefarious practices—money
laundering, most likely. After having been shut down under mysterious circumstances, it was now being opened to the public again
under even more mysterious ones. New York hadn't seen such a
gala cultural or artistic event in years. Romantic Continental art?
Something was rotten in the state of Denmark! Yet every one—
every one of us, that is—was planning to attend. They would wear
their fanciest clothes and play their assigned roles in the world
of the high and mighty, eating, drinking, lusting for each other's
partners, hobnobbing with the rich and the famous, and serving as
their moral and cultural fig leaves.

Where was the bar? Andrew was an old hand at events of this
sort, well versed in the social and professional rituals of grand
openings, cocktail parties, and fund-raising dinners, starting with
the scotch on the rocks (summer will soon be here—why not enjoy
its little pleasures like ice cubes?), the hors d'oeuvres, the meaningless small talk, and the prepackaged smiles. From there, the well-

oiled machine of institutional public relations would churn merrily along on waves of adrenaline, expensive perfume, and alcohol. But where was the bar? There had to be one somewhere. Did he need a drink to calm his nerves? Not him! Well, yes, maybe a wee bit. Yet why be nervous? It was just another opening. Ann Lee should be here any minute. She should have arrived by now, in fact.

Andrew found the bar in the northeast corner of the ballroom, half-hidden behind a massive pseudo-Mesopotamian column that looked like the large leg of a prehistoric beast, covered with onyx and sapphire scales. He surveyed the selection of liquor with a practiced eye. First-rate, absolutely first-rate! Price was no object, somebody was hell-bent to impress! There were over a dozen kinds of scotch, nearly all premium brands; all the leading cognacs— not just in their popular, lower-priced versions but in their superb, aged XOs; rare Armagnacs, interesting calvados; boutique-distillery Tequila, rum and gin, exotic varieties of grappa, and a large variety of intriguing European digestifs. It was Romantic Continentalism at its best, Exhibit A being a crushed ice bucket in which stood, not your ordinary, yellow-labeled champagne bottles of Veuve Clicquot but the diabolical-looking, round-bellied bottles of the legendary Dom Perignon. It went beyond the desire to impress; it could only be called the desire to overwhelm. Andrew scanned the labels on the scotch bottles. No comfortingly cheerful clink of ice cubes for him tonight: the single malts were simply too good! It was all a well-disguised display of power. Hesitating for a moment before a formidable row of bottles, he picked the amber nectar of a small distillery with an unpronounceable name that was touted by the bartender as "the next big thing." Although he considered asking for a double, he decided—a bit sheepishly, it might be—against it. His craving for whiskey had been getting stronger lately. Was it too strong? Nonsense! Not everything called for editorial comment. The party was just beginning.

The ballroom had suddenly filled up. Many of the men were in black tie. It was a different city, a different league. Someone had changed the rules of the game, turned around the equations of power and its representation. He sniffed his glass, inhaling the deep, complex aroma of the noble drink. It was indeed perfect, not too smoky and not too bland, a new blend he was not familiar with. He wasn't actually feeling nervous, was he? It was an event like any other: a bit more dramatically staged—a lot more, to tell the truth—but still, it was just another party.

He had hidden behind the column long enough. It was time to take his nose out of his glass and start mingling. Let the show begin! What time was it? Already seven. She still hadn't arrived. Where the hell was she? They didn't appear together in public every day, not at something like this, at any rate. It was important to both of them, so why was she doing this to him now after demanding, even twisting his arm, at a time when their relationship had cooled, to be his dinner partner on an evening at which the entire Who's Who of his professional life would be present? Never mind. He would manage. He always did. He just had to get ahold of himself, breathe deeply, take a nice sip of whiskey, arrange a smile on his face, and go forth to meet the world. The whiskey was truly excellent. It was too bad he had been embarrassed to ask for a double.

15

Ann Lee arrived at seven forty-five, just as the cocktail reception was about to end, wearing a short black dress and glitzy black high heels that Andrew had never seen before. On the whole, there was something about her that he didn't recognize, something disturbingly different that enveloped her like a dark halo. She didn't apologize for being late or offer an explanation. Nor did she owe him any, of course. "Get a load of that!" she said, pointing with her chin to the white bird's neck draped over the main table. "Is it at least dead?" She kissed Andrew lightly on the cheek. "Be a darling and bring me some champagne, will you?" Since when did she talk in that la-di-da way? He couldn't help feeling she was getting back at him for something. What did she have to be angry about? But there was no point in playing the innocent. He knew very well what it was. Champagne for her and another whiskey for himself, a double this time. It was going to be a long, hard night.

"I do believe it's my old friend Andrew!" The loud, familiar voice booming behind him made him turn around quickly. Standing there was Bernie Bernstein, president of the university, tall and elegant as always, his arms spread theatrically as if about to clasp Andrew to his bosom. "Andrew P. Cohen, professor of culture! If he's here, the organizers of this thing have real class!" Bernie rattled the ice cubes in his glass with a Hollywood flair. It was clearly not his first drink, perhaps not even his second. His cheeks were flushed and the boyish challenge in his eyes was like the irresistible grin of an ex–juvenile delinquent. His glance shifted from Andrew to Ann Lee, his eyes widening at her young, scantily clothed body in its shimmering black fabric. "And who is this enchanting lady?" asked the president of New York University. A good head taller than she was, he bent with a dandyish grace, his well-honed seductive instincts set in motion, took her small hand in his big, rough one, and kept it there considerably longer than was necessary. Taken by surprise, Andrew stammered an introduction. "Bernie, I'd like you to meet Ann Lee. Ann Lee is . . ." He looked for a way to end the sentence as banally as most sentences did on an evening like this, but Ann Lee cut him short. "Nice to meet you, I'm his midlife crisis," she told Bernie.

Bernie's eyes lit up with genuine interest. He liked women like this. "Is that so?" he said to Andrew. "You sly devil, you! Where have you been hiding her all this time?" He sidled up to Ann Lee and put an impish arm around her. "My heartfelt gratitude for thinking I could steal her from you!"

Ann Lee giggled flirtatiously. She was out to punish him tonight, no doubt. Bernie gave Andrew a cunning wink, his heavy, bearlike paw resting with playful possessiveness on Ann Lee's thin, sleeveless arm. Andrew was at a loss. What was he supposed to do now? Wink back with a complicit, hedonistic chuckle? With a grimace that might have passed for a smile, he tried, not very successfully, to respond. Not that he was in any danger. Bernie wasn't about to walk off with her. It was just his way of carrying on.

"Bernie, you old lech! Bet you'll tell me she's your granddaughter!"

Bernie turned to face the speaker, letting Andrew and Ann Lee slip from his field of attention. "Come on, Mike! You know me too well for that. You can't teach an old dog new tricks."

He released Ann Lee's arm, his fingertips gliding down it in parting, and turned to his new conversation partner, a balding, paunchy man with a pink silk pocket square that matched his tie. Andrew watched them embrace and slap each other's backs like two old gangsters in a film. Yes, everything had changed. Someone in the city had changed the rules of the game without telling him.

"Okay, I was nice to your boss." Ann Lee poked a small, sharp, mirthless elbow in Andrew's ribs. "I think I've earned my champagne fair and square."

Andrew looked at her, trying to relate the figure in front of him to the woman he knew and loved, but soon gave up. He hurried to get to the bar before it closed, bumping into already seated guests and skirting the main table while averting his eyes from the obscenely long swan's neck dangling from it. Once he and Linda had seen a pair of swans appear from nowhere, as if born from the ocean's foam. It was on the beach in Cape Cod. The girls were playing at the water's edge. Their little footprints, erased from the sand by each wave, were engraved in his memory forever, as if tattooed on the surface of the earth. Two long-necked, white swans were flying westward with infinite care. Their resolve, their self-mastery! A cool, shivery breeze blew from the water. Linda, as usual, was busy snapping her camera. It never ceased to annoy him, this need of hers to record every second. As if she knew that it would pass, that everything would pass, how transitory everything was. Where was the goddamn bar?

16

The meat was served in shameless, orgiastic quantities. Whole plump partridges were impaled on large, sooty iron spits to suggest that they had been roasted in the hearth of a medieval castle. Game birds, almost green from aging and smelling faintly of death. The quails came in nests of golden mashed potatoes, deep-fried to a crisp. Three small, spotted quail's eggs were nestled under the scrawny body of the dead bird. Waiters hovered silently at the guests' backs, filling and refilling glasses with a heavy, overbearing Bordeaux that suited neither the humid late spring evening nor the meat, which begged for something lighter, less dominant—perhaps a Burgundy? Even a nice California Pinot Noir would have been better. Andrew regarded the bird on his plate with revulsion. His stomach was turned by the over-explicitness of the visual metaphor as much as by the cruelty of it. The whole evening was wildly overstated. It was the victory of naked, unmediated power over the subtly discriminating mind. Everyone who was anyone in the city had been invited tonight: the mayor, the commissioner of cultural affairs, the curators of the large museums, the influential academics, and, of course, the wealthy art lovers. Raw, arrogant self-interest hung over the gathering like a cloud. What, really, was behind it? Were the city's masters poised for a real estate grab in which the Douglas-Sallon Building would be sold for a fortune to private investors as soon as it was emptied of the last of its dubious paintings? Was it some other scam? Something was indeed rotten in the kingdom, as rotten as the meat on his plate.

A shriek of laughter came from across the table. Ann Lee, sitting on its other side and half-hidden by a centerpiece of flowers, was completely drunk. She had been drinking heavily all evening, much too much. She had also been ignoring him while giggling in whispers with the man next to her. Himself a good twenty years older than she, he had an aging playboy's slicked-back hair and an artificial tan that painted him a lurid orange. Andrew turned sideways to survey the dimly lit ballroom. Its dull golds and crepuscular scarlets and indigos could have come from one of the museum's wretched paintings. All that was missing was a mysterious hand to write a wrathful prophecy of doom on the walls. Where was Bernie? It was irrational, he knew, but Andrew had been relieved to discover he was sitting nowhere near Ann Lee. Now, he spotted his Roman noble's profile at a VIP table near the speakers' podium, eating and drinking gustily while conversing with an expensively dressed, foreign-looking man whose laugh echoed through the ballroom. Although Andrew knew him from somewhere, he couldn't remember from where. Was he Indian? Perhaps Pakistani? Where had he seen him before? At some ceremony at the university, perhaps. His gaze followed the shafts of light rising to the ceiling. Little, carefully spaced spotlights beamed a thin, psychedelic lacework over the main tables, which seemed to hover above the floor. There sat the generals, the real power brokers. The rest of us are just foot soldiers, junior officers at most! They sit there, and he is sitting here, obsessing about the tastes of wines, the textures of foods, and his absurd tit-for-tat games with a woman young enough to be his daughter.

And yet power was something he had never craved. Knowledge was not a commodity! He had wanted something else, something more spiritual. One could laugh at his innocence or at the anachronism of his thinking, but he had wanted to be a seeker of truth. No, that, too, was ridiculous. Who knew what he had wanted? What person could seriously and honestly state he didn't care about power? Who knows what their true motivations are, anyway? Who could even think with all the loud blather and hearty guffaws, with all these smug, crass faces around him?

Another burst of drunken, unnatural laughter came from across the table. Andrew looked despairingly at Ann Lee through the serrated leaves of the tropical flower arrangement, in whose claws she appeared to be caught. She was so fragile and helpless—so young, so thin, so trapped in the bizarre, pointless role she was being made to play. His heart went out to her. If only he could lean across the table and stroke her cheek tenderly. If only he could go over to her, take her gently in his arms, and lead her away from here, take her home. But there wasn't a chance. It was impossible to leave now. The show must go on. He dug his fork into a quail, detaching a piece of gray, fibrous meat and putting it cautiously in his mouth. It was thick and cartilaginous, revolting. What now? How could he swallow such offal, which had aroused his repugnance from the moment it was served? But to spit it back into his plate? Into a napkin nonchalantly raised to his mouth? How could he do so without being seen?

A polite question coming from Andrew's left, not a word of which registered, put an end to his agonizing by forcing him to bolt down the meat stuck between his teeth. He turned to his inquisitor, a New York matron whose too tightly drawn skin and too perfectly arched brows testified to an expensive surgical intervention, trying in vain to decode what she had said. With a cautious smile—she had obviously been warned not to risk rupturing a perfect knife job by smiling too energetically—she repeated her question. Andrew felt a wave of nausea. The meat was creeping down his gullet, on its way to his stomach. What did she want? He couldn't understand a word. Had her face-lift affected her speech? What was that buzzing in his ears? He couldn't hear a thing. Smile, smile and nod—that always worked! It made them think you were in total agreement. Where was the restroom? He scanned the corners of the room, looking for a hidden recess. His stomach, queasily squeezing the dead bird's flesh, was determined to send it back. And now someone was talking on his right: he would have to face in that direction. He just mustn't throw up. He absolutely mustn't!

Andrew turned to the right, forcing himself to look up. At once, however, he looked down again with a feeling of vertigo: the woman sitting there looked like the identical twin of the woman on his left. They even had the same smile and dull, expressionless voice. Baring his teeth in a contorted smile, he rose half-instinctively, desperately gripping the table. Where was the men's room? He had to find the men's room! He straightened up, letting the white napkin on his knee fall to the floor, and groped his way blindly through the dim, sticky ballroom, holding on to columns and the backs of seats while bumping into the waiters, who buzzed angrily around him like bees whose hive had been breached. Ann Lee's contrived, hollow laugh followed him until he reached the restroom's heavy, soundproof door and closed it behind him, shutting out the insufferable din.

The toilet stall was cool and quiet, a little island of sanity amid the bedlam. He leaned forward, rested his palms against the wall, bent over the low toilet bowl, and tried to puke. His stomach turned over and he retched, his insides contracting like a boa constrictor, but nothing came out. He straightened up, gulped some air-conditioned air, and leaned back over the bowl. The great snake writhed wildly and finally ejected a gleaming, toxic yellow liquid. Was it whiskey? Bile? A terrible sensation of heartburn made him choke. *He was in a gray desert, stretching in all directions like an infinite, menacing ocean. A dreadful stench of death and desolation was everywhere. Wails of terror and sorrow pierced the noxious air like the blasts of a horn. The exhausted little birds flailed helplessly on the ground with gasping beaks, gray wings beating the drab desert dust. The stench, the fetor of rotting corpses!* He retched again. The toxic yellow liquid slashed his throat like a knife. *The gray little birds flailed helplessly on the ground. The rabble threw itself on them, crazed with hunger. Hardened fingers tore them apart, ripping open their innards, from which spilled mangled guts and little red hearts that went on beating in human hands until they stopped.*

Andrew returned haltingly to his seat, his face damp from repeated washing and his moist hair neatly combed in an unconvincing attempt to look refreshed. He had to find some way of making conversation with the women next to him. It was rude not to have spoken a single word to them all evening. He wasn't delivering the goods! What on earth was he doing here, anyway? The malignant doubt had gnawed at him all evening: he was defrauding the event's organizers, selling them an illusion of influence and importance he didn't have. Of course, that was ridiculous. His influence was considerable and would become more so when his new appointment took effect. Speaking of which, it was odd that Bernie hadn't so much as alluded to it recently, neither in their private conversations nor in the presence of others. Why the mantle of secrecy? All these Byzantine court intrigues were so out of place, so uncalled for. And this table, his empty seat sticking out like a missing tooth, the two women on either side of it sitting as straight and stiff as if embalmed by the doctors to keep their bodies from decaying still further, carefully chewing their gray meat with smiles that looked like they were pasted to their faces with superglue!

Enough negativity! To work! Andrew sat down, reached for his napkin that had been picked up, refolded, and put back in place by an alert waiter, and peered through the flower arrangement for a glimpse of Ann Lee. The table had grown suddenly quiet. Her hysterical giggles that had pursued him to the ends of the ballroom had yielded to a worrisome, ominous silence. Cocking his head to get a better view, he felt a chill run down his spine. Ann Lee's seat was empty, as was the man's next to her. Her scarf was gone, too, along with her handbag. She had left. Without telling him, without saying good-bye, without a word! Gone, she and her awful fake-tanned companion. She would never come back. Never! He caught his breath. His lungs gasped for air. His skin crawled as if a colony of ants underneath it were repelling an attacker. She was gone! He would never see her again!

An impatient voice blared near his left ear. It reverberated like the sound of a trumpet on some other floor of the building. His clothes felt tight, the wrong size, as if he had suddenly put on more weight. The strange voice blared again, more insistently. Andrew turned toward it. With barely disguised annoyance, a broad-shouldered waiter with a black satin bow tie around a thick neck was standing next to him, almost touching him, while extending a hand toward his plate. Andrew arched startled brows, shocked by the physical intrusion on his space. *The gray, exhausted birds fell from the air in midflight, hitting the ground with a dull thud like ripe fruit from an old, heavily laden tree.* The waiter repeated his question, his animosity more pronounced. The words reached Andrew's ears like thick bubbles from the bottom of the sea. "Sir, are you done? May I please take away your plate?" What an exaggerated, aggressive show of politeness! Andrew turned to look at his plate. The little gray corpse lay practically untouched, its orphaned eggs peering from beneath its stiffened body that still seemed to be retracting in fright, as though in the middle of rigor mortis. Andrew nodded, equally embarrassed and intimidated, watching his plate unceremoniously snatched by a hand powerful enough to be a boxer's. "Thank you, sir." The words rumbled like a crack of thunder overhead. She was gone. She would never come back. He peered through the flower arrangement again, hoping desperately to see her sitting there with her captivating smile. It was just a practical joke, wasn't it? A small, harmless joke! Soon she would return and they could go home together. She wasn't there. Her abandoned seat was still empty. Yet the aging playboy was back in place, holding his wineglass while chatting idly with the woman on his other side, ignored until now for his exclusive tête-à-tête with Ann Lee that had driven Andrew—no, everyone—to distraction. The scandalous incivility of it! A warm, almost triumphant feeling spread through him. What a relief! Joy! As chagrined as he was to admit it, he felt like a new man. No, it wasn't Ann Lee's disappearance that had tormented him. It was his jealousy, foolish, childish, and irrational.

But the relief did not last long, cut short by a shudder that ran through him. What if she had gone off with Bernie? That old fox, that serial skirt-chaser! Though painfully conscious of the absurdity of his fear, he couldn't defend himself against its predatory bite that sank its teeth into him. He fought to fend it off, struggling to restore the rule of common sense, yet he found himself casting an anxious, involuntary glance at the main table, praying to find Bernie there without her. Suppose she was there, sitting in his lap, the thin strap of her black dress, slipped from her shoulder, revealing a small, impudent breast in the lewd glare of the spotlights? Enough! Enough of this! He had to stop. Bernie was there by himself, oblivious to the neurotic drama taking place a few tables away, drinking, laughing, and talking loudly with the elegant Indian man sitting to his left. A strong, healthy, powerful man! Still, Andrew continued to indulge his tormented imagination a while longer: Bernie's strong, age-spotted hand lifting the hem of her short dress, stroking her smooth thigh with a proprietary air, slowly, pleasurably, making its way upward . . . There was nothing to stop him from torturing himself. How filthy, how putrid, it all was! Nausea welled up in him again, threatening to erupt like a volcano and engulf the room and its degenerate diners, the whole drunken bordello of them. What had they put in the food, for God's sake? How could a tiny piece of meat poison a grown man like that?

Andrew rose, letting the napkin fall to the floor again. The nausea, however, was gone. Abashed, he looked around to see if anyone had noticed his strange behavior, bent to pick up the napkin, and sat down once more, doing his best to look nonchalant. What, after all, had happened? Nothing to be that upset about. He took a deep breath and looked to his right, where his jilted neighbor had despaired long ago of his being her cavalier for the evening. Her twin on the left, who no longer resembled her as much, had found a way to occupy herself, too; taking a small makeup kit from her bag, she was busy redoing the lines of her face with the help of a rectangular little mirror on her powder box. Where could Ann Lee have gone? Should he go look for her? Where could she be? He couldn't just get up and leave now, before the last speeches. They hadn't even served dessert yet. He had no choice but to stick it out to the end.

An after-dinner speaker ascended the podium. The ceremonious, empty words resounded in the ballroom. Yet though the sound system worked perfectly and the remarks could be heard clearly at the farthest tables, Andrew had trouble following them. The annoying buzzing in his ears started up again and the distant trumpet blasts were joined by strange kitchen noises mysteriously emanating from the vents of the air conditioners, creating a cacophonous chaos. A second speaker mounted the podium. The audience's attention was flagging. Sounds of laughter and renewed conversation came from unseen places in the ballroom. Yet Bernie and his distinguished companions at the main table went on listening, a knowing expression of amusement on their sharply featured faces.

From time to time, they exchanged the sly, intimate whispers of an inner circle of confidants. Something was happening behind the scenes—something unclean, unethical, immoral. Where was she now? Had she gone home? She had planned to come back with him to his apartment tonight. Poor girl! She could be cruel when she wanted, but there was a childlike innocence beneath it all, a pure, honest streak that commanded respect. Andrew's glance wandered back to the centerpiece on the table. Something had changed in the course of the evening: there were new colors in it. The warmth and humidity had made some buds open their mouths and shamelessly show their orange palates to the world. The large, decadent flowers reminded him of something—something that aroused his longing. A deep orange, turning almost scarlet at the margins; at the center, a concentrated black. Long, ragged, translucent petals, the light streaming through them bringing you back to distant childhood. Gorgeous wildflowers—and so fresh. They sold them by the roadside on Cape Cod, in empty cans with half-peeled-off labels. Gay, casual bouquets in all the sizes, colors, and stages of blossoming and wilting. Fiery splotches of color, so in contrast to the restrained palette of the Atlantic coast, their pure vitality the gift of fast-approaching death. A blue-gray line runs from one end of the horizon to the other, filling it with fierce yearning. The pearly hue of the big bay beyond the front porch. The stubborn bushes turning yellow in the late summer sun beneath an enormous sky. So many stars, so much sky. If only he could be in the Cape now, bathing in the infinite purity of its sky and water.

17

The clink of bottles against glasses and forks against plates brought Andrew back to reality. He looked around as if waking from a dream, blinking in the dim light. Dessert! Dessert was being served. That was a good sign. Serving dessert before the speeches were over meant the evening wouldn't go on past eleven thirty. The pugilistic waiter reappeared behind him. "A dessert wine, sir?" His crisp courtesy showed no sign of his former annoyance or even of recognition. Andrew nodded, eager to avoid further complications, and the waiter bent to fill a long-stemmed glass with a viscous yellow liquid. Andrew raised it cautiously to his lips. It was a Madeira, oily and bitter as it was meant to be, but with none of the freshness of the pure rainwater that gave it its legendary name.

A small, gold-rimmed plate was set in front of him. On it was a piece of olive oil cake with coriander seed, drenched in an apricot compote that had the Madeira's telltale bitterness, too. The whole thing was too rich, too pretentious, too baroque. Like the entire menu—like the entire evening—it was overdone. What would have been wrong with an elegant Sauterne and a lighter, more summery dessert—say, an airy fresh fruit whip? His fork plowed through the heavy cake, which could have been cast in bronze. When might he get to the Cape? The sooner, the better. They had agreed that Linda would have the house for July and he would have it for August. But he couldn't wait for August, he had to have it before then! He took a sip of wine, made a face, swallowed the rest of the glass, and put it down. He had never liked Madeira. He preferred ports or Sauternes, even certain sweet sherries.

The waiter stepped up behind him and refilled his glass without asking. It had been refilled all evening—who knew how much he had drunk? And on a practically empty stomach! Ann Lee had had a lot, too; he had never seen her in such a state. As soon as the speeches were over, he would slip away and look for her. He couldn't get up and leave now, not in the middle of a speech. Could she have gone to his place after all? That seemed unlikely. In fact, there was no chance of it. His fork clinked against his empty plate. To his dismay, Andrew saw that he had eaten the entire piece of cake, the whole overly rich concoction he had sneered at. For a moment, he felt a childish, embarrassing urge to ask for a second helping, from which he refrained not only because he mustn't overdo it but also, and perhaps above all, because of the mockery he feared seeing in the hostile waiter's eyes. His nausea, which he thought his body had vanquished, was back again—not as violently as before, but still unpleasantly enough. Air! He needed some air. Why wasn't this place better ventilated?

Where was he? The white window frames, jutting out from clapboard walls turned gray with age, were like some mysterious script. Although in the really old houses the wood had turned almost black, its blue trim made it look younger, more alive. Empty rocking chairs graced the front porches, swaying softly in the sea breeze, the creak of their wooden runners keeping time with the boom of the surf. The house was gray inside and out. Every passing year had left its mark, like the annual marks of the children's height on the jamb of the kitchen door. Layer upon layer in the living body of the wood, their silent memories were faithfully preserved.

Andrew took a deep, desperate breath of over-conditioned air. A warm, salty sea mist tickled his nose, causing his upper lip to quiver as if he were about to sneeze. He had to look away to avoid seeing the little girl stretching her thin body as high as it could go, small heels pressed to the floor, the ruler on her head at a right angle to the wall, her eyes shining like dark suns, like stars. Our wonderful old kitchen. That peeling, crumbling, aging room. All the old cutlery with its ceramic, glass, and enamel handles, the heavy, antique, time-burdened spoons and forks. The last thing he had bought for the house was a set of new knives. It was right toward the end, during their last summer together: a superb, expensive German set of Wüsthof knives. All must be dull by now. Unlike the knives in his New York apartment, he had never sharpened them. Linda hadn't bothered to cut vegetables and meat on their wooden cutting board, preferring to do it directly on the granite counter, or on plates and trays. Her negligence had annoyed him. That was the way to ruin a good knife. They needed to be sharpened. Perhaps he would do it this summer.

The little girl was still there, jumping up and down excitedly, trying to read the numbers on the doorjamb. "How many inches, Mom? How many inches?" How stuffy it was. He couldn't breathe. He had to get out of here, now. Fuck all their speeches! Fuck them all! Andrew leaped to his feet without glancing at anyone, pushed back his chair, and headed quickly for the exit. Glass doors opened in front of him. A wave of hot, muggy air washed over him. Large, pitter-pat drops of rain fell on the sidewalk, drumming on the awning above him, which barely protected him from the summer storm. He looked to his right and to his left. The street was deserted. There was nothing but water and darkness. Turning up the collar of his jacket, he hiked up his pants and ran westward, into the storm, toward Madison Avenue. The warm, heavy drops poured down on him, drenching his hair, his clothes, the skin beneath them. Thunderless lightning flashed overhead. Andrew kept running, though he had no idea where he was going or what his mad dash would accomplish.

He saw her at the corner of Madison. How long was she standing there for? The thunder caught up there with both of them, crashing over them like a steamroller. She was dripping wet, soaked to the bone. Her black dress hung from her twiggy body like a wet rag, making her look spectacularly feminine and heartbreakingly thin. She didn't look at him and he didn't dare call her name. He approached her, slowing to a walk, and stood silently by her side. Long minutes went by before they were able to crawl into a large, night-cruising limousine that wheeled them away, each wet, silent, and withdrawn in a corner of the backseat. The car's worn tires spun along the wet asphalt, the city's lights glittering there like reflections in a black river flowing from nowhere to nowhere.

18
June 8, 2001

The 17th of Sivan, 5761

A gray, infinite, menacing desert stretches like a desolate sea all the way to the horizon. A stench of death in the air. Wails of terror and sorrow, the fetor of corpses. The dead birds pile up, gathered together upon heaps, their drooping wings caked with thin, ash-colored dirt, their beaks gaping in a helpless plea. Great plague rages through the stricken, delirious rabble. Noxious fumes rise from the heaps of rotting flesh that quiver in the merciless light. It's my baby, I gave birth to it. I clutch it to my breast and make my way past the columns of smoke and the dying, flailing bodies on the ground. Its soft mouth is tightly clamped on my right nipple. It nurses desperately, sucking the last life I have to give it. It mustn't stop. As long as I have milk for it, it will live, immune from the plague.

END OF BOOK FIVE

On other days he would take out [the cinders] with a silver coal pan and empty it into one of gold, but this day he took them out with a golden [coal pan], in which he was to bring them. In [the inner sanctuary] on other days he would take them up with a coal pan containing four *kabs*, and empty it into one containing three *kabs*, this day he took them out with one containing three *kabs*, in which he brings [the cinders] in, too. Rabbi Jose said: On other days he would take them out with one containing one *se'ah*, and empty it into one containing three *kabs*, this day he took them out with one containing three *kabs*, in which he also brings in [the cinders]. On other days the pan was heavy, today it was light. On other days its handle was short, today it was long. On other days it was of yellowish gold, today of red gold.

He took the coal pan and went up to the top of the altar, clearing the coals to both sides, took a panful of the glowing cinders from below, came down and placed the coal pan on the fourth terrace in the Temple Court. They brought out to him the ladle and the pan. [From the latter] he took his two handsful [of incense] and put them into the ladle, a tall [High Priest] according to his size, a short one according to his size, and thus was its measure. He took the pan in his right [hand] and the ladle in his left [hand].

The High Priest was given a coal pan. Light and long-handled, it was of a ruddy gold. He went to the altar, poked the hot coals, and filled the coal pan with glowing embers. Next, he was brought a pan of incense and a brazier that he filled from the pan. Holding the coal pan in his right hand and the brazier in his left, he walked slowly to the curtain between the Sacred Hall and the Sanctuary as if approaching a danger zone and disappeared behind it. From here on, there was no way of knowing what was happening. The priests and the people held their breath. No one dared say a word. All knew that if the High Priest's offering and prayers were accepted, neither sword, plague, nor hunger would prevail in the coming year—and that if, God forbid, they were not, the High Priest would be stricken dead and Israel would be orphaned and left exposed to every ill.

The Master said: "And the [smoke arising from the] pile of wood on the altar." But was there smoke arising from the pile of wood? Has it not been taught: Five things were reported about the fire of the pile of wood: It was lying like a lion, it was as clear as sunlight, its flame was of solid substance, it devoured wet wood like dry wood, and it caused no smoke to arise from it?—— What we said [about the smoke] referred to the wood from outside [of the Sanctuary]. For it has been taught: And the sons of Aaron the priest shall put fire upon the altar. Although the fire comes down from heaven, it is a proper thing to bring fire from outside, too.

Rabbi Oshaia said: When King Solomon built the Sanctuary, he planted therein all kinds of [trees of] golden delights, which were bringing forth their [golden] fruits in their season, and as the winds blew at them, they would fall off, as it is written: *May his fruits rustle like Lebanon*, and when the foreigners entered the Temple they withered, as it is written: *And the flower of Lebanon languishes*; and the Holy One, blessed be He, will in the future restore them, as it is said: *It shall blossom abundantly and rejoice, even with joy and singing; the glory of Lebanon shall be given unto it.*

[Mishna, Treatise Yoma, Chapter 4, Mishna 5] He went through the shrine until he came to the place between the two curtains which separated the Holy from the Holy of Holies and between which there was [a space of] one cubit. Rabbi Jose said: There was but one curtain, as it is said: And the veil shall divide unto you between the holy place and the most holy. The outer curtain was held back by a clasp on the south side and the inner curtain on the north side. He walked along between them until he reached the north side. When he reached the north side, he turned round to the south and went on along the curtain, to his left, until he reached the ark. When he reached the ark, he put the pan of burning coals between the two bars. He heaped up the incense upon the coals and the whole house became full with smoke. He came out by the way he entered and in the outer house he uttered a short prayer. He did not make the prayer long so as not to frighten [the nation of] Israel.

[Mishna, Treatise Yoma, Chapter 5, Mishna 2] After the ark had been taken away, there was a stone from the days of the earlier prophets, called the *shethiyah*, three fingers above the ground, on which he would place [the pan of burning coals].

[Babylonian Talmud, Treatise Yoma, Folio 53b] Our Rabbis taught: It happened with one High Priest that he prolonged his prayer. His fellow priests undertook to enter after him. As they began to enter he came forth. They said to him: Why did you prolong your prayer?——He said: Is it disagreeable to you that I prayed for you, for the Sanctuary, that it be not destroyed?——They said to him: Do not make a habit of doing so, for thus have we learnt: "He would not pray long lest he terrify Israel."

Each minute felt like an eternity. At last the incense was heard crackling on the coals. Soon clouds of smoke billowed from the Holy of Holies. The High Priest took a moment to pray, doing it quickly to alarm no one by his absence, and returned to the Sacred Hall. When the people saw him emerge from the Sanctuary safely, his face shining with an unearthly radiance, there was great joy. Only the somber mood of the day kept them from breaking into song and dance.

[Babylonian Talmud, Treatise Berakhot, Folio 7a] It was taught: Rabbi Ishmael ben Elisha said: I once entered into the innermost part [of the Sanctuary] to offer incense and saw Akathriel Jah, the Lord of Hosts, seated upon a high and exalted throne. He said to me: "'Ishmael, My son, bless Me!" I replied: May it be Thy will that Thy mercy may suppress Thy anger and Thy mercy may prevail over Thy other attributes, so that Thou mayest deal with Thy children according to the attribute of mercy and mayest, on their behalf, stop short of the limit of strict justice! And He nodded to me with His head.

[Leviticus, Chapter 16, Verses 14—19] And he shall take of the blood of the bullock, and sprinkle it with his finger upon the ark cover on the east; and before the ark cover shall he sprinkle of the blood with his finger seven times. Then shall he kill the goat of the sin-offering, that is for the people, and bring his blood within the veil, and do with his blood as he did with the blood of the bullock, and sprinkle it upon the ark cover, and before the ark cover. And he shall make atonement for the holy place, because of the uncleannesses of the children of Israel, and because of their transgressions, even all their sins; and so shall he do for the tent of meeting, that dwelleth with them in the midst of their uncleannesses. And there shall be no man in the tent of meeting when he goeth in to make atonement in the holy place, until he come out, and have made atonement for himself, and for his household, and for all the assembly of Israel. And he shall go out unto the altar that is before the LORD, and make atonement for it; and shall take of the blood of the bullock, and of the blood of the goat, and put it upon the horns of the altar round about. And he shall sprinkle of the blood upon it with his finger seven times, and cleanse it, and hallow it from the uncleannesses of the children of Israel.

The High Priest took the stoup of blood from Obadiah, who had been stirring it all along, and retreated behind the curtain once more. Now, his voice was heard each time he sprinkled the blood with a flick of his wrist in the Holy of Holies, first up and then seven times down: "One. One and one. One and two. One and three. One and four. One and five. One and six. One and seven." All hung on every word. Every soul felt stretched to the limit at the thought of Judgment Day.

[Mishna, Treatise Yoma, Chapter 5, Mishna 3] He would take the blood from him who was stirring it, and enter [again] into the place where he had entered, and stand [again] on the place on which he had stood, and sprinkle thereof once upward and seven times downward, aiming to sprinkle neither upward nor downward but [making the movement of swinging a whip]. And thus would he count: One, one and one, one and two, one and three, one and four, one and five, one and six, one and seven.

The Gate of Rebirth:

The impregnation of a cleaving soul takes place, as has been said, during a person's lifetime and is unconnected to his physical body, unlike the soul that enters the body at birth and is indissolubly joined to it until death. For this reason, if the body suffers from a physical ailment or affliction, the cleaving soul is unaffected and feels no pain. It is like a loan, or like a guest in someone's house who stays only as long as he pleases.

[Mishna, Treatise Yoma, Chapter 5, Mishnayot 3—6] They would bring him the goat. He would slaughter it and receive its blood in a bowl. He entered [again] into the place where he had entered, and stood [again] on the place on which he had stood, and sprinkled once upward and seven times downward, and he did not intend to sprinkle [simply] upward or downward but rather like one who cracks a whip. And thus would he count: One, one and one, one and two, one and three, one and four, one and five, one and six, one and seven. Then he would go out and place [the bowl] on the second stand in the Sanctuary. [. . .] He would take the blood of the bull and put down the blood of the goat, and sprinkle from it upon the curtains facing the ark outside, once upward, seven times downward, intending to sprinkle neither [simply] upward nor downward, but rather like one who cracks a whip. Thus would he count: One, one and one, one and two, one and three, one and four, one and five, one and six, one and seven. Then he would take the blood of the goat, and put down the blood of the bull, and sprinkle from it upon the curtain facing the ark outside once upward, seven times downward: one, one and one, one and two, one and three, one and four, one and five, one and six, one and seven. Then he would pour the blood of the bull into the blood of the goat, emptying the full vessel into the empty one. [. . .] He then began to purify [the altar by sprinkling] in downward motion. From where does he begin? From the northeast horn [of the altar], then the northwest, then the southwest, then the southeast. From the place where he begins [sprinkling when offering] a sin offering on the outer altar, there he completes [sprinkling] on the inner altar. Rabbi Eliezer says: He remained in his place and sprinkled. And on every horn he would sprinkle from below upward, with the exception of the horn at which he was standing, which he would sprinkle from above downward. Then he sprinkled the body of the altar seven times. And he would pour out the remainder of the blood at the western base of the outer altar. And on the outer altar he poured out at the southern base.

[Mishna, Treatise Yoma, Chapter 5, Mishnayot 3—4] Then he would go out and put it on the golden stand in the sanctuary. One would bring him the he-goat, he would slay it, receive its blood in a basin, enter [again] the place he had entered before, stand [again] on the place he had stood on before, and would sprinkle therefrom once upward and seven times downward. Thus would he count: One, one and one, one and two, one and three, one and four, one and five, one and six, one and seven.

[Mishna, Treatise Yoma, Chapter 5, Mishna 7] Concerning every ministration of the Day of Atonement mentioned in the prescribed order, if one service was done out of order before another one, it is as if it had not been done at all. If he sprinkled the blood of the he-goat before the blood of the bullock, he must start over again, sprinkling the blood of the he-goat after the blood of the bullock. If before he had finished the sprinklings within [the Holy of Holies] the blood was poured away, he must bring other blood, starting over again and sprinkling again within [the Holy of Holies]. Likewise, in matters of the Sanctuary and the Golden Altar, since they are each a separate act of atonement. Rabbi Eleazar and Rabbi Simeon say: Wherever he stopped, there he must begin again.

The High Priest reemerged and placed the stoup on a gold stand in the Sacred Hall. The goat was brought to him. He slit its throat, gathered the blood in a second stoup, and returned with it to the Sanctuary. Again he counted as he sprinkled the blood in the Holy of Holies: "One. One and one. One and two. One and three. One and four. One and five. One and six. One and seven." He returned to the Sacred Hall and placed the second stoup on a second stand. He took the blood of the bull and sprinkled it on the outside of the curtain, up and down, counting as before. He did the same with the blood of the goat, after which he poured the remaining contents of the fuller stoup into the emptier one, mingling the blood of the two animals. He went to the inner altar that stood near the candelabrum in the Sacred Hall and sprinkled blood on its four corners, starting with its northeast one and ending with its southeast one. Then he raked aside its ashes and coals until its gold was visible, sprinkled blood on that seven times, too, returned to the outer altar, and spilled what was left of the blood into its gutter. The priests and the people did not take their eyes off him for a minute. They followed every movement, large or small, for they knew the day's rites had a strict order that must not be departed from.

[Mishna, Treatise Yoma, Chapter 6, Mishna 1] The two he-goats of the Day of Atonement are required to be alike in appearance, in size, in value, to have been bought at the same time. But even if they are not alike, they are valid. If one was bought one day and the other the following day, they are valid. If one of them died before the lot was cast, another one is bought for the second one. But [if it died] after the lot was cast, another pair must be bought and the lots cast for them over again. And if the one that was cast for the Lord died, he [the High Priest] should say: Let this on which the lot for the Lord has fallen stand in its stead. And if the one that was cast for Azazel died he should say: Let this on which the lot for Azazel has fallen stand in its stead. The other one is left to pasture until it becomes blemished when it is to be sold and its value goes to the Temple fund. For the sin offering of the congregation must not be left to die. Rabbi Judah says: It is left to die.

[Mishna, Treatise Yoma, Chapter 6, Mishna 2] He then came to the scapegoat and laid his two hands upon it and he made confession. And thus would he say: I beseech thee, O Lord, thy people the House of Israel have failed, committed iniquity and transgressed before thee. I beseech thee, O Lord, atone the failures, the iniquities, and the transgressions which thy people, the House of Israel, have failed, committed, and transgressed before thee, as it is written in the Torah of Moses, thy servant, to say: For on this day shall atonement be made for you, to cleanse you; from all your sins shall ye be clean before the Lord. And when the priests and the people standing in the Temple Court heard the fully pronounced name come forth from the mouth of the High Priest, they bent their knees, bowed down, fell on their faces, and called out: Blessed be the name of his glorious kingdom forever and ever.

It was time for the scapegoat. The High Priest placed his hands on it and prayed:

"I beseech Thee, O LORD! The House of Israel has sinned, transgressed, and offended before Thee. I beseech Thee, O LORD! Atone for its sins, transgressions, and offenses! As is written in Thy Torah: 'For on that day shall He make an atonement for you to cleanse you, that ye may be clean from all your sins before the Lord.'"

This time, too, when they heard the great and terrible name of God uttered by the High Priest in sanctity and purity, the priests and the people bowed to the ground, every one of them, and cried in one voice:

"Blessed be the name of his glorious Kingship forever and ever!"

And the High Priest, concluding his prayer, proclaimed to them:

"Be ye cleansed."

[Leviticus, Chapter 16, Verses 20—22] And when he hath made an end of atoning for the holy place, and the tent of meeting, and the altar, he shall present the live goat. And Aaron shall lay both his hands upon the head of the live goat, and confess over him all the iniquities of the children of Israel, and all their transgressions, even all their sins; and he shall put them upon the head of the goat, and shall send him away by the hand of an appointed man into the wilderness. And the goat shall bear upon him all their iniquities unto a land which is cut off; and he shall let go the goat in the wilderness.

[Mishna, Treatise Yoma, Chapter 6, Mishna 3] They handed it [the scapegoat] over to him who was to lead it away. All were permitted to lead it away, but the priests made it a definite rule not to permit an Israelite to lead it away. Rabbi Jose said: It once happened that Arsela of Sepphoris led it away, although he was an Israelite. And they made a causeway for him because of the Babylonians, who would pull its hair, shouting to it: Take and go forth, take and go forth.

[Mishna, Treatise Yoma, Chapter 6, Mishna 4] They made a special ramp for him [the man who led the goat out], because of the Babylonians who used to pull at his hair, and say to him: Take [our sins] and go quickly, take [our sins] and go quickly!

[Babylonian Talmud, Treatise Yoma, Folio 66b] Rabbah bar Bar Hana said: These were not Babylonian [Jews] but Alexandrian [Jews, who were known for their thuggish ways], and because they [the Palestinian Jews] hated the Babylonians, they called them [the Alexandrians] by their [the Babylonians'] name. It was taught: Rabbi Judah said: They were not Babylonians, but Alexandrians. Rabbi Jose said to him: May your mind be relieved even as you have relieved my mind!

The Superior cut a strip of the scarlet band tied to the scapegoat and handed it to an acolyte, who hung it at the entrance to the Sacred Hall, while the High Priest transferred the goat to the care of whoever was charged with driving it into the wilderness, toward the dreaded Azazel. The driver of the goat waved a kerchief to frighten it, running behind it along a ramp that led them out of the Temple precinct. (Some say it was built to keep the onlookers from pulling his hair to make him run faster.) Ten huts stood at as many rest stops between Jerusalem and the wilderness, and any distinguished citizens not too wearied from the fast ran with the goat and its driver as far as the first stop to show their love of God's commandment.

[Babylonian Talmud, Treatise Yoma, Folio 67b] Our Rabbis taught: Azazel——it should be hard and rough. One might have assumed that it is to be in inhabited land, therefore the text reads: "In the wilderness." [. . .] Another passage taught: Azazel, i.e., the hardest of mountains, thus also does it say: And the mighty of the land he took away. The School of Rabbi Ishmael taught: Azazel——[it was so called] because it obtains atonement for the affair of [the wicked fallen angels named] Uza and Aza'el [of whom scripture says [Genesis 6:1—4] *And it came to pass, when men began to multiply on the face of the earth, and daughters were born unto them, that the sons of God saw the daughters of men that they were fair; and they took them wives of all which they chose.*

And the LORD said, My spirit shall not always strive with man, for that he also is flesh: yet his days shall be a hundred and twenty years. There were giants in the earth in those days; and also after that, when the sons of God came in unto the daughters of men, and they bore children to them, the same became mighty men which were of old, men of renown.]

[Mishna, Treatise Yoma, Chapter 6, Mishnayot 4—6] Some of the nobility of Jerusalem used to go with him up to the first booth. There were ten booths from Jerusalem to the *zok* [. . .]. At every booth they would say to him: Here is food and here is water. They went with him from booth to booth, except the last one. For he would not go with him up to the *zok*, but stand from afar, and behold what he was doing. What did he do? He divided the thread of crimson wool, and tied one half to the rock, the other half between its horns, and pushed it from behind. And it went rolling down, and before it had reached half its way downhill it was dashed to pieces. He came back and sat down under the last booth until it grew dark.

[Babylonian Talmud, Treatise Yoma, Folio 67b] Our Rabbis taught: Mine ordinances shall ye do, i.e., [this refers to] such commandments which, even if they were not written [in Scripture], they should by right have been written, and these are they: [the laws concerning] idolatry [star worship], immorality and bloodshed, robbery and blasphemy. And My statutes shall ye keep, i.e., [this refers to] such commandments to which Satan objects, and these are they: [the laws relating to] the putting on of a garment mingled of linen and wool; the loosening-of-the-shoe and spitting-in-the-face ritual [performed by the widowed] sister-in-law; the purification ritual of the leper, and the he-goat to be sent away. And lest you might think these are vain things, therefore Scripture says: I am the Lord, i.e., I, the Lord have made it a statute and [therefore] you have no right to criticize it.

At every stop, the goat's driver was offered food and water and accompanied by someone to the next stop, except for the last one, a mountainside that he reached by himself while watched from afar. When he arrived at it, he took the scarlet band from the goat's neck and tied one end of it to its horns and the other to a large rock. He gave the goat a push and it tumbled down the side of the mountain. Before it was halfway to the bottom, it was nothing but broken bones. The driver of the goat then repaired to the last hut and sat there until it grew dark.

[Babylonian Talmud, Treatise Shevuoth, Folio 14a] It is right according to Rabbi Simeon that Scripture mentions two confessions and the blood of the bullock: one instead of the goat offered within [the veil], one instead of the goat offered outside, and one instead of the scapegoat. But according to Rabbi Judah, why do we require two confessions and the blood of the bullock? One confession and the blood should suffice! One for himself and one for his household; as it was taught in the Academy of Rabbi Ishmael: Thus, the nature of justice is practiced: it is better that the innocent should come and atone for the guilty, and not that the guilty should come and atone for the guilty.

[Babylonian Talmud, Treatise Yoma, Folio 67a] AT EVERY BOOTH THEY WOULD SAY TO HIM: HERE IS FOOD AND WATER: A Tanna taught: Never did anyone [who carried the goat away] find it necessary to use it, [it being a fast-day] but [the reason of this provision is because] you cannot compare one who has bread in his basket with one who has no bread in his basket [i.e., the craving of him who lacks the opportunity to gratify it is much more intense then the craving of him who has such opportunity].

[Mishna, Treatise Yoma, Chapter 6, Mishna 7] He [the High Priest] came to the bullock and the he-goat that were to be burnt, he cut them open and took out the sacrificial portions and put them on a tray, and burnt them upon the altar. He twisted them [the beasts] around carrying poles and brought them out to the place of burning.

And at what point would his clothing become impure? From the moment he went outside the walls of the Temple Court. Rabbi Shimon says: From the moment the fire took hold of the majority [of the carcasses].

[Mishna, Treatise Yoma, Chapter 6, Mishna 6] From what time do they [the carcasses of the dead beasts] render garments unclean? After they have gone outside the wall of the Temple Court. Rabbi Simeon says: From the moment the fire has taken hold of most of them.

Meanwhile, the High Priest was busy with the slaughtered bull and goat, which were, in the manner of sin-offerings, to be burned rather than eaten. He severed their parts, removed the fat from the liver and kidneys, put it in a dish, and placed this in the coals for the sweet smell to rise. It was clearly an effort for him. Butchering an animal was hard work even for those who were accustomed to it, let alone for those who were not, and the smell of raw meat overwhelmed him. Yet no one could come to his aid, for the day's rites were his responsibility alone. He took himself in hand, finished the work, and tied the severed parts to the poles on which they were carried off and burned outside the city walls.

[Babylonian Talmud, Treatise Yoma, Folios 55b—56a] Rabbi Judah said: THERE WAS NO MORE THAN ONE STAND. Now, why was not two? Evidently because they might be mixed up! But then let him provide two and write upon them: This is for the [blood of the] bullock, and this for the [blood of the] he-goat? [. . .] Also: for the Day of Atonement let there be prepared two stands with such inscriptions! Because the High Priest is fatigued, he would not pay attention to them. For should you not agree to this consideration: he could really do without any such inscriptions, for one [contains] more [blood], and the other less. And if you were to say that he does not receive the whole of it, but Rabbi Judah said: He who slays the animal must receive the whole blood, as it is said: The whole blood of the bullock he shall pour upon the base of the altar. And if you were to say some thereof might be spilled; still, one [blood] is lighter [in color], the other darker. Hence you must explain that the High Priest, because of his fatigue, could not pay sufficient attention [to the difference in the blood]; thus is it here: because of his fatigue, the High Priest could not pay sufficient attention [to the inscriptions].

The Gate of Rebirth:

The pains taken by the cleaving soul increase its merits even though these are already great. Know, too, that the cleaving soul, being an impregnator that only wishes to assist rather than a sharer in rebirth, stands to be rewarded for the good deeds of the soul that it cleaves to but not to suffer for its bad ones. Indeed, if the soul cleaved to turns aside from the path of self-perfection and doing good, the cleaving soul departs from it. This is the hidden meaning of the saying of the Sages that the righteous soul in Paradise enjoys the fruits of both its own and its neighbor's labors.

[Mishna, Treatise Yoma, Chapter 6, Mishna 8] They said to the High Priest: The he-goat has reached the wilderness. And whence did they know that the he-goat had reached the wilderness? They used to set up guards at stations and from these, shawls would be waved; thus would they know that the he-goat had reached the wilderness. [...] Rabbi Ishmael said: But they had another sign, too: a thread of crimson wool was tied to the door of the Temple, and when the he-goat reached the wilderness, the thread turned white, as it is written: Though your sins be as scarlet, they shall be as white as snow.

[Babylonian Talmud, Treatise Yoma, Folio 39b] Our Rabbis taught: During the last forty years before the destruction of the Temple, the lot ["For the Lord"] did not come up in the right hand; nor did the crimson-colored strap become white; nor did the westernmost light shine; and the doors of the Shrine would open by themselves, until Rabban Johanan Ben Zakkai rebuked them, saying: Shrine, Shrine, why dost thou alarm thyself? I know about thee that thou wilt be destroyed, for Zechariah ben Ido has already prophesied concerning thee: *Open thy doors, O Lebanon, that the fire may devour thy cedars.*

Done with the task, the High Priest sought to recover his strength while hiding behind a column to prevent his fatigue from being a cause for alarm. He was allowed to rest for a few minutes, leaning against a marble pillar, until the Superior whispered to him, "My liege the High Priest, it is time to read from Scripture." As he was speaking, a stir ran through the Gallery. The priests turned to look and saw that the scarlet band tied to the entrance of the Sacred Hall had turned white, a sign that the scapegoat had perished in the wilderness. All rejoiced that the day's sacrifices had been accepted, as is written: "For if your sins be red as scarlet, they shall be made white as snow." The Superior smiled at the High Priest. The High Priest smiled back and said, "Let us read."

[Babylonian Talmud, Treatise Yoma, Folio 67a] Our Rabbis taught: In the beginning they would tie the thread of crimson wool on the entrance of the [Sacred Hall] without: if it became white they rejoiced; if it did not become white, they [the Israelites gathered in the Temple Court] were sad and ashamed. Thereupon they arranged to tie it to the entrance of the Sacred Hall within. But they [the Israelites gathered in the Temple Court] were still peeping through and if it became white, they rejoiced, whereas, if it did not become white, they grew sad and ashamed. Thereupon they arranged to tie one half to the rock and the other half between its horns. Rabbi Nahum Bar Papa said in the name of Rabbi Eleazar ha-Kappar: Originally they used to tie the thread of crimson wool to the entrance of the Sacred Hall within, and as soon as the he-goat reached the wilderness, it turned white. Then they knew that the commandment concerning it had been fulfilled, as it is said: If your sins be as scarlet, they shall be as white wool.

BOOK
SIX

1
June 8, 2001

The 18th of Sivan, 5761

Nine p.m. The remains of the light had drained out of the apartment, which was now immersed in a murky, irritable gloom. The rectangle of the laptop glowed in a corner of the room. Andrew was bent over it, as though trying to conceal it with his body. There was something unusual about his posture, as with the screen itself. Its usual bluish-gray background was now flesh-colored, the symmetrical lines of icons replaced with a jumble of intertwined bodies in a variety of odd positions that seemed too real to be anything but contrived.

Pornography. Just how did Andrew find himself in this remote corner of the Internet? It would be at best a half-truth to say it was an accident. He had been sitting at the computer all afternoon, in vain, trying to complete that same accursed article that ordinarily would have taken him a week or two, when he decided to surf the Web for inspiration. He needed something stimulating, radical, to restart his stalled thought processes: *Sluts R Us*—now, that was short and to the point! The site's lengthy list of categories was arranged alphabetically: *Anal, Bisexual, Cock Worship, Dwarves* . . . *Dwarves?* Andrew clicked quickly on the mysterious title before his inhibitions could get in the way and stared incredulously at what appeared on the screen: A little woman, three feet tall, wearing nothing but a ridiculous-looking pink tutu, stood in front of a tall young man whose head and face were cut out of the frame. She was slightly hunched over his large erection, her mouth tightly pursed around it, her misshapen face contorted in an expression that aroused both pity and revulsion.

Andrew grimaced involuntarily, quickly shut the window, and moved the cursor to X-out. But the little arrow never reached the small box framing the X. *No, not yet*. His research called for further investigation. He scrolled up and down the alphabetized categories, too embarrassed to choose any of them yet too curious to forgo one last, quick glimpse into the unknown worlds they concealed. There it was: *College*. College? What did that mean? Andrew clicked on it, his inhibitions weakening, and found himself in an empty classroom. Next to a blackboard on which was scrawled childish, pseudo-mathematical equations, stood a bizarro version of the stereotypical professor, a man in an old-fashioned bow tie and tweed jacket, his pale penis extruding limply from his fly. Fondling it was a bare-breasted young student with oversize, lensless, black-framed glasses and thighs bursting from a schoolgirl's short plaid skirt. What a dumb, primitive cliché! Who could be turned on by such a thing? Andrew regarded it disdainfully. Its banality relieved him: the entire genre was infantile, unimaginative, dumb. He X-ed out but decided to try one more before switching off his computer. No point in trying to write any more. After all, tomorrow is another day.

What else might be hiding in this virtual university of sex? As if it had any relation to reality. *College Fuck Fest*: the subtlety of these titles! The screen went suddenly dark. At its center appeared a shaky, grainy frame. A tangle of human figures that appeared to have been shot by a hidden camera. Several dozen strapping college students were gathered around a cleared space in the middle of what appeared to be a large basement, wildly cheering as if at a football game. The camera zoomed in on the clearing, maneuvering its way past a forest of brawny arms and budding beer bellies. The light intensified, as did the cheers, which grew so loud that Andrew had to mute the volume. For a second, the cheap home video lost its focus. Then, the delicate, vulnerable-looking body of a naked woman emerged from the blur, trapped in the hooting male circle. Andrew caught his breath. The unexpected sight grabbed him by the windpipe. The woman, very young-looking, crouched on all fours on the floor of a fraternity house, littered with cigarette butts and beer cans, her face down and her shapely white buttocks tilted upward in an inviting position. Two girlish braids hung down to the filthy floor like golden tassels.

There was a burst of noise. The sound had unmuted itself—Andrew's fingers, nervously playing with the keyboard, must have clicked on it by mistake—and was blasting. The cheers, made to sound even more primitively barbaric by the amateur film's changing volume and tempo, grew frenzied. The circle heaved and ejected into its center a tanned, muscular young man wearing designer sunglasses and a backward baseball cap. His bare chest and shoulders shone in the light of the room's single, overhead lamp, his half-lowered jeans revealing a distended penis so unreal-looking that it seemed about to rocket from his body. Seizing the young woman's pelvis, he lifted her lightly off the ground and rammed himself into her with a single quick motion. The cheers turned to roars. The circle went berserk. The young man, a smug smirk on his face, humped her white backside, which bounced up and down with a horrendous, hilarious jiggle. Just above it, at the base of the spine, the film slowed to reveal a light blue tattoo of a butterfly.

The screen suddenly went blank. What happened? Was the video over? No, it resumed, this time from a new angle. The camera had moved to the front of the young woman, whose now visible face might have been romantically misconstrued as having a rare, even spiritual beauty, while the young man, his cruel smirk grown broader, was at the far end of the unsteady patch of light. A loud, ugly laughter came next—the sound was out of sync with the picture—for now, the girl arched her back like a balky pony and stared at the camera with a hysterical, glassy-eyed whinny that was more like a muscular spasm than an expression of human emotion. Plastered to her face, her grin made one think of a grotesque carnival mask. "Man, he fucked her stupid," said a drawling, beer-slurred voice behind the camera. There was another loud burst of laughter—*Man, that was funny!*—and the screen went blank again.

That was it. It was over, leaving only its residue in Andrew's eyes and ears. Agitated, he rose from his chair and glanced vacantly around the room as if woken from a disturbing dream. The girl's convulsive smile appeared to be beamed on every object, refusing to fade away. The young man's hard stomach with its cubist planes of muscles kept flashing before him. That heartless, sneering smirk. That beautiful, white behind. *Man, what an ass! He fucked her stupid!* The small butterfly, bright to the point of transparency, fluttering over the clear fair skin. What should he do now? Should he watch it again? Make sure it was real, that he had actually seen what he thought he had? Yet suppose someone came. Suppose Ann Lee were to surprise him drooling over cheap porn like some old pervert? Ridiculous! Who was going to come? Ann Lee had no plans to drop by. Lately, she had been busy all the time, and when she did come, it was always late at night, when she was tired and grumpy. Although they had made up after that absurd evening at Cipriani's—half made up, anyway—things were no longer the same. Far from it.

A new, paranoid idea suddenly crept into Andrew's mind: Was this vile video now burnt into his hard disk, imprinted on it forever like a tattoo? What if he got rid of his laptop one day, or gave it to recycling, and someone found it, retrieved its information, and used it to publicly shame him, the celebrated professor of comparative culture? He breathed deeply, trying to calm himself. What an absurd, irrational thought! Who would do such a thing? His anxieties were running amok lately. He had to exercise more, eat healthier food, sleep longer hours. What time was it? Nine fifteen. The whole thing had lasted no more than a few minutes. And yet he felt as though it had gone on for hours and it was already the middle of the night. The apartment was dark, so dark. Time to turn on the lights. Should he watch the video again? No! Enough foolishness. Just turn off the damn computer.

2

June 8, 2001

The 17th of Sivan, 5761

The angel sits by my side, on the edge of the bed. He reaches out and touches me lightly. I wake from my sleep. For some reason, I am not surprised or frightened to see him there. He has something to show me, something important.

"What do you see?"

"I see a candelabrum."

"What kind of candelabrum?"

"A candelabrum all of gold with a bowl and seven wells for oil."

"And what more?"

"Two olive branches, one to the bowl's left and one to its right. What are they, sir?"

"You know very well what they are!"

"No, sir. I do not know."

"What do you not know?"

"I do not know the meaning of these two olive branches with the golden pipes running through them."

"They are the two anointed ones that stand by the Lord of the whole earth."

"And the wells?"

"They are the eyes of the Lord that run to and fro over the whole earth."

The angel rises from the bed and approaches the candelabrum, growing larger as he does until he looms like a mountain from the plain. He lifts an arm toward the towering gate arching over him from earth's end to earth's end, reaches up, and effortlessly removes its large headstone—the stone that bears the full weight of the arch, of the entire house. Afraid, I shut my eyes, waiting for the ceiling to collapse in a hail of stones and leave all in ruins. There is silence. Nothing has happened. I open my eyes: the building is unscathed. The arch is suspended over the void like the vault of the heavens, miraculously intact. The angel smiles and toys with the huge stone, tossing it from hand to hand like a ball. Who has despised the day of small things? They shall rejoice and see the plummet. Not by might, nor by power, but by my spirit, says the Lord. The house shall not lie in ruins unless the word is spoken, and the city shall stand on its foundation. This is the headstone, grace, grace unto it.

3

June 10, 2001

The 19th of Sivan, 5761

Eight thirty a.m. Andrew squinted in the blinding light flooding the park and glancing off the unwashed windshield of Ann Lee's car. The light seemed overwhelming for such an early hour. Or was it just ordinary light that his eyes, red from lack of sleep, couldn't tolerate? He lowered the sun visor. Lately, he had been sleeping poorly. In fact, it was hard to know whether to call it sleep or not. Striking yet unnerving visions kept flickering before his eyes, realistic and dreamlike at once. *He was looking through the heavy gates of an ancient shrine. Golden shovels, fire pans, and candelabra, strange, intriguing instruments that looked brimming with energy, as if they were about to burst into flames at any moment, gleamed magically inside its dimly lit interior.* Andrew yearned for these beautiful things, for the heady aroma of incense, the golden semi-dusk of the Temple's interior. If only he could walk through these golden gates and disappear there forever.

The old car jolted along. Andrew ground the gears, confusing first with third and second with fourth, unable to find reverse. The car protested with hoarse, animal-like grunts. His bad driving, especially when it came to stick shifts, was a standing joke between him and Ann Lee, but there was nothing funny about it now. It was depressing, humiliating. Having to borrow Ann Lee's car for Alison's monthly visits to Ethel had lost the charm of its irony. Ann Lee had made a face when he asked for it, or so he imagined. Not that she needed it for anything or that there was anything wrong with asking, but these days, everything between them was wrong. Nothing was right, period.

Andrew shut his eyes for a second to shield them from the fierce sun. A large, burnished gold candelabrum, the seven arms of which rose upward like the branches of a young tree, burned brightly behind his tightly shut eyelids, searing its image into the retina. He opened his eyes just in time to see a barrier closing off the entrance to Central Park. Still daydreaming, he swung the wheel to the left and then to the right without grasping what his hands were doing and turned onto the park drive that was reserved on weekends for joggers and cyclists. Yes, he was in a dream—or more precisely, in a nightmare. The eerily empty road awoke him with the awful knowledge that he had blanked out while driving, and driving Ann Lee's car at that.

Andrew slowed down, trying to cope with the unusual situation. What if this really was a dream? There wasn't a car in sight, not a single cyclist, not even a jogger. Like every Manhattanite, he knew the park was closed to motor vehicles from ten to three every weekday. He himself had biked through it hundreds of times during these hours. Now, though, he was there when he shouldn't be. The quiet around him was oppressive, unreal. He braked and almost came to a stop in the middle of the road, then remembered with a start that driving on this road on the weekend was strictly forbidden. Cautiously, he began looking for a way out of the park. Where was the nearest exit? Wasn't it 96th Street?

It seemed to take forever to get there. The childish relief he felt on seeing the exit gave way to a no less childish panic when he heard the siren of the police car that had been lying in wait, its full complement of lights flashing even though his was a simple traffic violation. It made Andrew think of a predator springing on its prey in some National Geographic documentary. Anxious to cooperate like a good antelope, he stepped on the accelerator instead of the brake, sent the car lurching forward, and snatched his foot from the gas while forgetting to floor the clutch. The car bucked and hopped almost clownishly, then stalled and came to a stop as though shot through the heart. Although the farce did not end, fortunately, like he imagined it may end—with his being surrounded by officers with their guns drawn, like an escaped convict—it was certainly bad enough when a crew-cut, baby-faced policeman approached him with all the excitement of a rookie cop and said, "Your papers, sir."

Andrew looked in the glove compartment, frantically searching it for the registration. He wiped beads of sweat from his forehead with a sleeve of the freshly ironed shirt he had put on that morning, now as damp and rumpled as a dishrag. The policeman looked at him with an intense stare. Where had she put the damn registration? It was perfectly clear now: he would be arrested and the car impounded. And just when Ann Lee had lent it to him so begrudgingly! He squirmed in the driver's seat, ransacking the glove compartment for a third time. No, the registration wasn't there. Despairingly, he straightened up and looked about. There, staring at him mockingly, protruding from the inside pocket of the sun visor, was the folded piece of paper he was looking for. The policeman took it without a word and studied it at length as if he had difficulty reading.

"Is this your vehicle, sir?"

"No, it's not. It's . . ."

"Whose is it, sir?"

"My partner's."

"Your partner's?"

"My girlfriend's."

"Your girlfriend's. Right."

The last word, though clearly uttered with no disrespect, grated on Andrew's already frayed nerves. How could it not seem judgmental to him? A fifty-two-year-old man driving a 1985 blue VW owned by his twenty-six-year-old girlfriend crashes a barrier at an entrance to a park! It was unseemly, if not suspicious, behavior. He didn't know what to feel more demeaned by: the absurdity of the violation, which was hard enough to explain to himself, much less to a policeman; being given a lecture like a schoolboy by someone no older than Ann Lee or Rachel; or his timid acquiescence in the face of the banal lecture, which clearly had been rehearsed in more than one simulated drill. Did he understand the seriousness of what he had done? He had endangered the lives of cyclists and joggers. He would have to stand trial at the traffic court at 346 Broadway. The details were on the back of the ticket. Due to the gravity of the offense, he would unfortunately have to appear in person.

It went on and on, the theater of the absurd without an audience. When the car's papers were returned to him, Andrew even found himself saying, "Thank you very much, Officer. Have a good day." It was an automatic reaction, everyone had it. He hadn't really believed he would be arrested, had he?

4

One day, it will all erupt. The city will shatter like a dam before an angry river, bursting volcanically with the energy stored in it from the first day of Creation, sweeping all that's in its path. A thick, black tide of iniquity will overflow and flood the streets like a gigantic, blocked sewage system. The outcry of the city's poor who lived and died unheard—the sufferings of its impoverished, helpless immigrants crowded into lightless dungeons— all has accumulated, all has been compressed by the city's weight into a liquid amalgam, a percolate of blood, sweat, bile, and tears bubbling beneath layers of asphalt, concrete, metal, and stone, a turbid, toxic fluid that keeps striving to force its way upward, into the open. Human passion, too, has been pressurized into a fiery, belching liquid that seethes behind facades and bakes the pavements until they steam and smoke with toxic fumes. Lust; gluttony; drunkenness; greed; pure, naked ambition: all the world's cupidity has come to the city to satisfy its craving, teeming with rivers of sperm, estuaries of sweat, torrents of saliva—and nothing cools, all stays at the boiling point, all grows hotter and thicker from year to year, a perpetually churning lava. It will erupt one day, annihilating everything: all animal life, all plant life, all matter. All intellect, too, the ideas upon which the city is built: abstract and concrete, rational and romantic, idealistic and self-serving. So much thought has gone into the city and its intricate architecture, from the complicated symmetries of the metal constructions at the base of its skyscrapers and the magnificent, perfectly proportioned grid on which it rests to the fabulously complex economic and administrative networks that have made it the world's capital. Never before has the human spirit been so intensively combusted in the cast-iron cylinder of technology, architecture, economics, and politics; never before has it been in such danger of exploding. The very earth, the primal foundations of Manhattan fertilized with the bones of its enslaved pyramid builders, will rise in rebellion. Deprived of light for one hundred years or more, choking under billions of tons of concrete, glass, metal, and meaning, the dark schist and granite will cast all off like a titanic beast breaking the chains of civilization and snapping the bonds of human conquest. Earth and air, fluids and flames: the destruction will be as infinite as was the city's glory.

5

June 18, 2001

The 27th of Sivan, 5761

Five p.m. It was exactly five in the afternoon when Andrew knocked on the new cherrywood door of Bernie Bernstein's presidential suite and was admitted by a receptionist with a practiced, professional smile. Although he had heard of the extensive renovations carried out in the administrative wing of the Tisch Building, this was his first chance to see them for himself. The refined luxury of Bernie's office was so in contrast to the stark, spartan aesthetics of the university's halls of learning, it was striking. Warm afternoon sunlight poured through the roof windows, illuminating a corner of the president's open office that was visible from the reception room. A beautiful antique Persian rug lay on its rich brown, brightly waxed floor; nearby, a collection of tawny-colored bottles stood on a mahogany bar. As lavish as a Hollywood studio, the suite impressed him, amused him, and left him somehow uneasy. Andrew returned the receptionist's practiced smile, as she knocked for form's sake on the open door and announced, "Professor Bernstein, Professor Cohen is here."

The president was alone, reading at his desk. *So they're not here yet*, Andrew thought, with no idea of who "they" were. The purpose of today's meeting was unclear. The notice he had gotten from the president's office had been diplomatic to the point of obscurity. Although presumably he had been invited to confirm his appointment as the new director of the Asch Interdisciplinary Program, he could only guess why this had not been explicitly stated as the official purpose of the meeting. It was probably another one of the president's theatrical whims. Bernie was not forthcoming about such things. He kept his cards close to his chest, whether or not there was a need for it. Now, his eyes lit up as he glanced from the document he was reading. Coming out from behind the empty desk, he shook Andrew's hand. Smartly dressed, he was his usual suntanned, pleased-as-punch self. "Well, here you are! It's good to see you. Can I pour you a drink? I have some interesting bottles here . . ."

A drink? The president, it seemed, wanted to give things a festive air. Should he have worn a fancier suit? Bernie steered him by the elbow to the mahogany bar, which was indeed well stocked with the best, and took his time with the drinks, rattling bottles and glasses with the overgrown boy's glee with which he did everything. Andrew used this time to take in his ostentatious surroundings. There was something astonishingly, almost surrealistically disproportionate about them. He speculated idly what the interior decoration had cost and where the budget had come from while Bernie chatted away in his normal, friendly, personal tone.

The old windows had been replaced with floor-to-ceiling stained glass that looked suspiciously like original Frank Lloyd Wrights. The elliptical conference table, around which a dozen black leather chairs were neatly arranged, was white oak. Academia, so it seems, had become a profitable—a lucrative!—enterprise.

Andrew looked at his watch. It was already five fifteen. Who else were they waiting for? Bernie turned to Andrew, handed him a big, beautifully crafted tumbler (*It's real lead crystal*, Andrew thought, informed by his grip even before closely inspecting the glass) filled almost to the brim with a dark, fragrant single malt scotch that was poured over a few large, clear ice cubes.

Motioning Andrew toward the leather seat in front of his desk, he said, as if reading Andrew's mind: "No one else is coming. It's only you and me today, dear friend. We have something important to discuss." These words were not uttered in his usual, jovially noncommittal tone. His entire body language had suddenly changed. His face lost its usual impish expression and, much to Andrew's astonishment, it seemed to have even forsaken its suntanned hue, making him look more like a regular middle-aged university administrator and less like an aging rich playboy. He sat heavily in his tall leather chair, carefully placed his drink on a black leather coaster, and slid another across the table toward Andrew who, sensing the mounting tension, suddenly pined for the usual Bernie-style banter about the rare quality of the scotch, the cost of the mahogany table, and the fact that the board would fire him immediately if he left a watermark on its supremely finished surface. But this was no day for banter, so it seemed. Bernie, his forehead furled and his thick eyebrows shadowing his eyes, started speaking, his voice hoarse and earnest.

"Listen, Andrew, dear friend," Bernie said as if picking up on an earlier conversation that they have recently had, "we need to talk seriously now!" The word *now* echoed in the room like a distant

reproach, as if they've both indulged in a childish game and someone had to finally put an end to it and assume the role of the responsible adult. "I am sure you know what all this is about, right?"

Andrew stared at Bernie, paralyzed by surprise. But Bernie's
face returned Andrew's look of disbelief. "I must say that I am a
bit baffled, I was sure that you were well aware of what's going
on. I did try to warn you then, in our meeting last winter. Not
that it would have mattered, the deed is done." Bernie lifted his
glass from the leather coaster, leaving a wet ring that shimmered
in the bright light of the table lamp, took a long sip from it, and
put it down again, slightly missing the round watermark stain and
leaving some of it exposed. Shocked at his inability to control his
racing thoughts, Andrew found himself wondering if the dampness would stain the black leather surface of the coaster or whether
it was processed to be water stain resistant.

"It was decided," said Bernie, "wait a minute, why am I saying
'it was decided'? I was part of the decision, I was in the room—we
decided, and by 'we' I mean the board, some members of the faculty and myself—to offer the position of the director of the Asch
Interdisciplinary Program to someone else."

It seemed to Andrew that lightning had struck in his mind,
trapping the air in his lungs for a few seconds before the thunder
of understanding followed. "I wasn't obliged by protocol to summon you here today and break the news to you in person," Bernie
said, "but it wouldn't have occurred to me, after all these years of
friendship, to let you find out tomorrow, with everyone else."

Bernie halted for a moment, stretched his hand toward his half-
empty whiskey glass, reconsidered, and laid it back on the table.
Andrew drew in a deep breath, forgetting to exhale. A loud static
noise buzzed in his ears, silencing everything around him. "Please
understand," continued Bernie softly, his voice free of the playful,
manipulative mannerisms that he developed over the many years

of his tenure as president. "Our world is changing, it is changing rapidly, and we, as an institute, must adapt to these changes or we will perish. Our choice did not take into account only the past and the present, it took into account the future as well, and this future is going to be very different from what you and I can possibly imagine. The future is no longer ours, dear friend. We're lucky we still have a slice of present to hold on to. We can't take that for granted, I'll tell you that!" He stretched an impatient hand toward his drink—diluted by the melting ice, it was now turned watery yellow—and downed it in one long gulp. "This may not sound very comforting now," he went on, slamming his damp glass back on the coaster, "but you really should not take it lightly: you still have your job, your tenured position, your long list of publications, your reputation, and they—I'm sorry, I mean, no one—can take that away from you!" Bernie shot a quick glance at his empty glass, returned his gaze to Andrew, and continued. "Listen, it's not so bad, what you have, not so bad. Do you think I don't miss it sometimes? The serious, straightforward life of a distinguished professor? Far away from all this . . ." He waved his hand contemptuously at the disproportional grandeur of their surroundings as if it were imposed on him by some mysterious external force. "You probably want to know who the new director is, right? Well, that's your prerogative. You do have the right to know before the rest of the world finds out." Bernie stared at Andrew curiously. "You know her. As a matter of fact, you know her well." Bernie paused for moment, his stare suddenly laden with new meaning. "We've decided to appoint Dr. Shirin Zamindar as the new director of the program."

For a second time, lightning struck inside Andrew's brain, this time more rapidly followed by deafening thunder. Yes, he did know Shirin Zamindar. He knew her well, very well. She was his graduate student, who transferred from Cambridge a year or so prior to their acquaintance. A daughter of one of the most affluent families in India, she spent her youth in a prestigious Swiss boarding school and moving between a few European capitals. Her work was somewhat undistinguished, not to say mediocre, her reputation in the department was owed mostly to her expensive taste in designer clothes and the rumors surrounding her wild love life. Her dissertation, named *Patriarchy Within Patriarchy: The Influence of Colonialism on the Oppressive Structures of the Traditional Family in India,* was comprised mostly of clichés, unimaginatively imported from the works of the more important thinkers of the schools of postcolonial and women's studies. But Andrew, in spite of all this, had supported her work in the department. He had done so out of the simple, intuitive, yet profoundly felt belief that the truth was arrived at by a multiplicity of voices, not by intellectual monotone. Andrew drew in another deep breath, trying to stabilize his racing thoughts, which rushed uncontrollably across his mind.

How very typical, he thought contemptuously, feeling the rage mounting inside him, ready to erupt. How very Bernie-like, to want to appear progressive and egalitarian while hiring a vapid, spoiled brat who slept her way into the faculty for lack of a better set of skills. How very like Bernie to adorn himself with the appointment of a young woman—and a woman of color at that!—but to choose one who could never threaten him, or anyone else for that matter!

Andrew's anger continued to rage for another second or two, filling him with self-righteous, vindictive vigor—but then it suddenly subsided, leaving behind an emptiness in which a different inner voice now sounded. That was too easy, way too easy! It was lazy and despicable of him to push Shirin into the demeaning slot of a trust-fund brat, a social climber or class slut. The truth is that there was something about her, hidden under the many layers of predictability and banality, that were the result of her academic training. Once the yoke of her doctoral program's expectations

was broken, she had actually become a more serious worker and
a more serious thinker. She spent more hours in the library and
seminar rooms—her tastefully chosen clothes and beautifully
quaffed hair a sharp, refreshing contrast to their usually drab and
inelegant surroundings. The articles she published became more
interesting, more original. A sudden, scary realization crept into
Andrew's mind, forced itself on him in a brutal clarity that made
him shudder: Could it be that it was precisely because she stopped
working with him that this change had occurred? Could it be that
it was his presence in her life that had caused her to cling to those
ready-made clichés and recycle them so tirelessly? Perhaps it was
him, Andrew, and not Bernie, who wanted to adorn himself with
the presence of this young woman while keeping her in the un-
threatening, banal slot he had chosen for her? Andrew flinched
visibly, as if he had been stung. What an absurd thought! How
could it be? Hadn't he, of all teachers and mentors, encouraged his
students to liberate themselves from what had already existed and
seek what was not yet put into words? Andrew's chest constricted;
breathing was an effort. Something swelled uncontrollably inside
him, setting his thoughts flying at a fast, frenzied pace. And there
was that other thing, too! That other thing, that he had so con-
veniently half-forgotten, in spite of it being such a rare—very
rare!—occurrence. After all, he was a man of strong moral fiber
and almost never strayed from the ethics of his profession. Had he
really forgotten their brief, very brief, affair that started right after
she submitted her dissertation and was, officially at least, no longer
his direct subordinate? A wave of panic rushed over Andrew: How
much did Bernie know? Is this the reason for that long, meaningful
look he gave him before mentioning Shirin's name? It would be a
total disaster if the rumors about his affair with her became public,
a total disaster! True, there was nothing illegal about it, not even
unethical, not really, and yet, it would be a terrible thing if this bit

of information became public. A chilling wave of paranoia slithered swiftly into Andrew's head, wriggling inside it like a venomous snake: Did Shirin tell Bernie? Were they in cahoots, resolved to bring Andrew to his demise? What if the whole thing had been planned? What if it all had been a diabolically clever sting operation meant to blackmail him, to force him to quietly step aside and allow her to take away the coveted appointment that until not so long ago was considered his and his alone? The poisonous serpent kept twisting and turning inside Andrew's skull, its jerky movements more and more violent. What a fool he was, allowing her to tempt him like this! He should have suspected it from the first minute! One couldn't put anything past her! The toxically euphoric realization that he had been deliberately set up by Shirin Zamindar sent a rush of adrenaline into Andrew's body, taking full possession of him and inflating him with rage before it ebbed suddenly, leaving him drained and depleted, again. Nonsense! That, too, was too easy. Too easy, and totally wrong! It would be a vicious lie to claim that she had set out to seduce him, a total, shameless lie. It's true, he did not court her while she was his research student, not openly at least—but the thought of it had often crossed his mind during the time in which they worked closely together. And that famous seduction scene, in that gorgeous Alsatian restaurant that had recently opened, not far from the New York Public Library, where they both attended a panel discussion one winter night? That seduction scene—preserved in his memory by the fragrance of the fruity Alsatian wines and the irresistibly alluring shimmer of the antique polished copper cookware that hung on the walls, lending the restaurant the air of a charming country inn—wasn't it his own brilliant, masterfully executed production? How lowly it was of him, how cowardly, to lay the so-called blame on her? And how lowly it was of him, how despicable, to forcibly forget the desperate, surprisingly vulnerable quality of her lovemaking!

How could he expunge from his memory her touching, almost childlike eagerness to please him when they were together? A sudden, silent, dry sob rattled Andrew's body. No, she had not manipulated him at all! What happened between them was not a part of her alleged faculty seduction crusade, the stuff of nasty corridor-rumors. As a matter of fact, these rumors were never substantiated, were they? Why then were they—no, why then was he—so ready to believe them? Why was he so eager to assume such ugly assumptions about her and her motives? Was she more of a threat to him than he had ever dared to admit? And why did he so forcefully deny the distinct feeling he had, the sense that for her this was not necessarily just a small, amusing, noncommittal fling as it was for him? It was the same feeling that caused him, truth be told, to abruptly end their affair, much more quickly than usual. And why, for heaven's sake, hadn't he bothered to tell her even once, out of simple courtesy, that he had indeed read her last publication and that it was, quite honestly, nothing short of brilliant? Was it really so preposterous to suspect that it might have been him, and their work together, that caused her to recycle those damned clichés for which he then disdained her? Was he semiconsciously pushing her into the slot of the ridiculous, predictable role of a knee-jerk rebel? Turning her into a crude caricature of herself? Why? Because she was a woman? Because she was Indian, or "a woman of color"? Did it enable him to ignore her as a true intellectual force to be reckoned with? And could it be—this thought made Andrew cringe in pain—that the choice to appoint her as the new director of the interdisciplinary program was actually the right decision? A seriously considered, professional choice and not just a fashionable, manipulative gesture as he automatically assumed it to be? Andrew leaped from his chair in panic. The intensity of his thoughts had suddenly become unbearable, and he tried in vain to push them out of his head, to unthink them. He is right, this dirty old lecher, Bernie, this greedy, power-hungry, heartless, cynical puppet master. He is right! Shirin Zamindar does represent the future while he, Andrew, is the one who's been recycling himself, repeating the same old, tested, pseudo-progressive tricks for the last twenty-some years, riding the wave of his now cold youthful promise. Andrew's knees gave in. He plopped his body heavily back on the chair, desperately struggling to push back this horrific possibility, this terrible realization, push it back so hard and so deep so that it would never be able to emerge again.

Bernie watched him patiently, sympathetically witnessing the wordless emotional roller coaster to which his old friend and colleague was strapped. He stretched his hand toward Andrew's untouched drink, the content of which was by now totally diluted by ice water, and gently pushed it toward Andrew—together with the black leather coaster that was by now soaking wet from the water condensed on the cold glass. Andrew mindlessly took the glass, lifted it to his lips, and drank its entire content in one gulp—swallowing the disgusting swill like Socrates drinking his hemlock. All was lost now. He knew it with humiliating yet liberating clarity. All was lost! There was nothing to be done anymore. The matter was out of his hands.

He was led like a blind bull to the ring. The great white bull! That's what Bernie had been trying to tell him on that winter morning in his roundabout, Machiavellian, now-you-see-it-now-you-don't way. He didn't really try to save Andrew, that was bullshit—he just wanted it on the record, so that Andrew couldn't say he hadn't been warned. They didn't even leave you the right to be angry, they robbed you even of that! What was he supposed to say now? He couldn't just sit there. He had to say something. He had to express his fury, which, he was forced to acknowledge to his chagrin, felt dangerously close to an insulted child's uncontrollable sob of grief rather than the roar of a wounded old lion.

Andrew realized his mistake as soon as he began to speak. His words came in angry, wildly aimed volleys. He was aware of it, aware he was destroying his last chance at convincing anyone. He understood it all with a painful lucidity, with a realer-than-real clarity—and still he couldn't stop. He suddenly had a feeling that there was something else, something that Bernie was hiding from him. He glanced across the table, consumed by hate . . . but his eyes could go no further. He couldn't bring himself to look at Bernie, the vile puppeteer who had made him dance before sacrificing him like a disposable pawn on the chessboard of power and influence. He broke off his tirade in the middle and sat silently, feeling powerless and ridiculous, staring at the empty glass in front of him.

"Another touch of whiskey?"

"No, thanks. Well, all right. Just a touch."

Another mistake, he did not need another drink! Whatever, what difference did it make by now? Bernie got up from his chair, went to the bar, and returned with two fresh drinks. Andrew mindlessly accepted the glass Bernie offered him. Although he knew he shouldn't have, he took it and emptied it in practically one gulp. He was drained. Even his anger was suddenly gone, vanished into thin air. That was Bernie for you, the ultimate seducer! One couldn't stay angry at him for long, no matter how hard one tried.

Bernie sat facing him in his chair, leaning forward with a movement that, in the movies, signaled that a frank disclosure was about to take place. He was a great moviegoer, Bernie, a great lover of Hollywood—of TV sitcoms, too, no doubt. Where did he find the time for it? A foolish question. Men like Bernie found time for everything; they devoured life like a slice of pie. Here comes the speech. It had already begun.

"My hands were tied, Andrew. You need to understand that."

Bernie wanted, as always, to have his cake and eat it, to get what he wanted without being resented. He had to know he still was loved. "The forces working behind the scenes were very strong, stronger than either of us." Voilà! So now they were comrades in arms again, two rational men upholding the pursuit of knowledge, not the opportunism that masqueraded as it. Did Bernie believe that himself? Apparently, he did. He always did. That's what made him what he was.

Bernie went on spouting empty phrases and Andrew, though no longer listening, let himself be lulled by their sympathetic tone. That was one more mistake, a serious one, but he needed all the comfort, however phony, that he could get. The whiskey festered in his stomach, emitting the sour vapors that were a sure sign of the heartburn to come. Home! He was going to be sick, he needed to sleep.

Andrew rose without excusing himself and went to the door, suddenly feeling drunk. Bernie regarded him in silent sorrow. His hand on the doorknob, Andrew reconsidered and turned back, looking at his old friend, or his ex–old friend, in the eye for the first time since realizing he had been set up, laying the unasked question at his feet. The glint vanished from Bernie's eyes, along with his patronizing tone. For a moment, surprising even himself, the good, old Bernie emerged from the shiny pleats of his presidential, twenty-five-hundred-dollar suit. "You understand, old friend, it wasn't me. I wasn't even asked. I was a pissed-on little pawn just like you. It came from above, from the board of directors. Have you heard of Koshal Pooldar? Pooldar, as in the new Pooldar Library? Yes, it's the man that I sat next to at that ridiculous dinner at Cipriani's two weeks ago. I know you know who I'm talking about, I saw you peering at us through that ghastly flower arrangement. I was sure you knew everything! It turns out he's Shirin Zamindar's maternal uncle, or godfather, or the second husband of her mother, or something like that. . . . Need I say more?"

There was no need to say anything else. Andrew left in silence without saying good-bye, gently closing the door behind him.

6

Dawn is breaking. The path leading to the Viceroy's Palace is
colored a bright indigo. Two large mastiffs sprawl on either side
of its majestic entrance a few dozen yards away, regarding me
with stony eyes. Then they come to life and turn into lions. They
recognize me. One bounds quickly toward me. I turn and run.
Ahead of me is a tiger. The lion is closing in. I run, leaping over
the gray rocks, frantically looking for a stone to throw at it. It's
breathing down my neck. I turn and throw a stone. It recoils and
takes to its heels. Now I'm chasing it. It turns into a naked boy,
his long hair smooth, wrapped around him like a royal robe. He
throws a stone at me and I prepare to be devoured. The second lion
is right behind me. I can feel it about to spring. A red light goes
on. There's a siren. The screen flashes: Direct Hit for Lion 1.
The screen blurs. Another red light: Direct Hit for Lion 2. *The*
screen fades out. The game is over. Darkness. The room is dark.
I'm shivering. It's cold. The air is electric. Without warning, a
heavy, tropical rain begins to fall.

7

June 25, 2001

The 4th of Tammuz, 5761

It was already eleven thirty. Where had the morning gone? Two
and a half hours of concentrated effort and he hadn't a single line
to show for it. Not a word. Every minute spent facing the computer
was a pure hell of blind, futile willpower fighting to get past a wall of
blank words. Again and again he hurled himself at it, injuring only

himself. Letters danced before his eyes like malevolent trolls. The tenser he grew, the more annoyingly his head buzzed. He wasn't a miracle worker! He couldn't squeeze water from a damn stone! How many days had gone by since that god-awful meeting with the president? A week already. Its shock and humiliation hadn't worn off. They were poisoning his body and mind, causing a general paralysis. He hadn't told anyone about it. No one: not Ann Lee, not Rachel, not even Linda. How could you talk about such a thing? What could you say? Never mind. He would think of something. The main thing was to concentrate on his work. That was the main thing! Publish or Perish was still the name of the game. It was a gladiator's arena, a fucking slaughterhouse. If only he could drop it all and go to the Cape with them. If only he could go to bed and never get up again.

Andrew jumped from his chair. What unadulterated crap! For the third or fourth time that morning he strode to the bathroom to wash his face, splashing water all over it. If the faucet had been higher, he would have stuck his head under it and turned it on full force. No, he would have been too embarrassed. Back to work! He dried his face with the damp towel and returned to the computer, pretending to feel refreshed. A shitty little article he once could have written in his sleep! He didn't even care about the magazine it was promised to. Why not just send them an apology? He was sorry to say he was too busy to meet the deadline. Everyone knew how busy he was, now that he was about to take on the added responsibility of . . . fuck! Fuck them all, every one of them!

Twelve thirty. Not a line. Swimming across the English Channel would be easier than writing a single clear, coherent paragraph. He needed inspiration, something to tear away the heavy, grungy curtain blocking him from writing. No, nothing online. Something classical, something solid to give him a fresh start. Barthes! Roland Barthes, of course! How hadn't he thought of it? There was nothing like Barthes for a suitable quotation; he was the Oscar

Wilde of literary criticism. *Writing Degree Zero*: perfect! He was at zero degree himself, and it wasn't even funny.

Andrew went to a bookshelf and took down a thin book that felt like an expensive bar of chocolate. Speaking of which, did he have any at home? A little pick-me-up wouldn't hurt. He tossed the book onto his desk with what was intended to be a kind of French, debonair gesture and went to the kitchen to look. Again and again he rummaged through the same cabinets and drawers, as if expecting some chocolate to turn up by magic. There was none to be found. Why should there be? He never kept sweets at home. Might Ann Lee have hidden some somewhere? Where would she have kept such a yummy little secret? Ann Lee. She almost never dropped by anymore. To hell with the chocolate! He would buy some later. To work! But wait. Mightn't there be some in a drawer after all?

It took Andrew a while to get over his childish disappointment. The sharp pang of it put him to shame. Returning to his desk, he picked up the little book—this time, not so debonairly—and opened it as if looking for an oracle. Still standing, he read:

> *It is impossible to write without labeling oneself. . . . Literature must signify something other than its content and its individual form . . . whence a set of signs unrelated to the ideas, the language, or the style, and setting out to give definition, within the body of every possible mode of expression, to the utter separateness of a ritual language.*

What the hell did that mean? What was there besides content and form? How could a set of signs unrelated to anything define something? He shut the little book and threw it disgustedly on his desk. Once so wonderfully friendly, it, too, had turned its back on him and disowned him. What was it about, for God's sake? Could someone please explain to him what it was saying?

His anger died as quickly as it had flared, yielding to an almost peaceful sense of emptiness. All those concepts that described nothing that actually existed, no outer or inner reality! Signifiers signifying nothing, floating in space until they vanished from one's field of vision like helium balloons slipped from one's grasp, magnificent birds beating their way toward a horizon never to be seen again. Reality was not so complex that it needed rarefied concepts to do it justice. It was what it was. The fluted cornice of a building rising against the blue sky. Birds hopping in the branches of a tree. Children playing baseball. Straight lines. Crooked lines. Love. Hate. Life. Death. If only he could get away from it all! If only he could leave it all behind and go with them to the Cape.

Andrew sank into a chair, overwhelmed by the knowledge that nothing would get written today, either, that nothing would ever get written. Writing and reading called for euphoric, if not manic states of consciousness—and he was so far from euphoria. He thought of the cartoons from his childhood with their comic-book villains dashing over the edge of a cliff in mad pursuit of their victim, still running without knowing they were in the air. There was always that cruel, hilarious moment when they realized it and stopped pumping their terrified legs, beneath which was a yawning abyss. Their eyes bulged ludicrously as they hovered in midair for a second before plunging with a long, dismal cry that trailed off and ended with a thud. *I'm over the edge. I'm falling. I should turn off the computer.*

8

A delivery truck stood outside the black gate, forcing Andrew to walk around it and onto the Columbia campus. Since when were trucks allowed to park here in the middle of the day?

He looked back at it disapprovingly. Half a dozen burly men in undershirts were unloading white garden chairs and folding tables for some event. A fund-raiser? Maybe a wedding? It wouldn't surprise him if universities started renting out their lawns for private events. Why not? It would be a nice source of income, wouldn't it? Isn't it all about income nowadays? Andrew brushed the thought aside, embarrassed by his own open bitterness. The men were too hard at work to notice his disgruntled stare. Just one of them, a tall, rude-looking fellow, put down the stack of chairs he was carrying, placed his hands on his hips, and stared back at him scornfully. Andrew instinctively glanced away and walked off, his heart racing irrationally as if he had been caught doing something wrong.

The summer sun beat down brutally, baking his surroundings and dazing him. Although he knew the campus well, it hardly seemed recognizable. The steaming lawns fidgeted in the muggy air. The metal cornices of the buildings were on fire. Even the statue of Alma Mater in front of Low Library, depicting the university as a wise goddess seated on a high throne with an open book in her lap. Nearby, twenty or thirty shockingly young-looking women lay on the lawn, their slim, sun-drugged, half-naked bodies a jumble of long legs, bare arms, and flat stomachs. One, lying with her mane of copper curls like a mermaid, wore a ring in her bare navel. Andrew regarded the scene in bewilderment, unable to make sense of its contrasts. What was going on? Who would have imagined the Low Library lawn turning into a nudist beach? Nothing was the same anymore. Things were falling apart, the center didn't hold. What was he doing here? What had he come for? Ah, yes: to sit in a library. Perhaps, in its grand space, he could finally get some work done. Turning his back to the ornate, ancient shrine-like building of the Low Library, he now faced the majestic, geometrically perfect facade of Butler Library.

Butler, the newer and bigger of Columbia's two libraries, was not so new anymore. It was one of Andrew's favorite buildings, an imposing neoclassical structure whose portico of heavy columns, each proudly bearing the name of a great figure of Western civilization, had unfailingly conveyed a sense of stability, grandeur, and intellectual responsibility. Today, though, Butler Library did not seem at all welcoming. He felt intimidated by it. Its large columns formed a barrier that couldn't be crossed, their tops a peak that couldn't be scaled. The names of Homer, Herodotus, Sophocles, Plato, Aristotle, Demosthenes, Cicero, and Virgil were like the hostile parapets of an impregnable enemy castle. Going any farther in their direction struck him as impossible. They were surrounded by a magnetic field antithetical to his own, which would send him reeling backward if he had to approach.

He turned back toward Alma Mater. Her black metal eyes rested on him with a dark indifference. Outstared too many times today, he returned her gaze, unwilling to submit without a fight. Approaching her more closely, he examined her for the first time. The black folds of her gown draped her proud figure like actual fabric. The noble leaves of her laurel wreath stood stiff and somber against the hazy summer sky, her royal scepter formidably piercing its faded blue. Was this she, the Nourishing Mother of All Wisdom? Was it at the foot of her unsparing, pitiless tyranny that he had sat these thirty years? He had been young, so very young, when first enthralled by the romantic pursuit of knowledge. There had not been a hint of cynicism in him. He wasn't really cynical even now. Bitter? Yes, that might be. Disillusioned? He wasn't sure. "Illusionless" might be a better word. Academic life was good to us, it let us be who we wanted to be and do what we wanted to do. We never let its careerism affect us—or so we thought. But something was lost along the way. Something wore thin. We let the magic of it dull. We learned to play it safe after all, became intellectual mediocrities without knowing it. . . .Why do I keep saying "we" and "us"? I don't know. Probably a defense mechanism.

Where now? Home? To the gym? No, he couldn't work out now. Maybe later that afternoon. Should he have something to eat? Who could even think of eating in such heat! The sun was like an inferno. Didn't these young women sprawled on the lawn know it caused cancer? Hadn't they heard about the hole in the ozone layer? He was beginning to sound like a grumpy old man. Andrew dragged his legs up the stone steps of Low Library, trying to overlook the sea of nudity that spread around him like a brightly colored fan. What were they doing here? Weren't they supposed to be on summer vacation? Reaching the broad landing at the top of the steps, he peered into the dusky interior of the grand building that had once housed all the university's books and now called to mind the temple of an ancient god or the secret headquarters of a Masonic lodge conspiring to rule the world. He turned to his right, roaming aimlessly under the ruthless sun that seemed so close it was practically touching him. Anything for some shade! A handsome, semicircular stone bench with the inscription FOR FELLOWSHIP AND LOVE OF ALMA MATER, DONATED IN 1911 BY THE YOUNG GENTLEMEN OF THE CLASS OF 1886 awaited him around a corner and welcomed him to its white lap. He leaned his head against its carved backrest, shut his eyes, and lifted them toward the orb of the sun. The insides of his eyelids were bright orange. He felt a childish, almost infantile comfort. She was an unattainable lover, Alma Mater, a jealous mother who cast her betrayers far beyond her black gates, but her lovers rested in her bosom forever as new babes laying aside all malice, and all guile, and hypocrisies, and envies, and all slander, nursing her white stone milk that they may grow thereby.

Andrew opened his eyes, blinking like a cat in the strong light. Around him were beds of anemically pale, long-stemmed irises,

their powder blue the color of the university's flag that drooped
with an aristocratic nonchalance from a white flagpole, its symbol a crown topped by a square cross. How nice it was here, how
regal and peaceful! He felt cradled in the warm white bosom of
Alma Mater. This was how it should be: bright, clean, and mo-
nastic. The colored posters, the art festivals, the baby carriages,
the naked women on the lawn—all were distractions from the
scholarly life. They created an illusion of freedom, of an easy flow
between town and gown. But the true ideal of the Academy was
different, severely insular, its beauty spiritual and abstract. Try
as they might, its trustees could not conceal the signs of it; the
black gates with their javelin-headed, heaven-thrust bars; the mysterious dome of Low Library; the well-tended lawns guarded by
black iron chains as heavy as the anchor chains of ships; the peacefulness. The peacefulness most of all. It was the peace in the eye
of the storm, brewed in mysterious alchemical laboratories in the
library's basement. The noises of the metropolis, the dull, never-
ending, all-penetrating roar of the great city, broke against it and
was repulsed by the iron gates that marked where the world ended
and the redbrick walls of academe began.

Such odd clarity. He couldn't say if it was acceptance or despair.
This wasn't his territory. He didn't belong to Columbia. He came
from the other end of the academic spectrum, from popular, progressive, culture-light NYU. He hadn't come to this place looking for an alternative. He had wandered into it, a lost vagabond
in search of shade and somewhere to lay his fever-hot head. And
his writing? All those years of prolific, creative, cutting-edge research? None of it had what it took. His articles wouldn't change the
world. That wasn't going to happen. They wouldn't even change
the world of scholarship, not even of the disciplines he had chosen
for his own. It wasn't that he hadn't worked hard, had wasted his

life, or sold out his dreams. He had had a good run for his money, grown intellectually and personally. In the end, though, he had not made the slightest difference. He hadn't rewritten the rules of the game, hadn't pushed back the frontiers or even the discourse defining the frontiers. All the omnipotent fantasies of youth—the wild optimism that believed the world lay before one, just waiting for a new god or Übermensch whose wisdom, courage, and intellectual integrity knew no bounds—his passionate infatuation with Alma Mater: All that had died within him today, buried with him under the white stone bench, surrounded by the beautiful light-blue irises that feed off the milk of words.

Andrew awoke with a start, his face sunburned. His hair was mussed and sweat drenched his neck. Had he fallen asleep? How long had he been sitting in the burning sun? He glanced at his watch. It wasn't there. Alarm ran through him: he had been robbed! For a moment, he let the thought get the better of him, even though he knew it was ridiculous. Who would rob him in the middle of the Columbia campus? A half-naked sunbather? A mad librarian? The university president? He had a sour feeling in his stomach, which felt empty although he wasn't hungry. He rose with an effort, stretching his stiff limbs and looking worriedly about, hoping no one he knew had seen him sleeping like a vagrant on a bench. The pleasurable, liberating clarity was gone. He felt wooden. *It's all over. There's nothing for me here anymore.*

Andrew brushed imaginary dust from his pants, glanced back at the bench to make sure he hadn't forgotten anything, and headed home. The scantily clothed bodies no longer commanded his attention. They were sunbathing—so what? He descended the steps, passing to one side of Alma Mater, and leaving by a side exit to avoid the unpleasant deliveryman. With a glance at Butler Library, the familiar names on whose columns evoked no emotion good or bad, he limply followed the walkway to the street. The unseeing iron eyes of Alma Mater stared at him with indifference as he grew smaller and vanished in the distance.

9

Accursed city! All boundaries are blurred here. The border among science, art, and pop culture, between truth and public relations, no longer exists. There are too many beautiful people, too many brilliant, ambitious, successful ones. They rub against one another, desire one another, exchange innuendos, smiles, and inner jokes. How can anyone stay sane? It simply can't be done. All the openings: of museum shows, of galleries relocated from SoHo to Chelsea, of fashionable restaurants, of artsy fringe theaters, all trapped in the bear hug of the city's cultural establishment. Exorbitantly priced French wines and unpasteurized cheeses outlawed by the Health Department. Artists, academics, models, and billionaires sit knee-to-knee in a dimly lit proximity that you would say was filled with cigarette smoke if only anyone still smoked. Pink cosmopolitans in martini glasses, you couldn't ask for a more diabolical drink! It's one big mental jumble. That stunning model over there, the one with the white, transfixing thigh showing through the long slit in her black dress, is a head taller than any man in the room. The head of the arts faculty, in a conservative, tailor-made suit, is chatting her up. What about? Neo-Marxist interpretations of Jackson Pollock? The inevitability of Roy Lichtenstein? And that dot-com millionaire with the three-hundred-dollar T-shirt, the black Hugo Boss jacket, and the wife, a well-preserved ex–beauty queen in a Ralph Lauren morning suit—what can they be discussing so passionately with the drunk, scruffily dressed off-off-Broadway playwright, the current enfant terrible of the theater world, and his girlfriend, or whoever she is, though whoever she is, she's completely stoned? The Enron scandal? The crazy real estate prices in Southampton? How did we learn the body language? Who taught us to feign three minutes of interest in what someone we've never seen before and will never see again has to say? How did we acquire the art of tilting our bodies at impossible angles as we go from person to person at cocktail parties, maneuvering ourselves between our hostess's silicone breasts and her teenage daughter's real ones without touching either while flashing each a polite smile to let her know she means nothing to us? And there's still more! What about the restaurants, the museums, the Madison Avenue boutiques? And those sexy bakeries that have been opening all over (à la Provence, à la Tuscany, à la English countryside, à la American colonial, all indistinguishably alike) with their brick walls, their thick wooden tables, their little jars of mass-produced, absolutely authentic jams! European-style, New England–style, Mediterranean-style, fig, citrus, strawberry, raspberry, blackberry! How expansive they make us feel! There must be something in the light, in the air, to make us so young and attractive. And then there are the liquor stores with their dizzying arrays of labels and differently shaped, colored, and textured bottles, each wine and spirit a window into a distinct terroir with its own sun, water, and air! Dozens if not hundreds of brands of different whiskeys, cognacs, premixed cocktails for the sophisticated palate! The extra-virgin olive oils from hundreds, no, thousands of artisanal presses in Italy, Spain, California, and the Middle East! And bread, every possible variety of bread! Coarse, rustic pumpernickels, gourmet loaves, whole-wheat, sour rye, five-grain, seven-grain, ten-grain breads! You could spend a lifetime sampling the delights of the great city, drunk with pleasure like love-sated Ulysses in Calypso's arms, the road home to Ithaca lost, forgotten.

10
June 26, 2001

The 5th of Tammuz, 5761

Three thirty p.m. Half an hour of cardio, *now*?! Although Andrew had somehow managed to survive forty-five minutes with his personal trainer, he didn't know where he would find the energy for half an hour on the elliptical, maintaining a heartbeat of no less than 139. Not that his session with his trainer had been particularly difficult today. Sergeant Andrew (who, finally realizing that the joke had gotten stale, no longer called himself that) had sensed Andrew's condition and behaved more like an occupational therapist or male nurse than like a martinet. After putting Andrew through some light drills, he had laid him down on a cot half-hidden behind a column in a corner of the room and stretched his limbs one by one, relaxing his cramped muscles and releasing the toxins that had built up in them. He had ended the session early, cutting it short by several minutes and intimately wrapping a warm, comforting white towel around Andrew's neck while imparting a few tips for staying in shape. It was as if they had decided that this was to be their final meeting. Even the jesting "And now half an hour of cardio and no goofing off—you know I always can see you!" sounded hollower than usual.

Andrew took hold of the machine and pulled himself into position, settling his feet in its broad, boat-shaped pedals. Taking longer than usual to enter his weight and set the resistance and incline, he stifled an unbecoming sigh and began, slowly and reluctantly, to pedal his way through the damned half hour. He hardly bothered to look at the screen; he would forget about working up to 139 today. What was on TV? The news? No, not for him. A cook-

ing show? Not today, either. Music . . . another news channel . . . a
talk show . . . stop! It couldn't be, not after such a long time. The
twins, "his" twins, the hideous-looking Jason and Aaron, the Jewish twins who wanted to look like Brad Pitt, they were back again!
Where had they turned up from? The channel must be rebroad-
casting the series; it was a way of filling screen time. The two of
them were lying in a room crammed with gadgets and electronic
equipment, the dream room of a Jewish American Prince. Though
their heads were swaddled in bandages that made them look like
mummies or creatures from a horror movie, Andrew recognized
them at once. By now they were almost like family. The surgeons
had broken every one of their aching facial bones so as to put them
together in conformity with the white American male beauty ideal.
You couldn't make an omelet without breaking eggs, could you?
Nor chop down a tree without the chips flying: everyone knew
that. The two weren't their old teasing selves. Their optimistic
smiles were gone, too. All that remained was pure misery, naked
pain. Andrew's heart went out to the pair, who seemed oddly orphaned. Aaron was crying. His tearful voice came through the
bloodstained bandages: "It hurts. It hurts so bad." Jason groped
for his brother's hand and gave it a tender, wordless squeeze. The
camera lingered on them for an obscenely long moment, focusing
on their two hands joined together. The MTV crew was nothing if
not professional. It wasn't about to let a visual gold mine like that
slip away unexploited. And now a short break for a commercial.

Andrew glanced at his watch. A mere seven minutes had passed
since beginning his cardio. Twenty-three more minutes on this
humiliating machine! He gritted his teeth and pedaled slowly, a
feeble ox turning a grindstone that was simply too heavy. These
commercials! What were they trying so hard to sell? Wonder di-
ets for instant weight loss, wonder solutions for credit debt, wonder drugs for bigger and better erections: a brave new world of

wonder. Two more minutes gone by. How many commercials
could they squeeze in between one segment and the next? It must
be a popular show if they could sell so much advertising time. A
thick, feverish perspiration ran irritatingly down his face. Reaching for the towel around his neck, he knocked it clumsily to the
floor beneath the pedal rods. Instinctively, he bent to pick it up,
letting go of one handle. At once his feet slipped from the pedals as
though they were stepping on ice, and he lost his balance. With all
his strength he clutched at the other handle, which rattled rapidly
as though trying to shake free of him, too, and managed to avoid a
painful, embarrassing fall. His muscles felt stiff and tight again. He
wiped his brow with the sleeve of his exercise shirt, looking with
vague, sorrowful guilt at the little white towel lying at his feet like
a dead dove. There was nothing to do but let it lie there and go on
pedaling. If he stopped even for a second, he knew it would be the
end. He would beat a hasty retreat to the locker room and never
come back.

The program resumed with the caption: "A Month Later."
There they were, on their way to a glitzy club in the Los Angeles
hills, pulling up in Daddy's black Mercedes. Their friends crowded
around them excitedly. Jason's kinky hair was a straightened, per-
oxide yellow—or was it Aaron's? Both were blond, their eyes an
ersatz, ghastly ultramarine. They couldn't be told apart. Which
was which? One wore a stylish light blazer, the other . . . but God
only knew what his sleeveless tunic was supposed to be. Still, as
much as one hated to admit it, who could deny that the golden lines
of their elegantly reconstructed cheekbones were a big improve-
ment? What's true was true. They were not nearly as ugly as they
had been.

There was Michelle! Short, pretty, and blond, too, she slunk into
view in a tiny evening dress. The twins approached her reverently,
a path cleared for them by their friends, who formed a ritual cir-

cle around them. Michelle, in the middle of it, looked bewildered and even alarmed. She clearly had not been expecting this. Live television at its best! Now the twins stood facing her with broad grins, their hearts pounding beneath the fashionable outfits that the program's costume designers had dressed them in. "Well, what do you think?" Cut. The camera pans out and in again on an interview with Michelle outside the club. Although the light isn't good enough to make her expression out clearly, her eyes do look moist. She seems in shock. "They look a lot better but they're still not Brad Pitt," she says. Cut! Another short break for a commercial.

Andrew took his eyes off the screen. No, they weren't Brad Pitt. Not quite. Still, the results weren't unpleasant. Nineteen minutes gone. Only eleven left to go. Just keep it up a little longer! But no, he'd had it. Enough for today. Maybe tomorrow. He dismounted clumsily, his spine jolted by the sudden stop, bent, picked up the no-longer-warm towel lying on the floor, wrapped it around his neck, and headed for the stairs to the locker room. His glance lingered on the familiar surroundings as if he might not see them again for a long time, perhaps forever.

11

June 26, 2001

The 5th of Tammuz, 5761

What time is it? They have taken my watch with my other personal belongings, leaving me in a short green smock that barely reaches my thighs. Terribly weak, I sit hunched on a bed trying to follow the doctor's explanations, which go wearyingly on and on. I don't understand exactly what the problem is. Something has gone seriously wrong in my genital area, there is irreversible damage that calls for immediate surgery. I will be operated on alongside someone else, the faceless man lying catatonically in the next bed, wrapped in blankets and sheets as though in shrouds. How can it have come to this? I try collecting my thoughts and concentrating on the doctor's words. If only I could stay focused on the soft, blinking eyes behind the thick glasses, I might grasp what has happened.

The doctor continues his patient explanation, his soft, monotonous voice barely audible above the buzzing in my ears. It has to do with my seminal vesicles. Something very bad has happened to them. They have fallen into my anus. A dim, malignant feeling of guilt sweeps over me. What neglect! How, I ask, nodding a bit too eagerly to show that I am following the doctor's remarks and want to cooperate, have I let myself deteriorate so? What luck that I am being offered a last chance to extricate myself, if only at a steep price, from the predicament I have gotten myself into!

Yet how steep the price was only dawns on me as the anesthesia dripping into my arm takes effect. The realization hits me like a bomb: my prostate, testicles, and penis are about to be removed. A cold, paralyzing horror creeps through me, causing my body, which is growing heavier and more numb, to writhe in a final paroxysm like a fish in a net. The needles dislodge, tearing the skin of my biceps into bloody shreds. Sturdy arms seize me from behind and hold me in their practiced grip. Although its use of force is degrading, this display of authority calms my panic. Yet a moment later, the thick needle jab between my vertebrae almost makes me pass out from pain. The anesthesia is working on my muscles, which suddenly feel weak and watery. The terrible pain is now gone, though. In its place is a sense of relief, almost joy. I have done all I can to resist. Now I can give in and go to sleep, diving into the warm depths of helplessness.

The hours pass. Perhaps days. Who can say? I open my eyes with great difficulty, forcing their sticky lids apart. They are bleary and sting as though from acid. I try lifting my hand to them, but it refuses to obey me and remains cold and lifeless on the sheet. I shut my eyes to let them rest. When I open them, they are met by a hideous sight: the elongated blue head of a young man was staring at me from a pillow next to mine. Certain it has been decapitated and diabolically placed near me, I shudder and shut my eyes again to drive the vision away. I take a peek. It is gone. The head, more pitiable than heartening, is now attached to the long neck of a youthful, astoundingly beautiful body. Its tormented look has a breathtaking, almost angelic beauty. The eyes flutter, the half-opened lips mouthing voiceless words that wake me from my anesthetized state. I know clearly now who the handsome young man is. It is Brad Pitt. Brad reaches out an arm to gather me to his maimed body. I strive to meet its embrace halfway, yielding to the desperate hug. We are both in such pain. Everything hurts. We are so wounded.

The days pass as though in a clear, uninterrupted dream. Now we are ambulant, bandaged hermetically, taking gingerly walks in long, white hospital gowns, supporting each other. We are inseparable, me and Brad Pitt. It is as if we share one body. I have to pee. My urine is making my wounds hurt. Where is the bathroom? We have to find the bathroom. A nurse, stern and uncaring, stops us on our way. No! You can't! You can't urinate like that anymore! You have no penis! You'll have to learn to pee sitting down. From now on you'll have to pee like a woman.

12

Andrew woke up suddenly from his nightmare. He was in his bedroom. Although part of him rejoiced in this sudden relief, another part wanted to return to the warm, total embrace of the blue man, whose anguished beauty went on shining even though it had been only a dream. Ann Lee lay on the other side of the bed, half-naked. She had thrown off the blanket. The light from the street, mistakable for moonlight, bathed her in a soft, romantic glow that flamed in him tremblingly, tenderly. He reached out a hand to her, his fingers aiming for the place where her bare thigh met the bottom of the man's shirt she wore as a pajama, then thought better of it. The movement was mechanical, volitionless. The struck match of desire went out quickly, leaving a trail of acrid smell. Lately, this had happened too often. What little sexual excitement he still felt vanished as fast as it was aroused. Though this worried him, he had no explanation for it; not knowing what to make of it or do about it, he preferred not to think of it. The last times they had tried having sex had not gone well, to put it mildly. The electricity between them was gone, its place taken by a cold make-believe that led to more anxiety than pleasure. Although you couldn't really point to any specific moment or thing that had spelled the end of their passion—but that was a lie! He knew very well that it had begun with that terrible night of the bloodied sheet; they no longer felt it. For the first time in his life, Andrew brooded about his ability to make love. It had become a major concern. Ann Lee was patient, perhaps more than she should have been. She seemed to have lost her sarcastic sense of humor and become unnaturally serious while prone to increasing fits of anger. Andrew had never been able to imagine life without sexual desire, especially for a young, attractive woman like Ann Lee. It was basic to his masculine identity. And yet the very idea of it now seemed improbable, almost unimaginable. He could hardly believe he ever had felt it. All his refined, richly nuanced, epicurean male sexuality now struck him as an illusion, an empty bubble that had burst against a gray, diminished, Eros-less reality. Memories of past lovers came and went: naked bodies, assorted positions, ribs rising from a woman's waistline; the elongated curve of a white thigh; the fine fuzz running down a spine: it all seemed distant, unreal. It had the cheap vulgarity of a bad novel or dumb movie, a triteness like the Vaseline smeared over the lenses of cameras in old X-rated films to give their nude figures a mysterious, dreamlike halo. The whole tiresome exertion of lovemaking, of arousing the minimal desire and curiosity needed to maintain an erection, had come to seem not only tedious but immature and even infantile.

Andrew pulled the blanket toward him and turned carefully on his side so as not to jostle the mattress, his face to the wall and his back to Ann Lee. All he wanted was to lie like this, by himself, semi-fetally curled beneath the blanket while surrendering to the wisps of thoughts and bright, golden visions that increasingly occupied him by day and by night. They bore him to far times and places, bound him to them with magical cords as if he had unfinished business there that he needed to complete. But tonight they did not appear. The doors of the shrine remained shut, excluding him from the enchanted light that filled the interior, gilding its implements and its smooth, cool marble walls. His half-waking fragments of dreams and memories were replaced by a strange, regressive stirring more like the vague desire of prepuberty than a normal, mature sexuality, the autoeroticism of the masturbating child who has no object in mind and is too young to ejaculate. He was having more and more of these cloudy, infantile episodes that evoked a lost sexual prehistory. Paradoxically, they occurred most frequently on nights when Ann Lee shared his bed, frustrated by

his lack of interest in her and forced to make do with a fatherly
hug and a good night peck on the cheek. Andrew would lie by
her side, waiting for her regular, childlike breathing to tell him
she had fallen asleep. As soon as she had, all the demons of his
imagination emerged from their hiding places to torment him with
images and snatches of scenes having nothing to do with his adult
self or its sexual proclivities: huge, white, flabby, sexless behinds;
heavy, pale bellies spilling over thick hips, their flesh crisscrossed
by bluish veins; thick, hushed voices whispering baby words he
did not understand, though they aroused in him a strange yearning. Sometimes a covert violence took control of this phantasmal
night world, trapping him in its crude, sterile, embarrassing lust. A
hand holds the elastic band of a pair of baggy underpants, stretches
it, and suddenly lets go. The band snaps back, thwacking loudly
against a bare bottom that quivers with a cry of protest . . . Andrew sat up with a start. An invisible hand has taken hold of his penis and milked—with a few sudden, rapid strokes—all the sperm
stored in his warm, sleepy testicles.

Panicked, he looked for the hidden hand. There was no one
there. No one had touched him. Ann Lee was still sleeping at the
other end of the bed, her position practically unchanged. The last
of the quick, deliciously painful contractions throbbed in his loins.
He peeked beneath the sheet and saw nothing. Taking a deep
breath, he stuck a hesitant hand in his pajama bottoms and pulled
it back quickly, his fingers covered with a layer of warm, sticky
goo. Incredulously, he stared at the viscous sperm shining dimly
in the light from the street. This had never actually happened to
him before, though of course he had heard about it as a boy. It was
a subject for locker-room talk, the "wet dreams" related by the
boys who had them in voices no less sticky and wet. The gluey
fluid had seeped through his underpants and was staining his pajamas. Andrew threw off the blanket with his left hand, holding his

right hand, on which the drying semen burned like a cold fire, in the air. Trying to keep it from touching anything, he extended it before him like a soldier while slipping out of bed and tiptoeing to the bathroom. Still using his left hand, he shut and locked the door and turned on the hot water. The faucet gurgled testily. Surprised to be woken in the middle of the night, it took a second or two to start filling the sink. Andrew scrubbed his sticky fingers, unable to recall when he last had encountered the batter-like texture of human semen. He dried his hands, which were stinging from the hot water, and turned his attention to the real disaster, the smelly, sticky mess in his pajama bottoms. He peeled these off cautiously, trying to avoid unnecessary contact, rolled them into a tight ball, and stuck them deep in the laundry hamper, hoping the pile of dirty clothes on top of them would keep their odor from permeating the bathroom. Next, he inspected his body. His sex and groin were almost completely covered with the sickening substance that whitened as it congealed, making his short, curly pubic hairs stiff and prickly.

How much goddamn sperm did he have in him? He had never imagined one ejaculation could contain so much. Although he would have given anything for a hot shower, the thought of waking Ann Lee was out of the question. The combination of shame, animosity, and self-pity that this made Andrew feel brought him to the verge of tears. He was trapped in his own bathroom, forced to act like a thief in his own home! Grabbing a washcloth from its bar by the sink, he wet it with hot water and set about cleaning himself of the disgrace as best he could. In the end, still feeling soiled and polluted, he made another little ball of the towel and thrust it into the hamper by the first. *Angie!* She was sure to find it, still damp, when she came in the morning and identify the smell at once! He would have to do something. Would there be time to retrieve it all and wash it with hot water and soap before she arrived? Fatigued

to the point of apathy, he leaned above the sink and stared in despair at his puffy, unshaven face in the mirror. Dark bags hung
under his eyes. His gray hair stuck out ridiculously like a rodent's
filthy fur. The sight disgusted and shamed him. He shut his eyes
and breathed deeply, struggling to recover his senses. *White, sand-
smoothened, wind-honed wooden oars. Whalebones, cleansed by the
sun and the years. A breeze from the sea would blow away all impurity.
The light would bleach it. The sand would scrub it clean of its apartness
and return it to the bosom of Unity. All matter would be pure again,
restored to what it once was. . . .*

Andrew came to with a start, startled by the sight of himself in
the mirror and the realization that he had fallen asleep standing
up: undressed from the waist down, his two hands gripping the
sink, his forehead almost touching the cold mirror. He was far too
exhausted to sneak back into the bedroom, open the dresser, and
take a fresh pair of pajama bottoms from a drawer. What would he
tell Ann Lee in the morning? It was too much to deal with now.
He would think of something. Perhaps he would wake before her
and manage to dress before she asked embarrassing questions. He
hobbled back to bed, groping his way with half-shut eyes, and lay
down, taking care to keep the blanket away from his still moist and
sticky genitals. He mustn't contaminate the bedclothes with even
a leftover drop of sperm! He let his eyes close and breathed in and
out to stay calm. A deep weariness overcame him. He yielded to
the sensation of it, maintaining his breathing while letting sleep
steal over him. . . .

13

The telephone rang sharply, close to his ear, tearing Andrew
from his sleep and hurling him into a panicky wakefulness.

Who could be calling at this hour? Something terrible must have happened! He grabbed the receiver and held it to his ear. Linda's voice screamed hysterically into it, her words so mixed with sobs that they were hard to make out. "Alison's gone! She's disappeared! Someone's kidnapped my baby!"

Andrew leaped out of bed and dressed hurriedly without turning on the light, groping for his clothes that lay on a chair like a dark corpse. One leg in his pants, he hopped out of the bedroom while trying to work in his other. His damp, itchy genitals rubbed against the rough fabric. There hadn't been time to put on underpants, every second counted. Sticking his feet into a pair of shoes, he grabbed his wallet and keys and ran outside, uncombed and unwashed. The long hallway, lit by a weak neon light, was like a labyrinth, every one of its gray doors alike. Low-wattage bulbs flickered over the emergency exits. Empty elevator shafts yawned with toothless mouths. Andrew kept pressing the button of the snail-like elevator to make it come faster, then dashed across the lobby and leaped into the dark street.

The taxi sped down Broadway and turned left at 96th, heading for the FDR. Its faceless driver weaved past flashing traffic lights and orange road-repair cones. As in a bad dream, the apocalyptically illuminated streets were totally empty. The taxi raced on. Andrew squirmed in the backseat, running his hand through his hair in a vain attempt to make it look presentable. The driver drove in silence, taking the streets to Brooklyn at an unbelievable speed. Was he shocked by Andrew's strange appearance? Could he smell the faint whiff of dried semen coming from his pants? What was he thinking, what was going on in his mind? Most likely, nothing. New York cabdrivers had seen everything. Nothing could surprise them anymore. They were on the FDR now, tearing by the exit at 42nd Street, at 34th, at 23rd. The tail end of the Williamsburg Bridge loomed in the corner of the front windshield, causing

Andrew's terrified heart to beat faster. The rapid ticking of the meter kept time with it as they neared their destination. Down Flatbush Avenue. Then right, into Park Slope.

The house was brightly lit with spotlights, as if a night crew were filming it. Linda stood in the doorway between the tall marble, Greek columns. Her wild black curls snaked like Medusa's, giving her the frightening look of a witch in an old movie. Tears melted her thick eyeliner, which coursed in black rivulets down her pale cheeks. Where was George? What had happened to him? He couldn't have left her alone at a time like this, not when he was always there when she needed him. Half-crazed, she ran to him. "My baby! My baby!" Her screams pierced the respectable, gentrified Park Slope night. He had to calm her down, get her back into the house. Soon all the neighbors' lights would start coming on. But she wouldn't be pacified. Her long, sharp, black-lacquered nails dug painfully into his palm, as they had once done in the delivery room, so many years ago. "You must find her!" Everyone knew there was a rapist on the loose in Park Slope, an insane murderer. Little girls had been violated and slaughtered in the bushes of their parents' backyards. You could hear the desperate cries of the searchers, calling their names over and over. Andrew felt his upper lip tremble. He mustn't panic, he had to stay rational! A mad idea crossed his mind like a lightning bolt: He was dreaming! It was all a dream, it couldn't be real! "Listen, Linda! I know this sounds crazy, but you've got to believe me. I think I'm dreaming. I'll shut my eyes tight and open them and try to wake up, okay?" Linda looked at him incredulously, not knowing what to make of such an absurdity. Andrew shut his eyes tightly. He gritted his teeth, clenched his fists as hard as he could, and suddenly released them. No, it wasn't a dream. Nothing had changed. Alison was gone. There was nowhere to run to, no one to blame. How could it have happened? She had disappeared from her bedroom. The murderer had climbed through an open window and snatched her easily from her bed. Who had left the window open? Linda looked at him with a terrible hatred. Her eyes were bloodshot, as if all their capillaries had burst. "What do you mean, who? You! You left her all alone! It's all your fault, yours!"

14

Wind-smoothed, sand-honed wooden oars. Whalebones, hollowed by the years. The breeze coming from the ocean will blow away all impurity. The sun will bleach it. The sand will scrub it clean of its apartness and return it to the bosom of Unity. All matter will be pure again, restored to what it once was. Matter in itself can never be impure. It always is clean. We, too, will be cleansed. Our bones will become white and dry. They will abrade and grow smooth with the passage of time. Our skulls will split along their seams into brittle conches, no longer scary, no longer repellent, no longer human. Their marrow will desiccate and turn to dust. They will grow as friable as the shell of a dead snail bleaching on a shriveled bush by the shore. There will be no more terror; no more memory; no more shame or sin. All will revert to sand and stone, chalk and dust. To matter, pure matter in itself.

15
June 27, 2001

The 7th of Tammuz, 5761

Ten p.m. The dim, reddish light of Beauty Bar, which Andrew might ordinarily have found soothing and sensually stimulating, was having an opposite, irritating effect on him. His long walk down 14th Street looking for the self-consciously hard-to-find place had left him out of breath and perspiring. Ann Lee had insisted on meeting him here, and at this late hour, which seemed to him like the middle of the night. Yesterday's phone conversation with her had given him a heavy, queasy feeling that increased as time went by and only grew worse now that he stood adjusting to the dim light.

Andrew squinted at the noisy, packed bar, searching for Ann Lee. The tense anticipation he had initially felt about meeting her had become an unbearable torment. Although he knew she wasn't there, he kept hoping to find her, threading his way between the trim young bodies talking animatedly in the tenebrous glow like beautiful devils in a designer hell. He had heard about this place, which had become one of the self-infatuated city's hot spots, but had never been in it. Beauty Bar had originally been an old-fashioned beauty salon with 1970-ish barber chairs and large spaceship-shaped hair dryers along one wall. The fashionable bar that took its place had made this its ironic retro theme, and its regular customers—the college-aged progeny of wealthy parents whose clothes and hairstyles suggested that they were students at film schools and art and design academies—took part in the production. Stylish kids crowded around the bar painting each other's nails with bright colors, or else sat in the barbers' chairs or beneath the hair dryers chatting with a youthful insouciance. Andrew was used to the presence of young people, but not in this kind of situation. Usually, he dealt with them across a semitransparent divide of age and professional status. He didn't socialize with them outside of the classroom and had no experience in dealing with them on their own territory. The longer he stood there, the more he felt his power peeling away like a cheap, old gold plate. The collar of his new shirt was damp with perspiration and its middle button, the one over his midsection, felt tight. What was he thinking, going for that slim-fit shirt? Did he think he was still a teenager?

It was too late to change that, though. What was done was done: you simply had to pay the price of having done it. He sucked in his stomach to ease the pressure on the button, which seemed about to pop and ricochet into space before the mocking eyes of the youths surrounding him. For the umpteenth time, he stared at the backs of the customers at the bar, hoping to make out Ann Lee's familiar, miraculously materialized form. It wasn't there. Of course not. It was twenty after ten. Where could she be? Andrew abandoned his observation post by the door and made his way to the bar. Could she be sitting there unnoticed? He knew perfectly well she couldn't be. Why had he worn this damn shirt? He could hardly breathe in it.

On any other evening, Andrew would have sat at the bar, ordered a drink, and waited, enjoying the trendy high voltage of the place. Now, though, he felt too nervous for that. He looked at his watch again: 10:25. She was seriously late. Once more he surveyed his dim surroundings, hoping against hope to spot the wry but loving smile that he adored. His glance fell on a corridor leading to a mysterious, perhaps even ominous-looking, back room. On a whim, he strode toward it. Suppose she were hiding from him there. A red velvet rope, of the kind used to cordon off lines and museum rooms, barred his way. Only half-aware of what he was doing, he sidestepped it and continued toward the back room, keeping close to the wall as if for protection. What if she were there, passionately making out with some young guy, his shirt hiked up past his flat stomach, his sharply outlined pelvis showing above his low-slung pants? The ridiculous thought had a chilling effect. He slowed his gait, afraid of what he might see when he peered into the room. What, for God's sake, was he doing here? Where did he think he was going? He knew he should stop, take a deep breath, get a grip on himself, and turn around. Yet his legs refused to obey him and he walked on, determined to reach the end—the dead end—that he was heading for.

"Sir!" There was a hard edge mixed with cruel amusement in the voice behind him. "Sir! The back room is closed to visitors." More impatient than the first, the second "Sir!" brought Andrew up short. "Excuse me," he murmured while turning to face his challenger, a husky, spiky-haired bouncer. Surprised by the exaggerated deference in his voice, he was even more startled to hear himself say, "I'm looking for the bathroom." The bouncer measured him up and down with narrow, close-set eyes, nostrils flaring scornfully as if he were able to read Andrew's mind. "It's back there," he said drily, pointing with his chin to a door on the other side of the velvet rope. "Didn't you see the sign?"

Andrew hurried to thank him, demeaned by his own lie. With a shaky hand he opened the bathroom door, slipped inside, locked the door behind him, and leaned against it as if afraid of being followed. The bathroom had the same camp decor as the bar. There was leopard-skin wallpaper, a synthetic fur toilet seat, and a red lampshade whose risqué glow called to mind a European brothel. Although he had no need to go to the toilet, Andrew unzipped his fly and forced himself to squeeze out a few drops as though to justify himself to the bouncer. He took his time at the sink, running the water loudly as additional proof, which he felt compelled for some reason to provide, that he had merely been looking for a place to wash up. The strong hot flow had a calming effect. He leaned over the sink and scrubbed his face until it was red and stinging. Near-scalding water spattered in all directions, staining his pants and shirt with dark splotches. He would look like a fool! It was a good thing the place was so dark that you could hardly make anyone out.

Andrew's chest, which had been feeling less tight, contracted again. Suppose there were students of his here! It was exactly the sort of place you would expect them to spend a free evening.

Although he knew no one in his introductory course by name, he would be recognized at once. All he needed was to be seen wandering around in wet pants like the city's village idiot! The whole university would know in the morning; the classrooms and corridors would buzz with sordid descriptions. *Stay calm! Don't lose your head!* Water ran down his cheeks in large drops. He groped blindly for the faucets and turned them off. A minute or two went by. The drops slowed to a trickle. He waited for the bathroom to grow quiet and summoned the courage to look in the mirror. All that water hadn't made him look any fresher. He had the red, unfocused eyes and pale, puffy face of someone who had been crying. His hair, a muddy gray in the bordello-red light, stuck out wildly. He tried brushing it with a hand and looked at his watch: 10:40. Enough! He couldn't go on hiding here all night. He had to go back out and face the music.

Andrew left the bathroom and headed for the bar without looking back. There was still no sign of Ann Lee. Could he be in the wrong place? Had he confused the time? Nonsense! He knew the truth only too well, as much as he hated to admit it. He detoured around a group of youngsters in heated conversation, sure they were making fun of his bumbling manner. They had seen him skulking like a prowler toward the back room. It was all over with! Tomorrow he would be the talk of the town.

Andrew pushed through the crowd to the bar, looking for a place to sit. Everything was taken. He debated and decided to order a drink and have it standing. Greater than his craving for alcohol was the need to hold something in his hand to give him confidence. New Yorkers that they were, the young people at the bar did not hurry to make way for him. They were too self-involved, too young and beautiful, to notice anyone. Andrew found himself pressed against their alien, unyielding bodies. The sensation, though intense, was not in the least sensual. Once at the counter, he couldn't manage to attract the attention of the female bartender at its far end. Was he being paranoid or was she deliberately looking through him? What had happened to his celebrated presence, his knack for making himself the center of things? He leaned forward and waved to her, trying to catch her eye. Those days of masculine potency now seemed like a distant dream, formless shards of memory. He looked again at his watch, angered by his weak nerves and willingness to take part in the ugly game Ann Lee was playing: ten forty-five. Where the hell was she? Yes, she sure was taking her sweet revenge.

The bartender was talking to a pale young man, leaning over the counter with her large white breasts all but spilling out of her low-cut dress. Andrew looked away and let his gaze wander. Above the mirror behind the bar, dominating the 1970s advertisements for shampoos and hair conditioners, was the brash sign: OVERSIGHTS CAN BE EMBARRASSING! PAY WHEN YOU'RE SERVED! SPARE YOUR-SELF THE EMBARRASSMENT! Andrew studied it. Although unsure how to interpret it, he felt certain it was meant for him. *Here am I*, he whispered, clutching at the quote as though at a straw, *an old Jewish gentleman*. The stiff, ascetic figure of Bernard Malamud appeared like a wraith in the fogged mirror above the bar and vanished, just as the pleasure of quoting him quickly dissipated, like a match blown out by the wind. Resting both elbows on the counter, Andrew called to the bartender in an impolitely loud voice. With a look of cold annoyance, she turned and walked challengingly toward him, her heavy breasts swinging like a cow's udders. "Yes, sir. What will it be?" The question took him by surprise. He had been trying so hard to get her attention that he hadn't thought of what to order. Although he wanted a whiskey, his acid stomach rebelled against the idea. He settled on a beer, asking the bartender, with the same deference he had shown the bouncer, to recommend a craft brew. Leaving a big tip that made no impression on her, he carefully lifted the wet glass from the damp counter and worked his way back through the crowd of barbed bodies while trying not to spill his drink.

There were no seats. The only available one was a high barber's chair standing by itself in the middle of the room. Andrew managed to clamber into it, holding his beer as though he was hiding behind it. His shirt tugged at its middle button and clung to the folds of his stomach. He sat as straight as he could to relieve the pressure on the button and took a sip of his beer, which was every bit as tasteless as he had expected it to be. How long was he going to put up with this childish ritual of humiliation? It was 10:50! Should he get up and walk out? What was keeping him in this nightmare? Nonsense, he wasn't going anywhere. He would sit and wait, sit and drain his hemlock to the lees.

"Excuse me, sir. Would you like a manicure?"

Andrew turned around, the beer almost sloshing from its glass. Behind him, a pudgy, bored-looking young lady was looking at him with indifference from a small table arrayed with colorful little bottles. A sign behind her said, MANICURE $10. DRINK INCLUDED. Yet another creative, self-satisfied shtick! Andrew murmured something that sounded like "No, thank you, maybe some other time" while pretending to overlook the manicurist's generously exposed though not at all sexy cleavage. What was it with these low-cut dresses? Was it an occupational requirement? She looked at him with round, vacant, bovine eyes, rhythmically chomping on a stick of gum as though chewing her cud. *A tired, apathetic old gentleman who has lived long enough.* What was he doing in this preschool? Why in the world had he agreed to come here?

Andrew got down from his chair and headed for the bar, promising to leave at the stroke of eleven. Although all the seats at the counter were still occupied, he succeeded in reaching it quickly and depositing his almost full glass, which had become a burden he was glad to get rid of. He looked at his watch: 10:55. Would he really walk out in five minutes? Perhaps he should have a scotch, after all. What brands did they have? Nothing special, that much was for sure. Looking for the bartender, he turned his head to his right and jerked it back quickly. What he saw, so near it could have been a close-up on a screen, was alluring and repelling at once— titillating, shocking, beautiful beyond words, and thoroughly revolting: a colossal, voluptuous kiss that as though had an existence of its own between the two faces that framed it. They were so young, so good-looking! The kiss was passionate to the point of being aggressive. The young man's hands held the young woman's two cheeks. His tongue, thrust into her mouth, moved beneath hers, wrapped around it like a naked snail. Her chest rose and fell so that you could almost hear her throbbing heart. Andrew stared at his reflection in the mirror, not daring to take another look at the young couple. Yet the vivid scene remained before his eyes, draining and exciting him. His weary mind was collapsing under the weight of too many impressions. He blinked hard and threw an involuntary glance in the direction of the kiss. It was gone. The seat next to him was empty. In the seat beyond it, a few steps away, sat Ann Lee. She was staring at him stonily, her face like a stranger's. Andrew's heart sank. His chest was a bottomless abyss. All was lost, that was perfectly clear. All was lost.

16

I'm tired of playing this game! It doesn't turn me on anymore— and it's not working for you, either, by the way. It was you who cast me in the role of the sexy, dangerous, innocent, child-woman, but you've had enough of it, too. I admit that at first it was exciting. The aura of mystery, the childish drama of 'Should or shouldn't I call back?,' 'Who's sleeping at who's tonight,' and 'Should I keep a spare toothbrush and pair of panties at his place?' Candlelight dinners in the nude on the rug with *Tosca* or *Carmen* in the background and breakfasts in bed at two in the afternoon with eggs poached in Burgundy, a fresh baguette, and red roses. Yes, it was wonderful, don't get me wrong! But it's no substitute for real life, for a real relationship between two adults. I feel we're trapped in a play you've produced to protect yourself from life. I feel expected to go to sleep acting and wake up acting. I feel as if a camera were following me and forcing me to play a part in a bad Hollywood movie. I'm fed up with it. I don't want to go on being a prop in a stage set designed by you. I want to be with you without always having to feel that I'm some character in a novel about an older man having a passionate affair with a Lolita young enough to be his daughter. I want to wash the dishes while you work or do my exercises in the bedroom while you're checking your e-mails and answering phone calls at the end of the day. I want to take care of you when you're sick and to know that you'll take care of me. I want to eat ordinary breakfasts with you—cornflakes, or a scrambled egg with toast—and grumble that you're reading the newspaper while you eat. I want to go out with you for dinner, to meet your friends, to get to know your world, to be a part of it. I want children! Not now, but someday I'll want children and a family. We're having a secret affair, for God's sake—can't you see how absurd that is when neither of us is married? I'm not your student anymore and you're not my teacher, you haven't been for a long time! You're as tired of it as I am. The role no longer fits, you're miscast in it. You try holding on to it, but everything around you is falling apart. The safe, perfectly designed little world you've created no longer works. The actors have stopped following your directions and so have you. Something bigger and deeper is going on inside you. I have no idea what it is. But you have to confront it, you can't go on denying it and pretending it doesn't exist. I'm leaving. Don't look so surprised. We both know it's been in the cards for a long time. I've been offered a grant to compose with a studio of my own for four months in San Francisco and I've decided to take it. I know I didn't consult with you about it. I never thought of that as a possibility. It wasn't included in the unwritten contract of our torrid love affair. I need to think and I would advise you to take the time to think, too—to think about the two of us. I'm not going to call you. You can phone me if you like when I get back, but only if you're ready to be my true partner, not an actor in a romantic comedy."

17

June 27, 2001

The 6th of Tammuz, 5761

Once more that noise out of hell, as if it never stopped, and the low-grade home movie that makes everything look like a bad dream. The title this time is *Michelle Likes a Drink Now and Then*. The camera zooms in jerkily on the same basement and focuses on the young woman. She is completely drunk, squatting on all fours on a low table like a little white rabbit, her bare bottom a bright patch against the dark background. The college students surround her, shouting and miming the repetitive, apelike movements of a cheerleading team. The young man behind her has already penetrated her and tosses her back and forth like a rag doll. Michelle's toneless muscles can't hold her up and she flops from side to side, a new wave of cheers urging her on each time she nearly tips over. Nonchalantly, the young man lifts her small body, straightens it on the table, and resumes his thrusting as if it never had been interrupted. Is she enjoying it? Resisting? Does she have any idea of what's happening? She's so drunk that there's no way of knowing. A second youngster, his pants down halfway to his knees, stands at the other end of the table and tries to stuff his erect penis into Michelle's mouth. She shakes her head with a stubborn, mulish obstinacy and struggles to spit out the foreign object, which he keeps trying to push past her flaccid lips.

The screen goes dark. A new scene. She's now flat on her back on the table, thrown this way and that by whoever is on top of her. Her round, firm breasts have fallen out of the blouse and bounce comically, up and down. The young man in front of her hasn't given up and is still trying to force his penis into her mouth. Michelle shakes her head disjointedly from side to side with stubborn helplessness.

The screen goes dark and is silent again. Scene Three. Michelle is sprawled, vanquished, on the stomach of a young man. (His face is not in the picture, but who cares about his face?) She is impaled on his erect penis. At some point, she must have passed out. Her miniskirt is pulled down and her goose-pimply bottom is clawed red. A drunk college student sticks his face into the rectangular field of the film. He waves a beer bottle in greeting, grins at the camera, and says something inaudible to Michelle. His checked flannel shirt, baseball cap, and vulgar self-satisfaction suggest a big game hunter photographed with a trophy. Darkness, The End. The video clip is over. How can such things be allowed to happen? It's rape, gang rape, pure and simple! There are laws against it. Poor little Michelle. What have they done to her? Those firm little breasts, the pounding piston-like thrusts. They didn't even bother to undress her. They ran her down like an animal, pulled up her skirt and had their fun. That sweet little, goose-pimply, red-streaked bottom! Is she cold? Is it cold in the satanic beer cellar she's been raped in by devils? They've pinched her, raked her skin, vented their bestial lust on the soft hillocks of her flesh. She lies without moving, spitted on a huge uncircumcised penis as though on a monstrous iron stake. Not even the twins can save their Michelle, their unattainable love. They lie far away in their beds, wallowing in their pain, powerless.

18
June 28, 2011

The 7th of Tammuz, 5761

Twelve noon. Andrew, pale and wan, sunglasses shading eyes red from sleeplessness, walked slowly eastward on West 4th Street, bound for the formidable redbrick building of Hebrew Union College. Standing in the middle of the NYU complex, it was a structure he knew but never had been in. He had been surprised to receive an invitation to a memorial gathering there to mark an academic year since the death of the celebrated Israeli poet Yehuda Amichai; he had no idea where the event's organizers had found his address or why they had added him to the list of invitees. Although Andrew had first met the Israeli poet when Amichai was a visiting lecturer at NYU and had kept up an acquaintanceship with him until his death the previous September, they weren't close friends and didn't move in the same circles. Nonetheless—if nothing else, his insomnia had forced a painful honesty on his usually well-defended mind—he welcomed the excuse to take a break from his routine and get out into the world. Above all, he was glad to take time off from the wretched article that he still hadn't finished.

What time did the memorial begin? He had left the invitation at home and couldn't remember if it was twelve or twelve thirty. A cup of coffee (it would be his third of the day) wouldn't hurt. It might restore his energy level, which had run down in the course of a morning that had started with waking far too early.

The traffic on Broadway, which roared like a rampaging river, broke Andrew's troubled train of thought. How had he gotten all the way to Broadway? Confused, he looked in both directions, unable to orient himself on the city's grid. The HUC building was farther west, near the Levitt Building. Feeling as woozy as if he had had a few drinks, Andrew turned around. Ahead of him, 4th Street now ran westward to the invisible river hidden behind the city's clutter. He blinked and shook his head, trying to get over his sudden dizziness. Where, damn it, was HUC? Could he have passed it without noticing? Hurriedly he began walking west. There was no time now for coffee or a bite to eat. The overhead sun, directly above him at its noonday zenith, seemed to saw the sky deafeningly, drowning out the sounds of the city. He walked on, carried more by his inertia than willful locomotion, blindly following the street to its next corner in the harsh light flooding the city. West 4th and Mercer. How could that be? He knew the area well. It was his home turf—or had been, anyway, until a few weeks ago—and he was certain that the building was not west of Greene Street. Could he be dreaming? Turning around once more as though sucked into a nightmare, he was startled to see, just a few steps away, the high, square entrance of Hebrew Union College looking down at him with unconcerned mockery.

Andrew breathed deeply, trying to pull himself together, and shuffled toward the entrance. He felt about to faint. Somehow, he had forgotten to eat today. Leaning one hand against the brick side of the building to steady himself, he removed his sunglasses with the other and stuck them in his shirt pocket. For a while, eyes covered by his fingers, he stood desperately seeking to regain a sense of reality. Voices echoed in his head. Fragmentary visions, the splinters of shadows, passed before his eyes, knocking on the gates of consciousness as if threatening to break them down and burst into the world. Pedestrians strode nimbly around him, regarding him with a moment's puzzlement that quickly receded into a customary urban indifference. The minutes went by, void and disconnected. His head was spinning more slowly now and the bitter reflux in his throat had retreated to his stomach. Uncovering his eyes, he pushed his way through the revolving door and entered the lobby. Passing the security guard and reception desk, he crossed the marble floor slowly, as if still unsure of his legs, and wandered through the cold, remote, ultramodern lobby of the Reform rabbinical school.

The walls of the lobby, painted a museum white, were hung with a dozen or so mediocre works of art displayed with pride in modest institutional frames. They were concerned with the usual variety of Jewish themes and conveyed in the simple, unimaginative, semiabstract style that was a feature of contemporary religious art. Andrew filed past them, regarding them with a mixture of disdain and—for some reason—vague guilt. They were so depressing. He turned to the lobby's display cases in which modern and ancient Judaica reposed lifelessly, protected by double-glazed panels. Hushed, hesitant voices were speaking to him. He was looking for something, something forgotten but important—but what? He glanced at the exhibits without mentally processing what he saw: Sabbath candlesticks, Kiddush cups, Hanukkah menorahs and wooden dreidls—unwanted, discarded objects, caged in glass, that life no longer had a use for.

A pristine, thrilling gleam of burnished bronze interrupted Andrew's brooding. A huge, rounded, seven-branched candelabrum, crafted with a skill belonging to an age gone by, stood grandly on a stand, shining with an inner light that illuminated its surroundings with an unearthly vitality. It was a thing of astonishing beauty. Andrew's breath was taken away. This was it! This was what he had been looking for—this ravishing, golden-hued artifact! He approached it with controlled excitement and halted a few feet away, his heart beating like a pilgrim's who has finally reached his longed-for destination. For a long time he stood looking at the glorious object, lingering on its magnificently executed details. Although he had seen such menorahs more than once, some of them in rare Judaica collections, this one was special. He thought he saw a strange halo surrounding it, an invisible electrical field.

A museum label at the candelabrum's foot described its provenance. It had been looted by the Nazis from a Jewish banker's home in Frankfurt am Main, only to turn up after the war at a shady antique dealer's in Philadelphia. Bought from him for a hefty sum by the wealthy American descendants of another Jewish Frankfurt family that had emigrated to the United States in the late nineteenth century, it was donated by them to the Reform movement in honor of their deceased father after he passed away at a ripe old age surrounded by his American progeny. Though intriguing, this history was only half-absorbed by Andrew, as was the information that the candelabrum was meant to be an exact reproduction, based on ancient Hebrew and Aramaic sources, of the renowned Menorah pillaged by the Romans when they destroyed the Holy Temple of Jerusalem in the year AD 70; supposedly brought to Rome and displayed with other sacred objects in Titus's triumphal procession, it then disappeared, inspiring esoteric speculation throughout the ages on its whereabouts. Andrew was in too much of a state to take all this in. His pulse hammered in his temples. The doors of The House opened wide and a river of light poured through them. Although the two candelabra, the one on the stand and the one in his vision, were highly similar, there were unmistakable differences. The oil bowls in the burnished bronze reproduction were smaller than the original. Its branches were set at a wider angle. Its base, too, didn't look quite the same, perhaps because it was portable and the candelabrum of his visions was not.

Suddenly, the doors of Andrew's vision slammed loudly shut. Its glow that outshone the lights on the lobby's ceiling faded away. As if a wire plugging a mental screen into a distant current had been severed by a sword stroke, Andrew was torn from the ravishing sight. He blinked in surprise, waking from his dream. The large, empty lobby was still there, its glass cases like striped gray rocks in an untilled field. Where was he? What was happening? What was he doing in this place full of dread? Right: the Amichai memorial. His visions. What was he going to do about them? He would go crazy, that much was clear. He would be locked up in a madhouse if they didn't stop. What time was it? Late, very late. He had to find the chapel.

Andrew cautiously pushed open the heavy wooden doors of the chapel, hoping his late arrival would go unnoticed. The vestiges of his vision ran through him like the ripples of an aftershock, flaring in his consciousness like the last flashes of lightning at a storm's end. The ceremony was already under way. The spotlighted front of the auditorium was full. The first row was occupied by the scholars, university professors, and lecturers whose demeanor bespoke the refined ennui of literary grandees. In the second row sat the New York Hebraists, a motley assortment of aging eccentrics reminiscent of musty old newspapers and high-minded intellectual debates. Rows three and four were taken by the rabbinical students, most of them young women with brightly knit skullcaps perched on their heads. Behind them, out of range of the spotlights, were the hoi polloi: poetry lovers, homesick Israelis, and the usual oddballs who filled the galleries at public events.

Andrew tiptoed inside, trying to blend with the shadows, and found a seat in the back, shrouded in semi-obscurity. The chapel resembled a small concert hall more than a place of worship. Only a few flimsy prayer shawls, neatly folded like theatrical props on an antique-looking wooden rack by the entrance, testified to its official purpose. He surveyed the scene with weary eyes. Although the speakers' remarks reached his eardrums, they failed to penetrate the circuits of his brain. He felt an ominous mixture of nameless anxiety, nervous exhaustion, incipient hysteria, and—surprisingly, considering that he and Amichai did not know each other that well—an unexpected sense of bereavement. The poet's warm irony and unique, clear-sighted humanity would be missed. . . . A memory connected to him was struggling to rise from the bottom of Andrew's consciousness. It was something that had fallen into the sea of forgetfulness, where it glittered in the depths like a bright, precious object whose refraction shimmered dreamily on the surface. He couldn't believe he had forgotten. Just a minute or two ago it had been there.

Andrew looked up and glanced at the audience distractedly, only half-seeing its profiles that were turned attentively toward the speaker. In a far row, a familiar face that he couldn't place roused him from his thoughts. For a moment, their glances met. With a flicker of recognition, the man smiled slightly in Andrew's direction. Embarrassed, as though caught peeking, Andrew looked down at the ground, still feeling the man's eyes on him.

It was his neighbor from 110th Street! The man with the two dogs, the man from Alison's Sunday school who was writing so passionately in the café! What was he doing here? Of course. He was an Israeli, he spoke Hebrew. Even if he didn't look like a literary type, he had come to pay his respects. Yet the sight of him had a powerful effect. Andrew felt drawn to him with an eagerness he couldn't describe and didn't know what to make of. He wanted to get up, cross the room, and say something. Had it not been so absurd, so insane, he would have said that the man held a key to the mystery that had taken control of his life, a secret code that might help decipher it.

He recalled their first meeting in the street. Dredged from his memory, it brought with it another, more substantial recollection, the one that had lain on the seabed of his consciousness all morning, unable to surface. When had it happened? He couldn't say. At least several years ago: his mind was too groggy to calculate more exactly. He was with a group in Jerusalem as a guest of the Kandel Institute for Social and Cultural Studies. His hosts, who attributed great importance to his presence, had gone out of their way to introduce him to the cream of Jerusalem intellectual society, no doubt in anticipation of similar treatment when they visited New York.

One of the high points of his stay in Jerusalem was a guided tour of the Old City, a fascinating personal glimpse of it given by none other than Yehuda Amichai, already then Israel's unofficial poet laureate. The tour took place on a Jerusalem spring day that was like summer in every respect. The luncheon preceding it had been heavier than was the norm in Europe or America, and the guests were drowsy and lethargic by the time they reached the narrow lanes of the restored Jewish Quarter with their asphyxiating, fortresslike atmosphere and the obscenely excessive use of local Jerusalem stone that felt like an arrogant, light-crazed architectural nightmare. The tour's climax was a half-comically intended visit to an out-of-the-way museum that displayed facsimiles, based on ancient descriptions, drawing, and engravings, of the implements used in the Second Temple. The rabbi who founded and ran the place, Amichai warned his charges with a friendly, ironic wink at Andrew, as was apparent from his last name, was himself a descendant of the ancient priestly clan and had a more than theoretical interest in his project. The museum was less a repository of the past than an "exhibition of the future" whose reproductions would serve as a basis for the Third Temple that would rise on the ruins of the Al-Aqsa Mosque, called by "our friends, the Bible-quoting fanatics," as Amichai referred to Israel's religious Messianists, "Desolate Abomination."

Amichai's ironic manner vanished as soon as they reached the entrance of the museum, replaced by a more vehement, judgmental tone that Andrew took to be an indication of distress. Although the poet continued to speak of the place they were in as a curiosity, one more bizarrely colorful feature of a sacred, wonderful, and thoroughly daft city, his increasingly frequent use of the words "insane" and "insanity" sounded like the apology of someone forced to introduce a guest to a deranged relative. As though fearing to be associated with such a person, he stressed that the museum represented the lunatic fringe of a sane society and was funded not by Israelis but by American Jews. (Here he threw Andrew another, somewhat less friendly but even more ironic look.) Andrew, sensing Amichai's discomfort, had come to his aid with some urbane comments on the invention of nationalism, the construction of the past in the image of the present, and the longing for an imagined golden age that accompanied all nation-building projects—"in this case," he said, pointing to the strange implements on exhibit, many of which were made of pure gold, "a quite literally golden one." Their surroundings now contextualized by the academic clichés they were accustomed to, the members of the group responded with relieved laughter. Amichai, too, smiled appreciatively, although his discomfort hardly seemed relieved.

The museum's founder, the rabbi-priest, now appeared, interrupting the intellectual banter. He wore a large white yarmulke embroidered around its edges with seven-branched candelabra in gold and indigo thread, and the open collar of his white shirt, neatly folded over his jacket lapel, reminded Andrew of his first trip to Israel. Yet the man was well spoken and sensible, and his riveting, far from trite lecture maintained a self-reflective humor even when touching on the final Apocalypse, which he described as if it were a pastel-colored daydream. Only the strange fire in his eyes, which made Andrew think of an evangelical preacher's, gave an indication of his uncompromising, dangerous zealotry. Andrew didn't listen to what he said very carefully. Not that it wasn't interesting. He was more captivated by the beautiful, pure gold objects and the large murals of sturdy, virile-looking black-bearded priests in their white linen garments and turbans, lighting oil wicks, carrying golden fire pans and censers, and prostrating themselves before a gold candelabrum on the marble floor of a great hall. . . .

A bolt of lightning struck Andrew's brain with a loud, explosive clap. The doors of the shrine swung open all at once, all but torn from their hinges. Bright light flooded the hall, and in it swirled a mixture of fiery ancient sights and drab everyday New York realities. An uncontrollable wave of fear turned his innards to ice as he toppled dizzily into a bottomless chasm in which there was no up or down, no possibility of finding his balance. His free fall seemed to last forever. Time and space ceased to exist. Terrified, he nevertheless felt the strange joy of plummeting willingly to his own destruction. A burning candelabrum blazed against the black background of a mountainous sky, its oil bowls and ornamental knobs and flowers living flames in the heart of the darkness. Desperate to stop his plunge and the inevitable crash it would end with, Andrew forced himself to open his eyes. His fall stopped, stranding him midway between heaven and earth. The chapel hovered in front of him, a small world apart, revolving on its axis. He saw it from a vantage point high above, astounded by the sudden clarity with which his mind registered every detail of his impossible situation. He shut his eyes hard. When he opened them, the chasm was gone. Space had returned to its ordinary dimensions. The chapel's air conditioner droned like a far-off echo of the speaker. Andrew instinctively turned to look for his mysterious neighbor from 110th Street. To his dismay, the man was no longer there.

Andrew leaped up and stumbled for the exit, bumping drunk-

enly against the wooden bench in front of him. He had no idea
where he was hurrying to or what he would do if he saw the man
in the lobby. What would he say to him? They weren't acquainted.
But that didn't matter. It didn't matter at all. He had to find him.
The loud screech of his shoes on the recently polished wooden
floor sent a ripple of protest through the chapel. Disapproving
stares followed him to the exit. Andrew, well-bred, perfectly mannered Andrew, neither noticed them nor did they slow his mad
dash. A gold fire pan with burning coals appeared so close to him
that he might have been holding it in his hand. An intoxicating
scent of incense tickled his nostrils. Dream state and waking state,
night and day, all were one. He had to find the man. He had to talk
to him, to somebody! A round of applause. A new speaker. The
opening lines of an Amichai poem resounded in the chapel and
escorted him out of it.

> On the grounds where we always are right
> no flowers will grow
>   in the spring.
> The grounds where we always are right
> are packed hard
>   like a yard.

19

A ndrew shot out of the chapel, its heavy doors banging behind
him. His eyes scurried across the lobby, looking for the familiar, mysterious stranger. He wasn't there. Could he have been a
figment of his imagination? Who was to say? Now wasn't the time
to think about it. Clearheaded! He must stay clearheaded!

He was back in the formal, empty, depressing lobby. The Judaica in its glass cases looked like scientific displays, dead fetuses preserved in formaldehyde. Andrew walked past them in a daze, oblivious to what he was looking at. Although the large, gleaming burnished bronze candelabrum beckoned alluringly from its stand, he did his best not to look at it, afraid of its burning intensity. He quickened his pace without knowing where he was going. What was he doing in this place? A half-formed thought was seeking admission to his mind. It took a while for it to crystallize. Yes, he was looking for a rabbi, a Jewish rabbi! He needed to talk to a rabbi! The knowledge of this embarrassed him, embarrassed him no end. Too desperate to be deterred by this, however, he swept it aside, promising to think about it later. A rabbi! He had to find a rabbi! There must be rabbis here, mustn't there? It was a rabbinical school, for fuck's sake! He glanced around him, looking for someone to ask. Two mousy young women stepped from an elevator and headed for the street. Their knit skullcaps pinned to their tightly woven hair made him think of the fiery, charismatic rabbi-priest of his Jerusalem tour, sending a new wave of anxiety down his spine. No, he couldn't ask them. He would only scare them. They would run from him as though from a lunatic.

Andrew headed for the exit, keeping his distance from the two women to prevent them from thinking they were being followed. In front of him was a small glass table spread with some bright, glossy leaflets. An amiable young man, a knit yarmulke on his head, too, stood behind it with a welcoming smile. Andrew approached him hesitatingly, trying to think of a sane way to phrase the question. "Excuse me, sir," he asked. "Do you know where I can find a rabbi?"

The young man regarded him with astonishment, permitting himself a polite smile in which the effort to avoid condescendence was a bit too obvious. "A rabbi? What kind of rabbi do you have in mind? There are many rabbis here. Perhaps they can help you at the reception desk."

The young man indicated a nearby counter, his neutral but well-meaning smile remaining rigidly in place. The reception desk, of course! Why hadn't he thought of it? Feeling reassured, as if some valuable piece of information had come his way, Andrew approached it. Yet the sight of the uniformed woman at the desk made him have second thoughts. His feverish brain could only too easily imagine the conversation that mustn't take place.

Sir, do you have some specific rabbi in mind? Do you have an appointment with someone in this building?
No, I have no appointment. I need a rabbi.
Sir, there are many rabbis here. I need a name to refer you to.
I'm sorry, but I don't have a name. I don't know any rabbis.
May I ask, sir, why you wish to see one?
I have to talk to him! I need to talk to a rabbi, now!
Please, sir, I'll have to ask you not to shout.
I'm not shouting! Who's shouting? I just want to talk to a rabbi.
Sir, I'll have to ask you to leave the premises. If you don't, I'll have to call a security guard. Security, this is Reception. I've got an urgent problem. Over to you.

Andrew took a quick step back and found refuge behind a large pillar near the entrance to the lobby. From there, painfully aware of the absurdity of his behavior, he peeked furtively out at the young man at the table to make sure he wasn't being watched. The young man was chatting pleasantly with two middle-aged ladies, patiently showing them his printed wares. Andrew left the safety of the pillar and crossed the lobby quickly with the busy air of someone who knows where he is going, praying the security guard wasn't hot on his heels. Dodging around the first corner, he dashed for the elevator, punched the call button repeatedly, and vanished into the first car to arrive. He picked a floor at random, impatiently pressing Close until the door shut.

The elevator stopped on the seventh floor. Andrew stepped cautiously out of it and looked around like a seasoned burglar. Long corridors ran in both directions, lit by greenish fluorescent lights. Uncertain which way to go, he let himself be pulled to the right. The long corridor with its offices was as oppressively empty as the lobby. It gave Andrew the uncomfortable feeling of being in a dream. Where was everyone? He passed closed doors, more, pointless-looking elevators, and a large library room with no one in it, its distinguished authors arranged in perfect order on richly stained wooden shelves. Just when he thought the empty corridor would go on forever, he came to a large, brass-handled door with the sign, RABBI ARTHUR SILVER, PROVOST. Andrew stared at the sign as blankly as if it were written in code. The one word that registered, reverberating in his mind, was "Rabbi." He wavered, took a deep breath, and knocked. There was no answer. He knocked again, less hesitatingly. No, no one was there. The office was empty. He stood facing the closed door, debating what to do. The voices in his head—near or far, he couldn't tell—caused him to throw caution to the wind. Pressing on the brass handle, he stepped into the office, keeping close to the wall as if expecting an ambush.

The front room was empty. The secretary, no doubt out for her lunch break, had left her desk. From an open second door, however, came loud sounds of conversation and lively laughter. Andrew stood there uncertainly. Should he barge in or slip away before he got into real trouble? The latter, obviously! What was he doing here, anyway? Systematically destroying what was left of his career? He shook his head as though trying to wake from a bad dream and resolved to make his getaway, go home, crawl into bed, bury himself between the cool sheets, and fall asleep. He would come no closer to the open doorway and the hearty voice booming beyond it.

He did the opposite. Standing on the threshold, a shabby-looking intruder, he peered into the room apprehensively as if fearing guards would appear to evict him. Rabbi Silver, a smiling, balding man in a light jacket and bright tie, sat talking on the phone at his desk, his stubby fingers drumming merrily on the desktop as though to the beat of unheard music. Andrew stared at him, surprised to be so disappointed that he was smooth-shaven and bareheaded. What had he expected? A Hasidic rabbi muttering ancient Yiddish incantations? The father from Chaim Potok's *The Chosen*? Still, he had imagined Rabbi Silver would somehow look different, less ordinary, perhaps less secular.

The rabbi, sensing Andrew's presence, glanced up at his haggard face from the fancy knickknacks on the desk. His smile grew broader and his eyes widened with delight, crosshatching his cheeks with jovial wrinkles that gave him the look of a favorite uncle. With a suspiciously familial wave of his hand, he signaled Andrew to have a seat in the leather chair facing the desk while half-covering the phone with his other hand and whispering amiably, "Just one more minute, all right?" Andrew, nonplussed, took a step toward the chair but remained standing. Why was this portly, energetic man behaving as if he knew him? Rabbi Silver kept talking for another minute, nodding vigorously and murmuring a few words of agreement before cutting the conversation short with the apology that he had an important visitor. He hung up, came out from behind his desk, and held both arms out to Andrew in greeting. "Professor Cohen! How are you, my dear friend?"

Andrew felt dizzy. His nausea revived, turning inside him like a trapped animal. It was a dream! It had to be. This couldn't really be happening. Where did this man know him from? For an embarrassing moment until he thought of reaching out a reciprocal hand, Andrew stared at the outstretched arms. Rabbi Silver, however, paid or pretended to pay no attention to his quandary. Clasping Andrew's cold hand in his own two palms that were as yeasty and warm as fresh rolls, he kept it there while seating him in the chair. Clearly, a mere memory lapse was not enough to disturb the composure of a man with such sharply honed diplomatic instincts. With an admirable casualness, he reminded Andrew of the panel on which they had met several years ago, proceeding from there to a subsequent article in the Arts and Leisure section of the *Times* in which Andrew had contradicted, or so it seemed, some of the views he had expressed on the panel.

Andrew stammered a few words in reply. He remembered neither the rabbi nor the panel. Stripped of the illusion that he could remain incognito, he struggled to adjust to a conversation with a fellow academic for which he was ill prepared. Rabbi Silver's doctoral degree, it turned out, was a joint one in anthropology and religion. For someone not professionally involved in the latest developments in cultural criticism, he displayed an impressive mastery of them, pleasurably rolling the common coinage of the field off his tongue. Andrew found it exhausting. The role of the brilliant polymath that he was expected to play belonged to another life lived thousands of miles away. Although he did his best to keep up his end of the conversation, it was beyond his power to convince himself that he was the eminence others thought he was.

The minutes went by. The time customarily allotted for the polite preliminaries had long since passed, but Andrew, who could hardly explain to himself, much less to Rabbi Silver, the nature of the question he had come to ask, prolonged it. The rabbi, too, seemed in no hurry to get to the matter at hand. In the end, however, feeling a need to address the elephant in the room, the rabbi asked, "So what brings you here today, my friend?"

Andrew felt his heart race. What, indeed, was the question that had brought him here? How was he to ask it? Too disconcerted to have planned his next move, he himself wasn't sure what his madcap pursuit of a rabbi was about. The possibilities that passed through his muddled mind all seemed absurd, one more than the next. He took a gulp of air, feeling as shamefaced as if caught with a prostitute or fortune-teller, held it in for a second, and quickly expelled it with a mumbled query that sounded like, "What can you tell me about the Temple in Jerusalem? I mean its implements."

The room fell silent. The vaguely worded, out-of-context question hung discomfitingly in the air. Andrew felt the blood rush to his face and immediately drain from it, leaving it cold and clammy. The silence persisted. Not even a public functionary like Rabbi Silver knew how to break it. He cleared his throat, leaned back in his chair, and looked at Andrew as if waiting for more. Andrew couldn't think of more. He nervously clenched his fingers that were resting on his knees like a chastised pupil's. An involuntary tremor of his eyelids made him think of the forgotten, bittersweet childhood sensation of giving in to importunate tears. He cleared his throat, too, desperately trying to think his way out of the predicament he had gotten himself into. He couldn't just change the subject. Nor could he just get to his feet, thank the rabbi for his time, and make a hurried exit from his office, which was beginning to feel like one of the glass cases in the lobby, like a space he was eternally trapped in. Rabbi Silver waited another second or two. Then, despairing of any rational explanation for Andrew's strange question, he launched into an orderly elucidation of the symbolic status of the Temple as an organizing metaphor for the post–Second Temple period Jewish experience. It was a lecture he had obviously given before—under more propitious circumstances, it was to be hoped. The neutral, scholarly tone of his remarks soothed Andrew's frayed nerves. He listened to them without understanding a word, allowing their familiar, buttery monotone to numb his tormented mind.

A chair scraped in the next room. The secretary was back from her lunch break. The bubble of quietude burst. The building came to life, humming like a beehive. The rabbi's expression changed, too. He glanced at his watch and gave Andrew a friendly but businesslike, end-of-conversation look. Once more he came out from behind his desk, held out both hands, and deftly escorted his visitor to the door, thanking him for dropping in so unexpectedly and handing him a visiting card with his private number. "Feel free to come by any time you'd like to talk," he said with an avuncular twinkle. Andrew expressed his appreciation for the rabbi's enlightening remarks and pocketed the card, which he found comforting, though he knew he never would use it. Stepping into the corridor with the sensation of having been rescued from a disaster at the last moment, he took the elevator to the ground floor, crossed the lobby without glancing at the candelabrum, averted his face as he passed the reception desk, and stepped from the building into the bustling, light-filled street. He didn't want to think about what had happened. He didn't want to think about anything. It was too much even to have to walk to the subway. A taxi. *Taxi!* Home! To sleep!

END OF BOOK SIX

[Mishna, Treatise Yoma, Chapter 7, Mishna 1] The High Priest [then] came to read. If he wished to read in linen garments he could do so, otherwise he would read in his own white vestments. The synagogue attendant would take a scroll of the Law and give it to the head of the synagogue, and the head of the synagogue gave it to the deputy, and the deputy gave it to the High Priest, and the High Priest stands and receives it, and reads.

[Mishna, Treatise Yoma, Chapter 6, Mishna 7] Then he would roll up the scroll of the Law and put it in his bosom and say, "More than what I have read out before you is written here. And on the tenth . . . ," which is in the book of Numbers, he recites by heart. Then he recites in connection therewith eight benedictions: for the Law, for the Temple service, for the thanksgiving, for the forgiveness of sins and for the Temple separately, and for Israel separately and for Jerusalem separately, for the priests separately and for the rest of the prayer.

The High Priest was stationed where all could see and hear him. The attendant of the Temple's synagogue brought a scroll of the Law and passed it to the head of the synagogue, who passed it to the Superior, who passed it to the High Priest. The High Priest read standing up. At first his voice was weak, for he was worn out from his exertions and it was difficult to hear. Soon, however, the words had an effect on him and his voice grew stronger. The elders, seeing that he was familiar with the text and understood what he was reading, relaxed. When he was finished, he rolled the scroll shut, clasped it to his bosom, and proclaimed, "More is written here than what I have read!" He then recited the eight blessings that follow a reading from the Law, to which the people answered "Amen." Handing someone the scroll, he hurried to the ablution pool.

[Mishna, Treatise Yoma, Chapter 7, Mishna 2] He who sees the High Priest when he reads does not see the bullock and the he-goat that are being burnt, and he that sees the bullock and the he-goat that are being burnt does not see the High Priest when he reads: not that he was not permitted but because the distance apart was great and both rites were performed at the same time.

[Babylonian Talmud, Treatise Yoma, Folios 69 a—b] THE SYNAGOGUE ATTENDANT WOULD TAKE A SCROLL OF THE LAW. May one infer from here that one may show honor to the disciple in the presence of his master? Abaye said: It is all done for the sake of the High Priest. AND THE HIGH PRIEST STANDS. From this you can infer that he [i.e., the High Priest] was sitting before, but surely we have learnt: Nobody may sit down in the [Temple] Court except the kings of the house of David alone, as it is said: *Then David, the king, went in and sat before the Lord.*

[Leviticus, Chapter 16, Verses 23—30] And Aaron shall come into the tent of meeting, and shall put off the linen garments, which he put on when he went into the holy place, and shall leave them there. And he shall bathe his flesh in water in a holy place and put on his other vestments, and come forth, and offer his burnt-offering and the burnt-offering of the people, and make atonement for himself and for the people. And the fat of the sin-offering shall he make smoke upon the altar. [...] And the bullock of the sin-offering, and the goat of the sin-offering, whose blood was brought in to make atonement in the holy place, shall be carried forth without the camp; and they shall burn in the fire their skins, and their flesh, and their dung. And he that burneth them shall wash his clothes, and bathe his flesh in water, and afterward he may come into the camp. And it shall be a statute forever unto you: in the seventh month, on the tenth day of the month, ye shall afflict your souls, and shall do no manner of work, the home-born, or the stranger that sojourneth among you. For on this day shall atonement be made for you, to cleanse you; from all your sins shall ye be clean before the LORD.

[Mishna, Treatise Yoma, Chapter 7, Mishna 3] If he read in the garments of linen, he would then sanctify his hands and feet, strip off his clothes, go down and immerse himself, come up and dry himself. The golden vestments would be brought to him, he put them on, sanctified his hands and feet, went out, offered up his own ram and the ram of the people, and the seven unblemished, one-year-old lambs. This is the view of Rabbi Eliezer. Rabbi Akiba said: These were offered up together with the daily whole offering of the morning, whereas the bullock for the whole offering and the he-goat, which is offered up outside, were offered up together with the daily whole offering of the afternoon.

The High Priest washed his hands and feet, undressed, bathed, emerged, and dried himself. Garments of gold were brought. He donned them and went to sacrifice two rams, one for himself and one for all Israel, and seven unblemished, one-year-old sheep. The superior arranged them for him in a line, for the day was rapidly waning and there was no time to waste. The High Priest slit the first ram's throat, let an acolyte finish the cut, and went on to the second ram. Then he slaughtered the sheep one after another with great speed. So quickly did the blood spurt from their throats that it was hardly possible to tell how any were still alive and how many were already dead.

[Babylonian Talmud, Treatise Yoma, Folio 47a] It was told of Rabbi Ishmael ben Kimhith that one day he talked in the street to an Arab [according to other sources, the king of Arabia], and a spittle from his mouth flew on his garments [thus rendering him ritually impure], whereupon his brother Jeshebab entered and ministered [as High Priest] in his stead. Thus their mother saw two [of her sons serve as] High Priests in one day. Furthermore, it is told of Rabbi Ishmael ben Kimhith that he went out and talked with a certain [foreign] lord in the street, and spittle from his mouth squirted on his garments, whereupon Joseph his brother entered and ministered in his stead so that their mother saw two [of her sons serve as] High Priests in one day. The Sages said unto her: What hast thou done to merit such [glory]? She said: Throughout the days of my life the beams of my house have not seen the plaits of my hair [i.e., a married woman would always cover her hair, as a sign of modesty]. They said to her: There were many who did likewise and yet did not succeed.

[Mishna, Treatise Yoma, Chapter 7, Mishna 4] He then sanctified his hands and feet, stripped off his clothes, went down and immersed himself, came up and dried himself. The white vestments would be brought to him, he put them on, and sanctified his hands and his feet.

[Babylonian Talmud, Treatise Yoma, Folio 69a] Come and hear: As to priestly garments, it is forbidden to go out in them in the province, but in the Sanctuary, whether during or outside the time of the service, it is permitted to wear them, because priestly garments are permitted for private use. This is conclusive. But in the province [it is] not [permitted]? Surely it was taught: The twenty-fifth of the month

As soon as he had slaughtered the last sheep, the High Priest hurried back to the ablution pool. He washed his hands and feet, undressed, bathed, emerged, and dried himself. White evening garments were brought to him; they were made of the finest Indian linen. He donned them, washed his hands and feet again, and went to retrieve the coal pan and brazier from the Sanctuary, for it was getting dark and the hour had come to light the candles and offer the evening incense. He returned to the ablution pool, removed his white garments, and handed them to the superior, who gave them to someone to bundle permanently away with his white morning clothes.

of Tebeth is the day of Mount Gerizim, on which no mourning is permitted. It is the day on which the Cutheans demanded the House of our God from Alexander the Macedonian so as to destroy it, and he had given them the permission, whereupon some people came and informed [the High Priest] Simeon the Just. What did the latter do? He put on his priestly garments, robed himself in priestly garments. Some of the noblemen of Israel went with him carrying fiery torches in their hands. They walked all the night, some walking on one side and others on the other side, until the dawn rose. When the dawn rose he [Alexander] said to them [the Cutheans]: Who are these? They answered: The Jews who rebelled against you. As he reached Antipatris, the sun having shone forth, they met. When Alexander saw Simeon the Just, he descended from his carriage and bowed down before him. They said to him: A great king like yourself should bow down before this Jew? He answered: His image appears to me and wins all my battles. He said to them: What have you come for? They said: Is it possible that star worshippers should mislead you to destroy the House wherein prayers are said for you and your kingdom that it be never destroyed? He said to them: Who are these? They said to him: These are Cutheans who stand before you. He said: They are delivered into your hand. At once they perforated their heels, tied them to the tails of their horses, and dragged them over thorns and thistles, until they came to Mount Gerizim, which they plowed and planted with vetch, even as they had planned to do with the House of God.

[Exodus, Chapter 28, Verses 31—35] And thou shalt make the robe of the ephod all of blue. And there shall be a hole in the top of it, in the midst thereof: it shall have a binding of woven work round about the hole of it, as if it were the hole of a habergeon, that it be not rent. And beneath upon the hem of it thou shalt make pomegranates of blue, and of purple, and of scarlet, round about the hem thereof; and bells of gold between them round about: A golden bell and a pomegranate, a golden bell and a pomegranate, upon the hem of the robe round about. And it shall be upon Aaron to minister: and his sound shall be heard when he goeth in unto the holy place before the LORD, and when he cometh out, that he die not.

The High Priest immersed himself, emerged from the pool, dried himself, donned garments of gold, washed his hands and feet, and prepared to reenter the Sanctuary for the day's final incense offering. He took the golden coal pan, filled it at the altar with glowing ambers, and placed it on the top landing of the stairs, exhausted from the fast, and from his exertions, and from mastering his inner trepidation. The Superior saw that his strength was failing and whispered, "My liege the High Priest, hold out a little longer, for we have done nothing until we have done all." The High Priest nodded as if to say, "You are right." He was brought a pan of incense and a brazier that he filled from the pan. Holding the golden coal pan in his right hand and the brazier in his left, he disappeared behind the curtain.

The High Priest walked slowly with his heel almost touching his toes, the coal pan weighing on his arm and its handle burning his fingers. By the time he reached the Holy of Holies, he felt dizzy and short of breath, and when he turned toward the place of the Ark, he tripped in a moment of reckoning on the marble floor and nearly pitched forward. Fighting like a quarried lion, he righted himself while gripping the coal pan with all his might, for if the coals spilled, God forbid, there would be no time to bring more and the world would be left mired in sin. As he struggled to keep his balance, the bells on his priestly garments rang like an alarum. The sound resounded in the Sacred Hall, causing consternation. A gasp hung in the air. All held their breaths, priests, Levites, and Israelites, men and women, the young and the old. Obadiah shook with fear and with joy. His fear was like everyone's. What would be if there was no atonement? His joy was his proud heart's alone. Yes, he thought, *He turneth wise men backward and maketh their knowledge foolish. The sages of Israel did not see what I did. I, a simple priest, saw right through the man. He has gotten an evildoer's deserts. So let all Thine enemies perish, O Lord!*

A second passed. Then another. All stood helplessly. And then, all at once, a cloud of smoke billowed up from behind the curtain. Soon it filled the entire Temple. The High Priest, all now realized, had simply been trembling in awe before lighting the incense. Exactly what behooved a man of his station! As he exited the Sanctuary backward, honoring the Ark's place by keeping his face to it while nudging the curtain aside with his elbows, all the day's worries vanished like smoke. Only a great happiness remained. All joyfully exclaimed as one man: *Thine, O Lord, is the greatness, and the power, and the glory, and the victory, and the majesty!* Over and over they repeated it, shouting themselves hoarse until the walls of the Temple shook.

Truly, how magnificent was the sight of the High Priest as he stepped forth safe and sound from the Holy of Holies!

As taintless as the tent of the heavens above
was the High Priest.

As bright as a beam of the splendor of the Seraphs
was the High Priest.

As radiant as the rainbow that shines in the cloud
was the High Priest.

As grand as the glory of God's creation
was the High Priest.

As ruddy as a rose in a garden of delights
was the High Priest.

As regal as a wreath on the brow of a king
was the High Priest.

As gladsome as a groom at his wedding feast
was the High Priest.

As shining as the star of the dawn when it rises
was the High Priest.

As awesome as an angel met on one's way
was the High Priest.

As clear as a candle burning in a window
was the High Priest.

As cheerful as the chimes of bells on a cloak
was the High Priest.

As splendid as the sight of the sunrise in the East
was the High Priest.

[Mishna, Treatise Yoma, Chapter 7, Mishna 4.] He would sanctify his hands and feet, strip off his clothes, go down and immerse himself, come up and dry himself. The golden garments would be brought to him. He put them on, sanctified his hands and feet, and went in to burn up the afternoon incense, and to trim the lamps. He sanctified his hands and feet and stripped. Then he went down, immersed himself, came up and dried himself. They would then bring to him his own garments. He put them on. They would accompany him to his house. He would arrange for a day of festivity for his friends whenever he had come forth from the Sanctuary in peace.

[Mishna, Treatise Yoma, Chapter 8, Mishna 9] For transgressions as between man and the Omnipresent the Day of Atonement procures atonement, but for transgressions as between man and his fellow the Day of Atonement does not procure any atonement until he has pacified his fellow. This was expounded by Rabbi Eleazar ben Azariah: from all your sins before the Lord shall ye be clean, i.e., for transgressions as between man and the Omnipresent the Day of Atonement procures atonement, but for transgressions as between man and his fellow the Day of Atonement does not procure atonement until he has pacified his fellow.

The High Priest washed his hands and feet and removed his gold garments. He was brought his own clothes and put them on, after which he was escorted to his home. Festive was the day on which he emerged safely from the Sanctuary! Happy was that people that such was its lot! Happy is the people that the Lord is its God!

When Obadiah, a simple priest, saw the High Priest emerge safely from the Sanctuary, eyes glowing like the sun, face bright as day, garments flashing like lightning, and in every respect like an angel of the LORD, his heart sank at the thought of having vilified such a blameless man. So dreadful was his contrition that his soul almost departed his body. The people took to the streets of the city with lanterns and musical instruments, escorting the High Priest home with song and dance, for they knew God had welcomed their penitence and forgiven their sins. Like a mourner at a wedding, crestfallen and shame-stricken, Obadiah let himself be swept along by them. While all around him rejoiced, singing and clapping, he trudged along with dull eyes on the ground like a pallbearer. The High Priest's home when they reached it was gleaming with lambent candlelight for the prominent guests invited to dine with him in celebration. Obadiah stood watching as the High Priest turned to face the people like a man giving thanks for a kindness done to him. "Go in peace, O righteous one!" he thought. "Go in peace, O modest one! Forgive me, I pray! Forgive my having thought evil of you when the evil was all mine."

Two burning tears of remorse rolled down Obadiah's cheeks. As Rabbi Hama bar Hanina has said: "Great is repentance, for it brings healing to the world," wherefore it is written in the fourteenth chapter of Hosea, "I will heal their backsliding, I will love them freely." And as Resh Lakish has said: "Great is repentance, for it turns crime to merit," and wherefore it is written by Ezekiel, "If the wicked turn from his wickedness and do that which is lawful and right, he shall live thereby." When the tears cried by Obadiah in his wretchedness were seen in heaven, his sentence was commuted and his crimes were deemed small sins and converted into credits, for love converts all sins. Such are tears and such are their wages. Rabbi Akiba said: *Happy are you, Israel! Before whom do you become clean? And who is it that purifies you? Your father which is in heaven, as it is said: And I will sprinkle clean water upon you and ye shall be clean. And further it says: Thou hope of Israel, the Lord!* Just as the fountain renders clean the unclean, so does the Holy One, Blessed be He, render clean Israel. Here ends the story of the simple priest Obadiah. May He who pardoned him pardon us and commute our harsh sentence and place Mercy before Justice and end our darkest Exile and build His house quickly and in our lifetime, amen and amen!

[Babylonian Talmud, Treatise Yoma, Folios 86a—b] Rabbi Hama bar Hanina said: Great is penitence, for it brings healing to the world, as it is said: I will heal their backsliding, I will love them freely.
[...]
Rab Judah pointed out this contradiction: It is written: "Return ye backsliding children, I will heal your backsliding," but it is also written: "For I am a lord unto you. And I will take you one of a city. And two of a family?" This is no contradiction: The one verse speaks [of a return] out of love or fear; the other, when it comes as a result of suffering.
[...]
Rabbi Johanan said: Great is repentance, for it overrides a prohibition of the Torah, as it is said: "If a man put away his wife, and she go from him, and become another man's, may he return unto her again? Will not that land be greatly polluted?" "But thou hast played the harlot with many lovers; and wouldest thou yet return to Me?" saith the Lord. Rabbi Jonathan said: Great is repentance, because it brings about redemption.

But the High Priest, who saw that wretched man in his sorrow and prided himself over him in his heart, though it is written: "Rejoice not when thine enemy falleth and let not thine heart be glad when he stumbleth." He marred his earthly stay beyond repair, on the holiest of days on which all fates are sealed for good or for bad. For this his soul was forbidden to return to its heavenly home and condemned to live again and again in the body of a priest until he shed bitter tears on the night of the Ninth of Av, when the Temple was destroyed. For on this day we have wept for generations, from a humbled and broken heart, for the ruined house.

BOOK
SEVEN

1
July 8, 2001

The 17th of Tammuz, 5761

Jesus Christ, it's hot. The city, faint with heat, is trapped in its sun-stricken daydreams. The walls of ruined ancient citadels flicker in the blue, blanketing haze, their pointed turrets stabbing the sun. The faded, melancholy colors of midsummer's flowers converge until they all look the same. The sightless pupils of the white marble statues stare reproachingly into space. The horned stone demon carved on the Firemen's Memorial at Riverside Drive and 100th Street irregularly spurts water from its rectangular mouth, spewing its greenish bile into a stone basin. At its foot, set among the cobblestones, there is a curious bronze plaque. Dismounted from his vehicle, a wagon driver raises his stick on a fallen beast of burden whose long neck is turned to him in anguished supplication. Above them stands a tall, winged, long-haired figure—an angel of the Lord, its sword drawn over man and beast alike.

The city is faint from the heat, but the large apartments of the blissfully rich stay pleasantly cool. Their controlled climate has its occupants shivering with cold and gratitude. Andrew, too, has decided to leave the air conditioner on tonight. He has taken the comforter from the top shelf of the closet where Angie put it while doing her spring cleaning and pulled it up to his neck, seeking in vain to find some comfort in it. He is praying for sleep. He needs it now more than ever. What a terrible month June has been, a month of horrors! He hasn't begun to process the latest events, hasn't absorbed what has happened. He has simply tried to ride them out and survive, one day at a time.

The air conditioner drones with a wet clatter. Why is it that every time you're sold a silent air conditioner it sounds like an old outboard motor after a year? Not that it matters. Nothing matters anymore. He has to sleep. He has to rise fresh enough in the morning to finish the damned article that has taken a year off his life. He shuts his eyes tight, desperately seeking sleep. Although he is still awake, his eyelids have begun to twitch of their own accord. The visions he sees are frighteningly vivid. The world is a mad, hallucinatory inferno—as if painted by Hieronymus Bosch. Red, boiling blood runs in the streets. The walls have been breached, the besieged city has fallen. The cries of raped women mingle with the bestial roars of the plunderers. A massacre is under way, a naked, vicious, foul slaughter. Men and women, young and old, are cut down indiscriminately, run through with a wild animal fury by spears, swords, and daggers. It is murder at its filthiest and bloodiest—rhythmic, nonstop, almost intimate. The burly arms of the soldiers wield their weapons like butchers' knives, cutting through bone, gristle, and fat. Stomachs are slowly sliced open. Greenish-gray intestines, looking more like pallid sea creatures than anything human, spill from them. Punctured lungs, bared to the sunlight with unspeakable savagery, wheeze in and out while jetting a crimson serum. Pregnant women are thrown to the ground. The swollen mounds of their bellies are a game won by whoever can slit them open most expertly, spear their unborn babies with a sword, and wave them high in the air like little red flags.

The distant voices are out of sync with the vision, like the uncoordinated sound track of an old movie. This split-second delay has a grating, nerve-racking effect and makes him acutely, violently ill. His stomach is turning; a vile-tasting acidic bile climbs up his esophagus, burning its way up his throat and into his mouth. If only the sound were synchronized, it would be like watching a Hollywood movie. The blood would be ketchup, the screams special effects. All would come to its appointed end and be forgotten, after which one could rest. But the horror goes on and on, replicated each time with the same nightmarish exactness. A large, hairy, muscular hand grips a baby's soft skull, swings it in a perfect arc, and smashes it against a stone wall smeared with clotted blood and grayish-white bits of brain. The little head bursts open with surprising ease, splitting along the touchingly vulnerable, heavenly-smelling soft spot of the cranium that anxious parents fret about in the first few months of a baby's life. Her eyes bulging with terror, mouth opened wide, the young mother stands paralyzed with horror, screaming as loud as she can. Her scream is inaudible. Either it has died within her or the horror it contains has driven it to frequencies too high for the human ear.

2

July 8, 2001

The 17th of Tammuz, 5761

One a.m. Andrew woke with a cry. He looked around wildly, unsure of his whereabouts. He was upright in bed—he must have sat up in his sleep—sweating and aching as if after some great exertion. Reluctantly, he let his mind take him back to the frightful scene from which he had been snatched. "What?" he gasped. "What?" A high-pitched sob, almost a howl, burst out of him—the uncontrollable sob of a terrified child—and turned into a fit of dry, hiccupy moans that came faster and faster until stopping as abruptly, as if running into a wall inside him, leaving him breathless and dazed. The silently screaming young mother would not go away. She remained before his eyes with a horrendous clarity. Why didn't she scream? His own helplessness made him want to cry. *Why don't you scream, damn it! Why?* It was somehow his fault. He must open his eyes. He must! They mustn't stay closed a minute longer. If they did, it would go on all night. It would go on forever. He had to get out of bed, go to the sink, and splash cold water on his face.

Andrew threw off the blanket, jumped out of bed in a single motion, and staggered to the bathroom, his skin bristling from the artificial cold. Although he knew that turning on the light would help him wake up and throw off his nightmare, something in him insisted on clinging to the horror of the dark. He groped his way to the sink and stood there, forgetful of why he had come. The baby's soft skull split in two like a ripe watermelon, splattering over the stone wall. *Keep your eyes open! Don't shut them whatever you do!* But they *were* open. They were open wide and getting used to the darkness. The dim shape in the mirror was his reflection. What was he doing here? Right: he had come to pee. He went to the toilet, lifted the seat, and began pulling down his pajama bottoms. His eyes were closing again. Too tired to stand, he lowered the seat and sat, swallowing a groan of defeat. He felt as bruised and exhausted as if he had been beaten. Every muscle was sore. His whole body felt black-and-blue.

Andrew's urine flowed slowly. He wasn't used to peeing sitting down. He cradled his head in his hands, feeling his sharp elbows dig into the pale skin of his thighs. How tired he was. He was dying for a sip of water. Its coldness would wash away his dream. Yet he did nothing about it. Sticky with sudden perspiration, he rose, pulled up his pajamas, and hobbled back to bed without flushing the toilet or wetting his face.

The visions began again as soon as his head touched the pillow. The little skull glides slowly on a perfect, silent arc toward its fore-ordained end. Its tiny brain spills out of it intact, dashed against the wall. Andrew felt nauseous. Afraid to throw up all over the bed, he jumped up and ran to the bathroom, colliding with the furniture. He quickly lifted the toilet seat, kneeled, and leaned over it until his head was almost touching the water. The smell of fresh urine made him feel even more violently ill. He retched and spewed a quick, sharp stream of vomit. Its filthy porridge splattered into the yellow water, spraying his face. The sickening smell set off another, longer fit of vomiting. It was as though his churning stomach was trying to eject itself from his body. Another minute passed. The paroxysms weakened. There was nothing left to throw up. Pushing against the cold toilet, Andrew rose heavily. He went to the sink, turned on the hot water, and scrubbed his face and hands until they were red. Although the water grew increasingly hot, he could not tear his hands away from it. In the end he snatched them away, red and itching, and switched on the light to make sure he was really awake. Bloodshot eyes, sunken in their sockets, stared at him from the mirror—set in a pale, puffy face covered by a gray bristle of beard. He had just shaved that morning—where had it come from?

Another, less intense wave of nausea racked his empty stomach. His muscles and joints felt like jelly. Too depleted to turn out the light or even cover himself, he dragged himself back to bed and lay in another round of nightmarish semi-sleep. Again and again the little head was smashed against the wall while the wild-eyed mother screamed silently, trapped in an endless cycle of horror. Cold, jarringly rapid tremors of fear ran through him. His mind tried desperately to protect itself against the horrific vision—to weave soft, silky threads of numbness around it, like an oyster forming a pearl around a sharp-edged object irritating its tender innards. Finally his visions grew more abstract, their details fading until all that was left was a skull's elliptical course and the circle of a screaming mouth. And yet a part of him refused to be sedated. It fought back, seething within him. Horror was everywhere: hanging over him, hiding around the corner, creeping under the floorboards. There was no respite from it. At any moment the illusory bubble of silence might burst, releasing a black wave of terror that would submerge him completely.

3

July 10, 2001

The 19th of Tammuz, 5761

Nine a.m. Andrew had been sleeping for more than twenty-four hours straight. His violent stomach virus had left him so limp that he could barely make it to the bathroom and back. He couldn't swallow a thing. Just thinking of food or water made him gag. He had thrown up several more times during the night, and his loose bowels kept expelling a gruel-like liquid that was halfway between stool and water. Later that evening, he felt better. Though he still hadn't eaten, he managed to drink and keep down a glass of water. The night went by passably and in the morning, despite feeling weak and running a slight fever, he was strong enough to get out of bed, shower, and put on fresh clothes. Sitting on the living-room couch, he slowly sipped a cup of tea (coffee was still out of the question) while staring dully out the window at the gray, depressing light of a summer morning. The day was as foggily dreary as was his mind. The night's horrible visions—the effect, so it would seem, of his virus—were almost gone, their place taken by other, more familiar images. Ann Lee's

lovingly mocking smiles. Her braids falling on her shoulders as on
the day he saw her in the Hungarian Pastry Shop. (Lately, she had
been wearing her hair in a more adult fashion.) The clear, ironic
vibrato of her voice over the telephone. The hint of a smile on Andrew's face changed to an uncertain scowl as he remembered their
last meeting at Beauty Bar. How hard and cold she had been. She
was no longer playacting as she was on that absurd, tragicomic
night at Cipriani's. This time it was for real. She had reached the
point of no return. There was no other way of understanding her
words. A piercing sorrow shot through him. He shut his eyes and
opened them again. The elegant but dreary apartment was like a
gray prison cell, a desolate land to which he had been banished. He
would never be able to stay in here alone until August. He would
go out of his mind.

August! What would happen in August? It startled him to realize that he had gone on thinking of August as if Ann Lee were still
coming with him to Cape Cod. Their separation had come as such
a shock that it hadn't penetrated. All their—his—summer plans
had revolved around their three weeks on the Cape. It would be the
longest vacation they had ever spent together—except, of course,
it wasn't happening. What was he going to do? Go to the Cape by
himself? Bury himself in the solitude of an empty house, once so
happy and filled with life, that would be as airless a dungeon as his
apartment? Cold, heavy fingers gripped Andrew's heart, their hard
tips digging into its tender tissues. How could he have not thought
about August? What was he going to do? Invite friends? The very
idea of picking up the phone and dialing someone made him ill. Not
go to the Cape at all? But what would he do all month? The city,
in August, was infernal—night or day, it made no difference. You
couldn't go out. No one would be around. Everyone would be gone,
taking advantage of the long academic vacation: in summer homes,
on family cruises, abroad. He alone would be stranded in an empty

apartment, by himself in a huge ghost town of a city. If only there were someone to talk to. If only he could talk to Linda now.

Linda! Why hadn't he thought of it? He would go to the Cape with them! With Linda, with Rachel and Alison, with good old George! There was plenty of room. He would sleep in the cottage, rent a car to be independent, and join them for meals now and then. Andrew laughed aloud with childish glee. He would eat well, sleep well, run on the beach every day. He would rent a bike and go on long, healthful rides with Rachel and Alison. He and Alison would finally have time together. Just thinking of her and her puppyish frown of concentration gave him a warm feeling, something to look forward to. They would go clamming, have picnics on the rocks by the sea, pick fresh corn at Morning Glory Farm and boil the sweet cobs in a big pot—three minutes and not a second more! He would buy fresh pies from the bakery every day: peach pies, raspberry and blackberry pies, and, best of all, those wonderful wild blueberry pies whose fruit maintained their texture even when baked. He would encourage them to stay for August, George, too, of course. Why shouldn't they? They would still be on vacation. Why return to the hellish heat of the city when they could remain with him in the most wonderful place in the world?

The apartment grew bigger and brighter at the mere thought of this possibility, and filled with rich oceanic grays and vivid maritime blues. The mist rolled in from the sea, shrouding the horizon with a dreamlike glow. A monochromatic play of color fanned out on the shoreline, shimmering on the wet sand, reflecting the early evening sky. Andrew's heart swelled with bliss and longing. It would be their best summer together, the best summer of their lives! Elated, he rose from his seat and ran to the telephone, his fingers quickly dialing the beloved number that they knew by heart, the number of their house in Cape Cod.

4

As usual, Linda picked up the receiver at the first ring. Euphorically, Andrew began to tell her his plan. There was a heavy, foreboding silence at the other end of the line. Andrew, his enthusiasm undampened, went on describing all the wonderful things that awaited them on Cape Cod. Linda interrupted him curtly. The friendly, bantering tone they had used with each other since deciding their divorce was amicable disappeared all at once. Her strained, grating voice made her sound years older, almost an old woman. His heart sank.

5

I honestly don't know what makes you think you can come waltzing into our lives whenever you crave some domestic bliss. Doesn't it occur to you that I might have plans of my own? A life of my own? Do you really think I sit by the phone waiting for you to call? Waiting for you to decide that you're sorry for what you did to me—to all of us—and come home? You know, for such a smart man, you're awfully stupid. You never did understand what you did to me, did you? What you did to Rachel, to little Alison! She was a tiny thing when you went off to live your picture-perfect life across town, at a safe distance from us. And do you know what the worst part of it was? The shittiest part of it all? It was that you never even let me— any of us—feel angry. God knows how you did it, but you got us all to play your game of the devoted papa bird who visits the nest now and then for an hour or two. I went along with it, too, I admit. Don't ask me why. Maybe because I convinced myself that it was good for Alison. Maybe I did it out of weakness. But you, you should have had the decency not to exploit that weakness to create your own convenient little guilt-free, responsibility-free reality. You know how long it took me to get over what you've done to me? You know what strength it took to build a new life for myself? I can't believe you can think of coming up here now to spend the ideal summer with your ideal family after smashing everything to pieces. Are you fucking insane, Andy? Are you fucking out of your mind?"

6

Andrew went on clutching the receiver, forgetting to put it back. His cheeks felt as hot as an oven. His giddy joy of a few minutes ago had gone as quickly as it had come, leaving a cold black pit into which, with one big spasm of pain, he was now falling.

Something was beeping. He stared blankly at the receiver, then put it down automatically. For a long while he stood there, shocked and unable to move. The awful things Linda had said ran through his mind without registering. The flush in his cheeks spread to his burning ears and neck. He felt a deep shame, a humiliation greater than any he had ever known—and with it, a paralyzing sense of guilt. The insidious thought occurred to him that Rachel might have been by Linda's side. Could she have heard it all and done nothing to stop her mother? Not even asked to talk to him herself? Andrew started to say something out loud, to whom he didn't know. His voice shook so badly that he couldn't understand his own half-articulate words. He shut his mouth tight, afraid of what he might say. His upper lip quivered like a small boy's. His face sagged. He took a deep breath, desperately trying to get hold of himself. A dam inside him was about to burst and flood everything. He mustn't let it! Nothing would remain intact if it did, nothing would survive such a cataclysm.

Andrew clenched his hands into fists, his nails cutting into his soft skin until it nearly bled. The pain was warm, comforting. As long as he felt it, he was still in control. He wished that the pain would settle in and stay there, maintaining its intensity, never losing its sharp edge. Yet it had already begun to recede as his alarmed body dispatched hormones to the disaster site, protecting itself. Little by little he unclenched his predatory nails that were loath to release their prey. Raising his hand to eye level, he stared dumbly at the deep, red, crescent-shaped marks he had made in them before hobbling to the couch, feeling weightless as though in a dream. Slowly, he sat down, leaned back against the pillows, took off his slippers, and hugged his knees to his chest as if trying to get as close to his feet as he could. Then he resumed looking at the dull gray light shining through the window.

7

Hell, hell on earth! Ironclad skies hang low above the heavy, gray, rasping air. The pavement melts beneath the feet, but the heat-stricken homeless people, still wrapped in their midwinter rags, lie on it helplessly, unable to move. Their maggoty bodies swell from day to day like giant larvae in which wasps have laid their lethal eggs. West Nile virus has claimed three victims to date, all slum dwellers. The crime rates have soared all month long in synchrony with the temperature. In Queens, the longest power failure in the city's history is now in its fourth day. Subway service has been completely disrupted and there are long lines at the bus stops. Bengali, Yemenite, and Pakistani grocery store owners, their refrigerators disabled, dump defrosted, rotten meat in the street, where it stinks like decaying corpses. Ambulances sound their sirens until they are hoarse. Police vans wail like stray dogs.

Yesterday, a poor little woman, three feet tall and wearing nothing but a ridiculous-looking pink tutu, walked slowly westward
on 42nd Street—hunched over with despair and weeping bitterly,
tears running down her misshapen face, swallowed in the folds of
her shriveled cheeks.

8

July 21, 2001

—————

The 1st of Av, 5761

Eleven thirty a.m. The heat wave clung to the city, but Andrew, who had not gone out for three days, was having re-
current chills. The air conditioner was getting noisier. It had been
running for seventy-two straight hours, recycling the stale, stuffy
air of the apartment through clenched teeth. An empty cup stood
in the sink. Andrew had drunk his coffee quickly, as though per-
forming a chore. His laptop had not been turned on. Half the day
had passed without pressing the power switch and getting down to
work. The last few days gave him no peace. They hung over him
day and night like the unrelentingly overcast sky. The more he
thought about them, the less sense he could make of them. He was
lost in an infinite labyrinth, holding a torn thread leading nowhere.

He had to finish the article, he simply had to! It was all he had
left. But how was he to do it? How was he even to begin? He put
out a hand to the computer and snatched it back as though he feared
being burned. Should he reread what he had written? How could
he work himself back into the mood of it? It didn't seem possible
that he had written its opening section just a few months ago. It
felt like ages! The smooth white pages crinkled in his hands. Their
letters danced before his eyes without becoming words, a swarm

of little flies whose wings never touched. What would become of him? It was hard to believe he had ever finished anything. Could he really have published two books with Stanford University Press? Edited an anthology of essays that won the 1995 Whiting Award? And what about all his articles? He couldn't possibly have been their author.

He propped his head in his hands and shut his eyes, trying to concentrate. His mind was in a fog. It was an effort to keep his heavy eyelids from drooping. Was he awake? Asleep? Who could say? I'm cold. I'm sad. I'm sick. I want to crawl back into bed, pull the quilt over me, and never get up again. I want to die. Something was droning behind his forehead as if an old motor had been left running there. *I'm weak. I feel empty.* He needed something to fill him, something hot, hot and salty. Soup! Pea soup! No, chicken soup! Chicken soup with noodles. A sick man's food, a wintry comfort food. How he would have liked to hear George's soft voice now—its modest, scholarly tone, the pleasing pauses for emphasis in its carefully phrased sentences. Whatever he said sounded right, clean, and uncluttered. With his short, graying beard and twinkling eyes, he was like a good grandfather. What would become of him? How would it all end? *I miss my wife's husband.*

A pang of ravenous hunger brushed the cobwebs of sleep from Andrew's mind, making him open his eyes and get up. Lunch! He must eat something, right away. He reached out to turn off the computer, forgetting he had never turned it on, his indignant fingers encountering its unraised lid without knowing what they had touched. He looked around him. Certain he had forgotten something important but unable to remember what it was, he headed for the door. The sharp ring of the telephone brought him up short. His heart skipped a beat. Who could it be? Linda? Rachel? Ann Lee? Both fear and hope vanished as he heard the phone say, "Hello! This is your last chance to eliminate your credit card debt!

Please contact us as soon as you can at the following number. This is a recorded announcement." The electronic voice recited some numbers and fell still with a metallic click that echoed in the room. Andrew stared at the phone, trying to quell his anxiety. The announcement wasn't meant for him. It was just an advertisement sent all over the city. There was nothing the matter with his credit card. He mustn't be paranoid, he can't turn every stupid little thing into an omen of doom. He strode to the elevator, rang for it several times, and then, impatient with hunger, headed down the emergency stairs.

9

A dull sky glowered over the city. The sun, more like a strange, cindery moon, made one think of an apocalyptic, dystopian film about the morning after a nuclear cataclysm. The two naked stone male figures on the building's front lost their sharp outline in the haze and turned the color of concrete, tormented by the knowledge that they were at last about to buckle beneath the weight of the thousands of tons of stone, iron, and glass that they've been carrying on their shoulders for more than eighty years. Andrew passed them quickly, stunned by the heat and humidity's assault on his drowsy senses. "Good morning, Professor," said the doorman, who was hosing down the sidewalk to cool it off. "Still on vacation, eh?" Andrew muttered a vague answer and headed for Broadway. The doorman's tone struck him as audacious. What did he want from him? And what made him say "Good morning" when it was already afternoon? Was he alluding to a professor's easy life? All these blue-collar workers don't believe we've ever done an honest day's work, do they? As far as they're concerned, we're on vacation all year round. He would have done anything right now to trade places with such a crude, uneducated man, to lay down the hellish torture of writing and live a simple, ordinary life. How wonderful to have no more to do than contentedly spray the sidewalk like a pissing horse while thinking of nothing, nothing at all!

Andrew's chest heaved. The hunger that had driven him into the inferno of the street was turning into a bilious, sick feeling. He knew he had to eat something but had no idea what. What could fill the void of a wasted morning of work? Not only was his appetite gone, the very thought of food made him gag. He kept walking absently up 110th Street toward Broadway, considering his options. There was the little Chinese restaurant on the corner of Broadway and 109th. There was the nice sushi bar next to the supermarket. There was Koronet Pizza, boasting one of the biggest, if not greatest, slices in the city. One by one, he vetoed them all.

Broadway was noisy as usual, its traffic spewing a thick smog of exhaust. A downtown train rumbled under his vibrating feet, causing the metal grates in the sidewalk to ring an alarm. Although it wasn't clear where he was going, he was impatient for the light to change. How lovable New York was at some times of the year and how detestable it was in summer! What was he doing here? He should have packed his bags and gone to the Cape. Rich oceanic grays and vivid maritime blues filled the air. The mist rolled in from the sea, shrouding the horizon with a dreamlike glow. A monochromatic play of color fanned out on the shoreline, shimmering on the wet sand, reflecting the evening sky.

For a second, Andrew felt immersed in the stillness of forgetfulness. He awoke from it with a bang. Linda's brutal, irrevocable words came back to him like a punch to the gut, nearly making him double over on the sidewalk. How could she have done it to him? How could she have said such things after all their years together? And yet she was right. He knew she was right: that was the worst part of it. He had to breathe deeply, he mustn't lose control. He straightened

up and took a breath of leaden air. The light was still red. As though
unable to bear the indignity of standing where he was a moment longer, he stepped off the sidewalk and dashed between the speeding
cars toward the island in mid-street, as angry drivers honked.

A few steps brought him there, sweaty and panting. Coming to
a stop as though awaiting further instructions, he wiped his face
with a white shirtsleeve, now more like a strip of gray rag, and
tried catching his breath. Taxis sped by as though on a racetrack,
trailing black wakes of burned diesel fuel that refused to dissolve
and snaked sluggishly through the muggy air. Where was he?
What was he doing here? Right: he was on Broadway. He was
crossing to the east side of it. He was looking for a place to eat.
His glance wandered to the empty bench where his homeless man
had always sat, hoping to see his comfortingly huge, blanket-clad
form. He wasn't there. Why should he be? He was gone for good.
In his place was a stout, Slavic-looking woman, her short, pudgy
fingers resting on the handles of a wheelchair that contained a
man so old that he scarcely looked human. He, too, was very fat,
as pale and flabby as a giant maggot. The two of them regarded
the sooty fumes in silence as though sitting in a green park. The
man was a waterfall of wrinkled, loose skin; it cascaded from his
cheeks, chin, and bare arms. A thick, feebly throbbing, sausage-
like tongue flopped from his half-opened mouth. Andrew stared at
him, hypnotized by the large, purple tongue. It was so ghastly that
he couldn't stop looking at it. How much tongue could fit into one
mouth? Where had the man kept it all the years of his youth? Was
there such a thing as a buried tongue, like a buried penis? Surgeons
had to cut a ligament to get it to drop and be bigger. He had read
about that somewhere, perhaps at the cardiologist's.

The woman stirred and rose from the bench, jostling the heavy,
lifeless body in the wheelchair. Brusquely, she wiped the man's
drooling tongue with her bare palm and then, without bothering to

wipe it off, she gripped the wheelchair's handles and began strenuously pushing its heavy load away from Andrew. Still mesmerized, it was all he could do to keep from turning around to follow
the old man, who was having a second, ugly infancy that brought
no parent joy. Andrew thought bitterly of the annual visit to Walter's grave. Jamila would remain standing by the car at a tactful
distance while Andrew and Ethel approached the sunken headstone overrun by the frostbitten grass. A cold wind would blow
through the trees, ruffling Ethel's thinning gray hair as she sat in
her wheelchair, staring with empty eyes that showed no awareness
of where she was. Andrew would stand behind her, his hands on
the rubber-coated handles, gazing at the distant hills between two
evergreens that framed the view. She, too, would die soon. She
didn't have much time left. And he? How much did he have? Not
that much. Thirty or thirty-five years—forty with luck. He, too,
would grow gross and mammalian, his body an old ruin. Would
his tongue stick out, too? Andrew slid his tongue awkwardly
around his mouth, experimenting to see how far it would extend. It
barely passed the line of his teeth. But suppose the surgeons cut its
ligaments. Would it suddenly flop out, frighteningly purple, and
hang down to his chin? How did the old man not choke on such a
tongue, how could he breathe?

Enough! He couldn't stand here all day thinking thoughts that
led nowhere. It was so humid. Who could live in a city like this?
It was impossible to breathe. A taxi. He had to find a taxi. An air-
conditioned one. It had to have air-conditioning.

10

Andrew threw himself into a cab that screeched to a stop, cutting off cars that honked in an irritable chorus, and slammed

the door behind him like a man on the run. The taxi started up
Broadway with a lurch, heading north. Why had he hailed it?
Where was he going? All he had wanted was something to eat.
The driver, an impassive Sikh in a blue turban, seemed unfazed
by the lack of a destination. Andrew leaned back against the soft
headrest, his eyes on the neatly tucked-in turban. It was spotless,
immaculate, its sky blue, reinforced by the breezy chill of the air
conditioner, creating a fragile, lustrous illusion that Andrew surrendered to eagerly despite its unreality. Rich oceanic grays and
vivid maritime blues filled the taxi. The mist rolled in from the
sea, shrouding the horizon with a dreamlike glow. Those happy,
blissful days on the Cape! In mid-July, the sea bass season would
begin. The restaurants would display special menus with bass as
the entrée, vying to see who could come up with the most original
recipe: charred bass with stir-fried vegetables, bass in a buttery
white wine sauce on a bed of saffron risotto, bass baked in Atlantic sea salt with garden herbs. He and Linda, great believers in
local traditions, never missed marking the occasion. They invited
friends, all bringing intriguing wines and frosty six-packs of beer,
for great, merry fish feasts. Andrew would go to the fishermen's
wharf and buy a huge fillet of sea bass, which he roasted in a marinade of olive oil, rosemary, and lemon juice and served with great
fanfare at the large porch table looking out on the sea. *The sun is
going down now. It's already past eight, late enough for a sunset dinner before the mosquitoes come out. A low sun gilds the clouds hanging
over the sea and glints in the windows of the houses across the bay. The
sailboats, back at anchor, rock gently on the rippling water, their tightly
folded sails swaying like hammocks. The clink of glasses. The merry
chime of knives and forks. A metal ice bucket, wine and beer peeking out
from it like flowers from a vase. Steamed baby potatoes in butter. Fresh
tomatoes, a green salad, three flavors of ice cream. Children frolicking
on the lawn, their cries of joy rebounding from the gray rafters of the*

porch. Dogs chasing imaginary rabbits through the bushes, returning filthy with their tongues out, drunk with the bliss of being alive. Andrew swayed excitedly in his seat, feeling the bliss of it. Fish. Yes, fish! A light, summery food, the food of the life-lover. He would have a fish meal at Barney Greengrass the Sturgeon King's.

The driver was as unruffled by Andrew's sudden command to take him to Amsterdam and 86th Street as he had been by his silence until now. He nodded acquiescently, worked his way into the left lane, and made a U-turn, heading downtown on Broadway, turning left at 86th, and dropping Andrew off on the west corner of Amsterdam by the entrance to Barney Greengrass's famous restaurant. Andrew, calmed by the cool quiet of the taxi's backseat, felt his appetite restored. Barney Greengrass's had never lost its charm for him. He liked the rough, familiar manners of the waiters, the brownish-gray Formica tables that hadn't been changed in years, and the logo of Poseidon that seemed less a Greek god and more like a brawny Lower East Side Jewish gangster from the 1920s. The ancient wallpaper with its grimy lilac bushes and large-wheeled carriages occupied by elegant passengers added a vintage touch that justified, at least partially, the sky-high prices. He paid the driver, tipping him generously, and stepped briskly, or so he thought, out of the cab, seeking to make the transition between one air-conditioned space and the next as rapid as possible.

He was surprised to find the place almost deserted. It brought him rudely down to earth from the mental lift he had gotten in the taxi. He had only been to the restaurant on weekends, when long, lively lines stretched in front of it, waiting patiently to be admitted to a fabled sanctuary of gourmet New York. The loud, laughing conversations at sunlit tables facing the street made Sunday brunches feel more like cultural happenings than meals in a Jewish restaurant. The weekday establishment he now saw was a less festive, more somber place. A fat man with horn-rimmed glasses and a trim beard sat in the corner talking to an older woman who appeared to be his mother. Two grim-looking, overly made-up women sat whispering in another corner. The place felt old, sleepy, and charmless. Andrew, disappointed, took a seat and waited for the bored young waiter to bring him a menu. What did he want? So the place didn't look quite the same—why should that make him so uneasy? Was it the lighting? The air-conditioning? No, it was something else. He had never before been here by himself, had never come here just to eat. He had always had company, usually of the other sex, with whom he could share the nostalgia of a place where so many memories and longings, his own and the city's, joined together. Where was the damn waiter? What was taking him so long? The restaurant was practically empty. What kind of service was this?

As though reading Andrew's mind, the elegantly unshaven waiter, a good-looking young man, finally appeared and handed him a menu. Andrew picked it up and put it down at once: its clear plastic cover was streaked with sticky grease stains that smelled faintly but stubbornly of fish. He made a face. The optimism of the taxi ride was gone, leaving him in empty solitude. He glanced around, hoping something might revive the old magic. No, it wasn't the same. Its faux-antiqueness now just looked run-down, the shabbiness of a place whose owners were too cheap to renovate. Its nostalgia was cloying. The airy weekend alchemy that had turned gray Formica and thirty-year-old wallpaper into chic decor was missing, perhaps because its dull colors weren't enlivened by the latest fashions on lithe, young, brightly dressed, snugly fitted bodies. *Things fall apart, the center cannot hold* . . . enough! Concentrate on the menu!

Andrew cast a desultory look at the fish and seafood that were listed in no apparent order, jumbled together like a basket of baby eels. Some things he was familiar with and some he wasn't. What should he have? Nothing on the menu appealed to him. The smoked whitefish was for those hale and hearty enough to cope with its strong, brash flavor. Some scrambled eggs or a salad? His gaze wandered off into space, lingering on the gray lilacs growing in tangled clumps between the carriages. Nostalgia was only for the healthy-minded. You had to be comfortably situated in the present to be able to smile at your longing for the past.

The waiter, suddenly efficient, returned too quickly to take Andrew's order. Unable to focus, he had difficulty choosing, the waiter's impatience arousing his temporarily lulled anxiety. What should he have, for God's sake? Smoked salmon? Eggs? A salad? He turned the menu this way and that, studying the appetizers. Smoked fish. Pickled fish. Salted fish. "Herring," he was astounded to hear himself say. It was as if someone else were speaking. "I'll have the herring with pumpernickel, please."

The waiter arched his brows. "Is that all, sir? Are you sure you don't want something else with your herring?" The way he said "herring" could only be interpreted as disdain for the miserly customer who had ordered the cheapest item on the menu.

Andrew looked up in bewilderment and shook his head. "No, thank you. For now, I'll just have the herring. Maybe afterward . . . ."

The waiter nodded, his scorn growing as he realized how small the tip would be. Andrew watched him take the menu away. What had gotten into him? Why herring? He didn't like briny fish. Was it too late to change the order to two scrambled eggs with whole-wheat toast? No, he wasn't up to facing more mockery. He would eat his damn herring, pay, and leave. There was nothing else to do.

Andrew took a sip of water from the glass in front of him and looked around again. How many times had he been in this place? Too many to remember. Two years ago he had sat here, perhaps at this very table, with an old friend who had just become his lover. He had brought her for a Sunday brunch on their first morning after sleeping together, as proud of the authenticity of the place as if he had created it. Their lunch together seemed to be taken out of the last pages of a great Jewish American novel. They saw none other than Philip Roth talking to Ted Solotaroff and a younger man, who was probably his son Ivan. They were at the table up by the window, accompanied by a surprisingly muscular old man, leaning on crutches, whose Israeli accent was too strong to misplace. Ever since then, his physical intimacy with this woman was linked in his mind to Philip Roth and the membranous texture of the eggs and the sour taste of the rye bread she had ordered. He felt his stomach turn over, whether from hunger or disgust he couldn't say. But why be disgusted? There was nothing disgusting about her. She was nice, clean, and polite like all the rest of them.

His feeling of loneliness was getting worse. He could feel it closing in on him like the walls of a deep pit. *Ethel's thinning gray hair ripples in the evening breeze, her unseeing eyes staring ahead. She gives no sign of knowing where she is or feeling anything. Jamila leans against the car, her heavy arms crossed on her chest, waiting patiently. The children's cries of joy rebound from the gray rafters of the porch, mingled with the breathless barks of the dogs scampering through the low hedges.* No, not here in public. He mustn't give in to it, he mustn't.

A white plate appeared as though from nowhere, cast provocatively, Andrew thought, on the table. The long, bloody piece of sliced herring made him think of a castrated penis, its horizontal cuts exposing an interior that looked full of pus. How could one eat such a thing? What on earth had made him order herring? *The old man's huge tongue sticking limply out of his mouth, hanging down like a thick, purple penis.* Andrew tried not to think of it and took a bite of the herring, shutting his eyes as though swallowing a medicine. The slimy, intolerably salty fish felt half-alive as he chewed it. It slithered down his throat like an eel and made him choke. He gagged, grabbed his napkin, and spat the half-chewed contents of his mouth into it. Folding it as many times as he could, he stuck its small square under his plate and out of sight. Glancing around to make sure no one had seen him, he drained his glass of water to rid his mouth of the scaly, finny taste, took out his wallet, quickly extracted a twenty-dollar bill, put it under the plate beside the little paper sarcophagus, and left without asking for change.

Although the torrid air hit him full blast, he was feeling too sick and hounded to pay it any attention. He strode uptown with long steps, glancing over his shoulder from time to time without knowing why. He halted for a moment at the corner of 87th Street, crossed the intersection, and had almost reached 88th when he was jolted by the thought that the waiter must be clearing his plate at that very moment and discovering the incriminating evidence. His heart pounded. It mustn't be allowed to happen! He had to go back, to get there before the plate was cleared. As if rehearsing his course of action, he shut his right hand like a pickpocket's over the imagined napkin and slipped it into his pocket. He could all but feel the revolting fish and smell its sticky odor as he furtively took out the small package and threw it in a garbage can. He saw it all clearly, right down to the look of surprise on the cashier's face when he returned. There would be anxious questions. Had he forgotten something? Was something the matter with the food? *Can we offer you something else on the house?* They were too well known at Greengrass's to risk harming their reputation. But the waiter! His sickening mockery fueled Andrew's fears. He might think he was a thief. They might detain him, threaten to call the police, insist on going through his pockets. What would he say? He needed a good alibi. He would say he had forgotten his cell phone! Cell phones were forgotten all the time, right? No, he would never go back there, never! He wouldn't even pass it in a taxi. He wouldn't let a driver turn up Amsterdam. Let them take Broadway, goddamn it! He had to find a taxi, an air-conditioned one. He had to get home, quick!

11

The taxi jumped lanes wildly, weaving in and out of the traffic like a speedboat. The driver, a bald, nervous man, kept stepping on the gas, missing the next green light, and cursing gutturally as he slammed on the brakes. The air conditioner hardly worked and the stale air reaching the backseat was lukewarm. Andrew clung to the door handle to maintain his balance and keep the savagely careening vehicle from making him seasick. He lacked the nerve to tell the driver to slow down. A fight with a hotheaded cabdriver was more than he could handle; it was better to grit his teeth and bear it. The streets flew by: 106th, 107th. 108th. How would he keep his nausea down until they got there? If it weren't so muggy, he would get off now. Then 109th Street. Another minute, a minute and a half. *Just don't barf now!* He leaned forward, gulping the cooler air in the front of the car and feebly asked to be let off at 110th and Broadway rather than on Riverside Drive. Not only couldn't he take being bounced around another second, he didn't want the doorman to see him getting out of a taxi in the middle of the day. Of course, that was ridiculous. Who was keeping track of his movements? Still, he felt transparent, as if anyone could read him like a book.

The taxi screeched to a stop at the corner, throwing Andrew forward so abruptly that he almost banged his head against the filthy screen separating him from the driver. He opened the door, threw the man a ten-dollar bill, and fled as if still running from the restaurant. Ankle-deep water was flowing in the gutter. His foot, suspended in midair, avoided stepping in it at the last minute. Where was it coming from? Some kids must have opened a fire hydrant to cool off. Planting his foot on the dry sidewalk, he pulled the rest of himself after it over the filthy stream—only to run smack into the black preacher, who was standing there in dishevelment. His crazed eyes stared at Andrew without seeing him. His mouth was opened in a shout. His hat was pushed back on his head, his tie was awry, and his collar stuck laughably up from his cheap polyester suit. "'Allelujah! 'Allelujah! 'Allelujah!" he shrieked in a hoarse, pitiless voice like a desperate, crazy old raven picking at his own feathers. The cries were not his usual, powerful but controlled ones. They were helpless, maniacal screams.

Andrew turned toward Riverside Drive, putting as much distance between himself and the preacher as he could. He felt a mixture of pity, anger, and fear. *Get ahold of yourself. Don't fall apart on me now. Don't lose it.* He broke into a run down 110th Street, his lungs on fire with the hot, heavy air trapped in them, dashed into the lobby of the building, and crossed it quickly to the elevator without stopping by the mailbox. It was silly, but he didn't want to run into the doorman. His foot drummed nervously on the floor as he waited for the elevator to arrive.

12

The sound of the shutting door and the precise click of its locks calmed him down a bit. It made him feel that his fears could be contained. He took off his shoes, kicked them into a corner, and tossed his sweaty socks after them, too tired to take them to the hamper. He wanted only to stand quietly with his eyes closed, feeling the reassuring reality of the parquet floor beneath his feet. The air conditioner, which he had forgotten to turn off, was still rattling away, weakly stirring the dense air like a propeller laboring to push a boat off a shore.

Andrew opened his eyes and surveyed the apartment as if he had not been in it for a long time. It was a mess. Dirty socks and underwear lay on the floor; unwashed dishes were piled in the sink with rotting food; a fifth column of black, greasy dust, the city's smoggy ambassador of ill will, covered the surfaces of things. How long had it been since anyone cleaned here? Where was Angie? He mentally reviewed the days, trying to remember which was which. No, she hadn't been here all week. He had been sick and home all the time. What had happened to her? He wandered from room to room like a stranger in his own house, oblivious of the view outside the windows. Angie's disappearance made him feel that everything was out of control. Where had she gone? She had left him without a word, without even saying good-bye! How could she just walk out on him? Everyone was deserting him. Where, why?

He had to calm down! There must be a logical explanation. Angie had worked for him for years, she would never do such a thing. He took deep breaths of the room's stale air. The explanation was somewhere. He could feel it hovering near him like a ghost. It wasn't just a matter of cleanliness, of the dirty dishes in the sink and the unwashed laundry. Angie was his one remaining link to the world, his last foothold in a widening gyre of emptiness.

Andrew went to the telephone on the kitchen counter, tripping over a pair of shoes and an empty paper bag on the floor. Seizing the receiver, his finger paused above the dial. Who should he call? Linda, of course . . . no, anyone but Linda! He would never call her again. Rachel! That was it: Rachel! They hadn't had a good talk in ages, he wanted so badly to speak to her. He began dialing her number in Princeton, humming a little snatch of something in his excitement, and froze on reaching the fourth digit. He had remembered! He knew what had happened to Angie! She had gone on her annual three-week vacation to Saint Kitts. They had discussed it. She had asked to go this year in July rather than August because a cousin of hers was getting married. She had even suggested finding him a temporary replacement, but Andrew had politely declined. It was too much to have to get used to someone new, he would get along without her for three weeks. How could he have forgotten? Everything made sense now. Everything was all right!

He emitted a nervous, involuntary chuckle. What a joke! He must tell Rachel. *You won't believe what happened to me a few minutes ago, sweetheart. Your father is getting senile!* He quickly dialed the rest of her number. The receiver came alive with anticipatory rings. The thought of talking with Rachel and amusing her with a funny anecdote filled him with incontrollable excitement.

The phone kept ringing. Lulled by its monotonous rhythm, he gave a start when he heard a deep masculine voice say, "Hi, this is Tom."

For a second, he couldn't place the name. Of course: Tom, Rachel's boyfriend! A nice young man. "Hi, Tom," he said. "How are you? This is Andrew Cohen."

There was an uncomfortable silence, then "Hi, Mr. Cohen, how are you?" Tom sounded confused.

"I'm fine, Tom, just fine. Is Rachel there?"

Another silence was followed by, "Mr. Cohen, Rachel and I haven't been together for quite a while. I thought you knew. She's not living here anymore."

Andrew caught his breath, feeling dizzy. He did know. They had broken up a month or two ago, maybe more. How could he have forgotten? He was losing his mind, there was no longer any doubt of it. His excruciating embarrassment caused him to break into a series of choked, broken apologies. "Oh, of course . . . Forgive me . . . I'm so sorry . . . I truly am sorry . . . Forgive me for bothering you . . . How are you feeling, Tom?"

Silence again. Embarrassing, embarrassing, embarrassing! How could he have forgotten something so important? Tom's hesitant voice filled the awkward void.

"Mr. Cohen, are you all right? Are you feeling all right, Mr. Cohen?"

No, he was not feeling all right. "Yes, yes, I'm perfectly fine, Tom. Thanks, Tom. I'm sorry."

Tom sounded more concerned than put out. "That's all right, Mr. Cohen," he said with a cautious note of commiseration. "Good-bye. Take care of yourself, Mr. Cohen."

Although Andrew knew he had to end the conversation, something in him kept clinging to it, refusing to say good-bye to this young man who had been until recently almost a member of the family. "Yes, Tom, I'm fine. Perfectly fine, thank you. How are you getting along, Tom?"

More silence. It couldn't go on. There was no real connection between them, they were simply two ghosts haunting the same abandoned house. "I'm fine, Mr. Cohen. I'll be fine. Good-bye, Mr. Cohen."

Andrew felt a great pang of sorrow. For whom was he mourning? Tom? Himself? Rachel? *For everyone. For all of us.* "Good-bye, Tom. Thanks for everything. Stay in touch."

Tom would not stay in touch. There was no chance of that. Why did this make Andrew sad? They had never had a relationship. Their lives had simply crossed for a few months, at most a year. "Sure thing, Mr. Cohen. I'll keep in touch. Good-bye, Mr. Cohen."

Andrew stared at the lifeless receiver. Thoughts he could not put into words chased each other through his mind, nipping at each other's heels. Poor Tom! Andrew's feeling of loss increased, as did his discomfort at having forgotten Tom and Rachel's breakup. He had no explanation for why he had. The more this stoked his fevered mind's distress, the more compelled he felt to find one. His reaction to the knowledge that he might never speak to Tom again was out of all proportion. He had never realized how attached he was to him.

Andrew shook his head to drive away the thoughts that were flocking to it. The phone, still in his hand, quivered like a small animal and rang. He snatched his hand away, feeling his blood pressure rise. Suppose it was Tom? Suppose he was calling back to scold him for his presumption? Suppose he knew everything, that he was still in touch with Rachel, that she had told him about his conversation with Linda? A second ring was followed by a third. In a moment, the speaker would announce the caller. It began to croak metallically, rattling off letters that sounded like a commercial name. Andrew relaxed, letting out his breath. It was the same announcement he had gotten earlier in the day from the mysterious credit card company. *Hello! This is your last chance to eliminate your credit card debt. Please contact us as soon as possible at the following number. This is a recorded announcement.* What on earth did they want from him? It shouldn't be legal to hassle people like that. There should be a law against it! Andrew grabbed the phone, deleted the message, and muted the speaker with a few violent jabs, leaving on its number recognition. He didn't have to let the whole world drive him crazy with its crap! It owed him some privacy. He was entitled to engage it when and where he liked.

Andrew turned away from the telephone. His anger ebbing slowly, he strode to his desk with a feeling of aggressive impotence, savagely pressed his laptop's ON button, sank into his chair, and waited with a nervous, tuneless whistle for his home page to appear on the screen. Although the thought of it made him sick, he had a strong urge to log on to the repellent blog whose babyish cretin of an author was in pursuit of the Lost Foreskin. But how could he feel nauseous when he hadn't eaten all day, or last night, either, come to think of it? What was taking the damn computer so long? Why was it so slow? It was only a year old. And why did they keep calling him about credit card debt? Could something be wrong? They stole your identity, they hacked your account and did what they wanted with it. Could it have happened during his visits to that porn site? He should have realized it was a trap all along.

Andrew tried banishing this latest worry from his mind while clicking several times on the Internet icon. Why wasn't the computer reacting? Why couldn't he get the damn blog? Something was holding it up. An announcement was flashing at the bottom of the screen. Andrew leaned forward, struggling to focus his uncooperative eyes on it. *Unfortunately, the site you have requested has been removed. We have no further information.* He stared dumbly at the small black letters, unable to comprehend their meaning. Where had the blog gone? Who had removed it? Had it been censored? Had its author realized the absurdity of his quest? What was he supposed to do now? Google "foreskin restoration"?

Andrew's fingers moved instinctively to his e-mail but refused to click on it. What if the letter he dreaded getting from the editor of the magazine were in his in-box, lying in wait like a venomous little snake? No, he couldn't deal with that now. Maybe later, that evening. He clicked on the Internet again. What now? More college fuck-fests? Another session with Princess Michelle of the Butterfly Tattoo? Those firm little breasts bouncing up and down in perfect rhythm? Those college boys with their giant erections? Hell, hell on earth! The abyss was yawning at his feet, he only had to let go and plummet into it. Quickly, he ran through the alphabetical list. *Pregnant.* He had already noticed it on his first visit to the site. What could it be about? Pregnant women having sex in public? Was that supposed to be arousing? The computer whirred softly. The screen blinked, went dark, and lit up again.

A young woman in her last months of pregnancy knelt, naked, before two muscular young men. Their shaven pubic hair made their penises seem unnaturally, bestially large. The young woman's tattooed skin, which at first glance looked stitched with black-and-blue marks, gleamed with an exaggerated whiteness. Her hands grasped the young men's penises while her mouth went from one to the other, desperately sucking. Eyes shut tight, her cheeks hollow, running her lips up and down the two moist erections that glittered in the bad lighting of the improvised projectors. Her swollen breasts with their widened nipples swayed in time to the strong, sucking movements of her mouth. Thrown forward by her breasts and her ponderous belly, she had to cling to the two penises to keep her balance like a monkey in the branches of a tree. Crouching over them, her gaping vagina seemed a diabolical and possibly intended parody of her approaching labor.

Andrew stared, mesmerized with disgust, at the awful scene. The swollen, bloodred vagina glistened like an open wound between pale labia that resembled drooping sails. A putrid, fishy odor assailed him. Sharp scales and bits of fin in his mouth. A thick, salivating tongue jammed down his throat, wriggling like a fat worm. His stomach convulsed violently, pumping bile into his throat. The sour reflux made him choke. He jumped up and ran to the bathroom, desperately trying not to puke on the living-room floor. Falling to his knees before the toilet, he stuck his head deep into its bowl. Smooth, slippery foreskins stretching and retracting, filling the mouth with their dead, unclean folds. A burning yellow fluid surged up his throat toward his olfactory glands, pricking their soft membranes with a needlelike acidity. He retched in agony, his teeth on edge, his throat tasting of sulfur. Phosphorus bursts of liquid shot from him like fiery arrows, on their way to the water in the toilet bowl, which they painted a garish, apocalyptic yellow. The burning in his throat was unbearable. His whole digestive tract felt like one bleeding, incurable sore. He gasped for air, breathing in the toxic fumes he expelled. His mouth opened and shut like a beak, struggling to eject the last poison from his system. He could feel the bile corroding the enamel of his teeth, eating its way toward their soft, sensitive roots.

With the last of his strength, Andrew pushed himself away from the toilet. All his muscles went limp, leaving him too weak to lean against the wall. With a slow, inanimate fatality, his body toppled sideways, yielding to the force of gravity. His cheek rested against the cool, befouled floor tiles. He shut his eyes. His breathing grew regular. The dark depths received him, their black gates shutting remorselessly behind him.

13

It is the black middle watch of the night. The dogs howl. The Angel of Death has come to the city. A distant, hollow barking echoes in its houses like a muffled but persistent omen, a savage forest sound unknown to places of human habitation. It is the frightful sound that we heard when sheltering underground like hunted animals on the outskirts of town, living in burrows and tunnels like moles, badgers, and foxes, hiding in tree trunks and the clefts of rocks. In the city, murder ran wild. The cries of the slaughtered and tortured turned the night red as flames. The fiends had no compassion: not on the young, not on the old, not on women, or children, or the littlest girls. They slit their throats like young pigeons, wrung their necks like turtledoves. From the jaws of a murderous red dog drips a hideous pink saliva. Its bark doesn't stop, there is nowhere to hide from it or flee. The harsh, terrifying sound of the Divine Mercilessness batters the walls, bounces against the ceilings, rebounds off the corners. Allelujah! Allelujah! Allelujah! The accursed preacher is shouting in the street again, praising God in his diabolical voice, over and over, day and night, a lifetime, an eternity, of satanic praise. A horrible bloodred dog, as murderous as a wolf, as big as a lion.

14

A ndrew barely managed to open his eyes, blinking in the darkness. He sniffed the air, trying to decipher its sour stench of
vomit, unflushed urine, and detergent. Where was he? What had
happened to him?

He shut his eyes again, uncertain if he was awake or asleep. He
opened them. The thick darkness around him dissipated, revealing murky details, shadowy hints of things. A round object like
the smokestack of a ship towered over him, its outlines visible in a
dim light coming from an unknown source. He had to concentrate
before realizing it was the toilet. He was in the bathroom. A chill
ran over him. How had he gotten here? Slowly, he stretched his
limbs, which were stiff from lying on the floor, and tried lifting his
head from the smooth tiles whose crisscross pattern was imprinted
on his cheek. The effort was too much for him. His weak, aching
body refused to cooperate and he gave up, letting his muscles sink
back into the cramped state they had been in all night. His half-
raised head dropped to the floor as though in hope of falling back
into a sleep that would shroud his waking nightmare. He lay in
the dark, breathing the fetid air in and out. Sleep failed to come.
Overwrought, he surrendered to the morbid wakefulness. Distant
shouts rapped on the windows, rattling their panes. "Allelujah! Allelujah! Allelujah!" Hell! Hell on earth! Why didn't the man shut
up, for God's sake? Didn't he ever sleep?

He couldn't go on lying in the bathroom like a dying beast.
He had to get up, immediately! Although he tried relaxing his
cramped muscles, they remained in spasm. Curled up on the bathroom floor, he felt panicked. He was paralyzed! He wriggled and
squirmed, fighting for dear life to gain control of his body. Dragging himself toward the toilet bowl, he gripped its rim like a buoy,

pulled himself into an upright position, stood, and went to the sink to wash his hands of their caustic filth. His frayed nerves recoiled from the hot water and he turned off the faucet. For a moment, he stood at the sink, debating whether to turn the water back on. Then, shaking his hands in the air to dry them, he wiped them disgustedly on his shirt as though to erase the stain of what had happened and went to the dark living room. In the sickly red glow of the streetlamps, it looked empty, inhabited by ghosts.

Andrew went to the microwave oven in the kitchen to check its illuminated digital clock. It was two a.m. He had been sleeping for twelve straight hours—if, that is, the cold, dark matrix he had been immersed in since early afternoon could be called sleep. His whole body was aching, but his mind was awake—not perfectly lucid, perhaps, but reasonably alert. Although he would have gladly slept another twelve hours, or even twenty, he knew he would sleep no more tonight. Should he turn on a light? His brain was too weary to cope with the profusion of detail it would reveal. Try to work? Watch television? He shuddered at the thought. He went to the window and leaned his head against its cold glass pane. An unseasonably strong wind was blowing outside, whipping the July night into a wintry storm. A torn piece of canvas flapped with the monotonous, unnerving rhythm of a metronome. The monstrously overblown trees tossed wild branches that threatened to break loose and dash themselves against the building. Riverside Drive, deserted, snaked below. A red traffic light was like a monster's eye in a horror movie. The park, dark and menacing, lay beyond its low granite wall. A whorish red neon sign blinked across the river. Its reflection shimmered on the water like a seductive call to swim to it and never return. The river was as dark and heavy as the Styx, a great, turbid mass moving blindly from nowhere to nowhere in a senseless, purposeless, meaningless flow.

Andrew turned queasily back to the room from the window. His eyelids felt lined with slivers of glass as though he hadn't slept in weeks. He walked distractedly about the room, his mind swarming with old angers, ancient insults, nameless fears, pathetic childhood anxieties. The air conditioner coughed and sputtered, alternately releasing blasts of cold and stale, tepid air. Andrew shivered, the fine hairs on his arms and neck bristling as if it were a cold winter night. His sour insides twirled like a balloon from which the air has been suddenly released. For a childish moment, he imagined the comfort of milk and cookies. The warm feeling this gave him vanished instantly: not only was turning on the kitchen light or opening the refrigerator door beyond his powers, the milk had run out two days ago and there hadn't been a cookie in the apartment for years. Frustrated, he returned to the living room and threw himself on the couch, tucking his legs as far under him as he could. The contact with the expensive leather on which he loved to luxuriate now made his teeth chatter. He lay curled with his head on a cushion, hugging his knees to keep warm. His chills persisted, subsiding and breaking out anew from time to time. Although he desperately wanted to lie under the comforter from his bed, something kept him from entering the dark bedroom. His amorphous fears of it were now a living, breathing terror that grew realer by the minute. To hell with the comforter!

The leather chafed his bare neck, which felt suddenly separate from him. Its sticky dampness felt alive, like the skin of a frog. *The skin of a frog?* He had never touched a frog in his life. He had hardly seen one since he was a boy. Why frogs? *A fat, greedy, evil-eyed frog. Calm down! Calm down!* He had to keep his wits about him. Why was it so cold? Something was wrong with the damn air conditioner. It was always too hot or too cold. Why did nothing ever work the way it was supposed to? Andrew jumped from the couch, dumbfounded by the jagged scream that he had loosed without intending to. He went to the antique linen chest that served as an end table, removed the old lamp that sat on top of it and other carefully arranged bric-a-brac, heaved it open, and took out the fleecy white cashmere throw, which he and Linda had bought in Italy. In winter, he draped it over the couch to give it an elegantly warm look. Without putting anything back in place, he returned to the couch and covered himself. The delicate fabric evoked long-forgotten sensations. Memories of any kind were more than he could bear. *The fourth- or fifth-grade nature teacher slits the frog open. He removes its male genitals with a pincer, places the tiny testicles on a glass slide, and shows his pupils their semen.* Why were children made to see such things? What was the point of it? He shook out the folded blanket, hoping it would cover the couch. Had the frog at least been killed first? The blanket wasn't big enough. He struggled to fit it over the couch's heavy bolsters until every last bit of leather was invisible—he didn't care that he was stretching it out of shape. No sooner had he lain down again than his body weight dragged it off the bolsters, its ends falling on him like tattered wings. He wrapped them around him, snuggling into them like a fledgling in its nest while shutting his eyes as if to shut out something he knew. *The Nazis used human skin. They upholstered chairs, bound books, and made lampshades with it.* A Jew-skin couch, the horror of it! What would become of him? How would it end?

He opened his eyes, staring at nothing in particular. The night stretched before him, as black and endless as a road to perdition. Although he knew he should turn on the light to drive away the demons that multiplied with every breath he took, he couldn't force himself to get up. Glued to the couch, he let cold flames of dread spread through his limbs. Only his eyes moved, running up and down the wall like a frightened mouse. The pale, garish light peeled the detached look of amusement from the antique tribal masks, exposing them for the dark epitomes of violence, ignorance, and evil that they were. A paralyzing dread took possession

of him. He could feel it entering his bloodstream and turning it
black as ink. He was being stared at by empty, malevolent eyes
whose large, crudely carved orbs bulged with hate. Black, cavernous mouths yawned, exposing uneven rows of sharp teeth. Pointy,
large-nippled wooden breasts projected above bellies swollen with
the flesh of dead, sacrificed infants. Wooden tongues vied with
menacing phalluses to see which was longer. Andrew felt violated
by their extravagant, grotesque sexuality. Their compactly car-
nal penises, stomachs, and breasts, stacked one on top of another,
threatened to invade his being. He shut his eyes and mouth tight
to keep them out. His pulse soared. His heart reared in its rib cage
like a wild stallion. He mustn't look! He mustn't! The dreadful
creatures would turn on him the moment they saw the whites of
his eyes, overrun him, and tear him to pieces. He felt a powerful
urge to tear the terrible masks from the wall and rip them apart.
He would sell them—he would give them away—he would burn
them—he would trash them! For a second, the thought of their destruction made him feel strong. Then an immobilizing reaction set
in as he pictured the nail holes in the wall, dotting its bare surface
like scars. What morbid, pathological thoughts!

Andrew tightened his grip on the blanket, gulping the inert air.
The aura surrounding the morbid figures on the wall was on the
verge of engulfing the apartment. Something tangible, abhorrent,
fluttered close to his face. He shrank from it with a cry, his eyes
wide with terror. Someone had touched him. Soft but deliberate,
the unexpected contact was terrifying. He tossed his head like a
frightened animal, moaning gutturally. His eyes grew bigger to
take in all the dim light that they could. No, there was no one there.
He was alone in the room. Its only sound was the rattle of the air
conditioner. But how could that be? Someone had just touched
him, he could swear it! In a panic, he ran to turn on the overhead
light and all the lights in the living room and kitchen. From there

he ran to the hallway and bedroom, groping for their switches with his eyes shut as if fearing for his sanity should he see something. Lastly, he turned on the light in the bathroom, searching the linen closet to make sure no one was hiding there. More deliberately, he returned to the kitchen for a look at the broom closet and the space behind the refrigerator where he kept the detergent and paper towels. Only after having checked every possible hiding place and dark nook in the apartment did he dare return to the living room, lie down again on the couch, and pull the cashmere blanket back over him.

What time was it? Every light in the apartment was on. The air conditioner wheezed consumptively. The bright light hurt Andrew's eyes. He blinked wearily, shaking off the cobwebs of sleep and ignoring the masks on the wall. No, he wouldn't take them down now. It was a crazy thought, and anyway, he didn't have the strength for it. Even turning on the television, or his computer to check his e-mail, was more than he was capable of. Shutting his eyes, he imagined his in-box, its unanswered mail arrayed on the screen like a court indictment, the fiery black seal of condemnation at its bottom a letter from the editor to whom he owed his article. He opened his eyes. The computer screen was gone. He mustn't fall asleep now! He absolutely must not! *He was in the ancient shrine again. How had he gotten here? He looked around him. The sheen of pure radiance faded from the curtain of the Sanctuary, retreating inward like the petals of a flower closing for the night. The soft splendor withdrew to the threshold, lingered there, and was gone. The Ark's two Cherubs, pristinely aglow just a moment ago, turned gray, their clear complexion blotched with darkness. The Temple's roof gleamed golden, catching fire in a bright flame that went out all at once. The wall of the Gallery glinted in a last sunbeam and darkened. The Altar flared up as its flames dwindled and died, collapsing into the ashes gathered at its feet. Although the city no longer could hold on to the light, the mount*

*in its midst clung to it a bit longer before letting go and sinking into a
sea of obscurity. The desert glimmered on until its soft hills, resigned to
their fate, let go of the day. Darkness. Utter darkness. Darkness and
great consternation.*

Andrew roused himself from the powerful reverie. He looked
at the window. Dawn was breaking. Shades of blue and green
streaked the pale sky. The night had fled, taking with it his desperate struggle, wrapped in black sheets. The Kingdom of Day
held sway. A deep weariness took hold of Andrew. He rested his
head on the pillow and breathed deeply. He shut his eyes, let the air
in his lungs run out through his nostrils, and set out with a slight
rocking sound on the quiet waters of sleep.

15

*Large, wet snowflakes fall haphazardly, like stray shots from the
sky. Harsh, skeletal German words rain down like hail. Distant
sirens wail in the night. Searchlights slash the darkness, crisscrossing the black sky. A black luxury Mercedes appears out of
thin air and brakes sharply by the little corpse, its wheels cutting
dirty tracks in the ice. The motor is still running. Large, bug-
eyed headlights beam two shafts that conjoin on the snowy earth
in a small circle, as though spotlighting a stage. Walter, naked
and stripped of his shrouds, lies curled on the ground. His dead
face, pressed to a grimy patch of ice, is chalk-pale in the strong
light. His eyes are wide open. His blue lips are pulled back in a
contorted grin, baring his long, old man teeth whose half-visible
roots protrude from receding gums. What's that scream? Who's
screaming like that? It's hard to say. It may be me.*

16

What time was it? He had no watch. He had fallen asleep. It was a dream. Andrew lay perspiring on the couch, staring at the distant ceiling while struggling to restore his sense of reality— any sense of it at all. How long had he been sleeping? Not that long. To judge by the light in the window, it still was early. The cashmere blanket was crumpled beneath him in a shapeless, uncomfortable ball. Throwing it on the rug, he forced himself to raise his head. He would clean up afterward. He wasn't up to it now. He wasn't up to anything. He needed to rest and get back his strength.

Andrew froze in an odd half-sitting, half-lying position, uncertain what to do. Go back to sleep? Get up, take a shower, and scrub away the memory of last night with hot water and soap? He wavered, wallowing in his helplessness, until his body decided for itself by slowly pushing itself up like a heavy piece of machinery. He stood shakily in the middle of the room, dizzily blinking to shield his eyes from the light. A shower? No, not now. The thought of the stinging hot water made him cringe. Unthinkingly, he went to the television, took the remote control from its little basket, and pressed the red button at its top. With a start, the TV crackled with electricity and came to life. A tide of color from the suddenly bright screen bathed the melancholy living room.

Hi, Bert. Are you sleeping?
Yes, Ernie. I'm sleeping.
But I can't fall asleep, Bert.
Try counting sheep, Ernie.

There was a lump in Andrew's throat. Warm, phlegmy tears welled in his sinuses. He felt as light-headed as if he had just drunk

a double whiskey or come down with a sudden fever. *Sesame Street!*
It was *Sesame Street!* Could it still be on the air? As if daydreaming,
he let himself be transported from an ordinary state of awareness
to the far, fanciful regions of cloudy memory. The lovable pup-
pets raced madly across the screen. He stretched out on the couch
with his feet extended before him, laughing half-apologetically
at the childish glee aroused by their comical voices, to which he
surrendered unconditionally. The scenes kept changing, revolving like a carousel. Large letters emerged from a swimming pool
to the accompaniment of a Hollywoodish sound track. Children
reported in excited voices what they liked to do best with their
fathers. Elmo, his strident voice too cute to be annoying, tickled
the cheeks of a fat, laughing baby in a high chair with loud, fleecy
kisses. Andrew relaxed and breathed evenly, soothed by the near
but distant voices. His shut eyes approached the rapid movement
of a dream state. *A repellent, lilac-gray sky hangs over the rooftops*
like an old sack. Sounds of pounding are heard. They grow louder and
quicker, as if someone were battering the city with a huge sledgehammer.
There is a sound like an avalanche. The legionnaires, drunk with rage,
swarm through the breached wall. A yellow summer sandstorm, sav-
age and merciless, interrupts the pillar of smoke rising from the altar,
blithely scattering it to the four winds.

17

The bright afternoon light hurt Andrew's eyes, half waking
him and forcing him to turn over on his side. He lifted the
back of his neck, sticky with perspiration, from the leather bolster, leaving a dark, elongated stain. He sat up and looked at it
indifferently, feeling a vague dread. What day was it? What time?
There was somewhere he was supposed to be! He had forgotten

something important. Whatever it was, he had to get there. Where was his calendar? Frantically, he racked his brain. He mustn't be late. It would be disastrous if he were. His fear surged and subsided like a wave breaking on the shore. His mind went blank. His eyes shut. His head fell back upon the bolster, his cheek nestling into its little pocket of sweat. At once he fell into a restless, dreamless sleep from which he awoke two hours later, feeling like an escaped prisoner who has been hiding in a ditch. The strong afternoon light streaming through the windows facing the river made him blink.

The television, which had been left on all day, was blasting away. Andrew sat up, snatched the remote control, and turned it off. The silence in the apartment was broken only by the anguished wheezing of the air conditioner, which was no longer cooling anything. He remained sitting on the couch, his wet shirt clinging to him, running a hand through his disheveled hair. It stuck up in tufts that made him look like a strange, horned creature. He hadn't shaved in a week. He must get up and take care of himself! Cumbersomely, he rose from the couch and went to the bathroom. His eyes stung despite all the sleep he had gotten in the last day. He felt as though he had a hangover. He had better buy some pills and get some real sleep! It couldn't go on like this. He wouldn't shave now. He was too weak. He had to eat something and have a glass of water.

Andrew showered in lukewarm water, without soap. He couldn't stand anything too hot or cold. Although this left him feeling somewhat better, he didn't really feel clean or refreshed. His closet looked half-empty. The stack of fresh shirts had shrunk and all his summer pants were creased and stained. When would Angie be back? In a week? A week and a half? He took the first pair of pants from a hanger, grabbed a polo shirt, dressed quickly, and went to the kitchen, not looking at the four living-room windows that were on fire with an intense, pre-sunset orange light. He automatically went to the coffeemaker, then removed his hand from it suddenly. No, not coffee. It would keep him up all night. Another night like the last one and he would collapse. He must buy sleeping pills.

He opened the refrigerator and surveyed its contents apathetically. There were a few bags of rotting vegetables, some cheese, and an empty carton of milk. Should he order delivery? No, he had to eat right away. He surveyed the meager pickings in the closet. On the middle shelf were a can of coconut milk, a jar of palm hearts, some jams and jellies, and a few bottles of sauces, vinegar, and oil. The top shelf had several boxes of cereal; their bright colors wove an airy fabric of childhood memories, some better than others, in his suggestible mind. He picked a box and started for the table, stopping at the refrigerator for milk, but, of course, it was empty. What should he do now? Although it was strange to think of cereal without milk, he took a bowl and spoon and continued to the table, sitting with his back to the living-room windows to keep his eyes from being blinded by the light. Emptying the remains of the box into the bowl, he dug the spoon into them and stuck it in his mouth. He chewed slowly, dutifully, finishing a spoonful and starting on the next. The stale cereal turned to mush in his mouth. How long had it been sitting in the closet? It tasted of cardboard.

He needed to drink something. Returning to the refrigerator, he hopelessly examined several bottles of white wine. A spasm in his stomach warned him not to open any. It would be foolhardy to drink wine now. A forgotten container of orange juice lay in the back. He reached for it, informed by its weight that it, too, was half-empty. Thirsty, he unscrewed it and brought it to his mouth, then decided to drink from a glass. He brought the glass to the table, filled it with the lurid, neon-colored juice, and drained it in several gulps, trying to ignore its sour, bitter taste. He poured himself a second glass, shaking out the last drops from the container, and chewed another spoon of the dry, flavorless cereal. He was beginning to get used to it, though he would have thrown it out under any other circumstances.

The orange light of the setting sun spread from the living room to the kitchen. It colored the memories evoked by the cereal, the juice, and the half-empty bowl on the table, conjuring up details long consigned to oblivion. *It's early in the morning. The kitchen window looking out on the yard is flooded with sunlight. Linda is packing Rachel's lunch in a bright lunch box, carefully arranging the sandwich, fruit, and dessert. Half-empty bowls stand on the table between crumbs of toast and puddles of milk.* Sesame Street *is on. Although the characters are hard to make out in the strong light, their voices give them away. They're Ernie, Bert, Big Bird, and Oscar the Grouch. There is a clatter of breaking glass. Grover, playing a waiter, has slipped on the floor of the restaurant. The dishes shatter, one by one on his blue head. His big, round eyes roll upward with comic despair before he passes out. The little girl is laughing out loud with short, breathless yelps of pure joy. "Rachel, darling, get a move on! Finish your cereal. The school bus will be here in ten minutes and you haven't brushed your teeth or hair."* The amount of sugar they put in those breakfast cereals! Longing. Regret. Pity. A moist, orange, sunset-colored feeling. It overwhelmed him, breaking through the barriers of self to a tender inner core. His desperate, embarrassed longing was entwined with bright floral patterns, painted with their colors, fiery with the light that trickled through their petals. What had happened to his passion for freedom? For the empty geometry of black-and-white space? For straight, infinite lines? The arrogance of it. The banal, childish immaturity. He blushed with a bitter, self-pitying sorrow that pressed on his overflowing sinuses.

Andrew jumped to his feet as though his chair were on fire and pushed the table away, his spoon clattering in its bowl. He must go to a pharmacy and buy sleeping pills! He had to, right away!

He hurried to the door, not breaking stride as he worked his bare feet into the shoes he had left on the floor two days ago. He patted his hair nervously, sweeping aside his discomfort at stepping out, unkempt and unshaven. He had enough to worry about as it was. His need to get to the drugstore was growing more urgent by the minute. His sole desire was to feel the little box of sleeping pills in his pocket. His mind clutched at it as if it were a talisman that could cure him and restore his control over his life, over himself.

18

Andrew crossed the marble floor of the lobby quickly. With every step his sweaty, sockless feet broke loose with an embarrassing squeak from the sticky leather of his shoes. The glass doors glowed radioactively in the orange sunset light. Although he knew the drugstore on the corner of Broadway was open around the clock, he was in a rush to get there, as if it might close at any minute.

"Professor!" The doorman's ironic voice tracked him down like a hunting dog just as he was stepping into the street. "Professor, just a minute!" Andrew, nonplussed, turned around. The doorman's mustache lifted with a smirk, revealed a missing molar. "There's someone here for you, Professor!" He pointed, for some reason highly amused, to a deliveryman holding a plastic package from Citarella's. Andrew reentered the lobby, abandoning the hot sunlight for its sour, air-conditioned chill. The deliveryman held out the bag with the ceremonial submissiveness of a tribute bearer. Bewildered, Andrew leaned forward to receive the mysterious gift, vainly racking his mind for the source of it. What could it be? Why was it being given to him? The deliveryman's expressionless face offered no clue. The package was heavy. It held something sinewy and snakelike that felt neither alive nor quite dead. It sent a current of shock through Andrew that went straight to his helpless brain. He jerked his hands away, dropping the package with a splat that sounded like a slap in the face. Stooping embarrassedly to pick it up, he bumped heads with the deliveryman, who had bent to retrieve it, too. The doorman, enjoying himself more and more, crossed his arms over his chest with a superior smile.

The package was in Andrew's hand again, its long, cadaverous contents, possibly bruised from their fall, more ominous than ever. With a self-effacing murmur that could have been either a thank-you or an apology, he pried its sealed top open and peered inside, uncertain of what he would find there. The tentlike interior, held up to the light, contained a second plastic bag in which, wrapped in pink tissue, a large, long object was steeped in a small pool of blood. Andrew turned away from the shocking sight, barely able to stifle a cry of fright and keep from dropping the package again. What could it be? The object looked like an amputated limb. The momentary conviction that he must be dreaming came and went, leaving him none the wiser. No, it was definitely not a dream. He was wide awake. He must get a grip on himself! There had to be some logical explanation. He took a deep breath and peered into the package again. At its bottom, he noticed, was a neatly folded sheet of paper. Trying to avoid contact with the bloody bag, he carefully put down the package, wiped his hands on his pants without thinking, shakily extracted the folded paper, and opened it. It was a receipt from Citarella's for advance payment by credit card for a cut of Black Angus beef tenderloin, dry aged for twenty-one days and weighing seven and a half pounds, at $39.99 a pound. A small credit card voucher was stapled to the receipt.

Andrew caught his breath at the sight of the astronomical price, blushing with surprise and embarrassment. Suddenly, it came to him. Of course! How could he have forgotten? He had, in a moment of hubris, ordered the meat at Citarella's shortly before that awful meeting in Bernie's office. How long ago had that been? A year? No, it couldn't be. It couldn't have been more than two or three weeks ago, a month at the most. He must sleep more at night if he was going to function during the day. It couldn't go on like this. He must start taking sleeping pills, now!

Thinking of Bernie made Andrew feel sick to his stomach. Bernie! He was to have been the guest of honor at the festive dinner whose pièce de résistance was the tenderloin. Andrew pictured it in full, mercilessly realistic detail: the president seated at the head of the table like a king at a royal feast, sinking his teeth into the tender meat, sipping Andrew's choicest wines while shamelessly flirting with Andrew's young girlfriend . . . Ann Lee! The thought of her on the brown leather couch, her bathrobe clinging ravishingly to her body, sent a warm wave of renewed desire running through him. It was dashed to the ground by the hard fist of memory. Ann Lee was gone forever. There would be no dinner, no guests, no anything.

What now? Andrew expelled an involuntary groan. What should he do with the damn tenderloin? It was no longer possible to return it. How much was $39.99 times seven and a half? The full amount, including taxes and delivery charges, was on the voucher. No, he wouldn't look at it now. It would be too humiliating, exactly what the doorman was hoping for. With unsteady fingers he searched for the pen in the breast pocket of the jacket he wasn't wearing. The deliveryman stared at him in deferential silence. Andrew tapped his breast again and asked as casually as he could if he happened to have a pen. Producing a cheap, greasy ballpoint pen from behind his ear, the deliveryman handed it to Andrew with a smile. Andrew took it warily, scrawled a shaky signature on the voucher, and handed it back. A tip, he had to give him a tip! He reached for the wallet in his back pocket while glancing sideways at the doorman, who kept shamelessly staring at him. What did he have against him? What did he want? Lately he had been acting as if he knew something about him that everyone but Andrew was aware of.

The wallet, which hadn't been opened in days, was stuffed with twenty-dollar bills. Andrew rifled through them frantically, looking for something smaller. A twenty-dollar tip was insane. Who gave that much to a deliveryman? He would ask for change. No, he wouldn't! The goddamn doorman was standing there, listening to every word, following every movement. Quickly snatching a twenty-dollar bill from his wallet before he could change his mind, Andrew folded it to keep the doorman from seeing it and put it in the deliveryman's hand. The deliveryman, overcome with gratitude, murmured two or three thank-yous, and disappeared in the dimming orange light of 110th Street, leaving Andrew alone with the doorman and the heavy package on the floor.

19

The orange light had retreated westward toward the river. Sweat, gasoline fumes, and an acrid gray soot coated the streets of the city. The night brought no relief from the heat. On the contrary: the sunset had stoked the air even more, making it almost impossible to breathe. Andrew hurried eastward toward Broadway, his feet sticky in their leather shoes. He was carrying the package from Citarella's by its two plastic handles. The striated cut of red meat was creased like a long tongue that curled upward at the bottom. Something about its serpentine form evoked a dim, frightening, and for some reason sea-tinted memory. He hadn't wanted to leave the package with the doorman, who was sure to examine it the minute he was gone—and although he could have gone back upstairs and put it in the refrigerator, he felt this would have aroused the man's gossipy instincts even more.

He had to get to the air-conditioned pharmacy quickly. A few minutes of this heat was enough to ruin the meat. Eating spoiled meat was dangerous, very. But who was going to eat it anyway? What was he going to do with it? It was better to concentrate on the sleeping pills. He reached the corner, turned quickly down Broadway, and entered the drugstore through automatic double doors.

The store was unbearably cold. Even the meat in the package seemed to stiffen, as if undergoing a second rigor mortis. Feeling frozen and weak from hunger, Andrew tottered like a drunk from shelf to laden shelf. What was he doing here? What was he looking for? Right: sleeping pills! Where could they be? The long, symmetrical rows of shelves were endless. Their brightly packaged products made Andrew's head spin. Should he ask someone? Embarrassed to approach another customer, he looked for a salesperson, yet none of the usually available help was anywhere to be seen. He would have to inquire at the checkout counter. Tentatively, he approached the line, debating whether to cut or wait his turn. He decided to wait. The heat-stricken New Yorkers did not look welcoming—and besides, the thought of asking his question with them as witnesses made him uncomfortable. A request for sleeping pills might be taken as a sign of weakness or helplessness. He stood there uncertainly, trapped between an angry older woman who kept muttering about the wait and a tall, young, anemic-looking one whose pimply skin was the same sallow color as his own in the dull fluorescent light. Although the package of meat kept getting heavier, he did not want to rest it on the dirty linoleum floor, which looked afflicted with an incurable disease.

The minutes dragged on. The cashier took her time, passing the same purchases over and over through the red beam of the scanner.

Andrew felt hollow and sluggish with hunger. He surveyed the
shortening line, trying to guess how long he still had to wait. The
rack by the counter was the usual candy bar trap. Feeling as though
an inner scaffold he was standing on were about to collapse, he left
the line, depositing the meat on the floor to mark his place, and
went to the crude, machine-made candy bars. Although he generally avoided rich desserts and never ate junk food, he felt an urge
to stuff himself with chocolate, caramel, and sugared nuts. Snatching all he could hold like a greedy child, he rejoined the waiting
customers while ignoring the grumbling behind him. He pushed
the package of meat ahead of him with one foot, reached the cash
register just in time, and dumped the candy bars on the counter,
where they scattered like dice in a children's game. The cashier
gathered them impassively and passed them one by one through
the scanner, which beeped indifferently with every sweet.

There was a final, longer beep. The cash register rattled and
printed out the bill. The operator took Andrew's twenty dollars,
handed him his change and a receipt, and pushed the bag of candy
bars with its stiffly rustling wrappers in his direction while staring
at some point in space behind him. He shoved the money into his
pocket without bothering to count it and headed for the door with
the bag. Halfway there, he heard the irritable voice of the older
woman call out, "Mister! Mister, you've forgotten your package!"
He returned, blushing, thanked the woman, who snapped something unclear, lifted the heavy package from the floor to which it
felt almost stuck, and hurried out, feeling faint.

Andrew staggered back into the hot, noisy street that sunk in
thick twilight. Jostled by the crowds to the corner, he rested a
hand against the pole of a traffic light and bent over a nearly full
trash can, prepared to vomit whatever remained in his stomach.
But though the hot, stinking fumes rising from the can made him
retch, that was it. He straightened up and looked around to get his

bearings. It was a pointlessly frenzied, smoggy, smothering New York summer evening. Whoever could flee the city had done so long ago. Only the pariahs had stayed behind to pick at the leftovers and rummage through the garbage. As he shifted the package from hand to hand, a rustle of wrappers reminded him of the candy bars. Reaching into the bag of them, he pulled out the first one, tore off its wrapper, and stuffed it whole into his mouth. Its gooey sweetness was overpowering. His scalp tingled. His palate felt fossilized by the soft substance. His teeth, sinking into a morass of caramel and nougat, stuck fast to one another, reeling from the sudden sugar rush.

He chewed the dense bar, swallowed it too quickly, and reached for another. The traffic lights changed. Cars honked. The day faded, yielding to the electric halo of the night street. The defrosted meat in the heavy package, which felt about to give out, was a limp mass rotting in its juices. Andrew stood on the southwest corner of Broadway and 110th Street, tearing off wrappers and bolting one candy bar after another, frantically gulping the industrial chocolate that was melting in the heat. His eyes raced in all directions. He was sure he was being stared at. What would happen if someone he knew spotted him, sweatily bent over a trash can while chomping on candy bars mass-produced for children and the sugar-addicted poor? As appalled and revolted as he was—couldn't he at least have waited until reaching the goddamn apartment?—he couldn't stop his mad gluttony. He ripped off the bright wrappers with his teeth, throwing them in the can like an alcoholic hiding empty bottles while gobbling chunk after chunk of candy, all the time aware that an inner cry as uncontrollable as his lust for chocolate was building up inside him, turning into a scream as he reached into the bag for the twelfth time, ransacked it, and found nothing.

Andrew crumpled the empty bag, threw it disgustedly in the

can, and headed back to the drugstore to buy more candy. The large glass doors slid open, greeting him with a violent burst of cold air that snapped him out of his trance. He halted, took a few short breaths, and turned back toward the street, his wild hunger yielding to a sick, sticky feeling. Gripping the smelly trash can, he felt about to vomit into it, spawning a great, brown, excremental blob that would lie there half-alive like a horror creature. Breathing deeply, he tried to overcome the desperate craving for still more sugar, turned westward, and made his way home.

20

He got there quickly. The toxic chocolate quickly entered his bloodstream and percolated through his sugar-drunk body. He felt light-headed. His bouncy steps lengthened. His glowing eyes took in the dimming remnants of the sunset on the horizon. Swinging the package of meat by its handles like a schoolboy swinging his bag, Andrew covered the block from Broadway to Riverside Drive in no time and skipped into the building, ignoring the doorman, with a playful wink at the cunning, pug-nosed demon grinning at him from the entrance. His sugar-tipsy mind was hard at work. *Why not?* Why not throw a grand dinner? He would invite an especially interesting complement of guests and serve the extravagant tenderloin. Tapping out a jazz rhythm on the lobby's floor, he whistled merrily as he waited for the elevator. He would live dangerously, aging the meat still more, bringing it to the very brink of decay before broiling it to such perfection that it would be studied in the future like a trailblazing cultural text.

The elevator arrived. Andrew strode briskly into it, borne on a wave of euphoria that rushed to fill the inner void. He felt his old self coming to life like a Phoenix spreading its wings. Should he push the concept to its limit by serving the tenderloin all by itself, with no first course, no vegetables, no dessert? A solo performance! A magnificent cut of red meat, served with decadence, accompanied by a great, iconic Old World wine: a Saint-Émilion or Saint-Julien whose pedigree declared itself with every sip. Rejuvenated, he rode the elevator like a drunken satyr bound for the bacchanalia of his dreams. Yes! The theme would be "Red on Red," or perhaps "The Red Banquet," a subtle homage to Matisse's *The Dessert: Harmony in Red*.

His brain effervesced with sugary excitement, he suddenly had an idea for a wonderful new article: the aging of meat as a metaphor for European culture vis-à-vis the New World ideal of the fresh steak. It would have fascinating footnotes combined with striking verbal and visual imagery: an Old Master Vanitas, a quote from Rabelais. The Aesthetics of Dissolution. Marco Ferreri's *La Grande Bouffe*. Serrated petals, redolent with sick, unrestrained sexuality, drooping limply to a brocaded tablecloth. A spectacle of feathers, no longer gripped by the pheasant's iridescent, rotting flesh, falling out of the picture one by one. And why just an article? It could be a video installation. He would get in touch with his old friend Barbara from Performance Studies. In fact, why not invite her, too? She was never dull. A stroke of pure genius! His brimming imagination was lord of all things. But wouldn't it, he wondered as the elevator continued its slow ascent, be wasted on the mainstream academic types he would have to invite? For a moment he felt proudly conscious of being, in his lonely refinement, an eagle trapped in the narrow world of country crows and street pigeons.

The elevator reached the tenth floor. Andrew sprang from it and flew to his apartment on new wings. He could all but hear them beating as they bore him along. He must write down the amazing thoughts that had come to him with a bang, like the clatter of coins from a slot machine. As he passed the neighbors' doors, he slid his hand into his pocket to search for the key, not wanting to lose a precious second. Almost breathless with excitement, he inserted the key in the lock. Then, his hand refusing to complete the turn it had begun, he froze.

All at once, without warning, the bubble of his euphoric high burst. The void was back. His wings fell apart. Their wax joints melted. The gray plume of their useless feathers followed his naked body's plunge into a blue sea. The absurdity, the complete absurdity, of it all! The juvenile, obvious banality! The dinner, the article, the installation—the same ideas that had caused him to soar a minute ago were now revealed to him in all their nakedness as the stalest of mannerisms, pure impotence masquerading as genius. His preposterous fantasy of a trendy media event made him cringe. He felt ill again. His bounce sagged beneath its own weight.

Andrew turned the key with difficulty, pushed open the door, and stood on the threshold, feeling too weak to take another step. The warm, repellent smells of the airless apartment paralyzed him anew. He squinted, his lungs preparing to fight for oxygen. Just shutting the door behind him seemed more than he could manage. And now, too, something was dragging on his arm, making him lean against the doorway to keep his balance. He looked down and saw the package of meat, its plastic handles stretched to the breaking point. Forcing himself to enter the smelly apartment and shut the door with his last strength, he hurriedly bolted and double-locked it as if fearing an imminent burglary. He turned to go to the kitchen, felt another sharp tug, and let out an exclamation of dismay. One of the plastic handles had broken, leaving the other to bear all the weight. A second later it snapped, too, and the package fell to the floor with a chilling plop. Andrew grabbed it frantically and ran with it to the kitchen, determined to banish it from sight. He looked wildly around him. Where could he put it? What was he supposed to do with the damn thing? Its two handles now drooped like the antennae of a squashed bug. He couldn't bear to look at it another second. Should he throw it in the garbage? At $39.99 a pound, that would be lunatic. Times seven and a half—how much was that? Not enough to keep him from opening the little cabinet beneath the sink, throwing the moist, heavy bag into the garbage pail, replacing the lid, and shutting the wooden door. In the sudden silence, the hidden meat seemed to fizz with an unheard but deafening sound. Andrew stood listening. Was that all he had needed to do? Could it really have been so easy? It wasn't as simple as that. In an hour, the meat would start to rot. Maggots would infest it. A corpse-like smell would spread from the pail, penetrating the wooden door beneath the sink and filling the apartment with its dark stench. Fat white worms. They were said to live in the flesh, waiting for the moment to breed.

The slow, hollow seconds ticked by. The strange fizzing continued. The dead tenderloin had come back to life, bubbling and gurgling behind the wooden door. Andrew opened the cabinet, lifted the lid of the pail, and peered into it, not knowing what to expect. The package lay there like a corpse in its shrouds. He overcame his revulsion, stuck in a hand, and pulled it out, smeared with rotting fruit peels and a cloudy liquid of unclear origin. Keeping his lips tightly shut and his nose turned away, he opened the package on the granite counter and removed its inner bag, which was sealed with a red plastic clip. The warm cut of meat in its pink tissue rested in its puddle of blood. He threw the empty package into the pail and scrubbed his hands thoroughly with warm water and soap. Should he throw the meat down the incinerator shaft? There was something liberating, therapeutic, in the thought of the hideous tenderloin plummeting down it, bouncing off its dirty walls and smashing to pieces at the bottom. No more tenderloin! It would be gone forever, taking with it all guilt, all sin, all worry, all of life's disgrace.

Andrew took desperate gulps of the unhealthy, endlessly recycled air, and suddenly he felt that he couldn't possibly step out of the apartment with such a thing. He couldn't step out of the apartment, period. Holding the inner bag in both hands, he opened the refrigerator with his knee. In the growing gloom of the kitchen, it cast a cold, greenish light. He leaned forward, feeling sick, chose a far corner of the bottom shelf, maneuvered the meat into it, shut the refrigerator, and ran from the kitchen as if the tenderloin were a murder victim about to rise up, break loose, and chase him through the dark apartment. Although turning on a light might have helped repel the nightmare, he groped his way to the bedroom in the dark, without lighting it.

The stuffy heat was unbearable. The exhausted air conditioner wheezed quietly in the darkness like a large sea mammal cast ashore. *Enough!* He couldn't go on like this. Why not just end it? He would crawl into the bathtub with a bottle of whiskey and a box of sleeping pills, or else slash the veins in his wrist and marvel effetely at the red flowers of blood spurting smokily into the hot water. *Cut it out!* There wasn't a dumber or more self-pitying fantasy than dying in the bathtub like a Hollywood diva. Whiskey and sleeping pills, really! Sleeping pills? He had forgotten completely about them! He had been so obsessed with the crappy candy bars that he hadn't remembered to buy them!

Andrew gave a start and turned to go to the front door, which was barely visible in the dimming light. Yet the thought of the doorman standing with his arms crossed, a crooked smile on his face and a gleam of what Andrew felt sure was sadistic pleasure in his eyes, made him realize that he couldn't go anywhere. It was simply out of the question. He would get along without the goddamn pills, at least until tomorrow.

Andrew shuffled out of the living room with his eyes shut, hands groping in front of him, experiencing the degradation of blindness. The allure of it, too, for he continued that way to the bathroom,

running into walls and doorways and cautiously seeking the medicine cabinet above the sink. Only when he found it did he open
his eyes, sorry to part with the peace of seeing nothing. He looked
for the little bottle of Tylenol in the dim light of the streetlamps
shining through the back window. He unscrewed it, shook out two
pills, swallowed them without water, and replaced the bottle on
its shelf. Not that he knew what good they would do, but sending them on their scratchy path down his throat made him feel he
was doing something. Without drinking or brushing his teeth, he
went to his bed and lay down with his hands gripping the mattress.
Once more he yielded to the pleasant illusion of being blind. The
distant, familiar sounds of the city drifted in and out. His eyelids
twitched. Time passed unnoticed. He lay without moving, unsure
if he was asleep or awake.

A loud ring startled him, waking him from an anesthetizing
dream of nothing. Who could be calling at this hour? What did
they want from him? He turned over on his side, drawing his
knees up and covering his ears with his hands, trying to ignore the
persistent ring. He knew what would happen if he picked up the
receiver. He could hear Walter's severe, wintry voice pronouncing
its harsh verdict. *She's dead! I thought you were with her. I thought you
were watching over her.*

*Hello, Dad? Is that you? What do you mean, Mom is dead? How
can that be? She was just calling to me a minute ago. She asked me to
come to her room, but I wanted to stay by the window looking out at the
infinite depths, at the big blue sharks swimming so far down that they
look like aquarium fish.*

He mustn't break now. He had to stay focused, to keep the
hot, choking tears from erupting and sweeping everything before
them. *The minister will send the limousine tomorrow, but who will help
me carry the coffin? I can't lift it by myself, I need help. A simple box
coffin, made of rudely cut pine.*

21

Four forty a.m. Andrew's eyes opened all at once, as if released by an invisible spring. He lay without moving, staring at the ceiling, bound to the sheet by spidery threads. A shiver ran through him, making its way upward from the soles of his feet with the tortuous slowness of a CT scan. A childish, irrational dread evoked dim scenarios of horror. There was someone in the apartment! A menacing being was lurking in the dark's dreadful void, lying in wait. He shut his eyes tight in the no less childish belief that this would make him invisible. The shiver traveled in an exact line, crossing his diaphragm on its way to his neck. He felt he was choking. Fear gushed from every pore.

Andrew jumped out of bed, threw off the sheets and blankets twined around him like the arms of an octopus, bounded to the door, and flicked the light switch. Light flooded the room, driving away the shadows and flattening the imagined depths between them. He looked around fearfully, surprised how little there was to see. Taking a deep breath, he stepped into the hallway, restraining himself from breaking into a panicked run. He made the rounds of the apartment quickly, turning on every light while resisting the urge to look behind doors and into closets. *Get a grip on yourself, man! Get a grip on yourself! Don't fall apart on me now! Don't lose it!* The lights, switched on one by one, awakened the dark apartment from its slumber. Bathed in an eerie glare, it looked like the site of an all-night party to which no one had come.

How could anyone live all alone like this? It was unnatural! Andrew stood wide awake in the living room, stunned by the light. Although it had indeed chased away the demons that drove him from his bed, the false daylight had wormed its way into him. It was the middle of the night. Everything was closed. What was he supposed to do now? Instinctively, he turned to the computer lying neglected on his desk. Of course! He would check his e-mail and surf the Web to see what was new. No, Andrew shuddered at the thought, he turned his back to his desk and wandered aimlessly into the dark kitchen.

22

The stainless-steel door of the refrigerator gleamed under the light's assault. Andrew yanked it open, held his breath, and peered inside. The long tenderloin, rescued from dark oblivion, was clearly visible in its blackening pool of blood. It seemed to have turned gangrenous in the course of the night. Andrew slammed the door as though to lock it up forever and escaped to the living room, rubbing his hands as if cleaning them of the blood they hadn't touched.

Like a sleepwalker, he wandered through the overly bright living room, bumping into furniture as if it were invisible. Even away from the refrigerator, the thought of the long, cylindrical cut of meat with its pointy, sensitive-looking tip haunted him. The sea-tinted memory struggled to rise again. Shapeless shadows drifted upward from the depths, splinters of a distant, haunting vision, thrashing the water, surfacing and vanishing once more. A morbid curiosity sent him back to the kitchen. Breathing heavily, he stood for a long while before the large coffin of a refrigerator while mustering the resolve to open its door. The tenderloin lay by itself on the bottom shelf as though having driven away all else. How, Andrew asked himself in astonishment, had he failed to see it immediately? It looked just like a huge, uncircumcised penis! He stared at it in disgust, overwhelmed by the obvious metaphor.

The haunting fragments of memory, rising and sinking through all the levels of consciousness, suddenly meshed. A curious, forgotten item from long ago sprang to life in Andrew's mind. It was a primitive piece of scrimshaw, one of those whale-hunting scenes that sold for absurd prices in the antique shops of Cape Cod, Martha's Vineyard, and Nantucket, with a grim black-and-white engraving of a dead, giant sperm whale lying helplessly on the deck of a ship between barrels and coils of rope, awaiting its dismemberment. Its huge sexual organ—a shockingly long, flexile black appendage—lay beside it as though mocking its owner's demise. The impression it made on Andrew was so disturbing that, in the hope of mastering the disquiet it caused him, he thought of buying the strange object and bringing it back to New York. In the end, of course, he didn't. It was no doubt too expensive and who would want such a horror in his home, anyway?

The memory burst with an unpleasant splatter. What was he to do with the damn tenderloin? There had to be some solution. He couldn't just leave it to rot in the refrigerator. What did rotten meat look like? Once it had been a common sight: the carcasses of animals by roadsides, bloated human bodies crawling with worms. Nowadays, you didn't see such things—not in America, anyway, not in New York. He had to get away from such morbid thoughts. Should he make a meal of it after all? Turning to his cookbooks, he chose several colorfully illustrated volumes and carried them to the living room, clinging to their glossy solidity as if it were a guarantee of sanity.

The light was too strong. How could he read? Andrew threw the cookbooks on the coffee table and sank heavily into the couch. The air conditioner, which was on its last legs, had begun to leak during the night, causing a puddle to form on the floor and nearly touch the black rug. The wet, shapeless rag of the cashmere blanket lay at his feet like a skinned, wrinkled hide. Andrew kicked it aside. The whale's amputated sex lay beside the hulk of its dead body. Why were they called sperm whales? What an off-putting name! It made one imagine them swimming in great, sticky halos of milky semen or else masturbating all day long. Wasn't Moby Dick a sperm whale, too? He wondered if they really had such big penises. Where did they keep them? In their stomachs? Buried under their skin?

Andrew leaned forward and took a cookbook from the top of the disorderly pile. *The Encyclopedia of Meat: Everything You Ever Wanted to Know.* He leafed impatiently through the illustrations in the opening pages, which made him think more of an anatomy textbook than of anything having to do with food. Venison. Fowl and Game. Wild Boar. Duck. Partridge. Where was the beef? Filleting a goose breast. *The meat is separated from the bone with a short knife. Start with the neck and work toward the lower abdomen, making sure to cut with the grain.* The fatty meat clung desperately to the scarlet muscle, its soft tissue crumbling from the effort. A jet of reflux surged up Andrew's throat, which contracted spasmodically to block its passage. He slammed the book shut and pushed it away, shutting his eyes and trying not to think of the deboned breast, its skin hanging in driblets. The cruelty of the knife left him aghast.

But he couldn't stop reading now. He had to do something with the tenderloin. He picked up the book again and searched in vain for the beef section. There were a staggering number of illustrations of raw meat. The long muscles, the round muscles, bones sawed lengthwise and crossways, ligaments, fat, cartilaginous joints. The illustrations were hyperrealistic, thanks to the latest state-of-the-art digital cameras. Where had all those nice old cookbooks with their down-to-earth, practical advice gone? They made you feel at home, not in some goddamn slaughterhouse. Beef. Beef. Beef. Here it was. Aging. Assado. Barbecues. Beef bourguignon. Demi-glaces. Goulash. Marinades. Stews. *Strips of lard are inserted with a special hollow knife into tough, chewy cuts of red meat.* Andrew stared transfixed at the color photo. The strips of lard were burrowed in the meat like maggots in dead flesh, their soft, little tails wiggling helplessly on the glossy paper. What ever happened to that fat blogger and his lost foreskin? He must once have been a chubby infant clutching desperately at a blue-veined flap of skin to save it from the knife. *The tenderloin flops heavily, screaming with pain, onto the red-hot skillet. The white worms shrivel in terror, fleeing into the charred cut of meat. Soft baby penises.* Slash them. Burn them. Yes, burn the fucking meat! Stick it in a high-temperature oven and let it go up in smoke. It would fight. It would writhe in the oven's inferno, begging for its life. Not for long, though. The fire would get the upper hand. First would come the fat. It would turn golden, then brown, then black, then carbonize completely. Next were the cartilage and the joints. The muscles would dry, stiffen, burn. Their fluids—their blood, their plasma, their water—would slowly evaporate. The tenderloin would surrender, give up its hold on life, shrink inward, shrivel to a hard concentrate. It would cease to be itself and disappear forever. No more meat. No more anything. Just black, nameless matter. What happened to the bones there, at Auschwitz? Something of them must have remained in the ovens. They couldn't have all gone up the chimneys. But what did bones have to do with it? There were no bones in a tenderloin. There were bones in penises, though. Yes, most mammals had a bone in their penis. He had read it somewhere. Something about blue whales. They had a huge penis bone that could come to six feet or more. What was done with it when the whale was cut up? Was it used for anything? Carved? Thrown back in the sea?

Andrew's mind went blank, collapsing under the weight of so many thoughts. He shut the book, knocked it from the table to the rug, kicked it beneath the leather couch, and looked around as if waking from a dream. The light in the room seemed softer. He gazed out the window, his tension draining as he saw a ruddy streak.

Thank God dawn had broken! It was morning. What time was it? Six forty-five! He didn't know whether to laugh or cry from joy. He had been waiting for this moment all night without knowing it. *Sesame Street! Sesame Street* was on in fifteen minutes! Reaching for the remote control, he eagerly turned on the TV and felt an almost hysterical happiness when the opening jingle came on.

Sunny day,
Sweeping the clouds away
On my way to where the air is sweet.
Can you tell me how to get,
How to get to Sesame Street?

He stretched out on the couch, too exhausted to be embarrassed by the emotion he felt. How had he remembered the song? So many years had gone by since he last heard it, and he hadn't known it by heart then, either. But what did it matter? Now came the next stanza. He shut his eyes and hummed it along with the television, basking in its blessed, eternal sunshine.

Come and play,
Everything's A-OK
Friendly neighbors there,
That's where we meet.
Can you tell me how to get,
How to get to Sesame Street?

Yes, sunshine! A kind sun shining through the leaves of a green forest. He knew the place, he had been in it before. A party was under way, a wedding, birthday, or celebration of an equinox. Who could remember? The enchanted cottage belonged to two long-haired lesbian hippies; their shapely legs that hadn't seen a razor in years showed beneath the hems of their white robes. A naked, angelic baby tottered among the trees. The fat, unpracticed soles of its little feet trod the rich leaf fall. The little plume of its male sex danced between its chubby thighs like a sweet little tail. What an awesome, magnificent sight: a whole, uncircumcised child! But wait a minute. What was going on here? Something was wrong, all wrong. How could the trees be green when there were so many fallen leaves on the ground? Was he confusing two different memories? No, that couldn't be. He had only been here once. He had never been here at all. But why then this sudden, uncontrollable, longing? For what? It never happened, it was a dream!

23

The stilted digital voice drilled into Andrew's brain like the buzz of a mosquito: *Rosenthal, Abigail, Rosenthal, Abigail.* Who the hell was Rosenthal, Abigail? He fought against opening his eyes, unwilling to part with this magical, comforting dream. The telephone fell silent, then sounded a lively beep. Someone was leaving him a voice mail. When would he listen to all his messages? Suppose it was something important. No, not now. Anytime but now! Soon. Later. First coffee. Yes, coffee. When had he last had a cup of it? He couldn't say. He had lost all track of time. Things fell apart, the center didn't hold. Who was this damn Abigail Rosenthal? He didn't know any Abigail Rosenthal. A wrong number? Impossible. The beep was preceded by his recorded announcement. Could it be the editor of the magazine? No way. The editor's name was Greenspan. He knew the man. Could he have been fired? But who in the world would fire him? He had to stop this paranoid thinking. It led nowhere. He had to get up.

Andrew made his way to the kitchen, sidestepping the wet stain

eating away at the black rug and turning it even darker. The thought
of coffee was both inviting and repellent. An espresso would be too
strong. He was weak, he was sick; he needed something easier on
the stomach. Perhaps a nice latte with lots of sweetened, foamed
milk? The thought of the hot milk slowly mingling with the aromatic brown brew brought a smile to his lips. He opened the refrigerator. *What?* There was no milk! He had finished it two days
ago. The smile vanished. Andrew sucked in his breath. Something
was hiding in the refrigerator—something he had done his best
to forget. He fought back the urge to slam the stainless-steel door
and run from the apartment. *Get a grip on yourself, man!* Forcing
himself to look, he saw the tenderloin in the refrigerator's sallow,
operating-room light. Pathologically black, it lay in its corner. He
stared at it in horror. It seemed to have swelled and lost its shape.
Its once succulent meat made him think of a dead, rancid animal.
Plunged from his dreamy, still sleepy state into a cold bath of hy-
perawareness, he felt the violent, urgent need to tear the malignant creature from its lair—to sweep it into the garbage pail—into
the incinerator shaft—into the river . . . *the river*! That was it! He
would throw the hideous thing that had taken possession of his
apartment, of his life, into the Hudson. He would stand watching
it sink slowly into the polluted, chemical-infested river, breathing
its last in a few final bubbles before disappearing in the metallic
gray water.

For a moment or two, flying high on the renewed euphoria of
a mad notion, Andrew felt an almost infinite power. Then, losing
altitude, he crashed on the hard ground of his helpless depression.
No, he would never dare do such a thing. Not now. Not ever. He
wasn't capable of such drama: it was one more ridiculous, juvenile fantasy. He shut the refrigerator with an empty feeling and
returned to the living room, forgetting the coffee he had craved
a minute ago. His mind whirled obsessively like a carousel with

no one to stop it. Impatiently, he turned the pages of the cook-books, still hoping to find in them the answer to his predicament. *But what was this? Unbelievable!* Last to emerge from the pile of books was the friendly, familiar, long-forgotten *Joy of Cooking*, the classic once found on every kitchen shelf in America. He hadn't known he still had it. Certain that their well-thumbed family copy had stayed behind with Linda in Brooklyn, he hadn't thought of it for years. He ran his fingers over the dog-eared volume, whose jacket was torn here and there, as moved by it as if he were stroking the cheek of a beloved woman or child. He leafed through its pages, lingering over the old black-and-white illustrations. It all came back to him now. Smells, tastes, and textures burst through the dam of memory. The loud, sticky oilcloth on the table. The pots and pans whose age showed in a broken handle or dent. The knives that stayed blunt no matter how often they were sharpened. The wooden spoons, blackened by the remains of the innumerable meals they had stirred, which had become part of them despite their frequent scrubbings. Where had the book been hiding? He had missed it so badly all these years without knowing it.

Andrew went on reading, carefully separating pages stuck together by grease and grains of sugar. Although he felt that he was in a whirlpool of different, contradictory, and even self-destructive emotions, he tried putting these out of his mind and remaining with his first, spontaneous reaction to the rediscovered lost book. Meat! Simple, hearty meat recipes. A French country casserole, home cooking at its best. *The onion, carrots, and celery are browned well before the wine and beef stock are added to the pan.* The wooden spoon scraped the charred, fragrant, flavorful bits from the bottom, folding them into the hot, brown stew whose lard gave it a special, silky texture . . . A sudden sob, sharp like a puppy's yelp, escaped Andrew's mouth. He shut the book and pushed it away. Propping his elbows on the table, he rested his head in his hands and kneaded his soft eyeballs. How would it all end? When?

Rosenthal, Abigail, Rosenthal, Abigail . . . The telephone's robotic voice made him sit up with a start. He mustn't answer. He mustn't! What did they want from him? Why did he have to answer every time someone called? The nerve of calling him at home over one shitty little article! Ten pages all in all, two of them bibliography. Furious, he rose to go to the phone. But what was he doing? Hadn't he decided not to answer? Not now. He would answer when he felt like it, when he had something to send. Meanwhile, he would show them. He strode to the phone, which had begun to quiver and growl again like a nasty little dog, reached quickly for its cable as if afraid of being bitten—*just not now, don't let anyone call now!*—and yanked it from its socket, letting it drop to the floor. Then, trying to forget the idiocy of his action, he beat a safe path back to the rug, now half-soaked with water from the goddamn air conditioner, from where he proceeded to the kitchen and opened the refrigerator door so savagely that it almost flew off its hinges. The tenderloin, unrepentant and shameless, was where he had left it. He threw it a hateful glance as if about to engage it in hand-to-hand combat, summoned all his strength, pried it from its place, and stuck it, the rare, aged-to-absurdum cut of meat, as far back in the freezer as it would go, behind bags of frozen vegetables, frost-covered vodka bottles, and cartons of ice cream. With a last glance at the freezer door, he slammed it shut and hurried to the bathroom, holding his hands out to keep them from contaminating the rest of him, until he could wash them.

24
July 28, 2001

The 8th of Av, 5761

Ten a.m. The tinkling chimes of an ice-cream truck penetrated the closed windows of Andrew's stifling hothouse of an apartment, bouncing off each other as if in a game of marbles. Andrew, his face still in his sleeve, shot out of his dream like the human cannonballs he had seen at the circus as a boy. He turned on his back, stretched, and listened to the fading music-box echoes while trying to put himself in the proper frame of mind to cope with the weekend. What was he going to do? He had no plans— nothing! He forced himself to sit up on the leather couch, feeling stiff all over. He couldn't stay by himself in this apartment another day. He would rot, he would go mad.

The park! Should he go for a bike ride? Get a breath of fresh air and some exercise? The green, open spaces of Central Park, he imagined in a new spurt of euphoric glee, were charged with health and vitality. They called to him. He roused himself. Should he shower first? He hadn't showered for the last two days or more and probably reeked to high heaven. No, not now. His bike helmet would hide the greasy mess of his hair and he would work up a healthy sweat, not like the night's sticky perspiration. He had to get out of here! Another minute and he would burst out crying like a little boy. *Get out, get out as fast as you can!*

25

Even before he reached the street, the effort of extricating his bicycle from the pile of junk that had accumulated on top of it in the basement had drenched his workout clothes in sweat. The shorts were big on him, hanging loosely down from his hips and stomach. He kept wanting to hike up his underpants. When had he lost so much weight? He pushed the bike through the lobby, relieved to see the doorman wasn't there, opened the heavy door, and stepped outside.

The asphyxiating heat hit him at once. One never got used to it, never developed the slightest resistance. He stood staring blindly at the street, his senses a frightening, heat-stricken blur. Where was he? He tried to piece together his surroundings. The gray, chipped bricks of the building's facade suggested a fortress or prison. An empty, rotting sky, the nondescript color of rusting metal, hung like a sack over the empty, rotting city. Should he turn around and go home? No, he had passed the point of no return. Onward! He steadied the bike, swung an awkward leg over the seat, settled into it, and began pedaling laboriously eastward, toward Central Park. More than the bicycle was carrying him, he felt he was carrying it.

Eleven fifteen. The park was already full of New Yorkers defying the heat. Joggers, strollers, and bikers thronged the lawns and paths. He pedaled with effort, as he threaded his way through them. He felt none of the relief he had hoped for, he was in the same prison in which he had been in his apartment. The sky was an impenetrable gray, rusting iron. An apocalyptic sun, pale and sickly, hid behind the curtain of haze. The burning hot asphalt stuck to the bicycle's wheels. He had known he had made a mistake from the moment of stepping outside, he just hadn't had the strength of character to turn back. His eyes stung. His lungs ached. He was thirsty and could feel the onset of heartburn. He needed to rest. To drink. Coffee. Juice. Water. When had he last gotten down anything solid? Two, maybe three days ago. He needed to eat. Maybe a bagel? Corn on the cob? Andrew made a face . . . Ice cream? Chocolate ice cream! Why not some ice cream? A goddamn ice-cream cone wouldn't kill him, would it? He could feel the yen for its sweetness go to his head as if he had already swallowed a tablespoon of sugar.

Andrew pedaled faster, scanning the park for an ice-cream wagon and almost panting with expectation when he saw one with a long line of customers in front of it. By now reduced to a single, all-consuming desire, he rode toward it so fast that the line was forced to jump back, muttering an angry protest as he braked at the last moment to avoid hitting a signboard with garish illustrations of the wagon's overpriced wares. Andrew ignored the indignation, which united the random collection of park-goers in a moment of solidarity directed against him, the violator of the unwritten law. Sliding his sore rear end off the seat, he planted both feet on the ground and studied the sign while awaiting his turn with open impatience. The vendor, overwhelmed by the heat and the fussiness of his customers, kept rummaging through his freezer to meet their demands. The heat hadn't bothered Andrew when he was in motion. Now, molten and stupefying, it hit him again.

Come on, move it! How long did anyone need to find a fucking Popsicle? His fit of anger nearly made him scream out loud. *Get a grip on yourself, man! Don't lose it, not in the middle of the park.* He inhaled some heavy air and held it in his lungs as though he were smoking a joint. When was he supposed to meet Mitchell his investment adviser again? When was the last time they had met? And what were those phone calls about his credit card debt all about? What goddamn debt were they talking about? He didn't have any debt! *Calm down! Calm down this minute!* He needed to take a deep breath and let the wave of anxiety roll over him and break nearer to the shore. But . . . *Move it, goddamn it!* How much time did the idiot need to count out change? What was that smell? There was smoke somewhere, a fire. Someone was burning dead branches. Or garbage. Or something.

26

Exhausted by the heat, Andrew asked for a large, family-size container of chocolate ice cream. *You only live once, right?* He gritted his teeth at its outrageous price and went looking for a private spot to eat it in, pushing the bike ahead of him. Far from feeling hungry, he suddenly felt disgustingly full. Braking sharply, he came to a sudden halt, almost falling from his bicycle. He found a place on the grass, half-hidden by a row of bushes, and took some deep breaths, opened the container, stuck his plastic spoon into it, and began to eat methodically. The half-chewed gobs of brown chocolate slid down his throat as though down the throat of a snake that had swallowed a live rodent. Unenthused by its first solid food in a while, his irritated stomach reacted apathetically. He ate at a fast, steady pace, combing his surroundings like a stray dog that fears its bone will be snatched from it. The less interested he was in what he was eating, the more he began to realize that the privacy provided by the bushes was an illusion. He looked uncomfortably at all the attractive, half-undressed bodies sprawled on the lawns around him while spooning up the last of the ice cream from the bottom of the empty container. On the grass a few steps away lay a self-absorbed young couple who were making out in full view like actors in a film. As though in a fog, Andrew stared at their carefree bodies that were twined around each other with a youthful, do-not-disturb innocence. He felt light-years away from

sexual passion. He was outside the circle of human sexuality entirely, a pariah banished from the camp. His ice cream—crammed
stomach, now determined to thrust out whatever had been thrust
into it, hung over the penis beneath as if shielding a cowering little mouse. Andrew belched loudly. The whole shocked park, or
so it seemed to him, stopped what it was doing to look his way.
The nearby couple disentangled itself and stared at him. He turned
quickly away, his cheeks burning with a shame he hadn't felt since
childhood. Getting to his feet in what he hoped looked like a casual manner, he steered the bike back to the path by its handlebars
while holding the empty container in his other hand. What was he
so ashamed of? Having belched? Been caught peeping at the couple? But he hadn't peeped, he hadn't! What was he supposed to do
with the goddamn container? Where were the goddamn garbage
pails when you needed them? Not that anyone ever ate so much ice
cream in one sitting. It was insane. Now he would be sick to his
stomach in the middle of the park. Just what he needed!

Andrew threw the container into the first garbage pail, feeling
sicker and sicker. Again he sniffed the burning smell. Who was
burning wood on a weekend? Couldn't they have waited until
Monday, when the park was empty? Hot, weak, and weary, he re-
mounted his bike and pedaled dutifully with no clear goal in mind,
conscious of a thick curtain of loneliness descending on him. Although he knew he should be heading uptown, back toward home,
he kept cycling downtown without asking himself why. More
and more bicycles were on the path. The park was filling up with
perspiring, scantily clad bodies that moved like wraiths or desert
mirages through the haze: bare shoulders, clean-shaved heads, uncovered breasts, naked thighs and stomachs. He swung the handlebars to the right, cutting across several cyclists, and banked at
high speed into a side path to get away from the crowds, which he
felt surrounded him, like a city under siege.

The smell of burning grew stronger, filling his mouth and nose with its black, astringent odor. *Flames licked the felled cedar beams that were strong as iron and the large stones that screamed with pain like living creatures.* Andrew braked with a screech, throwing himself sideways to avoid landing on his top wheel, and stood breathing heavily by the side of the path. The air was dense, noxious. What now? What should he do? He forced himself to look around, searching for something to latch on to that would help him out of the abyss. The stench was getting worse. He instinctively sent a hand to the collar of his shirt to unbutton the button that wasn't there and started out again, his thigh muscles straining to turn the stubborn pedals. His destination, unclear to his mind but known to his senses, was hiding just around the corner of consciousness. It was somewhere where he had forgotten or left something, somewhere where he had unfinished business. He kept heading downtown, crossing Strawberry Fields and turning left at Cherry Hill Fountain with Sheep Meadow on his right. The magical names in which he had always taken such pleasure now echoed dully in his mind, as meaningless as everything that appeared out of the haze and vanished back into it, like the fragments of an undeciphered dream. Circling the little lake, he followed the boathouse path toward the east side of the park and turned northward, drawn by a strong though invisible gravitational pull that grew stronger with every turn of the sprocket chain. A heavy, semi-opaque, impenetrable veil hung between him and reality. The glossy treetops resembled artificial, green plastic mushrooms rising above the haze. The lawns looked like Astroturf, their occupants scurrying ants. Even the majestic avenues bordering the park now felt like a stage set, a cheap Technicolor production.

The sweat ran down Andrew's neck, soaking his collar even more. His breathing grew as labored as if he were pedaling uphill, even though he was on level ground. Where was he going in this heat? What was he looking for? It would have been logical to turn right toward Fifth Avenue, stick the bicycle into the trunk of the first taxi to come along, and head for home, away from this inferno pretending to be a field of strawberries. He peered ahead, looking for a fork in the path that would lead him out of the park. A light breeze blew the burning smell, which was getting stronger all the time, in his face. From beyond a hedge came distant sounds of childish laughter, seeding his blank mind with bits and snatches of memory. A small, round pond. Little battery-operated boats. A large telescope aimed at the cornice of a luxury apartment building where a proud, stubborn pair of hawks had chosen to nest, the male shielding the female with his handsome, spotted white body.

Andrew strained to listen. The laughter seemed to be coming from nowhere, from a dimension in which ordinary space and time did not prevail. He braked, dismounted, and carefully walked the bike toward a stairway with graceful stone banisters, advancing slowly so as to preserve the delicate balance between the remembered past and the experienced present. His eyes widened in astonishment at the strange but familiar sight. It was a large metal sculpture. The cavernous curves of its sleekly cascading bronze made him think of a huge sea monster dredged from the depths. His nostrils dilated, sniffing the metallic air. He knew this place, knew it well. Years ago he had come here often with Alison. No, not with Alison. With Rachel. By the time Alison was born he was too busy, too irritable, too impatient. Something forceful, like a sneeze, was pressing on his forehead. It was Alice, Alice in Wonderland!

Andrew descended the steps slowly, his bicycle bumping down them, and reached the round space ringed with benches in which the statue stood. He circled its brown, metal mass over which laughing children swarmed like bright insects, his glance lingering on the grotesquely large head of the Mad Hatter. A swan-necked

Alice, seated on a large toadstool, appeared to be listening to him while regarding the dormouse in her lap, while the White Rabbit stood looking at his watch. Had he ever read the book to Alison? Who could remember? His breath came in shallow spurts. The raging waters pressed against the dam, threatening to smash it and drag him to destruction. With his remaining strength, he fought to stave off the deluge. Tearing himself away from the statue, he gripped the handlebars and pushed the bike back up the steps. His planned escape route up Fifth Avenue was forgotten. The bitter smoke thickened as if he were getting closer and closer to the center of the fire.

27

The smell grew stronger, permeating everything. What was burning? A building? A forest? But how could that be? There were no fire engines. No one looked perturbed. No one seemed to smell smoke except him. The path curved to the right, ran around a large boulder on some grassy turf, and let him abruptly out of the park on the east sidewalk of Central Park West. Andrew stood there in a daze, gasping for breath like a drowning man washed ashore. Crowds were still flocking to the park. Taxis sped by, their off-duty roof lights showing they were taken. Andrew swallowed a sigh, wiped his sweaty forehead with a sleeve, and waited for the light to change. Tourists were gathered by the Dakota, busily photographing the John Lennon memorial plaque. He passed them indifferently and walked along 72nd Street toward Columbus Avenue against the flow of human traffic, feeling like a man in a shrinking glass cage whose walls soon would crush him. He was too exhausted to push the bicycle any farther. What should he do with the damn thing? Leave it in the street for someone to take and rid him of it? That was ridiculous. Who left bicycles in the street? A taxi! He would do anything for a taxi. Where had all the taxis gone? The smoke was killing him. The air was full of soot and ashes. A huge fire must be raging somewhere nearby; whole blocks were going up in flames. And not a fire engine or police car was in sight! Nothing! Should he stop to rest at a café, have a bite to eat? A bowl of chicken soup at Fine & Schapiro's? Out of the question. Home, right away. He couldn't take another minute of this goddamn street.

A squeal of tires and the smell of burned rubber rescued Andrew from the vortex of his thoughts. A taxi pulled up at the curb to let off a young couple that looked as spruce and fresh as if clipped from the cover of a fashion magazine. Leaping for the open door in defiance of both safety and good manners, Andrew clutched its handle while pleading with the driver to open the trunk. On the verge of collapse, he shoved the bicycle into the filthy baggage compartment with no thought of possible damage, banged the lid shut, and threw himself into the backseat, hoarsely croaking his address. He shut his eyes and leaned back, determined to feel and think nothing until securely home. He would never go out again.

28

The claustrophobic atmosphere assailed Andrew the moment he stepped into his apartment, depriving him of the solace he had hoped for. The air felt like a semisolid mass weighing on the parquet floor. The thick smoke had followed him inside, hanging there in heavy coils. His lungs gasped for oxygen. No, he can't stay here! Fighting the urge to turn and run back out, he stumbled to the living room and turned on the TV without bothering to lock the door or take off his shoes. This fire must be huge! There was nothing like a national crisis or natural disaster for producing an adrenaline-rich cloud of news. He didn't know the local New York channels. Never having taken the slightest interest in their bulletins of fires, floods, police raids, and gossipy court cases, he went nervously from one to another.

All had only the usual stale coverage of the humid heat wave. Nothing about a fire. How could that be? There was enough smoke for all of Riverside Park to have gone up in flames. Andrew turned away from the television in frustration and wandered to the bathroom. A hot shower? A cold one? Coffee? Something to eat? The sour blob of chocolate in his stomach burbled like a sewer about to overflow. He returned to the couch and lay down with his sneakered feet hanging over it to keep from scraping the leather. The TV, playing some sports channel, kept babbling away with an obscene amount of pointless information. If he had had the strength to get up, he would have turned it off or looked for something more interesting—an old-time movie, a cooking channel, or even *Sesame Street*.

Sesame Street! The thought of it, like a distant flash of lightning, sent a painful current of longing through him. If Ann Lee were here, she would have recorded every program for him. She would have nursed him and cured him, saved him from himself. *What nonsense! That's ridiculous. It's hopeless.* The smell of smoke was unendurable. He shut his eyes and took a breath of its overbearing stench, giving into it as if sinking into a foggy, bottomless pit. It was getting hotter and hotter. The flames licked the edges of the Temple, their long tongues profaning its purity with their alien, insolent presence. Andrew squirmed on the couch like a worm on a hook, trying to rid his mind of the fiery sight. It was dangerous to stay in this place! Loud cries for help echoed in the hollow of his skull, alarms rang frantically. Women screamed as loud as they could, begging for mercy, their voices breaking from terror. He fought to drive the raging flames back. Home, home! He mustn't stay here. All was lost. He writhed on the couch, flailing like a drowning man fighting for breath. *Sun streamed into the kitchen through the window, glinting off the puddle of milk and the half-empty bowls on the table, outdazzling the screen. Although you couldn't see who was on it, their familiar voices gave them away: Ernie, Bert, Big Bird, Oscar the Grouch.* Sesame Street! *A clatter of broken dishes fills the room: Grover, playing a waiter, has slipped on the restaurant floor. The little girl laughs out loud with yelps of pure bliss. Let's get a move on, sweetheart, the bus will be here in ten minutes and you still have to brush your teeth and hair. The sugar they put in these cereals!* A warm tide was rising in him, probing his weak points, breaking through to his self's soft core. A bittersweet sorrow surged behind his forehead. Its lava threatened to erupt and annihilate all in its way.

Andrew leaped from the couch in a fright, no longer recognizing the room. A ghastly scarlet light glowed in the thick smoke, setting the walls apocalyptically on fire. He ran breathlessly to the window, flung it open, and leaned out. Neither light not dark. Neither day nor night. A last twilight followed by nothing. The smoke was not there. It was not outside him. It was within. It swirled all around him, getting in his eyes and choking him mercilessly. He backed away from the window, only half grasping where and who he was. Where was all the smoke coming from? Everything was full of it—his clothes, his skin, his bones, everything. It was coming from him. It was he who was on fire.

Andrew turned slowly, transfixed by what he saw. Red, fearful flames raged out of control, ravenously consuming the Temple and its implements. Terrified and helpless, he stared at them, feeling the walls collapse one by one under the impact of the destruction. Broken, animal cries resounded in his ears, drowning out the crackling flames and the horrors. Who was crying like an animal—like a child—crying and crying? *It's me. There's no one else here. It's me*. Uncontrollable sobs racked his chest, shaking him like a rag doll. His whole face trembled. The wave inside him was about to sweep all before it. His head felt light, as if he were going to faint. His muscles went slack, casting off his mind's authority. He sank slowly to the ground with his back to the wall until he was sitting on the floor, rocking back and forth to the rhythm of his sobs. The flames engulfed him, devouring the Temple. A large, round tear rolled down a cheek that had forgotten what a tear was like. The embossments on the ceiling were melting in the heat. Their liquid gold dripped to the charred floor in burning drops. The priceless curtains were consumed by the flames. The white marble walls were turning black, their delicate veins covered by thick soot. Two new tears trickled down either side of his nose to the corners of his involuntarily trembling mouth. He blinked as if trying to call them back, but more and more coursed down his cheeks like summer rain. The upward-raised arms of the molded candelabra toppled one by one beneath the weight of their unanswered prayers.

Andrew let out a short, high-pitched wail that was cut short at once, frightened by its own sound. The tremor spread from his mouth to his upper lip and nose. The warm, salty tears at the back of his throat were forcing him to swallow in waves. His mouth opened wide, as though of its own accord. The tears ran in hot rivulets, streaking his face. He raised one shoulder and wiped them in an ancient, forgotten childhood reflex. They poured down faster, unrestrained. Through a portal in the ceiling, he saw the gates of heaven open over the great city and all seven celestial spheres come into view. Errant souls flitted like shadows from world to world, one alone bright to the point of transparency: an ancient priest, his head wrapped in a linen turban and a golden fire pan in his hand. Andrew sobbed harder, all defenses gone, his body rocking back and forth. The room was dark. The portal was gone. The last outlines of day were gathered up by the dusk. The flames subsided, flickering in the embers. Andrew remained seated on the ground, rocking. He held his face in his hands. The tears ran through his fingers as though from a bottomless well.

29
July 29, 2001

The 9th of Av, 5761

Dad? Dad?" Rachel's hesitant voice sounded in the apartment. For a moment she stood in the doorway, nervously clutching the key she had somehow forgotten to return to its copper bowl on her last visit. Kicking off her sandals, she went to the living room, where a man and a woman were arguing noisily in a singsong Spanish. The scene that met her eyes was alarming. The TV was on, filling the apartment with the loud, melodramatic dialogue of a telenovela. The air smelled sour. Her father was sitting on the floor by one of the shut windows, pages of newspapers lying around him like autumn leaves. His head of wild hair was clasped between his knees.

"Dad, what's wrong?" Rachel hurried to Andrew's side. Gently, she raised his head until he was looking at her. "Are you all right? What's going on? I've kept calling you. Your answering machine is full—there's no room for more messages."

Andrew looked at her red-eyed, as if either half-asleep or awakened from a bad dream.

"I've been in town for a few days staying with friends. A friend. I have so much to tell you about, Dad. You're so thin! Are you on a diet or something?"

Rachel took Andrew's hands in her own and helped him to his feet. He rose slowly and stiffly, like an old man. She led him to the

couch, cleared it of newspapers, and sat him down. "You don't return phone calls, you don't answer e-mails—you honestly had me
worried. What's going on here? I've never seen your place look so
messy. The rug is soaking wet. It's so stuffy here! Why are all the
windows closed? Have you eaten anything today?"

Her uncharacteristically low-key manner, which barely concealed her worry, was reassuring enough to send Andrew, his
sense of reality partially restored, to the shower. Rachel turned
off the television and air conditioner, opened all the windows, collected the newspapers and trash from the floor, and ordered a light
lunch from the Japanese restaurant on 112th Street and Broadway.
She considered opening a bottle of white wine, thought better of it,
and brewed some herbal tea. The food arrived in fifteen minutes.
She took it to the kitchen, arranged it on plates, and brought it on
a large tray to the coffee table, which she had cleared and wiped
clean. Hair wet from the shower, Andrew sat on the couch in fresh
pajamas, his white bristle of a beard making him look older than
he was. Rachel sat next to him and edged the tray toward him.
Although he managed to get down only a bit of solid food, he liked
the miso soup and nearly finished his bowl of it.

After eating, the two of them drank tea and watched *Philadelphia Story* on TCM, sitting together on the couch with a blanket
over their knees as if it were a winter night. Andrew watched in silence, giving no sign of whether he was following the action on the
screen. Rachel did her best to appear relaxed. Although something
bad, something that would have to be dealt with, had clearly happened, her instinct was not to talk about it now. When the movie
was over she helped Andrew, who had barely uttered a word all
evening, to the bedroom. She brought him a glass of water and
a homeopathic tranquilizer that she found in the medicine chest,
said good night, and went to sleep on the living-room couch. She
already knew where to find the sheets, blankets, and towels.

Andrew lay in bed, his mind a blank and his half-opened eyes staring at the rhombus of light on the ceiling that came from the door left ajar by Rachel in case he needed her. He could hear her whispering on the telephone, clearing away dishes, and putting the living-room furniture back in place. The domestic, nighttime sounds evoked a mélange of childhood memories that he had no time to sort out before falling fast asleep. (The medicine was apparently more potent than its pseudoscientific label made it out to be.) At two a.m., he awoke with a loud cry. Rachel hurried to him. But he had already gone back to sleep, curled in a semi-fetal position. In the morning, he drank some coffee with a large amount of milk and ate half a fresh bagel that Rachel brought from Absolute.

Although the blankness of the night remained, his movements were more alert and less mechanical. Rachel phoned Dr. Nesselson's office and made an emergency appointment for that same day. Andrew was too dazed and tired to resist. He talked sparingly, and Rachel didn't press him. She went to the kitchen and spoke to someone in low tones over the phone. At midday, there was a buzz on the intercom. It was the doorman to tell "Miss Rachel" that someone had left a suitcase for her. Not wanting to leave Andrew alone even for a few minutes, she asked that it be sent up in the elevator. That afternoon they went to see Dr. Nesselson. He examined Andrew thoroughly and referred him to a colleague, a psychiatrist at Mount Sinai Hospital on the Upper East Side. Though still drowsy and apathetic, he seemed in a less hazardous state. When Rachel brought him a cappuccino from the coffee machine as they were waiting in the corridor, he made a face at its taste but drank it anyway.

A nurse ushered them into the psychiatrist's office. Andrew was cooperative throughout the interview. The doctor's remarks when it was over were directed mainly at Rachel. "I've spoken with Dr. Nesselson. Professor Cohen has obviously been through a severe psychological crisis, but its dynamics are difficult to understand. Something serious has taken place. We just don't have the usual symptoms that would point to a psychotic episode. These things are known to happen. What makes this case so unusual is that it almost seems as if an external force took possession and let go of the patient with none of the customary traces. We don't have an explanation for every physical and psychological phenomenon. Sometimes it's best not to look for one but simply to concentrate on the recovery process. We see no reason to hospitalize him at this time. Our recommendation is full rest under close supervision. I'll prescribe some medicines and would urge that they be taken regularly." The psychiatrist was now speaking to Rachel alone, since Andrew had shut his eyes and did not appear to be listening. "I need to emphasize that these are tranquilizers and not psychiatric drugs. I think we should wait a few more days before considering anything more aggressive. I take it you're his daughter. Can you stay with him for a while to look after him?"

Rachel nodded thoughtfully. She was amazed at how quickly she had adjusted to the new situation. She would never have guessed two days ago that the first object of her newly awakening maternal feelings would be her father.

30
August 1, 2001

The 12th of Av, 5761

Ten a.m. Andrew lay in bed, blinking in the strong light coming through the south window of the bedroom. After seeing the doctor, he had slept through the entire afternoon, evening, night, and next morning, waking only to eat a bit, take his pills, and sip some water, tea, or orange juice. It was Tuesday morning when he finally got out of bed. He showered, ate something, and sat in the living room for an hour and a half. Rachel sat with him for a while and then went back to working on an article she was writing with a colleague from Princeton. Andrew didn't touch the newspaper or the remote control that she had left for him on the coffee table. Like a child clutching its tattered security blanket, a part of him clung to his blank state. He went back to bed and slept through the night without waking. A conversation in the living room between two women talking and laughing quietly found its way into his dreams and was forgotten with them. The tranquilizers were effective. He let them do their work and made no attempt to remember his dreams or remain in them. The last weeks now seemed a distant memory, as if they had happened to someone else.

He threw off his light blanket, rose slowly from the bed, and made his way cautiously, as if learning to walk, to the bathroom. Washing his face with cold water, he regarded its bristles in the mirror and went to the kitchen. Compared to the two previous days, he was stronger and clearer-headed. Rachel, noticing the difference with a smile, offered to make him coffee. The small smile she received in acknowledgment was encouraging. Her father was clearly emerging from his zombielike dream state. They talked a bit, skirting any difficult topics. Both felt the change for the better. Andrew glanced at the headlines in the paper, lay down to rest on the living-room couch, had a second cup of coffee in the late morning, and went to the bathroom to shower and shave. Although he felt more himself again once clean-shaven, some of the fears quelled by the tranquilizers returned now, too. He took a deep breath and tried to drive them back beneath the protective cover of the medicine. He knew he would have to confront them sooner or later—that afternoon, that evening, perhaps the next day. There was much he needed to understand.

He dressed and returned to the living room, glad that Rachel was there. The day went by leisurely. Rachel came and went, careful not to be absent for more than half an hour at a time. Andrew sat thinking, more willing as time went by to put aside the forgetfulness in which he had shrouded himself. What had happened to him these past weeks? Where had he been? Although he had no answers, the questions seemed less frightening. In the early afternoon he felt a wave of anxiety and asked Rachel if it was time to take his medicine. She gave him two pills and helped him to lie on the couch and rest for half an hour. The attack flared and died down, leaving behind a bitter, unpleasant taste. Rachel ordered supper over the phone and made some tea, after which they watched the first half of *Gone with the Wind,* smiling at its never-failing power to play on their emotions. At ten, Andrew took two sleeping pills, brushed his teeth, and got into bed. Rachel stayed awake in the living room, talking on the phone. Although her voice reached the bedroom, Andrew couldn't make out what she was saying. It was like a strange lullaby that soon lulled him to sleep.

31

August 2, 2001

The 13th of Av, 5761

Nine a.m. Andrew woke to the notes of Mozart's Clarinet Concerto in A Major and smiled with satisfaction at Rachel's tasteful choice. It was so good to have her with him! How many days had she been here? He tried calculating, then gave up. He shut his eyes, his head falling back on the pillow, and let himself be rocked by the adagio that he loved. Although he knew this domestic Eden would not last, its tender intimacy had been good for him. And not just for him: even in his precarious, uncommunicative state, he could feel they had been good for Rachel, too, that they had repaired something that was broken long ago. Perhaps it could never be put back together again, but its shattered pieces would be less painfully sharp. Rachel would resume her life. And he? How was he going to resume his?

Nonetheless, he managed to overcome his anxiety. He would have to come to terms with reality. He had no choice. It just wasn't the time for it yet. Maybe soon. Coping with his fears made him feel stronger and more together than he had felt in a long time. Yes, it was good to be with Rachel. Not to have to talk and be witty and brilliant all the time. To be allowed to be weak. It made her milder, brought out the best in her. The music kept filling the room, lapping at its walls like the waves of a calm sea. Andrew let them pass over him as if he were a patient shore used to their rise and fall.

After breakfast and a shower, he let Rachel talk him into getting dressed. Wearing a white, short-sleeved linen shirt and a pair of khaki shorts, he drank a second cup of coffee on the leather couch. They chatted, both heartened by the progress he was making. He was still weak. He felt vulnerable. But the apathy in which he had taken refuge was gone. Rachel asked him what had happened. He didn't know where to begin. It was hard to find the words for it. He thought of the strange visions that had taken hold of him in recent months, surprised to realize that they had stopped completely since that dreadful evening after coming home from the park. He remembered the fire, the terrible destruction, and his uncontrollable weeping as he sat helplessly on the floor of the Temple. It was all so inexplicably strange, as if it had happened in another incarnation.

He debated telling Rachel about it and decided not to. She wouldn't understand him and would think he had lost his sanity. And who was to say that he hadn't? Although she sensed he was in conflict, she chose to overlook it. Encouraged by his improved condition, she didn't want to do anything that might cause a relapse.

After lunch, Andrew went to the bedroom to rest. He lay in bed and let his mind wander, no longer afraid where it might take him. He thought about Rachel and about the change in their relationship. About how patient and gentle she was with him. Yes, he had hurt her, hurt her terribly—and at an age when she had needed him the most. He hadn't wanted or been able to face up to that. Now, he no longer had a choice. He had to acknowledge it to himself and perhaps—not necessarily today or tomorrow, but sometime soon—to her, too. How was he going to do it? By apologizing? How did you apologize for what had happened so long ago? What did it mean to do it?

Never mind. He would find a way. A solution would present itself. And Linda? Although the thought of their awful phone conversation was still deeply painful, he no longer tried to repress it. Much of what she said had been true. Did he regret leaving her and starting a new life? Not necessarily. It had been unavoidable— perhaps. *Still, you can't deny the price she paid for it, the price we all paid.* A deep, dull sorrow came over him. He had to force himself to breathe. His eyes hurt and large tears ran down his cheeks, streaking his face. He lay without moving, letting them flow without attempting to stop them or wipe them away. An odd but comforting warmth suffused his face. Little sobs broke loose from him. Although he hoped Rachel didn't hear them, he didn't want to keep them in. Nor could he have. If she did hear, she didn't let on. He lay there for a long time while the quiet sobs kept coming.

Later that afternoon, Rachel went out for an hour or two, having decided he could be left alone for longer stretches. Andrew

thought about Linda some more, this time more calmly. Taking
a few deep breaths and warning himself to stay composed, he
thought about Alison, too. He missed her so badly that it made him
ache. Surely, it wasn't too late. The damage could still be repaired,
if only in part. Why not have her sleep over now and then? True,
the apartment wasn't set up for that. He had thought more of his
own comfort than of hers. She couldn't be expected to sleep on the
living-room couch and she had to have a space of her own. Should
he hire an architect to redesign the apartment and make another
bedroom? No, that would be too complicated. Too expensive and
dramatic, too. He would find some less flamboyant way to handle
it. There was no need to decide now.

Rachel returned toward evening, bringing a large illustrated
book about aesthetic archetypes of sacred space. "The girlfriend I
was staying with lent it to me. It's a topic she's researching. Don't
you think it's interesting? Oh, Dad, I've got so many things to tell
you . . . but it's too late to start talking about them now. Maybe
tomorrow. Let's have something to eat. What would you like for
dinner?"

Andrew took only one pill before going to sleep, leaving another
on the bedside table to be safe. He leafed through the beautifully
designed book that Rachel had brought and trembled when he
came to the chapter describing the Temple in Jerusalem. Its handsome gold implements, the regal space of its great hall, the spacious
galleries surrounding it—all were nearly as he remembered them.
The similarity frightened him, causing him to slam the book shut
and push it to the bed's other end. He lay awake, his heart pounding. His mind refused to stay still. In the end, though, he reached
for the book and retrieved it without opening it. Not now. Maybe
tomorrow. When he had the presence of mind, he would glance at
the illustrations again. Perhaps he would consult some scholarly
literature on the subject. He would find out what was available on

the Internet. Not that he had any idea what he would do with it. Still, it would be wrong to dismiss his visions of the past year or to absolve himself of the need to look into them.

That Friday morning, after coffee and a shower, he switched on his computer for the first time in three weeks. Rachel was sitting nearby. Although she was at work on her laptop, her company gave him confidence. He went through the accumulation of mail in his in-box and sent, with Rachel's assistance, a short note to the editor of the magazine in which he apologized for not being able to write the article due to an unusually heavy workload. Politely requesting to be excused, he expressed his thanks and his readiness to be turned to again in the future.

His appetite kept improving and he ate almost a full meal for lunch without feeling nauseous. Rachel helped him to go through his voice mail, most of which consisted of her own messages. In the afternoon they went to the park, where they bought ice cream and sat on a bench overlooking the river. Cars traveled up and down the West Side Highway, their muffled motors sounding like distant surf. Children were playing football. Joggers and cyclists filled the paths. Families and couples stretched out on the grass. A ripe, plump sun was dropping westward, painting the wavelets on the river an orange-pink. That night Andrew slept without sleeping pills. He passed the night in a deep, uninterrupted sleep. Before waking in the morning, he had a dream. He, Alison, and two of her friends had gone for a walk in Central Park. As they were leaving it, they passed the row of merrily decorated horse-drawn carriages that waited for tourists on 59th Street, opposite the Plaza Hotel, and stopped by one that was harnessed to a big, snow-white horse. Its coachman wore a top hat with a colorful peacock feather stuck in its velvet band. The girls began to giggle and blush, pointing at the white horse, which had a jaunty feather, too, in the brow band of its bridle. Andrew looked at it and began to laugh, too. It was pissing, its long black member spouting a flood of urine into a puddle on the sidewalk. The horse pissed and pissed. The girls were doubled up with laughter. The coachman laughed, too. He lifted his hat drolly and exclaimed: "That's my boy! Pisses just like a horse!"

Andrew awoke with a smile. Clear morning sunshine filled the room. Rachel was still asleep. There was a weekend quiet in the air. He lay on the pillow, reliving the funny scene of the urinating white horse. He still had a long way to go. Nothing had been solved, not really. The process of repair had only begun. He was conscious of that. Still, in spite of it all, he permitted himself, for the first time in a long while, a small, harmless dose of comfort.

END OF BOOK SEVEN

Epilogue
September 18, 2001

The 1st of Tishrei, 5762

Suddenly, everything seemed back to normal. After seven loud, nerve-racking days of endless CNN, droning helicopters, and wailing sirens, it was as if nothing had happened. The rain—the mocking rain that fell on the proud city licking the wounds that had wrenched it from its complacency, the largest of them a gaping hole in the ground where had stood the two towers that were wonders of the new world—the same rain that had thwarted the rescuers and condemned the last of those buried beneath the ruins to their deaths—the rain, too, had stopped. Among the thousands of inscriptions on the improvised memorial wall of the rescue operation's command post on Chambers Street, someone had written, FOR THIS IS THE WHOLE OF MAN.

A tentative autumn sun shone down on Riverside Drive, filtered by the still green branches of the trees. Although they had yet to turn, pale yellow blotches had appeared here and there like the early onset of gray hair, foretelling the autumn. On the northwestern corner of 110th Street and Riverside Drive a small crew of movers busily struggled to maneuver the carefully packed parts of a grand piano, which were too large for the prewar service elevator, up the emergency staircase to the tenth floor. Andrew stood in the street below amid a pile of items still waiting for the movers. Ann Lee's portable laptop was slung over his shoulder and a carton of her mementos, photographs, and correspondence was gripped firmly in his hands. She had gone to get coffee from the Starbucks on the corner, and perhaps also something to eat.

He looked around him, struck by the sudden tranquility. An Orthodox Jewish family walked by at the stately pace reserved for Sabbaths and religious holidays and turned toward the park. Andrew smiled fondly. "*Tashlikh, Rosh Hashanah . . .*" He said the words out loud as he had learned them in his distant Hebrew school days. A couple started down 110th Street, a swarthy, average-height man walking hand in hand with an attractive blond woman of fine bearing. Two dogs, one white and one brown, romped around them, winding their leashes around their owners' legs as if binding them together. Andrew blinked in amazement as he recognized his Hebrew-speaking neighbor, who was now clean-shaven and dressed in a starched, white shirt. Their glances met in a momentary flash of recognition and mutual, unstated understanding. The man nodded briefly. Andrew, for some reason feeling embarrassed, half nodded in return. The dogs leaped on each other in puppyish play, excitably dragging the couple toward the river.

Yes, it had been a hard year, very hard. But things were beginning to settle down. He would start teaching again when the fall semester began, and there had been hints from the administration of a highly desirable appointment in the not too distant future. Rachel was finishing her doctorate and would be coming to live in New York with Abby Rosenthal, her new partner. Although it was too early to talk about it, they were hoping to start a family. It hadn't yet been decided which of them would have a child first, but what difference did that make? They had plenty of time to think about it. Ann Lee was launching a career as a soloist and would be offering her own course in the university's Department of

Performance Studies. She hadn't made up her mind whether to en-
roll in a doctoral program; she thought she might prefer the life of
a dedicated artist to one of discoursing on the arts. Might she, too,
one day have a child with Andrew at his no-longer-young age?
It would be a bright, lively boy whom he would love with all his
heart and with whom he would miss no opportunity to play baseball on Saturday mornings on the sidewalk of Riverside Drive.
The haunting dreams and visions of the winter, spring, and summer of 2001 would never return and would slowly be forgotten as
the years went by. Time would go its way, its bright river flowing
onward. He would even once more see his fat homeless man, who
for some reason had moved to the steps of a church on 86th Street
and Amsterdam Avenue, where he reposed with regal ease, a huge
cigar clenched in his fist, absorbed in his chessboard as though it
were a crystal ball, a magic looking glass in which the whole world
was reflected. Everything would be the way it was, almost. Only
a whisper could still be heard where once stood the ruined house.

END

Acknowledgments

I would like to thank my many friends, family, and colleagues, who supported and enriched the long and, at times, excruciating process of writing this novel. They say it takes a village, but in this case it felt more like an entire city.

Special thanks go to my dear friend and editor of the Hebrew version, Dr. Haim Weiss, to whose boldness and determination I largely attribute the success it enjoyed; my larger-than-life translator, Hillel Halkin, whose hard work and unrivaled talent allowed him to render this novel, considered by many to be untranslatable, into beautiful, transfixing English prose; my able agent, Susan Golomb, from the Writers House Agency; my wonderful publicist, Lynn Goldberg, from the Goldberg and McDuffie Agency and the creative and devoted Nicholas Davies and Jennifer Murphy from Harper, for their excellent work; the authors Amos Oz, Colum McCann, Anne Roiphe, Dara Horn, and Lauren Belfer, who read the novel and offered their keen observations; my dear friends, Nicholas Lemann and Judith Shulevitz, who went above and beyond to help facilitate this translation; David Koral from production editorial, for his meticulous and painstaking work; Leah Carlson-Stanisic for brilliantly and laboriously designing the interior, and especially for taking on the complex and unprecedented challenge of creating the Talmudic pages; and above all, I owe the deepest gratitude for the tireless work, courage, rigor, and wisdom of my brilliant editor, Sofia Groopman, who saw the visions of this novel and turned them into reality. Working together with her on this manuscript was the most gratifying experience an author can wish for.

Finally, and most importantly, I want to thank my beloved wife, Carolyn, and most adored daughters, Leah and Talia, whose presence in my life feeds me every day and enabled me to reach this moment.

About the Author

Ruby Namdar was born and raised in Jerusalem to a family of Iranian-Jewish heritage. His first book, *Haviv* (2000), won the Israeli Ministry of Culture's Award for Best First Publication. *The Ruined House* won the 2014 Sapir Prize—Israel's most important literary award. He currently lives in New York City with his wife and two daughters, and teaches Jewish literature, focusing on biblical and Talmudic narrative.

Jerusalem Syndrome

F/ Book Club 2018　　　* You cannot escape
　　　　　　　　　　　　　　　who you are

- Andrew Cohen - a "פ"
　- what is means to be a jew in 21st century
　- can't get away from the biblical times/
　Temple
　-2 narratives　　　　　　　-his dinner parties -meat
　　parallel　　　　　　　　　-The temple sacrafices
　Andrew:　　　The Temple
　-obnoxious
　-unlikable
narrarotor: draws us in
　　　　:slightly critical of Andrew

?having a Jerusalem Syndrome in NYC
　-doesn't want to be jeeeish
　　then has 'talmudic visions'

　　　　　　　　　　　-starts Sept 2000
Ruined Houses　　　　　-ends Sept 2001
　-The temple
　-His family/home
　-The twin towers

(The Talmudic section, in each book, the most
　impt time Y.K ve, the אבודה, when the High Priest,
　cohen repents for all jews

Parallels -Btwn Andrew & diff Jewish observances
　-eg don't shave before Tish B' Av
　when Andrew: has ✓ rash
　Shaves - on Lag Baumer
　Jewish Dates - matter in Book

* You can't escape
who you are

Andrew Cohen - or "D.J."
- what is means to be a Jew in 21st century
- can't get away from the biblical times/
Temple
- 2 narratives   - his dinner parties ← most
parallel   - the temple sacrifices

Andrew: The temple
- obnoxious -
- well liked -

narrator: Cluaus US in
Slightly critical of Andrew

? having a Tensotton Syndrome in NYC
- doesn't want to be Jewish
- then has Jednusalic visions

                                            - Starts Sept 2020
Ronald Moses   Ends Sept 201
- the temple
- his family/home
- the twin towers

(The Talmudic section, in each book, the next
thing I have 9.k is the parable when he figured
when repeats to roll) coss

Parallels - Ronn interview at H - Truth observed
- don't show before Tish B'Av
      later Andrew: has + max
Shaul es   - on Yad Bachirah
2 Saner Fates - heath in Book